I0582144

Lore of the Wicked Wood

HILLARY RAYMER

Copyright © 2025 by Hillary Raymer

All rights reserved.

No part of this book may be reproduced in any form or by any electronic or mechanical means, including information storage and retrieval systems, without written permission from the author, except for the use of brief quotations in a book review.

Cover art by Yosbe Designs & Angela Chen

 Formatted with Vellum

for everyone who has been waiting for my sex fae book, may this burn be the slowest one yet

Trigger Warnings

- Violence
- Sexually explicit themes/scenes
- Adult language
- Death
- On page attempted assault
- Kidnapping
- Emotional abuse

One

Stardust Night at the Grand Cru meant two things—
Everinne Auvyre was going to be covered in iridescent
glitter before the night was over, and she was going to find
a male to warm her bed.

Lucky for her, the options were endless.

The Grand Cru was alive, pulsing with magic and extrava-
gance. It was one of the most dazzling parlors in Starysa, Prava's
capital city, where immortals and mortals alike would gather to
dance and drink their cares away. Violet and navy blue lights
swirled overhead, bouncing off the decadent crystal chandeliers
like shattered starbursts and casting the packed dance floor in an
ethereal glow. Spiral staircases rose on either side of the massive
space, leading to soaring balconies, safely tucking away the exclusive lounges where one might attempt to sell their soul for a peek
inside one of the premier rooms. Not that Everinne had ever tried.
She knew how to have a good time, and it never involved mingling
with the city's elite.

A mahogany bar wound itself along the outer walls of the
club, offering some of the finest indulgences. Anything from
shimmering alcohol and candied cherry shots to frothy ale and
bottles of sparkling wine that cost more than her most expensive

pair of shoes. But the shining star of the Grand Cru was its ceiling. A splendid glass dome stretched over the entire interior, showcasing the dazzling night sky and winter's first crescent moon.

Her fae blood hummed in response.

"Everinne!"

She spun at the sound of her name being called above the blaring music and spied Zoryana Daleth moving through the crush of bodies toward her. Zoryana was Everinne's best, and quite possibly only, friend. Her long brown hair fell in tiny spirals around her, and she'd clipped half of it back to showcase the navy beaded earrings dangling from her ears. She wore a short satin dress that spilled around her like liquid gold, setting off the rich bronze of her skin, and a pair of spiky black boots came all the way up to her knees.

"Zory!" Everinne squeezed through the crowd of dancers and reached with one arm, finally grabbing her friend's hand.

Zoryana pulled her in close, and though they were pressed against one another, she still had to shout to be heard. "Aren't you supposed to be at the palace tonight?"

Everinne groaned. The last place she wanted to be was at the damn palace. It didn't matter if it was a sprawling castle with hundreds of rooms, had a pool the size of a small lake, or was situated on a lush cliffside and offered some of the most stunning ocean views of the Ladova Bay. The imperial palace of Prava was cold. Forbidding. Charged with a kind of strained tension that made her skin crawl with unease. She hated the way she always felt like she was being watched, like the walls whispered whenever she walked past their obsidian surfaces.

Veros, her older brother, had requested her attendance there tonight, and though she initially agreed, she had no intention of going. Being surrounded by haughty nobles and other excessively wealthy members of society might sound like a dream to some, but to Everinne it sounded like torture. There was nothing worse than being surrounded by those who thought the world of themselves and enjoyed spreading malicious gossip.

If that wasn't bad enough, she would be forced to play nice with Atlas Skye, the Imperial Prince of Prava.

No, she would much prefer to be here, where the thrumming music and swaying bodies kept the chaos of her emotions locked away.

"The palace is overrated." She gave a flippant shrug, then swayed her hips to the rhythm pumping around them. Already, beads of sweat gathered at the back of her neck as the swarm of dancing bodies pitched to a frenzy.

Zoryana plucked two glasses of spiced wine from the tray of a passing server, and when he flicked her a look of disapproval, she smiled sweetly, then tucked a gold piece into the front pocket of his shirt.

There was the faintest current of power, coupled with the teasing scent of sage and juniper. The server's brows furrowed, then smoothed, as though he hadn't considered scolding her. "At your service all night, *milazk*."

That was the purely fantastic thing about Zoryana's witch magic—she absorbed emotions. The kind no one liked to feel, the types rarely ever spoken about or expressed calmly. Anger. Grief. Jealousy. Hate. The heavy, damaging ones that darkened souls and blackened hearts.

Zoryana turned back to Everinne and handed her a glass. "*Dravska.*"

Everinne clinked her glass against Zoryana's, then smiled. "*Dravska.*"

"You know," Zoryana drawled, swirling her drink, "Veros is going to be furious you didn't go tonight."

At that, Everinne downed the contents of her spiced wine. It was a drink only served when the chill of winter replaced the jewels of autumn and was meant to be savored. But she refused to let talk of always disappointing her brother sour her mood, and the warmth of the wine helped ease the thought of knowing she'd face another lecture tomorrow.

"He'll get over it." She shoved her dark hair back from her face, wishing she'd worn it up instead of down. "He always does."

"Yes," Zoryana began, tilting her head in that way she did whenever she was trying to make Everinne see reason. "But Veros—"

"No more talk tonight of how I constantly fail to meet my brother's expectations." Everinne grabbed Zoryana's free hand, luring her further into the swell of dancers. "Let's dance before the stardust falls."

Everinne couldn't be sure, but she could've sworn she heard her friend sigh.

Suspended above them, looking as though they were floating in the moonlit sky, were sparkling chandeliers dripping with star-shaped crystals and stained-glass moons. The violet and blue lights darted all over the nightclub, flashing in time with the music and splintering through the stars and moons like dozens of prisms. Any moment now, stardust would fall from the glass ceiling like rain and cover anyone on the dance floor in iridescent glitter.

It was one of Everinne's favorite themed nights at the Grand Cru and she'd specifically dressed for the occasion, despite the chilly temperature outside. Her dress was entirely too short, but she didn't care, it was lavender, strapless, and covered in dozens of silver beads. Hanging from her neck was a silver chain with a round black diamond pendant and a dark gray leather choker studded with polished amethysts. The thin, ice-pick heels she wore pinched her toes, and she knew she'd have blisters in the morning, but she ignored the dull ache in favor of dancing. She let the tempo overtake her, throwing her arms up over her head so the stack of silver bangles tumbled down her wrists like a sparkling waterfall.

Every so often, a phantom hand would caress her stomach or hip. She brushed it off on the fact that the Grand Cru was absolutely packed and there was no other way to make it through the crowded dance floor without accidentally touching someone within a five-inch proximity of their personal space. But if a male lingered a little too long with a touch, she simply cut them down with a glare and usually they were smart enough to back off. At least the mortal men could take a hint. Immortals, on the other hand, took a bit more convincing. Mostly by force.

Unfortunately for one unlucky male in particular, Everinne wasn't in the mood to be groped.

She shifted, dodging his initial grab. But then he foolishly snaked his arm around her waist, yanking her to him. Everinne whipped around in his arms, curling her fingers beneath his chin. He grinned down at her, displaying a pair of prominently pointy canines. A vampire, then. Lovely. She flicked her thumb along the band of her favorite ring—ornate silver and etched in runes with a sizable amethyst in the center—and a tiny blade sprung free, lightly jabbing the underside of the offender's neck. Just enough to warn him.

"Touch me again," she purred, "and I'll slit your throat."

The vampire's yellow eyes widened, but he didn't release her. "Sorry, *milazk*. I didn't mean to upset you."

"You haven't...yet." She kept her gaze on him, cool and even. "But I'm not your sweetheart."

"Ah, come now, little faerie." His fingers dug into her hips, and she clenched her jaw against his unwanted advance. "I only want to have some fun."

Everinne tilted the tip of her blade, ensuring he felt its bite, and he hissed through his teeth.

His breath reeked of cheap alcohol and stale smoke.

The corner of her mouth curved. "Not at my expense."

The vampire rolled his eyes but let her go, his hands falling to his side. He turned away from her then, shoving his way through the dense crowd. She waited until she couldn't detect a trace of his pungent scent before turning back to face Zoryana.

"Do you want to get out of here?" Zoryana asked, carefully

avoiding the drunk mortal girl who almost toppled into them. "The vibe is all wrong tonight."

As much as Everinne hated to admit it, Zoryana had a point. There was no denying her claims. The air in the Grand Cru was infused with a kind of restless energy. Like heightened anticipation just bordering on the edge of danger.

"Besides," Zoryana added, her gaze skimming the crowd of swaying bodies mesmerized by the hypnotic beat. "I feel like we're being watched."

Of course they were being watched.

Everinne wasn't naïve, she knew very well they caught the eye of almost every male in the general vicinity. Zoryana was striking. Tall and slender with spiral curls down to her waist and jade green eyes, she was never without male companionship. Not to mention she had the demeanor of a goddess and attracted others to her like a summer bee to honey. Everinne was quite the opposite. She was curvy where it mattered and wore ridiculously high heels to make up for what she lacked in height. Apparently, her face was less than approachable. She'd been called a bitch more often than she cared to remember, and had a lengthy list of ex-lovers, some of them whose names she could no longer recall.

She stole a glance at the timepiece on the far wall, where the dials ticked in warning. It was too early and the night was still young. If she went home now, there would be too much time to think. To dwell. To regret.

"I'm going to stay a little longer." Everinne looked up at the ceiling once more, and a slow smile spread across her face. "The chandelier is calling my name."

Zoryana pinned her with a look of disdain. "Everinne..."

"Zoryana..." Everinne said, mimicking her tone. "You know you want to do it with me."

"Absolutely not," she huffed, crossing her arms over her chest. "But I can't leave until I make sure you don't fall to your death."

"As long as Veros doesn't find out." Everinne winked.

She hated it when he called her reckless. Or careless. Or

foolish and dangerous. But the truth was, she wasn't any of those things. It wasn't as though she didn't consider the consequences of her actions, because they ultimately crossed her mind once or twice, but she simply didn't care. Not really. It was incredibly difficult to pretend the world was a beautiful, wonderful place full of hopes and dreams when you knew it to be a lie.

So no, she wasn't impulsive or stubborn. She was death-touched, and it had led her down a slippery slope of self-destruction.

At least she could admit it, even if her brother was in denial.

Everinne held up her finger. "One spin."

Zoryana rolled her eyes. "Fine. One spin."

Everinne pushed through the throng of bodies, smacking away hands that attempted to grab her, as she nudged her way closer to one of the curving staircases leading to the spacious balcony outlining the upper level of the Grand Cru. She climbed the dozens of onyx stairs, ignoring the pain as the leather strap of her shoe rubbed against her ankle. When she finally made it to the top, she gripped the railing of the balcony and stared up at the glass ceiling. She didn't even care that her feet ached from dancing, she didn't care about the music that was more like a dull hum. Up here, it was just her and the midnight sky. She felt like she could touch the stars. Like maybe, for a brief moment, she could be worth more than the pain she inflicted upon others.

But then her magic stirred, dark and deadly, as though it heard her silent call.

She shook the notion from her mind, and carefully shimmied over the edge of the rail. There was just enough space to stand with her toes hanging off the edge, and so long as she kept her hand firmly gripped on the railing behind her, she knew she wouldn't fall.

The chandeliers of the Grand Cru spun slowly, twinkling and sparkling, alight with a kind of magic of their own. All Everinne had to do was wait for one to get close enough. Her dress wasn't exactly the right fit to do any tricks, it was far too tight, but she would still be able to spin and twirl. And that freedom alone made it worth every heart-pounding second.

One of the chandeliers floated closer. The crystals seemed to call to her. The curve of its gold loop was just within reach.

Everinne leaned forward, stretching out her arm. Her fingers curled around the cool gold metal, and without a second thought, she shoved off the balcony.

Exhilaration coursed through her, filling her with a tantalizing rush that caused her entire body to tingle. She gripped the gold loop with both hands and spun, imagining she was one of those ballerinas on pointe she'd so often seen at the ballet. Back when Veros still used to take her, of course. Blinking the miserable thought away, Everinne focused on the crowd below her, on the gasps of shock and shouts of excitement as she twirled through the air above them. Using all her strength, she clutched the loop with one hand and slowly released the other, unfurling her arm out to one side. Her muscles burned and her abdomen clenched, but she'd done this a dozen times before, and all of it led to the thousands of sensations she felt when the rest of the world seemed miles away.

The music faded, the cacophony of voices drowned it out as they cheered for her. Loved her.

Everinne swung from the chandelier, whirling with it, dancing on air. The next one came into her line of sight, the crystals winked like they knew exactly what she had planned. All she had to do was get a little bit closer and then she'd leap from one to the other, in a grand finale.

A squeal sounded above the rest of the voices on the dance floor, and there was a shift in the air. The sudden commotion was no longer one of awe and wonder, but more like a fever pitch of delirium.

Her brow pinched together.

What the hell was going on?

Everinne strained over her left shoulder to see what could possibly be the cause of everyone below her losing their godsdamned minds. Between the play of shadows and glaring vibrant lights, she saw him.

Her heart dropped.

Standing in the elaborate entrance of the Grand Cru with a swell of worshippers surrounding him, was none other than Atlas Skye, the Imperial Prince of Prava.

And his piercing green eyes, the ones with swirls of gold, were focused directly on her.

Two

The last thing Atlas Skye expected to see tonight was his best friend's sister dangling from a chandelier, looking like a damn sex goddess.

What the fuck was she thinking?

She moved like a sultry ballerina, grasping the golden arm of the fixture with one hand as she arched and twirled. The dress she wore barely covered her curves and the heels of her shoes reminded him of daggers poised to strike.

On any given day, Everinne Auvyre was wildfire. Impulsive and reckless. She didn't care what anyone thought of her, in fact, Atlas wasn't sure she gave a damn about anything at all. Her mouth spewed words sharper than his finest blade, and her eyes could send the most loyal of males to their knees. But suspended from the ceiling like that, she looked like she was dancing among the stars. Like she was forged from dreams and nightmares. A fantasy in the making. Her graceful movements held him captive a moment longer until she peered over her shoulder and those eyes of hers landed on him.

Pools of turquoise with bursts of gold around the center, laced with venom.

He maneuvered his way further inside the Grand Cru,

carrying himself with the sort of authority one would expect from him. Careless, with his hands tucked into the pockets of his pants and a cocky half smile on his face. Besides, he was the heir to the throne of the Korvny Fae, and he was acutely aware of the effect he had on those around them. The nickname they gave him kept him up at night—the playboy prince. He reigned over pleasure, possessing the ability to elicit lust and desire with barely lifting a finger, and everyone knew it.

It was also the main reason he could count the number of people he trusted on one hand.

A cluster of females surrounded Atlas, cooing, simpering, and fluttering their lashes. His gut clenched but he forced an easy smile. "Ladies."

"Your Highness." One of the females preened, tugging on her red top in an effort to put the fullness of her cleavage on display. "It's such a pleasure to see you tonight."

"The pleasure's all mine."

"I bet it is," she murmured, and Atlas arched a brow. Her insinuation was not lost on him.

It wasn't as though the females encircling him weren't attractive. On the contrary, they were lovely creatures. He could take his pick if he wanted. Hell, he could probably have all three of them at once and guarantee they'd be on board with the idea if it meant they got to fuck the prince of Prava. Whispers of his bedroom activities were widespread, even though he only used the sexual nature of his magic when the willing participant asked for it—begged for it, more like—but tonight he wasn't in the mood for mindless sex.

Not since his father had berated him in front of his entire court earlier in the day by calling him a *walking whorehouse*. Atlas's blood boiled at the thought of his father's booming voice, of his constant ridicule.

Another female, this one with skin the color of freshly fallen snow, looped her arm through his, pawing at his bicep. He spared her a withering glance.

"Bold of you, *milazk.*" Atlas disentangled himself from her clutches. "But I choose who to take to my bed. Not you."

Her mouth fell open in shock. She looked like he'd struck her. *Good.*

He could easily morph from lackadaisical prince to royal asshole.

Shrugging away from the brazen female, Atlas put space between himself and everyone surrounding him, then summoned his wings. Magic thrummed through his blood when they appeared, sleek black feathers streaked with gold. Unfortunately, all they did was garner more attention, including that of his ever-vigilant Captain of the Guard.

Caedian Trivaris took one step toward him in warning. His brow furrowed in concern. "Your Highness…"

Atlas held up his hand. "I'm not going anywhere. I just have to take care of something."

"And by something, you mean—"

But Atlas didn't give him a chance to finish. Instead he shot upward, then aimed for the massive chandeliers rotating around the expansive ceiling of the Grand Cru, where a particular female was about to find herself in a shit ton of trouble.

Behind him, Caedian's stream of curses faded away under the blast of music.

He flew a little higher, close enough to where she would hear him, but far enough away to avoid her fist if the opportunity arose.

"Everinne." He crossed his arms over his chest. If Veros found out about this little stunt, he was going to be pissed. "What the hell are you doing?"

Her icy glare cut to him. She hated him, and for good reason. "None of your business."

"Are you trying to get yourself killed?" He kept his voice even, but when she released the chandelier and simply held onto it with one hand, his heart almost stopped.

"No," she spat, then dragged one ankle up to her knee.

Her skin looked like velvet, all smooth and supple, and Atlas forced his gaze to stay focused on her face.

"Showing off your wingspan a little early tonight, aren't you, Your Radiance?" She smiled then, but it was poisonous.

He wanted to wipe that stupid grin off her pretty little face. There was nothing he loathed more than when she called him *that*. His next words held a bite.

"No more than you're showing off whatever it is you're wearing under that pitiful excuse of a dress."

"Joke's on you." Her smirk sharpened. "I'm not wearing anything under this pitiful excuse of a dress."

His jaw clenched. Godsdamn, she was trouble.

Everinne lengthened her leg, and suddenly all the lights in the Grand Cru went out completely. A roar of excitement sounded from the swelling ocean of people beneath them as shooting stars exploded across the glass dome ceiling. The music pitched, the once frenzied beat dulling to a more calming rhythm. Orbs of silver flashed in incandescent beams of faerie light while glitter fell around them like a waterfall of confetti.

The glitter collected on the collar of his shirt, coating his forearms and boots. It would take months to get this sparkly shit out of his wings.

But Everinne, her face was tilted upward like she was walking in the sun. Her hair shimmered, her body glowed. It clung to the pointed tips of her ears, where purple stones pierced each one. She looked as though she'd been kissed by the stars. The makeshift stardust sprinkled across her cheeks and nose, down her neck, then further still to the swells of her breasts. Atlas tore his gaze back up to her face only to find her watching him.

He shoved his hands back into his pockets, then shifted, stretching his wings.

"If you'd excuse me, I'm trying to finish my performance." Everinne's gaze dipped to the crush of bodies below them. "So I can have a celebratory drink."

Atlas glanced down and spied Zoryana in the throng of

people. He didn't miss the look of worry in the witch's eyes, or the two glasses she held in her hands. One nearly full of spiced wine, the other completely empty. He had no doubt which one belonged to Everinne.

A scowl marred his brow. "I think you've had enough to drink."

"You're not my babysitter, Your Radiance," she taunted, reaching up to grab the chandelier with both hands. "Or are you going to run back to the palace and tell my brother?"

"I might," Atlas snapped back, his anger rising. It infuriated him that she cared so little for Veros, no matter how many times he came to her rescue. "Especially since you blew him off tonight."

There was a brief look in her eyes, an emotion he couldn't place, but then it was gone. She simply stared at him.

"Do you mind?" Everinne's voice dripped with disdain.

Atlas flew back, a little lower, just in case. "By all means, Wild-heart, be my guest."

Her jaw clenched at the use of the nickname, but it encompassed her in every essence of the word. Whether she liked it or not.

She spun away from him, her unruly dark waves tumbling down her back, glimmering in the splashes of silver light. In the next moment, she was swinging, rocking back and forth, using the momentum from the chandelier to assist in launching herself to the one across from her.

Atlas held his breath when she let go.

Everinne's fingers just grazed the gilded arm of the fixture, but it wasn't enough. Her painted nails clawed at the metal, yet she couldn't find purchase. The gasps and screams of everyone watching her little show echoed in his ears as she fell.

With his heart stuck in his throat, he shot forward, wings ripping through the air. He caught her in his arms, soaring over the dancers, and a collective cheer rose up around them when he landed by the bar.

If she didn't already hate him, she certainly would now.

"Veros was right," he muttered as she struggled against his hold. "You do have a death wish."

She scowled up at him, her mesmerizing eyes flashing with fury and something else. Something darker. "I don't have a death wish."

Atlas set her down, and she tugged on the absurd length of her dress in a poor attempt to straighten it. She took one step away from him and stumbled. He grabbed her arm and hauled her backward, spinning her so she faced him fully.

"Oh really? You just fell from a fucking chandelier. What if I hadn't been there to catch you?"

"I'm sure someone else would've saved the day instead." She tried to wrench herself free of him, but he only tightened his hold, not caring when she winced at the strength of his grip.

"Look around you, Everinne." He spat out her name like a curse. "Last I checked, I'm the only fae in Starysa with wings. No one would have saved your ass."

The brilliant purple and blue lights from before returned, flashing across her, cutting through the darkened corner where they stood. She attempted to yank her arm free again, but his hand slid to her wrist, pulling her closer.

"Let me go," she demanded, glaring up at him.

She was quite possibly the only female in the realm who could ever get away with demanding *anything* from him. And it was strictly because he'd known her for a miserable eighty-seven years.

"Why?" he sneered, daring an inch closer. "So you can keep ruining your life?"

Everinne bristled. He could hear the racing of her heart, sense the pounding of her blood. Her cheeks flushed. Not with embarrassment, with anger. She was furious. She was never good at concealing her emotions.

"Well, considering you already did that for me once, I don't see the harm in doing it again."

The scent of her magic slammed into him—blooming midnight lilacs. He was careful not to inhale too deeply.

"Careful, Ever." Atlas leaned forward, until his mouth was barely a breath from her ear. The purple studs lining their smooth points twinkled. "Your magic is showing."

She went rigid in his grip, and he released her.

Zoryana appeared then, quietly taking Everinne's hand in her own. Instantly, Everinne relaxed. Her shoulders slumped, her breathing evened.

"Apologies, Your Highness." Zoryana dipped into a curtsy, shielding Everinne from him. "We were just leaving."

"See that you do." His words were clipped. Cold and unkind. He knew it wasn't fair of him to direct his anger at Zoryana, who was merely trying to save her friend from imminent disaster. Either way, his tone had the desired effect.

Zoryana nodded quickly and draped one arm around Everinne's shoulders, guiding her in the opposite direction.

He watched them walk away, and when Everinne tossed one final look back at him, those turquoise eyes with center rings of gold were filled with enough fire to turn him to ash and dust.

Too bad something so beautiful could be so dangerous.

Atlas sensed his Captain of the Guard before he appeared beside him.

Caedian Trivaris rocked back onto his heels and let out a low whistle. "Damn. No wonder Veros doesn't bring her around the palace much."

Atlas's blood simmered. No. It boiled. He fisted his hands by his sides until his nails bit into his palms. Any deeper and he would draw blood. "She's off limits."

Caedian cocked a mocking brow. "For who?"

"Everyone," Atlas ground out, then jerked his head toward one of the spiral staircases, roughing a hand over his face. "Let's go to the Midnight Lounge. I find myself in want of a drink."

They shuffled their way through the crowd and climbed the stairs. Atlas slid back into the reputation he'd created for himself, once again becoming the playboy prince. He winked and flashed his most charming smile, making sure his dimples were on full display. He kissed hands and wrists, letting his magic slip just a little so the females were damn near feral, and even some of the males were stunned into silence. His sexual appeal knew no bounds, he was in his element. Limitless.

Until he caught sight of his own reflection in the ornate mirror hanging just outside the door to the Midnight Lounge.

Unkempt dark blond hair that always looked messy. Strong jaw and high cheekbones. Eyes that were sometimes gold, then sometimes green. A smile that could win hearts and break them just as quickly. A prince who loathed his father and mourned his mother.

Atlas looked away then, refocusing his attention on the task at hand. He strode into the Midnight Lounge, the most exclusive area in the Grand Cru where only Prava's wealthiest nobles and merchants could find a seat. The balcony was enclosed with reflective glass, so he could see out, but no one else could see inside. Here, the music wasn't loud and pulse-pounding. It was smooth and sensual, a low hum that echoed through his bones. Sleek, black leather sofas were scattered about, with small granite tables for idle conversation, and dark corners for more intimate encounters. The lounge had its own private bar and bartender. All Atlas had to do was raise a hand and a server would instantly appear to answer his beck and call.

This time, he stalked right up to the bar, ordered two shots of honeyfire, and downed them both. The golden liquid tasted like sweetened smoke, though the burn down the back of his throat did little to ease the frustration coursing through him. Caedian's brows narrowed slightly at the quick consumption, but he said nothing. He'd grown accustomed to his prince's indulgences, even though he knew much of it was forced.

Atlas found an empty sofa near the balcony overlooking the dance floor, knowing he wouldn't be alone for long. It was only a matter of time before some female charmed her way onto his lap.

But for now, he had an excellent view, where he could see everyone and everything. Including a certain dark-haired faerie with stardust on her cheeks.

No matter how much Atlas tried to relax, no matter how much he wanted to drink and smoke as many stigs as possible, something else took up residence in his mind. Despite everything, he couldn't shake the image of Everinne leaping from that chandelier, or the heart-stopping fear that pierced him when she fell.

Three

"Come on, Everinne." Zoryana dragged her through the crowd, toward the exit of the Grand Cru.

But if Everinne was being completely honest, her knees were still trembling from that damn near disaster, and the heels she wore were making it far too difficult to walk.

She didn't turn around to look at him again, but she'd already witnessed Atlas disappear into the Midnight Lounge, and she highly doubted he would come back out. Especially not to scold her. He probably already had some willing female straddling his lap with her breasts shoved up into his face while she was busy getting him off.

Everinne rolled her eyes, ignoring the wave of dizziness that swept through her.

Typical.

If Atlas hadn't distracted her, she would've made that jump. Now, he looked like the hero and she looked like she'd fallen on purpose just so he would catch her.

He was infuriating.

Maddening.

"Everinne." Zoryana's soft voice jolted her from her spiraling thoughts, and Everinne blinked, refocusing on her friend.

Zoryana's jade green eyes clouded over and she laced their fingers together, pulling her closer. There was the faintest hint of sage and juniper as her magic coasted over Everinne, stealing away her anger. Goosebumps pebbled her flesh, and it was as though Zoryana wrapped the thread of wrath around her finger, then gently tugged, luring the aggressive emotion from out of Everinne's heart.

"I'm fine." Everinne loosed a shaky breath, calming herself. Her blood cooled, quieting the cruel monster she struggled to keep locked within its cage. And her magic—so violent in nature, it granted her the ability to inflict unimaginable pain—fell silent once more.

But Atlas's words continued to haunt her.

Careful, Ever. Your magic is showing.

She'd almost slipped in front of him, had almost exposed that singular part of herself she hated more than anything. He knew, of course, what she was capable of doing. Just as he knew the kind of suffering she could inflict. Atlas was one of the few who could get under her skin, who could trigger her emotions enough to send her into a turbulent spiral. It was one of the main reasons she couldn't stand to be around him. It was why Zoryana was the only friend she'd ever managed to keep. She'd witnessed the darkest parts of Everinne, all her jagged pieces, and she'd stayed by her side in spite of it all.

Because when Everinne lost control of her emotions, she also lost her restraint. Her vicious magic scraped its way to the surface, unleashing a swell of raging agony. Anyone who stood in her way would fall victim to her torment. She was powerful enough to break hearts and shatter minds, to hurt and wound beyond repair, leaving nothing more than a husk of a soul. The worst was when she killed someone.

It had only happened once, but the memory of it was marked upon her flesh. A tattoo had formed around her wrist in the shape of a vine, and from it, a flower appeared. A blood rose, with crimson petals tinged by black, because the bloom always looked as though it was weeping blood.

She stole a hasty glance down at her wrist. "I need another drink."

"Absolutely not." Zoryana shook her head and sent her rich brown spirals tumbling. "I told Prince Atlas I was getting you out of here."

She tugged lightly but Everinne slipped free. Taking a step back, she fell into the outlying shadows of the Grand Cru, where the blinding dance lights didn't quite reach. "I can't go home, Zory. Not yet."

She sent her a pleading look, silently begging her to understand.

If she went home now, to the deafening quiet of her apartment, it would only be a matter of time before she was consumed by the nightmares that plagued her. Either she drank herself into oblivion in an effort to fall unconscious, or she didn't sleep at all. There was no in between.

Zoryana's stern expression softened, but her kohl-lined gaze flicked to one of the balconies jutting out above them. "If he finds out you stayed, you know he's going to tell Veros."

Everinne grumbled a swear and wrapped her arms around herself. Her mouth twisted to the side. "He probably already has, but don't worry, I'll be gone and back in my own bed before he leaves the lounge."

If she got lucky, Atlas would have far too much to drink and forget all about her escapade, then at least she would be able to avoid Veros's scorn.

"Are you sure?" Zoryana pressed, rubbing her lips together. She glanced around the magnificent dance floor once more, but when she looked back at Everinne, there was a glimmer of concern in her eyes. "I don't feel comfortable leaving you here by yourself."

Starysa was the only safe haven in all of Prava. It was also the only place on the continent of Aedran where mortals and immortals lived together peacefully. It was a conglomerate of fae, vampires, witches, humans, and shifters. During the day, it was breathtaking, filled with remarkable shops and lively markets selling any number of crafted artisan goods and oddities. The constant buzz from the bustling harbor was more like music, where dozens of ships took to port and traveling merchants came to trade their eccentric wares. But sometimes when dusk fell and the moon took to the skies, the energy shifted. The lurking Deszvila Forest pressed in on the walled city, the threat of its wicked wood and the fearsome stories of its past enough to make Starysa appear like a glowing beacon of protection. But the night was when shadows walked. There were obscure alleys, unlit corners, and the sprawling underdark of the occult beneath the city's center, perfect for conducting dark deeds and striking nefarious bargains.

But Everinne could take care of herself.

Of that, she was sure.

She lifted both hands, feigning innocence. "I'm only going to sit at the bar. I'll order one more glass of spiced wine and then I'll leave."

Zoryana debated, tucking the corner of her bottom lip between her teeth. She shifted her weight, then stole a look at the glass ceiling. The moon was barely visible behind a stretch of inky clouds. "Alright, if you're certain. But my door will be unlocked in case you decide you don't want to make the trek home."

Zoryana's apartment was only a few blocks from the Grand Cru, whereas Everinne lived in the shopping district, surrounded by darling shops and half of the city's pretentious elite.

"Thanks, Zory." Everinne leaned forward and pressed a light kiss to her friend's cheek. "I won't be out late. Promise."

She extended her arms and wrapped Zoryana in an embrace. Her friend squeezed once, tightly, before finally letting her go. "See you tomorrow?"

Everinne nodded. "Of course."

She watched as Zoryana made her way through the throng of

bodies on the dance floor until she disappeared from view completely. Everinne had promised she would only have one more drink and if that was the case, then she was going to make it a strong one.

Spinning on her heel and only teetering off-balance once, she headed for the bar. Not surprisingly, there was nowhere to sit and barely anywhere to stand. Nudging her way between a vampire with alabaster skin and bronze hair and the female human trying to seduce him, she reached over the slab of mahogany wood and hailed the bartender.

"Excuse you," the female spat, crossing her arms so her cleavage became more prominent. "We were having a conversation."

Everinne's gaze flicked over to the vampire in question. He pressed his lips together and gave the slightest shake of his head. She took that as her cue.

"Were you?" she cooed, eyeing the female from the tips of her hideous sequined shoes to her lime green dress that stretched around her like lizard's skin. "I hadn't noticed."

She winked at the vampire.

He chuckled, muttering his gratitude before returning to his drink. The woman scowled, and Everinne could feel the heat from her glare burning into her back, but she paid her no mind when the bartender appeared before her.

"What can I get you?" he asked, his voice gruff, his black eyes never quite meeting hers.

Everinne gave her best smile. "One glass of spiced wine, please."

He answered with nothing but a grunt, and a moment later, a glass of the delicious wine was set before her. Everinne slid two notes across the bar, grabbed her drink, and went in search of somewhere to sit. Or at least somewhere less crowded to stand.

She whirled around, but the thin heel of her stiletto didn't twist. It lodged itself between the wooden beams of the floor and when she jerked her leg forward to remove it, the momentum from her upper body sent her tumbling forward. The deep burgundy contents of her wine sloshed over the rim of the glass, and she instinctively threw one arm out as she careened toward the ground. Everinne yelped and braced for impact until a strong arm wrapped around her waist and pulled her upright.

"Easy there." A deep, rumbling voice coated the back of her neck like frosty ice. "I've got you."

Everinne turned in the arms of her rescuer, looked up into his face, and her mouth fell open.

She snapped it shut quickly enough, but not before devouring the fine specimen of a male who held her.

He might've been mortal—he lacked the distinctively pointed ears of a fae and his smile failed to reveal the sharp fangs of a vampire—but there was definitely something different about him. His warm brown hair was swept to the side, only partially hiding his handsomely sculpted face. Deep honey-colored eyes stared down at her from beneath dark brows, and when the corner of his mouth curved again, her knees softened. He wore all black, from his crisp shirt to his sleek pants, and on almost every single finger was a silver ring molded to look like a skull. One in particular had a pair of glittering ruby gems for eyes. She sucked in a breath and if she was a lesser female, she would've swooned. Whatever cologne he was wearing was enough to make her mouth water. He smelled woodsy and sensual, with a hint of amber. He was stunning, and by the feel of his solid, muscular arm still snared around her waist, she would bet anything he was good in bed.

Since Everinne was already covered in glitter, all she had to do now was find someone to take home, and her plans for the night would be complete.

Testing the waters, she sank her teeth into her bottom lip and a little thrill of pleasure shot straight to her core when his eyes tracked the movement.

"Can I buy you another drink?" he asked smoothly, nodding to her nearly empty glass. "Half of yours seems to be on the floor."

Everinne shifted closer to him, gently pressing herself against his solid chest. "Absolutely."

His answering grin had her wanting to drag him out the door right now and straight to her bed.

He edged his way back to the bar, bringing her with him, his hand maneuvering to the small of her back. Her entire spine tingled from his touch and goosebumps pebbled across her flesh. "What'll you have?"

She didn't care. "Whatever you're having."

He laughed, low and rumbling, and a flush spread through her. Swift and heady. "Are you sure about that?"

She simpered, offering him a throaty laugh of her own. "Pick your poison."

The mysterious male signaled the bartender. "Two soul snatchers."

The bartender nodded and started mixing their drinks. Everinne kept her eyes glued to him the entire time. When he handed them their beverages, she eyed the strange green liquid dubiously. She took a small sip and instantly regretted her choice. The flavors of tart apples and sweet berries mingled on her tongue. The soul snatcher wasn't only delicious. It was downright dangerous. Perfect for passing out in a drunken stupor and escaping an evening full of nightmares. She took another gulp, like she was dying of thirst.

Skulls, as she aptly dubbed him since she never bothered to learn the names of the men she slept with, turned to face her. He watched her over the rim of his glass, his gaze skimming the swell of her breasts before following the length of her neck, then settling on her mouth. He lifted his drink to his lips, slowly draining the entire thing.

"Where'd your friend go?"

"Home." Everinne swallowed down the rest of her soul snatcher, matching him. Two could play at this game, and she was never one to back down from a challenge. But almost as soon as she set her glass back down on the bar, the world tilted, blurring in a swirl of colors, and she swayed into him.

He caught her easily enough, his hand settling comfortably on her waist. Cold seemed to emanate from him, the coolness from his touch seeping through her dress so it was almost like he was touching her skin.

Skulls shifted, his molten eyes lingering on her mouth once more. "What about you?"

She blinked, trying to force his devilishly handsome face back into focus. "What about me?"

"When are you going home?"

"When I feel like it." Everinne swallowed hard. Her words were already slurring into one another. Whatever alcohol was in that green drink worked quickly, clouding her senses so she had to make an effort to remember how to speak properly.

"I can walk you back," he offered, his thumb tracing idle circles along her hip. "If you like."

Oh yes. She would like that very much.

Everinne hummed in agreement, leaning closer. "I think that sounds...like a wonderful idea."

Everything about Skulls seemed like a wonderful idea. She knew from previous experience that it would take nothing more than tracing one finger along the stiff collar of his shirt or fluttering her lashes with the promise of temptation to convince him to stay the night. Feeling more than a little adventurous, she cautiously placed one hand on his upper arm and the muscles beneath her palm flexed.

Her smile turned purely feline.

Oh yes, he would not be a gentle lover. He would take her hard and fast, just the way she liked it. She imagined him bending her over the kitchen table while her nails dug in, clawing at the soft wood. Or perhaps he'd hoist her up in those muscular arms of his and pin her to the wall of her bedroom as he pumped himself into her until she forgot her own name. Hells, he could take her out the back door of the Grand Cru and have his way with her in a dark alley for all she cared. The mere thought of it caused warmth to pool low in her belly and she squeezed her thighs together, suddenly desperate to be anywhere else that involved no clothing and no promises.

Skulls eyed her empty glass on the bar, his hand gradually moving from her hip to her lower spine, pulling her into him. "Can I get you another?"

"Can't." Everinne shook her head, then squeezed her eyes shut, leaning backward against the assault of alcohol as it sloshed through her. When she opened them, the Grand Cru blinked back into focus. "Promised I'd only have...one more and...then go home."

His teeth scraped along his bottom lip as his eyes lingered on the short length of her dress. "It's cold out tonight."

Everinne shivered, despite the sweltering temperature inside the parlor. The cold coming off him almost matched the frigid winter breeze outside. She reached up, locking her arms around his neck.

"You could keep me warm."

His hand dipped lower, cupping her bottom, and she was ready to climb him like a fucking tree. "If you insist."

"Oh," she purred, "I do."

Skulls stood, wrapping an arm snugly around her as he led her toward the exit of the Grand Cru. She leaned into him, somewhat for comfort, but mostly to keep herself from falling on her face. Whereas she usually had to struggle to get through the pulsing dance floor on her own, everyone else simply moved out of the way for *him*. She wished she held that kind of power.

Yes, this was exactly what she needed. A night of wild sex with no strings, no emotions, and no nightmares.

Four

The giggly female vampire sitting on Atlas's lap ran her nails up and down his chest, whispering promises into his ear about how she *swore* she wouldn't use her fangs on his cock, but he was hardly listening. He was simply going through the motions expected of him. She was stunning—deep ebony skin, eyes that reminded him of topaz, and sleek black hair that fell in a thick braid over one shoulder. His fingers tapped a restless rhythm against her slender waist, which she took as her cue to sidle closer. Every inch she moved sent her velvet skirt creeping higher up her thighs. She leaned in, her glossy berry painted lips primed for a kiss, but Atlas leaned back, craning his neck to peer over the balcony behind them.

And then he saw her.

Everinne was tangled in the arms of Jarek Zima. If it had been anyone else, Atlas told himself he probably wouldn't care, but if Everinne thought she was going to take a demon summoner back to her bed, she was highly mistaken.

When Jarek's hand slid lower to palm the curve of her ass, Atlas's pulse hammered in rage.

Over his dead fucking body.

"Excuse me, *milazk*." Atlas lifted the vampire off his lap, despite her pretty pout, and deposited her on the sofa beside him.

He stood, glanced over the balcony, his gaze zeroing in on them once more. Without another thought, he stalked toward the door of the Midnight Lounge.

"Your Imperial Highness."

Damn it.

Caedian appeared from the shadowed corner of the lounge, always on duty. He stepped forward, tucking his hands behind him. "Where are you going?"

Atlas lifted a hand, waving him off. "Stand down, Captain. I'm just going home."

Caedian arched a suspicious brow, the glass ceiling of the Grand Cru proving it was going to be an earlier night than usual. "Already?"

"I forgot I have something I need to take care of," Atlas muttered.

He stalked out of the lounge and closed the door soundly behind him. Almost instantly a flock of females descended upon him, but he was in no mood to wage war against the females of Starysa. His wings exploded from behind him, forcing them to stumble backward, away from him.

"Apologies, ladies. No time to play tonight." He gripped the railing of the staircase, swung both legs over, then let his wings carry him across the dance floor. Soaring lower, he ignored the gasps and shouts of his name, then dropped right in front of Everinne and Jarek, effectively blocking their path.

Everinne didn't notice him at first, her face was angled up toward the demon summoner, her eyes glassy from too much drink. She stumbled along beside him, holding onto him like she'd fall over if she let go. If she wasn't careful, she'd break her ankle in those damn shoes.

Atlas stretched his wings wider in a full display of power. No one approached him, no one spoke to him, but everyone watched him. He shoved his hands into his pockets, clenching his fists, and offered a slow smile.

"Evening," he drawled.

Everinne's gaze swung to him, and Atlas didn't miss the way Jarek's finger dug into her hip before he went rigid next to her.

"Your Imperial Highness." Jarek bowed, but Everinne's face hardened.

"Make anyone orgasm yet, Your Radiance?" she asked, her smile sharp.

"Not yet." Atlas rocked back onto his heels, then winked, just to piss her off. "But the night is still young."

Her jaw went slack but she recovered quickly, her full lips pressing into a firm line. She tugged on Jarek's arm, trying to steer him around Atlas, and lost her balance. He righted her, but she swatted at Atlas's wings in an effort to move past him. He fluttered them once, just to annoy her further.

Her brow furrowed, and those turquoise eyes of hers cut to him. "Move out of the way, playboy prince."

The slight was a little too loud, and his blood simmered at her public display of disrespect. It was one thing to mouth off to him in private, it was something else altogether when his citizens were watching.

He reached out, snaring her by the chin, and forcing her to look up at him. She struggled but he tightened his grip, holding her in place. She sucked in a sharp breath, eyes widening.

"Mind yourself, Wildheart," he murmured softly. "You might be my best friend's sister, but I'm still your *prince*."

Her scowl deepened.

"In a hurry tonight, Everinne?" He released her.

She stumbled backward, and Jarek's hand darted to the small of her back to keep her from falling. If the demon summoner wasn't careful, Atlas would cut off the offending hand one finger at a time.

"Yes, actually." Everinne slid one finger down Jarek's chest, then hooked it into the waistband of his pants. Atlas's jaw clenched. "As a matter of fact, I'm going home with..."

Her voice trailed off and a pretty shade of pink flushed her cheeks.

Atlas arched a mocking brow, then smirked down at her. Ah. So, she didn't even know the name of the guy who was escorting her out of the Grand Cru.

"Jarek," the demon summoner supplied for her, not at all embarrassed by her lack of knowledge.

"I would've asked," she ground out, shoving her dark waves back from her face.

"When?" Atlas asked, knowing exactly what to say to rile her up. "Before or after you sleep with him?"

"Fuck off, Atlas," she spat, swaying lightly.

"I'm taking her home." Jarek's voice was low and calm, but there was a hint of challenge reflected in his eyes.

"Like hell you are." Atlas held Jarek's stare, daring him to contradict him. Undercurrents of tension throbbed between them, drawing a thick crowd of onlookers. Many of them were partygoers out for a night of fun, drawn in by the spectacle of someone coming to a standoff with their beloved prince. The other half were royal guards, simply waiting for him to give the word.

Everinne barreled forward, poking Atlas in the chest with her finger. "Get out of my way."

He snared her wrist and leaned forward, ensuring his lips grazed the lobe of her ear, all while keeping his hard gaze trained on Jarek. She went utterly still, her breath hitching. "And what do you think Veros will say when he learns his sister spent the night with a fucking demon summoner? Do you really want to explain to him how little you care for your own life?"

She turned her head then, her lush mouth suddenly less than a breath away from his own. The apples of her cheeks were still dusted with iridescent glitter, and so was the tip of her nose. He didn't want to think about where else those sparkly little flecks were hiding. Her turquoise gaze dipped down to where their lips almost touched, then darted back up to his eyes.

"A demon summoner?" A breathy gasp left her and her lashes fluttered. "Perhaps I should let him steal my soul."

Atlas knew his next barb would strike true. "That would only work if you had a soul worthy to take, Wildheart."

She made to slap him, but he leaned back, dodging her hand, and she stumbled. Her ankle buckled, and the thin heel of one of her shoes snapped off completely. Everinne yelped, and a fleeting look of pain flashed across her face before she toppled into his arms.

Atlas held her tightly while she pummeled his chest with pathetically weak punches. He could specifically recall a time when one solid punch from her would actually threaten to leave a bruise. But this thrashing about was pitiful. He told himself it was probably just the alcohol—he hated to think she was wasting her life away, but the truth of the matter was she hadn't been the same since...well, since she took that wretched human man's life.

"Let me go!" She struggled against him, her mess of hair tickling his chin.

"Not a chance," he muttered.

When her knee came dangerously close to hitting him in the groin, he decided he had enough. In one swift movement, he lifted her up, tossing her over his shoulder like she was nothing more than a sack of sand. When his royal guards closed in around them, she froze, her fists slacking as she rested her palms against his back.

She may be the sister of the Lord of Time, but an assault on the Imperial Prince of Prava could still land her in the dungeon for a night. If anything, it would be worth it to teach her a lesson.

Atlas leveled Jarek with a cold stare. The male didn't even flinch. Just cracked his knuckles, all those skull rings he wore glinting like shards.

"Go find another toy to play with tonight." He clamped his

hand over the back of Everinne's thighs, ensuring his grip was strong enough to leave prints should she attempt to fight him again, while also making sure he covered her nearly exposed ass. "This one's broken."

At those words, Everinne fell limp against his shoulder.

But Atlas didn't have time to feel guilt for his insult, not while facing off with the demon summoner.

Jarek didn't retort. He wouldn't. Not with everyone watching. He stayed where he was, but even as Atlas turned away and stalked toward the exit with Everinne in tow, he could feel Jarek's hardened eyes launching daggers into his back.

* * *

The brisk winter air cut through Atlas's shirt, freezing his lungs on the first inhale, and from over his shoulder, Everinne shivered.

"Should've brought a coat," Atlas chided. But he held her tighter.

"P-piss off." Her entire body clenched, and he could feel the goosebumps pebbling her thighs against the palm of his hand.

He stalked toward the curb where the *valade* was parked, waiting for him. It was a sleek black vehicle powered by arcane magic. The windows were heavily tinted, the interior was svelte and luxurious, with numerous compartments and amenities— like chilled sparkling wine. Two guards flanked him on both sides, and one darted forward, opening the door for him. Atlas grunted his thanks.

"P-put me d-down. Now." Everinne's harsh whisper echoed around them and she flicked his back. He barely felt it. "You're acting l-like a j-jerk."

He could almost hear her teeth chattering over the wind.

"And you're acting like a petulant child." He bit the words out, then plucked her off his shoulder and dumped her unceremoniously onto the backseat of his *valade*.

She sprawled across the smooth black leather, hissing through her teeth. Atlas slid in next to her, the door closing soundlessly behind him, and she scrambled over to the other side. Like she couldn't stand to be near him. Good. He couldn't stand her either, especially not when she was drunk.

Everinne refused to look at him. Instead, she fidgeted with the compartments along the interior of the vehicle, running her fingers along the glossy edges and curves. For a moment, she stared at the reflective partition separating them from Atlas's driver, but then her gaze drifted to the glass ceiling where the stars were hiding behind layers of clouds and Starysa's bright city lights. She wrapped her arms around herself, then snagged her bottom lip with her teeth, and reached down to touch her ankle.

Her fingers jerked away and even in the slash of dim light coming in through the car's windows as they drove away from the Grand Cru, Atlas realized her ankle was already beginning to swell.

"Let me see it," he demanded, his kindness having long ago evaporated. Along with his patience.

"No," she snarled, crossing her arms.

Another tremble wrecked her, and Atlas reached over, tugging the silver fur blanket from the bench across from them. He tossed it on top of her and he tried again.

"Everinne." He patted his thigh, meeting her glare with one of his own. "Give me your ankle."

She huffed out a breath of annoyance, burying herself beneath the fur, wincing when she tried to adjust her position. "I said no."

"Fine." Atlas stretched his legs out, crossing one ankle over the other as the city passed by in a blur of colored lights and ornate buildings. "Let it swell, then you can hobble up seven flights of stairs by yourself because you're too stubborn."

She paled slightly, but a tiny line formed across her brow. Sliding against the leather, she shifted, revealing the length of her leg from beneath the protection of the fur blanket. Carefully, she propped her injured ankle upon his thigh. It was quite possibly the most sensual thing he'd ever witnessed.

Atlas immediately shook the traitorous thought from his mind.

This was *Everinne*.

Veros's sister.

Not only was she untouchable, but she was unpredictable. Risky. Venomous. The last thing he wanted to do was get tangled up in imagining what those smooth legs of hers might look like wrapped around—*no.*

Atlas blinked and stared down at her ankle resting upon his lap.

The skin was already mottled with splotches of bluish-purple. Granted, it would heal in no time with her fae blood, but that didn't mean he couldn't help speed up the process. He pressed one of the gold buttons on the side of the door and the small compartment flipped open. Hidden inside was a dagger with a golden wolf's head carved into the hilt and fire rubies for eyes, a pack of stigs, a small box of matches since he couldn't control fire, and a glass jar filled with a healing salve.

He pulled out one of the stigs—dried skullcap tightly wrapped in a passionflower stem, perfect for smoking—and pinched it between his lips. Grabbing one of the matches, he struck it against the bottom of Everinne's jeweled shoe. She jerked, her turquoise gaze flaring in the faint glow of the tiny orange flame.

"The fuck," she mumbled, but Atlas ignored her.

He lit the stig, inhaled deeply, then blew out a puff of floral, minty smoke. Almost instantly, his muscles relaxed, the tension crawling along the back of his neck and shoulders eased, and his mood mellowed.

"You shouldn't smoke." Everinne notched open one of the windows and a frigid gust of air fluttered the tendrils of dark hair curling at her neck. When he refused to answer, she huffed in annoyance and tried to pull her leg back. Atlas clamped one hand down on her knee, preventing her from moving. She sighed dramatically, her bottom lip sticking out in what he assumed was supposed to be a snarl but looked like more of a pout. "It's bad for you."

"That's not the only thing that's bad for me." Atlas rolled the stig to the corner of his mouth and grabbed the jar of salve. He twisted off the top, scooped out a small amount of the slightly yellow ointment, and carefully applied it to her swollen ankle.

Everinne's head lolled back against the seat and her eyes fluttered closed, her wispy lashes casting indistinct shadows across the very top of her glitter-covered cheeks. He continued to gently rub the salve into her skin until it dissolved completely and an almost imperceptible sound of pleasure escaped her.

His gut seized.

"What is that stuff?" she asked. Her eyes were still closed and her breathing was becoming deeper.

"It's a healing salve." Atlas closed the jar and returned it to the compartment, clicking it shut. "A friend of mine picked it up during his travels."

"Which friend?"

"You don't know him."

She made a noncommittal noise of disinterest and a few moments of silence passed between them until she said, "Atlas?"

"Hm?" He took another drag of the stig, his hand still casually placed on top of her knee.

"Don't tell Veros about..." She yawned, stretching and drawing her other leg up onto the seat, stretching it out across him. "Skulls."

Skulls? What the fuck was—oh. The demon summoner. Because she didn't know his name.

"I don't keep secrets, Everinne." His blood simmered and he studied the burning tip of the stig, rolling it between his thumb and forefinger. "Especially not when they involve your safety."

"You kept one," she whispered.

Right. *Her* secret.

The fact that she harbored a dangerous magic very few even knew existed.

"That's different." Atlas slung one arm around the back of the seat, keeping his gaze focused on the reflective panel in front of him. They were almost to her apartment.

"Of course." Everinne snuggled into the blanket. "It's always different."

His *valade* pulled to a stop in front of a building in the shopping district. The outside was made to look like the townhomes on either side of it, complete with pale blue shutters outlining each window and bronze balconies barely large enough for two people. But instead of housing one family, it was made of seven apartments, each one stacked on top of the other, and Everinne was on the seventh floor with only the gilded rooftop above her.

Atlas snuffed out his stig, then reached over and gathered Everinne, blanket and all, into his arms. His driver opened the door, and he stepped out, carrying her against his chest.

"Do you need any assistance, Your Imperial Highness?" His driver asked, bowing.

"No, I've got her." His gaze slid to the vehicle that had been trailing them the entire time, and he nodded once to Caedian in the passenger seat. "I'm going to take her upstairs and I'll be right back down."

"Of course, Your Imperial Highness."

Atlas could've taken the lift up to the top floor of Everinne's apartment, but instead he climbed all seven floors to her level. Her head rolled against his shoulder, her breathing even and deep, and he shifted her into one arm to grab the door handle.

Not at all surprised to find it unlocked.

Her place was spacious and tidy, but in a chaotic kind of way. Dozens of half-melted candles flickered to life with faerie light the moment he walked in, illuminating the space with a soft glow. The walls were all painted varying shades of purple and gray, and there was a large onyx bookshelf positioned against one wall that was completely devoid of any reading material. Instead, it was overflowing with different types of crystals—selenite, amethyst, aura quartz, and citrine. Some of them Atlas recognized, but there were a few others he'd never seen before. Bundles of dried sage lined the windowsill in her kitchen, looking out over the city that had not yet gone to sleep. Three empty wineglasses were sitting in the sink, each one of the rims marked by her lipstick, and there was a half-full bottle of sparkling wine sitting on the counter. Her balcony was just off her kitchen, where an oversized crimson sweater was tossed over one chair, like she'd simply forgotten about it.

Or perhaps she spent a lot of time out there. By herself.

Atlas carried her farther, noting the strangely personal art lining the halls in silver frames. Vibrant landscapes, golden splashes representing Starysa, and abstract images, all dark and moody. But there wasn't a single mirror to be found. He almost tripped over a pair of shoes on the wooden floor and gripped her tighter as she mumbled something into his chest.

Her unintelligible words seared through the fabric of his shirt, warming his skin.

He blew out a breath, finally finding her bedroom, and nudged the door open.

Everinne's scent assaulted him. Not the scent of her magic, but of *her*. Warm caramel beneath layers of rose and blackcurrant.

It was entirely too tempting.

He needed to leave before his thoughts betrayed him again.

Atlas laid her down on a plush silk comforter, then covered her with the fur blanket from his *valade*. He turned to go, when something sparkly strewn over the bedpost caught his eye. It was a piece of black lace fabric, studded with little diamonds, likely what she'd considered wearing beneath that dress before deciding not to wear anything at all.

He swallowed a curse before glancing back at her sleeping form one more time.

Not one to linger, Atlas stared at her a minute longer, then shook his head, shoving a hand through his unkempt hair. "Sleep without dreams, Ever."

Then he left, locking her apartment behind him, and wondering why Veros never used his magic to heal his sister's broken soul.

Five

Pain split through Everinne's temples, the sharp ache throbbing in time to the beating of her heart. The agonizing stabbing splintered from the space between her shoulders all the way down to the base of her spine. Her muscles were stiff, her joints sore, like she'd slept in the same position all night. The inside of her mouth was gritty and gross, and the taste of stale alcohol still coated her tongue. Each time she rubbed her lips together, it was like grains of sand had been glued to them. Despite the opaque black curtains hanging from the windows in her bedroom, slashes of angry sunlight slanted across her bed, blinding her.

Everinne groaned, throwing one arm over her eyes.

She was never going to drink a soul snatcher again.

Then again, the nightmares hadn't plagued her, so maybe those tart apple beverages weren't such a bad idea after all.

At the mere thought of alcohol, her stomach revolted, and she rolled onto her side, quickly regretting her decision.

If she could just get to her kitchen, she could cure herself of this godsforsaken hangover. There was a specialty tea she purchased from one of the street vendors in the shopping district, and once she realized the blend of ginger, mint, and a few other herbs instantly relieved her of the night-after agony, she bought a small case to stock her tea drawer.

She crawled out of her bed, shoving her tangled hair back from her face. Then she spied the silver fur blanket. The one she'd used in Atlas's *valade*, after he carted her out of the Grand Cru over his shoulder like he was disciplining a spoiled brat. Bleeding skies, she wouldn't be able to show her face there again for at least two weeks. Maybe longer.

Somehow, the Prince of Prava always managed to ruin everything.

Everinne kicked off her shoes. The one with the broken heel would have to be fixed, but she would deal with that later. She peeled off her dress from the night before, debating if she could make it to the bathroom to shower without passing out from dehydration, and thought better of it. Food and water first, then she could rinse off the parlor's reek.

And the *glitter*.

It was everywhere. Her bed. Her skin. Her hair. The fake star-dust was probably all over her face too, along with smudged liner around her eyes, and smeared lipstick. There was a reason she never kept a mirror in her room. Or anywhere else for that matter.

She rummaged through her drawers, pulling out a pair of black leggings and an oversized blue shirt that most definitely did not belong to her. Perhaps the male witch who shared her bed with her last week had left it behind.

Oh well.

Tugging it on over her head, she padded barefoot across the hardwood floor, reached the threshold of her room, and froze.

The scent of freshly brewed coffee, warm buttery biscuits, and a very distinct blend of tea filled the air.

It could only mean one thing.

Veros was here, and whatever conversation they were going to have would not be a good one.

Everinne sighed, trudging out into the hall, then rounding the corner to where she discovered her brother seated at the small table in her kitchen.

Veros was leaning back in the wooden chair, with his ankle propped up on his knee. In one hand he had a cup of coffee, as black as her soul, and in the other was a book on keys and realms. His hair was dark, just like hers, not black but more of a deep ash brown. It was shorter on the sides, but full and thick on top, so the longer pieces swept across one half of his face. He possessed the same startling eyes as her, but whereas her facial features were softer, his were hard and strong. As always, his clothing was impeccable. Slate gray pants, polished black shoes, and a cream-colored sweater with a small gold wolf stitched upon the upper left chest. A solid gold chain dangled from his pocket, and she knew it connected to the timepiece he always kept safely tucked away.

Sitting on the table across from him was a lavender teacup, already filled to the brim with the steaming hangover remedy. A basket of untouched biscuits wrapped in a napkin was in the middle, and Everinne's stomach rumbled when she caught a whiff of their savory scent.

Veros didn't look up from his book when she sat down at the opposite side of the table. He didn't even acknowledge her.

Everinne pulled one knee up, propping her heel on the edge of the wooden chair. She blew lightly on her tea, then took a small sip, watching him carefully from over the rim.

Seconds of uncomfortable silence ticked by, the tension becoming more palpable with every minute that passed.

Finally, he took a drink of his coffee, then set it down, his turquoise and gold gaze landing on her.

"Do you want to tell me about last night?" he asked, closing his book. "Or should I tell you what I already know?"

Fucking Atlas.

Everinne sipped her tea, meeting the intensity of his stare. "I was at the Grand Cru with Zoryana and had two drinks."

His jaw ticked. "And?"

She was prepared for this, for the inevitable fight. This is what it always came down to between the two of them—Veros would scold her, remind her that she was ruining her life, and toss out idle threats hoping she would promise to change her ways. In turn, Everinne would remain defiant, eventually apologize, and lie to herself about being the sister he deserved.

"And that's it," she mumbled, picking at a loose thread from the hem of the shirt she wore.

His brows narrowed, pulled tight by the final shreds of his restraint.

"So, you didn't swing from a chandelier and then fall? And you didn't almost bring a fucking demon summoner back here to spend the night?" Veros fisted his hand, his knuckles whitening. "And the Prince of Prava didn't have to throw you over his shoulder and carry you out?"

Everinne took a drink of her tea, wishing it would scald her throat. It would be better than dealing with his anger.

Her gaze flicked to him. He looked at her with such utter disappointment, such regret, that her stomach soured. But the spiteful words slipped from her mouth, anyway.

"If you already knew, then why did you ask?"

A tiny vein popped along his forehead. The same one that always appeared when he was furious. Recently, she only witnessed it when he spoke to her.

"Because I wanted to hear it from you." He ground out the words, sitting back in his chair. His hands flexed once. Twice.

"Why?" She tucked her legs beneath her and leaned forward, letting her elbows come to rest on the table. "So I can relay in my own words how much of a fuckup I am?"

"No, Everinne." He shook his head, pushing his swath of dark hair out of his face. When he looked at her again, his eyes had gone cold. "So you can hear how the decisions you're making are becoming more dangerous."

Veros slid the basket of biscuits across the table to her.

She grabbed one, silently grateful it was still warm, and

secretly hoped it would soak off some of the alcohol still sloshing around in her belly. At least the ache in her bones and her head had subsided.

Her attitude, however, had yet to fade. "Are you sure it has nothing to do with your little sister tarnishing your gleaming reputation at court?"

Veros inhaled through his nose. "I don't give a fuck about my reputation, Ever. I care about *you*."

A twinge of guilt pierced Everinne's heart of stone.

"You are my responsibility. Since Mother and Father..." He hesitated then, unable to say the word "died" even though they'd been gone for eighty-seven years. "I vowed to myself that I would keep you safe."

This time, remorse chipped away at her, carving whorls into the hardened wall she'd erected around herself. She hadn't made it easy for him.

The passing of time had not made the agony of their parents' deaths any less difficult to manage. Seasons would pass and Everinne would feel nothing, carrying on with her life as always, then all of a sudden an unbidden wave of grief would slam into her, drowning her. For a fleeting moment, she wouldn't be able to breathe. The sensation would leave her stricken, kicking and clawing her way to the surface, desperate for air.

Being fae, Everinne thought she would have a lifetime with her parents. Hundreds of years, at least. Far longer than that of a mortal. But they'd been taken from her and Veros much sooner than expected. Veros had already been at court with Atlas when the Deszvila Forest crept closer toward their village of Ravski, slowly devouring it. Gnarled roots slithered into windows, shattering the glass—they crumbled stone and brick, destroying everything in their path. Evergreens sprouted overnight, their thick branches fanning out with layers of dark leaves, shrouding all traces of sunlight. Everinne had watched, helpless, as her parents were snatched by ravenous vines and bound to trees, where their life-force was absorbed. Their beautiful faces, twisted in horror, were engraved into the dense trunks, their bodies frozen in time, as though carved directly into the wood.

When Atlas had come to save Everinne from Ravski, he'd discovered her alone and terrified in what was left of their village's square, surrounded by trees sculpted from the dead.

She watched her brother from across the table. As the Lord of Time, Veros couldn't exactly leave court whenever he pleased. His presence was always demanded by Kralv Oldrich Skye, Prava's monarch, but his friendship with Atlas was why he stayed without complaint. Veros's magic gifted him the ability to control time. To weave it. To move through it. But it was not always a blessing. Such magic came with its own burdens, its own cost, and though he never expressed frustration with the heavy obligation placed upon his shoulders, Everinne knew it troubled him.

Almost as much as she did.

Veros slung one arm around the back of his chair, stretching both legs out. He crossed one ankle over the other, considering her. "Which is why you can't go on like this."

"Like what?" Everinne asked, wary. There was something about his tone that set her nerves on edge. The hairs along the back of her neck prickled in response.

"The drinking. The partying." He waved one hand lazily between them. "The not giving a fuck."

She pinched off a piece of biscuit and popped it into her mouth. The melty, buttery flavor suddenly tasted stale and dry. "What are you saying, Veros?"

He straightened, ran one finger along the collar of his sweater, then leveled her with a look. "You're cut off."

"What?" Everinne almost choked. She forcefully swallowed the lump of biscuit, then took a hasty gulp of tea. "You can't mean that."

"You've left me with no other choice, Everinne."

She stared out her balcony, where the floor-to-ceiling window displayed rows of perfect, colorful townhomes with dark red and gold roofs, each one decorated with ornate bronze spires. The shopping district of Starysa was home to the capital's elite—fae families who boasted privilege and rank, ancient vampire clans with exorbitant amounts of wealth, and a small coven of witches who could afford it because no one dared to cross them otherwise. Veros put her up in an apartment in the safest part of the city and gave her an allowance, and despite the underlying tension between them, she was grateful he afforded her to live such a sumptuous lifestyle.

The thought of him taking it all away left her palms sweaty.

"What about the apartment?" She scrubbed her hands against her leggings, unable to look away from the intensity of his gaze. He wasn't joking. "If you—"

"The apartment is in my name, Everinne." He rolled his neck, his dark brows drawing closer together, cementing the seriousness of his threat. "I will continue to pay your rent, but you will be on your own for everything else. Food, clothing, your ridiculous number of shoes..."

"But—"

Veros lifted one hand, silencing her. He held more command in that simple gesture than anyone else she knew. Except for maybe the kralv. "That means if you want to waste your funds on alcohol and whatever else it is you do in your spare time, that's on you. But I will no longer support your destructive habits."

"Is this because I didn't show up to your little party at the palace last night?" Everinne ran her fingers under her eyes, grimacing when the tips came away smeared with kohl liner and glitter. Certainly her brother wouldn't stoop so low as to hold this over her head. It was just a party, he invited her to one almost every month.

"No. It's because you *never* show up." His voiced was laced with anger and something that could've been mistaken for defeat. He slammed one fist down on the table, rattling her teacup. Then his hand relaxed and his posture stiffened, pained with disappointment. "Because I realized I can't rely on you anymore."

Her brother's words hung in the air between them, the truth of their fraying relationship. "I can't trust you."

Everinne recoiled at the harshness of his admission.

She knew things were strained between them, but she didn't realize he'd grown so agitated by her behavior. It was one thing for him to shun her or express his constant dismay. But he was the only family she had left, and for him to no longer *trust* her...

"Veros, I—"

"I don't want to hear your excuses." Again, he refused to let her speak. A flash of pain was harbored in the depths of his eyes, but it was replaced by determination in the next blink. "You can only hide from your magic for so long, Everinne, and until you find a way to embrace it, that power will always be in control of *you.*"

He rose from his seat, smoothing away the invisible wrinkles from his pants.

Everinne stumbled out of her chair. She had to find a way to stop him, to change his mind. To beg him to give her one more chance.

Veros strode across the kitchen and threw open the door to her pantry. He heaved a heavy sigh, one that was filled with exasperation, and he dipped his head to his chest, shaking it lightly. The shelves were bare, save for a nearly empty bottle of honeyfire, a loaf of stale bread, and half a jar of blackberry jam.

Everinne scraped her teeth along her bottom lip, wrapping her arms tightly around herself.

She never allowed herself to be embarrassed. It was a rare occasion for her to feel mortified or humiliated anymore. She'd taught herself to ignore what others said about her, to shield her heart and mind from caustic insinuations, to keep herself from feeling *anything*. But standing there in her kitchen, with Veros's back to her and his shoulders taut with displeasure, shame colored her cheeks.

He reached into his back pocket and pulled out a bundle of pale blue notes. He licked his thumb, counted out an indiscernible amount, and she watched as he popped his jaw, then took the fistful of notes and slammed them onto the table. His eyes darkened, meeting hers.

"You will receive nothing else from me."

Somehow, it seemed as though he was talking about more than money.

Without another word, her brother turned to leave. His perfectly shined boots echoed softly against the hardwood floor.

Everinne's chest squeezed, and she absently rubbed the area above her heart where pain seemed to radiate.

"Veros?" Her voice was far more unsteady that she would have liked.

He stilled, reaching for the door.

"What do I do?" she asked.

Veros spared her a glance from over his shoulder, refusing to meet her gaze. "Go shower, Everinne. You reek of sweat and alcohol. Then I suggest you find some kind of employment, or else you'll be starving before winter thaws."

Everinne pressed her lips together as her brother walked out of her apartment, leaving her alone in her misery. But she couldn't allow herself to wallow in the anguish that settled around her like a suffocating cloak. No, she would have to bury that emotion. Because if she thought too deeply about losing Veros, if she paid too much attention to the feelings she hid away in the darkest part of her soul, then the violence of her magic would awaken, tearing through her like a heinous monster. It would devour everyone in its path, taking her with it.

Sucking in a shallow breath, reminding herself everything she did was out of necessity, Everinne went to sit out on her small balcony, the one place where the rest of the world could not reach her.

Six

The dining hall was quiet save for the sound of Veros idly pushing food around on his plate.

Atlas watched his oldest friend, taking note of the way Veros poked at the hash and eggs with his fork, not realizing the yolk was running over the edge of the dish. Dropping the fork, he propped his elbows on the arms of the plush chair and interlaced his fingers together. His dark brows were pulled down and his gaze was drawn toward the arching windows where frost etched the shimmering panes of glass.

Gossamer drapes of gold framed the windows, doing very little to keep out the chill, the lengths of thin fabric whispering against the slate floor. Veins of gold ran through each stone, splintering off in different directions like streaks of golden lightning. Onyx pillars, so glossy one could see their reflection perfectly, rose to the towering ceiling to support beams of smooth ebony. Situated above the expansive length of table were two massive chandeliers—the crystals dangling from them tinkling lightly like an enchanting melody.

The corner of Atlas's mouth curved.

He reached for an apple from the overflowing fruit bowl set in front of him, ran his thumb along its ruby flesh, then returned his focus to Veros.

Usually, conversation was easy between them.

But the line of consternation had deepened across his brow, and there was only one faerie who was always the cause of Veros's disquiet.

Everinne.

Atlas tossed the apple into the air, caught it, then took a bite. "I take it you went to see your sister this morning?"

Veros nodded once, though his gaze remained trained on the gardens beyond the windows, where winter roses of ivory and silver bloomed, where stark trees stood, the remnants of their ruby leaves clinging to them.

"Yes. After your enlightening revelation last night, I figured something had to be done."

It made no difference if Everinne had asked him to keep quiet on the matter. Atlas refused to keep secrets from Veros, and when they pertained to the well-being of his younger sister, then all bets were off. If it had simply been her performance on the chandeliers at the Grand Cru, he might have kept his opinions to himself. But the moment he'd caught her in the arms of Jarek Zima, he knew there was no way he could remain silent. Veros had to be informed—better he hear it directly from Atlas than some snobbish noble with nothing better to do with their time than spread rumors.

He bit into his apple again, chewing slowly. "And what did you decide?"

Veros adjusted the sleeves of his sweater, slowly rolling the cuffs. "I did the only thing I knew would get through to her. I took away her financial privileges."

Atlas almost choked.

He grabbed a glass of water, chugging the cool liquid down to help dislodge the chunk of apple. Pounding on his chest with one fist, he cleared his throat. "You *what*?"

Finally, Veros glanced over at him. But there was no humor in his gaze. "She's spiraling, Atlas. You know it just as well as I do. I can't sit back and watch her destroy her life while I provide the means to do so."

He ran his fingers along the bottom of his jaw, easing back in his chair as a sense of melancholy fell around his shoulders, dragging them down. "If she wants to party and drink herself into oblivion in an effort to escape her fate, then she'll do so on her own. Without my help."

Atlas dropped his apple onto the table. He scrubbed both hands over his face, then raked them through his messy hair. He hadn't expected Veros to take Everinne's discipline so far. Truth be told, he thought he'd hand her another slap on her wrist, and she'd continue with her reckless ways.

"Veros, as much as I commend you for taking a stand, this will be a huge change to everything she's known. Everinne hasn't worked a day in her life."

"She'll learn." His voice was cold and lacking empathy.

Atlas rubbed the back of his neck, glancing up at him from beneath a swath of his unkempt blond hair. "You don't think that's a little harsh?"

Veros turned to face him, rapping his knuckles against the hardwood of the table. "What would you do if you were watching your sister become a shell of herself? If every day and every night, she was getting worse, becoming damn near unrecognizable? All because she's too afraid to accept the magic coursing through her blood?"

Damn.

He made a valid point.

But still...

Atlas scooped his apple back up, pointing it casually in Veros's direction. "You know she does it to avoid her nightmares."

Veros slammed both of his hands on the table so abruptly, and with so much force, that the plates of food rattled and more than one grape tumbled to the floor.

"Nightmares she wouldn't be having if she controlled her

magic instead of allowing it to control her!" His chest heaved and he slumped in his chair, roughing a hand over his face. "Forgive me, Your Highness. That was out of line."

Atlas scoffed. "Don't you give me that royal title bullshit, Veros. You're afraid for her. I get it."

Hells, he was afraid for her, too.

"I did what I thought was best." He pinched the bridge of his nose, then straightened his spine, something he always did whenever he refused to back down from anything. "Everinne is stubborn, but she's also determined. I have no doubt she'll be able to find employment decent enough to keep herself afloat. Whether or not she stays in one place for more than a few weeks is another matter entirely."

Atlas couldn't imagine Everinne working anywhere. She wasn't exactly known for her...pleasant disposition. "I can make a few calls on her behalf and—"

But Veros shook his head. "While I appreciate the gesture, this is something she needs to do on her own."

Lounging in his chair, Atlas slung one arm over the back. "You're really throwing her to the wolves this time, aren't you?"

Veros stared at him, lifting one mirthless brow.

Wolves were the Skye family crest, the crown jewel of the Korvny fae. A lone wolf was emblazoned upon their seal and coat of arms—sleek black fur and slate eyes—and could be found in almost every room of the palace as well as scattered about all of Prava. Its image was woven into uniforms, sewn onto tapestries, carved as figureheads lining every entrance of the palace, and its likeness was mimicked with thousands of mosaic tiles on the floor of the ballroom.

Atlas shifted, tugging on the stiff, formal collar of his dark green shirt. He even had the wolf tattooed upon his flesh. One on his forearm, its jaws open like it was ready to snap through his veins, and another that wrapped around his left shoulder to the center of his chest.

He reached for his glass of water, downing the rest of the

contents in an effort to ease his suddenly dry throat. "She'll hate you for it."

"No more than she does you," Veros replied. "If the Prince of Prava can withstand my sister's hatred for so long, I'm sure I can as well."

His tone was light, but the words somehow twisted through Atlas like a sharpened blade.

The door to the dining hall swung open and a guard entered, dressed in the svelte black and gold of Korvny fae. He bowed, his movements stiff.

"Your Imperial Highness." The guard's gaze slid to Veros, and he inclined his head. "Lord of Time."

Veros returned the gesture.

The guard puffed out his chest as though he was preparing to make a proclamation. "His Esteemed Imperial Majesty, Kralv Oldrich Skye."

Atlas silenced a groan, rolling his eyes where rainbows danced and flickered around the chandeliers. His father, the Kralv of Prava, was a pompous asshole. Only he would find it fitting to use his excessive title when entering the same room as his son.

A moment later, his father strolled into the room.

Oldrich had been on the throne for nearly three hundred years, and though fae aged far differently than most and lived an immensely longer life, he'd gained a few faint lines around his eyes. His hair was a dark brown and threaded with strands of gray at the sides, and his beard was trimmed, though longer than Atlas's mother would've liked, were she still alive. He was a boulder of a male, large and intimidating, with a broad chest and meaty fists capable of crushing a windpipe. Dressed in black pants and boots, with a deep gray shirt and a vest stitched in gold, he carried himself like a male who knew the world he ruled bowed to him.

Atlas, however, imagined it had more to do with Oldrich's magic than any real kind of fortitude. His father's magic allowed him to sense and prey on someone's fear, and he used that ability to his advantage by forcing others to bend to his will.

He tried not to recoil at the sight of his father, but he stood from his seat out of habit, not out of respect. Veros followed suit, bowing before the kralv.

"Veros, I hope the prince isn't wasting too much of your time." Oldrich gave him a hearty clap on the back and to Veros's credit, he didn't even falter.

"Not at all, Your Imperial Majesty." He clasped his hands behind his back, straightening.

"Good, good," Oldrich muttered, already disinterested. "You wouldn't mind giving us a moment? I need to speak with my *son*."

Contempt dripped from his voice.

Atlas's relationship with his father was strained beyond measure. It had been that way since he was born and had only amplified following the death of his mother. Oldrich loathed the fact that he resembled his mother, claiming that because of his looks, Atlas would never be threatening. Coupled with his "sex magic" as his father so aptly described it, Atlas was relegated to a disgrace of an heir. A disappointment. A mistake.

Skepticism lined Veros's face but he nodded once. "Of course, Your Imperial Majesty."

It would only be a matter of time before Veros learned what was discussed after he left the room. The walls within the palace whispered, and Oldrich was never known for maintaining a calm demeanor, especially when he wanted something.

And the only time he ever approached Atlas was when he wanted something.

As Veros left the dining hall, Oldrich seated himself at the table. He demanded a servant fill his plate, and once it was placed before him, he ordered everyone to clear out of the room immediately, leaving Atlas alone with his father.

It must be a serious matter indeed if he didn't want to speak in front of the palace staff. A prickle of unease trekked its way down Atlas's spine.

"Sit." Oldrich pointed at him with a knife, then carved into his roasted beef. "Now."

Disgruntled but not willing to start an argument before the sun had barely reached its highest point, Atlas obeyed.

Beats of tense silence passed between them while his father gnawed on a hunk of beef, washing it down with a large pint of frothy ale. Atlas stared at him, his guard raised, and debated asking if he could be dismissed when Oldrich finally spoke.

"It's time you take a wife."

The words curdled in Atlas's stomach like sour wine. He blinked, not sure he'd heard him correctly. "I'm sorry?"

"Don't be a fool." His father shoveled another forkful of beef into his mouth, chewing noisily. "You heard me."

Atlas rolled his neck, cracked his jaw. There was no fucking way he was going to find a bride. There were more important matters at stake. "I have no desire to marry."

"Of course not," Oldrich chuckled, but it was tainted with hostility. "You'd be more than happy to spend the rest of your days between the legs of some willing wench, and I don't blame you."

He took another swig of ale. "Once upon a time, I felt the same way." Before Atlas could object to the crude remark, Oldrich set his merciless gaze on him. "But you have a duty to your kingdom. A duty to me and your subjects. You owe me an *heir.*"

Atlas's blood ran cold.

"An heir," he repeated numbly.

"A son preferably, though I'd accept a female," Oldrich proclaimed, as though it warranted no further discussion. His tanned cheeks turned a ruddy shade, a sign of his rising hostility. "I've tolerated your shameful foolishness long enough. You're going to find a wife, bed her, and after she births a healthy babe— preferably one with a useful kind of magic—then you can have as many affairs as you please."

"Are you serious?" Atlas countered, slowly sliding his hands beneath the table where he clenched them into fists so tight his nails bit into his palms.

"Of course I'm serious." His father returned his menacing glare.

"All you care about right now is marrying me off?" Atlas leaned forward, his own vexation imploding like an ominous cloud of storms on the horizon. "I know you've heard the reports from Captain Trivaris. Immortals are *vanishing*. Before too long, the ones who've taken notice will start blaming the humans and then we'll have civil unrest on our hands."

He couldn't believe it.

He couldn't believe his father could be so ludicrous, so absolutely mindless.

"And your main concern is about whether or not I find a fucking *wife*?" Atlas reared back, shaking his head in disgust.

Oldrich's complexion deepened, turning an almost hideous purple shade. The veins along his temple bulged, and his grip on the knife he held was so tight, he bent the blade in half. The acrid scent of sulfuric smoke permeated the air, stealing into Atlas's lungs so his eyes watered and his chest burned. It was a silent threat, a promise that his father would use his magic against him if necessary.

"Now you listen to me," he snarled. "You will host a ball, and you will find a wife, or else I will choose one for you. And if you dare refuse me, I will have your ass on the next ship out of here heading for the Karmorva Mountains. Do you understand me?"

Atlas paled.

The Karmorva Mountains were only reachable by sea, the Deszvila Forest had made them entirely inaccessible any other way, and they were also the home of Rizenrok Forge, a camp where thieves, miscreants, and other unfortunate souls were sent to mine for fire rubies. The extent of their crime made no difference, anyone who broke the law was sent to Rizenrok Forge. While there was a dungeon below the palace, Oldrich much rather his prisoners work for their freedom than sit in a cold cell and be of little to no use. If a subject went against their kralv, they spent their sentence in the frigid mountain range bordering the northernmost point of Prava. Atlas knew if his father dispatched him there, he wouldn't be overseeing with the guards. He would be forced to mine.

Oldrich reached over, snagging a fistful of Atlas's shirt collar, and hauled him close. His breath reeked of yarrow and spiced beef. "Do I make myself clear?"

Atlas's jaw clenched and he swallowed the retort on the tip of his tongue.

"Yes," he ground out. "Your Imperial Majesty."

"Good." Oldrich released him, shoving him back into his seat. "Now, get out of my sight so I can finish my lunch in peace."

Atlas pushed up from his chair and stormed out of the dining hall. He stalked through the glittering corridors, wanting nothing more than to shatter every reflective surface he passed. His chest heaved with simmering rage, his thoughts a volatile torrent in his mind. How could he be expected to host a ball and choose a wife in one night? It was absurd, the sort of bullshit one read about in fairy tales. If his father had his way, he'd marry Atlas off to some snobbish fae noble whose only goals in life were to wed a prince and buy expensive dresses.

Fuming, he rounded the next corner. The double onyx doors with the intricate wolf carvings ingrained in the wood stood before him and he barged through them, where he was immediately greeted by a cold gust of winter air and the clang of swords.

None of the soldiers training in the courtyard spared him a glance.

They knew there was only one reason he was out there.

Atlas unbuttoned the top of his shirt, hastily rolling his sleeves. From the corner of his eye, he saw Caedian shove off the far wall. His Captain of the Guard peeled off his coat and draped it over one of the rustic wooden tables littered with practice swords. Caedian grabbed two of them, then sauntered over, the corner of his mouth ticked up in a slight grin.

"Rough morning, Your Highness?" he called out, tossing the one with a black blade in the air.

Atlas caught it by the hilt, appreciating the way its familiar weight settled in his grip.

"Less talking." He readied himself in an attack stance, facing off with Caedian. He cut the sword through the air. Once. Twice. "More fighting."

His captain nodded once and Atlas lunged, stepping into the assault.

Oldrich might be threatening him with the mining camp and marriage, but Atlas had no intention of giving up without a fight.

He would go down swinging if he must.

Seven

"Veros wants you to work?" Zoryana gasped, aghast by the suggestion.

"I know," Everinne mumbled softly. "My thoughts exactly."

She shoved her hands into the pockets of her tight leather pants, freshly annoyed at the prospect.

Together they strolled through the rolling cobblestone streets of the market square at the heart of the shopping district. *Valades* and other vehicles weren't allowed down the uneven avenues, the shopping district was for walking patrons only, which made it easier to browse and peruse as one's leisure. Row after row of quaint little shops were pressed next to one another, the narrow, pastel-hued storefronts showcasing their exceptional wares behind pointed arching windows. Each wooden door was intricately carved, depicting whorls, runes, or some other archaic emblem. Stores owned by witches were always easy to spot—tinkling bells and crystals wrapped with twine hung from every doorknob. The rooftops were all a burnt orange color, many of them boasting curving spires that pierced the sky, and when the early morning or late evening light hit just right, the city was crowned in gold.

The early winter breeze swept through the maze of buildings, and though afternoon sunlight spilled into the square, Everinne still shivered. She knew she should've grabbed a coat, but the deep teal sweater she'd chosen was too pretty to cover up. It fell lazily off one shoulder and was cropped at the waist, but she was beginning to regret her decision.

Everinne and Zoryana continued winding their way along the slightly uneven path as vendors with rolling carts and brightly colored awnings offered an array of fashionable goods. There were displays of expertly crafted daggers with jeweled hilts, lustrous fur cloaks for the coming winter, and the finest selection of fire ruby necklaces she'd ever seen. Yesterday, she easily would've purchased such superfluous items, spending unseemly amounts of money on dresses that sparkled when she moved or perhaps even a few more bottles of honeyfire. Now, however, she actually had to buy things of worth...like *food*.

As though mocking her bitter mood, the mouthwatering scent of whipped lemon cream pastries wafted over to her from one of the stalls.

Her stomach growled, but she ignored it.

"I've never worked a day in my life, Zory." She wrapped her arms around herself in an effort to ward off the goosebumps pebbling across her flesh. "Employment is for..."

Not for someone lesser, exactly. But definitely not for her.

"For everyone else?" Zoryana suggested, pausing to run her fingers along a bolt of vermillion silk, a color that would look decidedly gorgeous against the deep bronze of her skin.

Everinne sighed, shoving her dark waves back from her face. "It sounds awful when you put it that way."

Zoryana's berry lips twisted to the side. "Working sounds awful in general."

She reached into the navy leather satchel slung over her shoulder and handed some notes to the vendor. In return, he put the entire bolt of silk into a brown paper bag, then passed it to her.

Everinne grinned. "What are you going to do with a whole bolt of fabric?"

"I'm not sure exactly." Zoryana shrugged, shifting the bag from one hand to the other. "I suppose I'll have to ask my dressmaker."

She took one step forward, then stopped suddenly, grabbing Everinne's arm. "That's it!"

Everinne glanced over at her, confusion knitting across her brow. "What's it?"

"Dresses, of course! You could see if Whispering Threads is hiring." Zoryana linked their arms together and started walking, taking Everinne along with her. "You love their clothing, and I know you already own a dress from almost every collection. Plus, I bet you'd get an amazing discount."

"Yes." Everinne laughed, but it sounded hollow to her ears. "And then everything I make would be spent on the latest style."

"Mm, that would be unfortunate." Zoryana led her further down the cobblestone walk of the district. The air was slightly tinged by the scent of the sea as they neared the harbor of the Ladova Bay. She snapped her fingers. "Oh, what about that adorable atelier a few streets over? The one with all the magical baubles?"

"Belladonna's?"

"That's the one. Everything she creates is unique and one of a kind. Rare." Zoryana leaned in close, her smile soft as she winked. "Like you."

Her implied intention was not lost on Everinne. "Isn't she a witch?"

She wasn't entirely sure if a witch would be willing to hire a fae. It wasn't as though they weren't amiable with one another, but witches were often demanding and held everyone to tremendously high expectations. Whereas Everinne had been known to disappoint on more than one occasion.

"Yes," Zoryana drew the word out, then winked. "But *I'm* a witch. I could put in a good word for you."

"I suppose it's not too bad of an idea. And I do love her wares." Everinne had been inside Belladonna's Atelier a number of times and was always utterly fascinated. Belladonna had a remarkable assortment of enchanted crowns, glass baubles that would reflect the owner's favorite place, charmed jewelry, and other wondrous items she'd spelled with her magic. "Okay, yes. Let's go see Belladonna, and if she says no, I can always see about getting a position at the Dancing Nymph."

"Ever!" Zoryana clutched one hand to her heart as though she'd be thoroughly scandalized. Her jade gaze darted around their general vicinity. "Keep your voice down."

Everinne smirked.

The Dancing Nymph was one of Starysa's notorious parlors, for lack of a better word, where females and males alike took part in the art of provocative dancing. They performed on stages in elaborate costumes, slowly stripping away one piece of clothing at a time, until they were eventually fully nude. Everinne had never been to the Dancing Nymph, but she imagined there was quite a bit of money to be made if one was willing to dance naked for its patrons.

"I bet I'd be pretty damn good at it." Everinne started to move and sway her hips, and Zoryana laughed, joining her in dancing to the whistling wind and call of the sea.

Everinne shimmied once, then spun, bumping soundly into something solid. At first, she thought she'd knocked into one of the vendor's stalls, but then a firm hand gripped her shoulder.

"Nice moves."

That voice.

Dark, icy, and dangerous.

She caught the flash of silver skull rings before turning to come face to face with Jarek Zima, the demon summoner.

"Imagine seeing you here," Jarek mused, biting into the flesh of a golden peach. Its shimmery juices clung to the corner of his mouth, and he swiped his thumb along his bottom lip, licking it clean.

From beside her, Zoryana made an indiscernible noise.

Everinne blinked, forcing herself to look anywhere but at his mouth. "Skulls, I mean...Jarek. What are you..." She glanced up and down the market's street. "What are you doing here?"

He gave the peach a little squeeze, then took another slow, if not slightly intentional, bite. Licking his lips, he grinned. "Shopping."

Zoryana cleared her throat, shuffling closer.

"Oh, apologies, Zory." Everinne turned toward Zoryana, gesturing to her friend who was practically salivating at the sight of the man eating his piece of fruit. "Jarek, this is my best friend, Zoryana Daleth."

"It's a pleasure," he murmured, leaning casually against one of the stalls. He kicked one leg out, crossing it over the other. His sleek black pants were stitched around the pockets with silver thread, and he'd tucked in his smoke gray shirt. Despite the cooler temperatures, he wore no coat and his rolled sleeves revealed toned forearms. "Where are you ladies off to this fine afternoon?"

Jarek tossed the rest of his peach into a bin behind the stall, ignoring the furious scowl from the vendor on the other side.

Everinne pointed toward the end of the market square, where the road split off in different directions near the harbor. "We were about to head over to Belladonna's Atelier."

He tilted his head, a loose strand of dark brown hair falling across his face. "That's the shop with all the magical baubles and quirky gifts, right?"

"That's the one." Though she wouldn't call Belladonna's quirky—extraordinary maybe, but not quirky. "It's a favorite of mine."

Jarek nodded, his molten gaze flicking to Zoryana then fixating on Everinne. "Anything in particular you're looking to buy? I hear she designs these crystal spheres that look like you're holding the world in the palm of your hands."

Everinne glanced at Zoryana, and a slight frown marred her forehead. Where before she was damn near salivating at the sight of him, now she was studying his manner, noting the skull rings on his fingers, and the constant cold permeating the air around them. Her brows pinched and the jade of her eyes darkened. She shared a look with Everinne, one she recognized well.

Warning.

"Actually," Everinne twisted the ends of her hair together, tossing it over one shoulder. "I was going to inquire about a job."

A stab of shame pierced her, flushing her cheeks.

Jarek didn't seem to notice or care. Instead, he shoved off the stall and stepped forward, towering over her. "Are you looking?"

Everinne rolled her shoulders back, refusing to acknowledge the sting of her own humiliation.

He shoved his hands into his pockets, studying her. "You want to work at a place like Belladonna's?"

"And what's wrong with that?" Zoryana slung her satchel of fabric over one shoulder and crossed her arms, glaring up at him. "Belladonna runs a perfectly respectable shop, just because she's a witch, doesn't mean—"

"Easy there." Jarek lifted both of his hands in defense and held his ground, not even flinching beneath the harshness of her stare. "I have no problem with witches, it's only that—"

"That what?" Zoryana spat, drawing out each word with an intentional pause between them.

Jarek nodded toward Everinne, the afternoon sunlight splintering in between the rise and fall of rooftops, dousing them in gold and cloaking him in shadows. "I would imagine a place like Belladonna's requires a certain type of disposition, and Everinne doesn't seem like much of a people-pleaser, does she?"

Everinne huffed out an annoyed breath.

She wasn't *that* terrible.

"Well..." Zoryana weighed Jarek's words. "When you put it like that..."

"Zory," Everinne admonished, lightly jabbing her friend in the ribs with her elbow.

"He's not wrong," she fired back, pretending to swat her

away. Her lips pulled into a small smile. Not a real one though, this one didn't reach her eyes. She was wearing a mask in front of Jarek, and likely for good reason.

"Then what else do you have in mind?" Everinne liked to think a chocolatier would be a good option for her. She could work in the back of the shop, not have to deal with customers, and be surrounded by raspberry chocolate creams all day long. They were her favorite candy, after all. She shook the dream from her mind, her stomach grumbling in protest. "Because as of today, my brother told me I'm officially on my own."

Zoryana sighed, shaking back her spiraling curls from her face. Her shoulders dropped and she gave a half-hearted shrug. "I suppose there's always the Dancing Nymph."

Everinne stared at her friend for a full minute before a laugh escaped her, loosening the knot of anxiety in her chest.

"Honestly, Zory." She sucked in a breath of the cool winter air tinged by the scent of sugared toffee scones and the sea. It was hard to remember the last time she'd laughed. Fully. Freely.

"I might know a place," Jarek mused, running his knuckles just beneath his left eye so the ruby gems of his skull ring glinted faintly.

"Oh yeah?" Everinne tilted her head and tapped one glittery silver fingernail against her chin. "What kind of place?"

He ran his teeth along his bottom lip, his gaze skimming above her and Zoryana's heads. The next time he spoke, his voice was lower, barely audible above the hushed call of the wind. "Have you ever heard of the Mystic Obscura?"

The Mystic Obscura.

The name was familiar, but it was the sort of place that could never be found. Unless one was invited. Whispers of its magic were shared in murmured conversations, stories of its mesmerizing shows were surrounded by gasps and shrouded in awe. She'd overhead some of the Mystic Obscura's captivating performances involved females who breathed fire and males who danced on water. There were contortionists. Illusionists. Those who partook in a dazzling feat of the death-defying and sensual, a dramatic display of alluring acts.

The Mystic Obscura was an emporium of the extraordinary.

"I hear it's fantastic," Zoryana said quietly, her jade eyes wide and sparkling with wonder. "It's exclusive and enchanting, and entry is only available to those willing to pay the price."

Jarek nodded. "It's all those things and more."

The Mystic Obscura sounded like the perfect place for her. Yet a tingle of apprehension pricked its way down her spine and she shivered. She pinned Jarek with a pointed look. "And you think I should work there?"

His grin was devastating, but the tiny hairs along the back of her neck stood on end.

"I know you could, especially after your performance last night at the Grand Cru." He leaned close, then winked, his dark lashes highlighting the gold of his eyes. "They have the most beautiful chandeliers you've ever seen."

Everinne eased back, peering up into his face. The handsome planes of his cheekbones gave no tell. There was no hint of mockery, no jest. He truly meant what he said, he thought she could do it.

Intrigued, Everinne considered the demon summoner's proposition.

Perhaps Veros forcing her to make her own way was more of a blessing than a curse. She would much rather perform in front of an audience than sell magical baubles to haughty customers all day. Besides, if the rumors she heard were true, the Mystic Obscura was only open in the evenings, and Everinne thrived at night.

She ducked her chin, burying into her loose sweater, then shifted her weight from one foot to the other. "Do you think you could introduce me to someone? Preferably someone with the authority to hire?"

Jarek adjusted the rolled sleeves of his cuffed shirts, where tattoos of skulls and unrecognizable monsters marked his flesh.

"I can do you one better. I can introduce you to the owner." Again, he scraped his teeth along his bottom lip, but she forced herself not to look. "She's a friend of mine."

"Is that so?" Everinne swallowed the bubble of hope, toying with the tiny amethyst daggers dangling from her ears. She couldn't show her excitement or her gratitude. Not yet. "If you're certain you think you can help me, I'd appreciate—"

Jarek raised his hand, silencing her. "On one condition."

Her breath caught and Zoryana sidled closer to her. Of course there would be a price. Nothing was ever free.

Wary, she eyed him coolly. "And what's that?"

"You let me take you out tonight."

Zoryana snorted, her laughter caught between a giggle and the inability to breathe. She waved a hand in front of her face, fanning herself. "A date. He only wants a date as payment."

But Jarek's piercing gaze was latched onto Everinne, holding her captive. "Let me take you to dinner tonight, then we'll go to the Mystic Obscura to meet Reine."

Reine.

Everinne filed the owner's name away in the back of her mind, then she stuck out her hand. "Deal."

Jarek caught her wrist, slowly letting his cool fingers slide over hers like icy silk. He raised her hand to his mouth, pressing a gentle kiss to her knuckles. "I'll pick you up at sunset."

With that, he turned and walked away.

"You don't even know where I live!" Everinne called after him.

He stilled, tossed a glance at her from over his shoulder, and winked again.

Then he gradually vanished into the sea of merchants, vendors, and patrons, disappearing from sight completely.

Once he was gone, Zoryana grabbed both of Everinne's shoulders, spinning her so they were face to face. "When did you meet *him*? I want to know everything."

"There's not much to tell, at least not yet." Everinne shrugged out of Zoryana's hold. "Though I imagine I'll have a story or two tomorrow."

"Oh, you better." But then the amusement faded and her eyes darkened, her pupils nearly devouring the pools of brilliant green. "Be careful there, Everinne. His intentions seem genuine enough, but there's something about his aura, about his vibe, that doesn't quite sit right with me."

"Don't worry," Everinne assured her, looping their arms together and continuing their stroll through the market square. "I'll be careful."

The lie tasted slightly bitter on her tongue.

Everinne might not always be cautious, but no male, demon summoner or otherwise, would dare fuck with her. Not if they knew what was good for them.

Eight

Atlas showered, scrubbing away the salt from his sweat, hissing as the warm spray hit the nick on his shoulder. The tip of Caedian's sword had stung slightly, but already the wound was healing. He ran his hands through his damp, dark blond hair, shuffling them around until he was happy with the wavy pieces he could never quite tame. He stalked from his bathing suite, fully nude, into the adjoining bedroom.

Maxim, his valet, had laid his clothing out across the imposing four-poster bed—Atlas had long ago told Maxim that he was perfectly capable of dressing himself. But that didn't stop him from at least trying to make decisions easier for Atlas. While the ash-colored pants and shiny boots would work well enough, the black shirt and gold-stitched vest would have to go. If there was one thing Atlas refused to do, it was to wear his father's colors. Gold and black dripped from every crevice of the palace, making Atlas's skin crawl.

His chambers were a sanctuary, a haven from the excess and glittering politics of the court. The walls were painted a deep grayish-blue, reminiscent of the surrounding mountains, when winter blanketed all of Starysa. A navy blue silk comforter was draped over his bed, but once the first frost arrived, it would be replaced with silver fur. The only symbol of his birthright was the large painting on the far wall by his wardrobe. Enchanted by magic, it depicted the black wolf running through the mist-laden Deszvila Forest, darting between trees, its slate gaze locked on whatever it chased in the distance.

The Desvila Forest was a daunting expanse of woods that stretched across most of Prava. Dark and cumbersome, the forest started just beyond Starysa's walls and the only thing stopping it was the chain of mountains curving along the Ladova Bay and winding along the frozen north where the mining camps were situated, where the imprisoned and enslaved were sent to mine, and eventually die, for fire rubies. At one time, it was said the forest devoured entire villages, creeping in slowly over time. Trees with thick canopies would sprout up in the middle of homes and buildings, overgrown roots would destroy paths and trails leaving the townspeople to wander lost and alone, and unruly vines would shatter windows and crumble hearths, until the forest swallowed away every last remnant of life. A few villages remained, most of them located on the outskirts of the woods, warded by witchcraft or archaic magic, and reachable only by those who knew where to find them. The tale of the Deszvila Forest was a folktale, but even the seeds of lore grew from truth.

Atlas's own mother had told him that story more times than he could count.

Atlas tugged on the pants and boots, then fastened a leather belt around his waist. He plucked the black shirt off the bed, then yanked open his wardrobe, shoving it to the back in the hopes that months would pass before Maxim found it again. Opting for a trim shirt in an evergreen shade, he pulled it on, leaving the top two buttons undone. If he were going out for the night, he might grab a tie or coat to look the part of a prince, but he had no plans to head into the city this evening.

Nor did he desire to be overwhelmed by lackluster company.

His gaze was drawn to the double doors where the late afternoon sun was already creeping to the west, streaking the sky with ribbons of amber and crimson. Beyond the doors was his verandah where dense shrubs rose up like a wall, surrounding his personal pool, and offering him a shred of privacy. Its smooth surface reflected the leaves and early winter blossoms, reminding him of a looking glass. Curls of steam floated over the turquoise waters—all the pools on the palace grounds were kept cool in spring and summer, and warm in autumn and winter—but Atlas couldn't remember the last time he'd actually been able to enjoy any of the pools without feeling like he was on display.

Filtered sunlight sprinkled onto the desk in the corner of his bedroom, highlighting a pile of sealed invitations to parties he didn't want to attend, and a decanter of honeyfire.

Atlas walked over to the desk, ran his fingers along its grooved edge. Slowly, he pulled open the smallest drawer and removed a wooden box. He swiped his thumb across the top, removing a fine layer of dust, revealing the worn initials carved into its surface.

VS.

Valentyna Skye.

Sighing, he flipped it open.

Cushioned on a pile of scarlet velvet was a ring.

It belonged to his mother. She'd given it to him years ago as a gift, for whenever he chose a wife. Set in gold was a large, oval teal sapphire. It wasn't the ring his father had given her when he proposed marriage, but this one, well, it had been her favorite. The ring had been passed down through generations of fae royals on his mother's side, usually to the daughters. But since Atlas had been the only one born to his parents, she'd given it to him in the hopes that perhaps one day she would have a new daughter through marriage.

The beautiful ring was all he had left of his mother.

His gut clenched and a twisted vine of anger and despair knotted its way through him. He snapped the lid closed, replacing the coveted piece of jewelry in the safety of the drawer. If his father had his way, that ring would be on the finger of one of the wealthiest females in Prava. Some female who likely didn't give a fuck about the former queen and would pout and protest that she hadn't received a fire ruby with a halo of pearls instead.

Atlas locked his jaw, grinding his teeth together so fiercely, a dull ache took form in his temples.

Leaving his room, he aimed for his study at the far end of the wing, the one place that was farthest away from everyone and everything.

Fuming, he shoved open the door, bypassed the shelves of books that he never bothered to read, and went straight to the bronze rolling cart in the corner. He grabbed the crystal decanter of scarlet whiskey—stronger than honeyfire but tasted like oak and bitter thyme—and poured himself a hefty amount.

He plopped down onto the plush sofa and deposited the decanter on the round wooden table before him. Propping his feet up on the table, he kicked one ankle over the other and stared into the stone hearth where a fire crackled.

Atlas had just brought the glass of whiskey to his lips when Veros appeared in the open doorway.

"I thought I might find you here." Veros walked in, then lowered himself into one of the winged high-back chairs.

Atlas glamoured another glass, poured some of the pungent alcohol for Veros, then handed it to him. "Can't say I've got anywhere better to be at the moment."

Veros swirled the murky golden liquid. He took a sip, then settled back, stretching his legs out. "So...marriage, huh?"

"I don't want to talk about it." Atlas glared at the flickering flames of the fire, where sparks jumped and danced, filling the study with a comfortable warmth. Of course Veros would already know about Oldrich's demand. If the palace was good for anything, it was the expedient spread of rumors.

"You knew it was coming." Veros tapped one finger on the rim of his glass. "It was only a matter of time."

An absurd turn of phrase coming from the master of the hour himself.

Atlas pushed his unruly hair from his face and took a large gulp of his drink.

"Even still, I thought I'd have time to get to know her first. But apparently my father thinks I should pick one, then fuck her until she's pregnant." He held up one hand. "And before you respond, yes, I'm aware of my current reputation. Whoever I pick, however, will be the next Kralvina of Prava, and will likely have to deal with my father's bullshit until the day he dies."

Veros nodded slowly, then pulled out a pack of stigs from his front pocket and tossed one to Atlas. Veros reached over into the blue bowl on the table next to his chair and fished out a lighter. After two clicks, a midnight blue flame appeared. He lit his stig, then handed the lighter to Atlas.

"About this future bride of yours," Veros continued, balancing his stig between his fingers while still holding his glass. "She'll need specific qualifications, then."

"Yeah," Atlas said around the stig dangling between his lips. The flame flared and he inhaled deeply, blowing out a cloud of floral and mint scented smoke. "She'll have to be fucking brilliant. She'll need to possess a spine of cold iron but know when to keep her mouth shut."

"Because of the kralv."

Again, not a question. Simply a stated fact.

"Exactly," Atlas agreed, then took another drink. He would love to find a breathtaking bitch of a queen who could win hearts just as easily as she could crush them. It would be even more preferable if she didn't take shit from his father. At the same time, she would have to know when to tread carefully. He couldn't allow her to be sent off to the Rizenrok Forge for crossing the kralv.

"What about her magic?" Veros asked, pulling a drag from his stig.

Atlas barked out a laugh but it was harsh, grating to his own ears. "As long as it's not sex magic, I doubt it will matter. She could be able to spit fire or conjure pastries with a flick of her wrist, and she would still be considered a superior match."

Veros chuckled before shaking his head.

"Do I hear laughter? That's a rare sound within these walls." Caedian tapped lightly on the open door, then walked into the study. He'd cleaned up after sparring with Atlas and looked fresh enough to go for another round. Not that the elite warrior ever needed down time. "What are we discussing?"

Atlas grunted, finishing off his drink. "My future wife."

Then he poured two more glasses of the *bovgka* whiskey. One for himself and one for Caedian.

"Yes." Veros nodded in Atlas's direction. "And apparently she'll be able to conjure that raspberry chocolate cake you're so fond of."

Caedian's face remained blank as he dropped onto the seat next to Atlas. He turned to face him. "Did you say wife?"

Atlas arched a brow. "You haven't heard?"

"Oh, I have." He rubbed a hand along the back of his neck, shifting uncomfortably. "I didn't realize you'd found her already."

"I didn't." Atlas took a final inhale from his stig, then tossed it into the hearth. The flames turned a deep violet from the skullcap, then returned to their normal fiery hue.

Veros smirked. "We're simply going over some of the necessary qualifications."

"I see." Caedian swirled his glass, thoughtful. "And raspberry chocolate cake is a qualifier?"

"Might as well be," Atlas muttered.

Caedian leaned forward, resting both of his elbows upon his knees. His gray gaze landed on Atlas. "How are you going to find this mystery female?"

"My father seems to think I should host a ball," Atlas scoffed. The mere idea of being forced to dress in court regalia while being fawned over like he was nothing more than a walking sex toy was enough to make the alcohol warming his insides sour. "Because what better way to find my future bride than by choosing her from an overabundance of females all vying for my attention?"

To anyone else's ears, his complaints might sound vain. But Veros and Caedian knew him, they knew he was more than the reputation he'd built for himself. More than the prince of pleasure.

"I wonder why the kralv is so intent on you throwing a ball." Veros set his empty glass on the table, and a line of concern creased his forehead. "Seems a bit coincidental, if you ask me."

"Yeah," Caedian agreed, roughing a hand over his face. "Because it's probably serving as a distraction."

Atlas's gaze slid to the door. He listened for any passing servants, any hint that the words they spoke would find their way back to the kralv.

Understanding his intent, Veros stood and quietly closed the door, then returned to his seat.

"Has it happened again?" Atlas asked, keeping his voice low.

Caedian sat back, nodding. "I'm afraid so, Your Highness."

"Who was it this time?"

"Khiran Vespertine."

Fuck.

Khiran belonged to the Morvayne, a clan of ancient and exor-bitantly wealthy vampires known for their lavish parties in the underground of their estate. Not only that, but they produced and marketed a concoction that allowed anyone to be bitten without fully turning. Atlas had attended quite a few of their sexually charged festivities, had been given a personal tour of their extensive wine cellar, and was on a first name basis with Valaina, the clan's leader. In fact, she'd almost convinced him to fuck her until her mate threatened to cut off his cock.

Would've been nice if she mentioned she was taken at the time.

"They won't let this disappearance slide." Atlas blew out a breath, shaking his head. Valaina would take the head of anyone who stood in her way.

"No," Caedian agreed. "They won't."

Already seven immortals had gone missing. Khiran made eight. Not that any life was insignificant, but those who vanished so far had seemingly gone unnoticed by the general public. Khiran, however...

It was only a matter of time before the entire vampire population was in an uproar. Before all of Starysa found out that immortals were disappearing without a trace.

"Does the kralv know?" Veros asked, his face a mask of indifference.

Caedian nodded sharply. "Yes, my lord. He does."

A beat of heavy silence passed between them.

"And?" Atlas prodded.

"And nothing, Your Highness." Caedian glowered, his frustration evident. "He didn't ask any questions, he only mumbled something about bothersome pests, then walked away. He didn't even care."

Fucking bastard.

Oldrich didn't give a damn about Prava. He might have once, before, but not any longer. His greed for wealth far outreached the safety of his subjects. But these vanishings, they were not some little conflict that could be shoved into a closet or swept under a rug to be dealt with another day. They would inevitably cause a rift between the mortals and immortals, especially in regard to where the blame was placed.

Veros leaned back in his chair, clasping his hands across his lap. "Perhaps I made a mistake in taking away Everinne's finances."

Atlas's brows pinched together with confusion. "How so?"

Veros rubbed his lips together, thinking. "All the immortals that have disappeared so far, what is the one thing they have in common?"

"They're similar in age?" Caedian suggested.

Atlas thought for a moment. No, age would not matter. It would have to be something greater, something more significant.

Shadows fell across Veros's face. "No. Their magic."

"But, my lord." Caedian sat up straight, then ran a hand through his white hair. "None of their magic is similar."

"You're right." On his next breath, Veros closed his eyes. When he opened them again, a swirl of an emotion Atlas had never seen before lurked in their turquoise depths. "But each of their magic is *rare*."

Oh shit.

"Oh, shit," Caedian murmured, echoing his sentiments completely.

Veros made a painfully valid point. All eight immortals were blessed with obscure kinds of magic, and the only people who knew about Everinne's magic were the ones sitting in his study. The only reason Caedian knew was because he'd witnessed it. Once.

"If I don't protect her," Veros whispered more to himself than to them, "who will?"

"We will." Atlas looked to his Captain of the Guard. "I want Everinne watched at all times, but only send your best soldiers. The ones who move with the shadows, who track and remain undetected. The ones who stay out of sight."

Veros made a derisive sort of noise, but the corner of his mouth tugged upward. "If she finds out she's being spied on, I'll never hear the end of it."

"None of us will." Atlas grinned, knowing full well Everinne would make their lives miserable. Then he returned his attention back to Caedian. "I want reports of her every movement. Daily updates of her whereabouts. If she so much as *breathes*, I want to be informed. Do you understand?"

Caedian nodded, pressing one fist to his heart. "Yes, Your Imperial Highness."

Atlas stole a glance at Veros. Worry haunted the planes of his face. There was a sliver of fear there too, the deep, terrifying realization that he may not be able to protect his sister.

"Relax, Veros." Atlas leaned back, confident in his abilities to at least do *one* thing right. "We won't let anything happen to her."

He told himself he'd do it for anyone, that he would put such extreme precautions in place for anyone else. But it was a lie. Everinne might be careless and a thorn in his side at times, but by the gods, she was *powerful*. If she fell into the wrong hands, if her magic was controlled by someone with a corrupt heart, it would be devastating.

Atlas glamoured a deck of cards on the table in front of him, and a healthy stack of gold coins. He bent forward and started shuffling. "Who's up for a round of Cups?"

Caedian's robust laughter filled the study, pressing down on the tension until it dissolved completely.

"Last time we played Cups, you took all of my money." But then he pulled out a velvet pouch and gave it a shake. The jingle of coins echoed loudly. "Deal me in."

Atlas arched a brow, eyeing his best friend, wishing he could offer him more reassurance. "Veros?"

He reached into his pocket and pulled out the gold timepiece he always wore. The chain glinted in the soft light. The face was made of a shimmery blue stone and silver dials spun in multiple directions at different speeds. Runes were engraved along the outer edge, and while Atlas knew Veros controlled time, he'd never quite figured out the complexities of how his magic actually worked.

Veros slid the timepiece back into his pocket and then pulled out a stack of notes, dropping them onto the table.

"One round." He grinned. "Hope you're ready to lose those precious cufflinks of yours, playboy prince."

Atlas laughed. Loudly. Fully.

Those fucking cufflinks were hand-cut sapphires and worth more than all the coins and notes on the table combined.

Atlas smirked. "Bring it on, time lord."

Nine

Dinner with the demon summoner was...fine.

It wasn't as though Everinne didn't enjoy Jarek's company, on the contrary. He was respectable, made easy conversation, and there was something about his voice that caused her to stare at his mouth more often than she cared to admit. All of which were perfectly acceptable, even desirable, qualities.

And yet...

The way he looked at her left her unsettled. He didn't watch her the way other males did—there was no leering, no lust-filled longing. He didn't undress her with his eyes, or act like he couldn't wait to fuck her against a wall until she forgot her own name. No, Jarek *studied* her. Every movement she made, every word she spoke, she could almost see him committing every detail about her to his memory. From the moment she sipped her fire-bomb martini and smoke curled around her lips, to when she fiddled with the black diamond necklace dangling at her throat. He tracked all of it.

After dinner, just as Jarek promised, he brought her to the Mystic Obscura.

At least, she hoped that was where he'd taken her.

They climbed out of the *valade* and Everinne found herself standing before a dimly lit alley in the pulsing heart of Starysa. Around her, the city was alive, full of vibrant music and raucous laughter as everyone wandered down the streets in search of the next best party. None of them noticed her standing there with Jarek, hesitant to take that first step into the alley where the filtered gold light from the streetlamps didn't quite reach. In fact, every soul who passed by them never even glanced their way, as though they were invisible.

Jarek nodded toward the alley, gesturing before them. In the seeping darkness, his eyes burned bright like molten gold. He winked. "After you."

Everinne blew out a low breath that misted before her as the chill of the night settled into her bones. There was no going back now. And though she couldn't quite shake the undercurrent of unease humming just beneath her skin, her curiosity couldn't be silenced. She swallowed the knot of trepidation threatening to choke her and walked forward, stepping right through a shimmer of glamour. Magic coated her skin, the feel of it reminding her of cool satin. Behind her, the sounds of Starysa were muffled. The music was distorted, the voices garbled and distant. Slightly crumbling, aged stone walls surrounded both sides of her, but at the very back end of the alley, a door appeared.

Glossy, midnight blue wood with bronze-dusted whorls and spirals took shape, complete with a curving gilded handle.

Slowly, Everinne edged nearer, aware of Jarek's closeness to her.

Whether he intended to protect her or lure her in, she couldn't be sure. She considered asking him as much when a sign materialized above the door.

It was the same shade of blue as the door, with swirling silver edges, and in faint lettering, two words were scrawled in a bold, elegant script.

Mystic Obscura.

Everinne leaned back a bit, taking in the dilapidated exterior of the building and the door that was so shiny she could see her reflection. It was hardly an imposing entrance. If anything, it was lackluster and disappointing.

She cocked one hip to the side, crossing her arms. "It's not quite what I was expecting."

"Nothing ever is." Jarek opened the door, then turned to face her, holding out his hand.

Beyond him, the alluring music of a violin and piano called to the depth of pain she kept hidden away inside her. The place she never let anyone see.

She hesitated for only a moment before accepting Jarek's hand and allowing him to lead her inside.

The entryway was more like a maze, a confusing pattern of vanishing corners behind silk curtains of deep sapphire and bronze that seemed to move and shift and breathe. Fractured, mirrored spheres glowing with gold fire sent splintered beams of light and shadow flickering across the high ceiling. A faint silver mist curled around her feet, spilling over her heeled boots, concealing the floor from her view. Jarek's grip on her hand remained firm and steady, then he reached out in front of him, pulling one of the thick curtains aside.

Everinne's jaw dropped.

He inclined his head, tilting it toward the grandeur glimmering right in front of them.

"Welcome to the Mystic Obscura, Everinne."

She had never seen anything so wondrous in all her existence.

Grand chandeliers sparkled like lustrous topaz above a massive theater where a center stage hovered, suspended in the air by magic. A female dressed in a nude bodysuit covered in diamonds twirled across the stage, wrapped in thick ribbons of scarlet silk. Her body twisted and flowed to the music, flawless and fluid, as murmurs of awe and applause echoed through the elaborate hall. Rows of decadent balcony seating swept up to dizzying heights along every wall, and while many suites were occupied by some of the city's wealthiest patrons, others were hidden away behind deep blue draperies, lending to their allure and intrigue. The mist around Everinne's feet had cleared, and she realized she stood upon a floor of iridescent mosaic glass with veins of dark gold spiraling off in different directions.

While it seemed as though the balcony seats had the best view of the stage, it was the area around and beneath it that was brimming with all the fantastical wonders that gave the Mystic Obscura its namesake.

There were fountains carved from lapis lazuli where sparkling wine flowed freely into towers of wine glasses. Females wore next to nothing, save for the swaths of satin hugging their lithe bodies while every other inch of their flesh dripped with jewels. Some of them danced, the sound of their heels clicking in time with the mesmerizing beat of music. Others served refreshments, balancing trays of glimmering drinks that caught fire, sending blue sparks shooting into the air. The males donned bronze pants with chains that hung around their waists, and black top hats. They wore trim coats layered with an excessive amount of midnight feathers and their chests were bare, revealing sculpted muscles and intimidating tattoos.

At first glance, it didn't appear as though the males had anything better to do than stalk about with permanent scowls creasing their brows.

But Everinne quickly realized they weren't haughty performers who curled their upper lips at any patron who passed by too close.

No, that wasn't the case at all.

They were *watching* the females. Protecting them from any unwanted advances or crude remarks.

"This is the menagerie." Jarek spoke in hushed tones, draping his arm casually around her bare shoulders.

She'd left her coat in her apartment, opting instead for a strapless silver dress that dipped down low in the back and was covered in crystals that swung and tinkled as she moved. Not her best idea, considering the freeze of winter was growing colder each day, but she'd assumed a place like the Mystic Obscura would be warm, if not overly stuffy. Unfortunately, the cold emanating from Jarek caused her to shiver, and he took it as his cue to draw her in closer to his side.

Everinne turned, feigning interest in a massive wooden wheel painted in swirls of washed gold and brilliant blue. A rack of assorted daggers with leather-wrapped hilts and gleaming blades was positioned next to it. She carefully eased out from underneath his hold.

"That looks interesting." She nodded toward the wooden wheel, where leather bindings were attached to four outer corners.

"I suppose." Jarek's golden honey eyes sparked in the slash of light, illuminating the predator within him. "If you're into bondage and blade play."

She tilted her head, considering. "I could be."

Jarek laughed but it was rough, and he smothered it with one hand. His molten gaze skimmed the length of her, his thumb and forefinger running along the edge of his jaw. "I'm not sure you have what it takes."

Everinne reared back, affronted.

She cocked one hip to the side, fully prepared to tell him she would absolutely strap herself to that wheel while some shirtless male threw daggers in her direction, but he snared her wrist instead, pulling her in the other direction.

"Ah, there she is." Jarek gently tugged Everinne through the crowd, maneuvering her past performers who breathed fire while others juggled orbs of spinning water.

He drew to a stop and standing before Everinne was the most stunning woman she'd ever seen. She definitely wasn't fae, but there was something otherworldly about her presence, giving her an air of magnificence.

Her skin was a rosy umber, and gold dusted the apples of her cheeks. She'd painted her lips a deep red shade, and heavy liner framed her amber eyes. Silken brown hair fell to her waist, half of it braided back and pinned into place with a comb of golden pearls. She wore a gown of black that covered one shoulder and arm, then pulled tight around her waist. Strands of chains woven with the same pearls were draped around her hips, and when she moved, the fabric of her gown glinted like polished obsidian.

"Everinne." Jarek gestured to the beautiful woman. "This is Reine, the owner and reigning madame of the Mystic Obscura."

Jarek placed his hand on the small of Everinne's back and urged her forward. "Reine, I'd like you to meet my friend, Everinne."

"Hello, Everinne." Reine's voice was sultry, like tendrils of smoke curling into the air after a midnight fire. "Such a pleasure to meet you."

"This place is..." Words failed Everinne. It was nearly impossible to describe all the sights and sounds blending around her like a dazzling display of the wondrous. "Well, it's remarkable. I've never seen anything so breathtaking."

Reine clasped her hands together, the corner of her mouth lifting into an almost-smile. "The Mystic Obscura is designed to be a wonder to all the senses, with an obvious emphasis on the visual delights. We take great pride in the extraordinary and curious."

Visual delights, indeed. With any luck, Everinne would be one of them.

As though reading her mind, Jarek gave her a gentle nudge.

"Everinne is currently looking for employment." His gold gaze slid to Everinne and he offered a friendly wink. "She's incredibly talented."

"Oh?" Reine tilted her head, slowly folding her arms. Her rich amber eyes glinted with interest and her deep red lips curved. If Jarek studied her like he was something he wanted to absorb, then Reine watched her like she was a coveted treasure she couldn't wait to exhibit. "And what is it exactly that you do, Everinne?"

She drank.

She partied.

She wasted her life away in an effort to avoid the nightmares of her past.

"Um, well. I..."

"I've seen Everinne perform on the chandeliers of the Grand Cru," Jarek interjected smoothly, and Reine's brow lifted. "She's fearless."

Reine sauntered closer, inspecting every inch of Everinne, from the strapless cut of her beaded dress to the absurdly high heels she wore.

"Heights don't bother you?" she asked, pursing her lips together.

"Not in the least." Everinne shook her head, tucking her messy waves behind one ear. "There's something freeing about being so high above everyone else. You almost feel untouchable."

"Mm, I like your energy." Reine placed the tip of her pointed nail below Everinne's chin, tilting her head up. "Uninhibited. A little intense in the eyes. Beautiful face."

Reine stepped back, nodding sharply. "I think the hoops would suit you nicely."

Everinne glanced around the menagerie. "Hoops?"

Jarek bent down next to her, then pointed up to the main stage where bronze gossamer curtains fell from the cavernous ceiling, concealing the scarlet silk dancer from view. When they lifted a moment later, the dancer and silks were gone, and rain had begun to fall on the stage as a group of males with chains bound around their chests and shoulders appeared.

"The level we're on is the menagerie. The hoop dancers perform on the main stage, up there." Jarek bumped his shoulder against hers, already knowing he'd won her over. "For all to see."

Excitement hummed along Everinne's skin. This was exactly what she wanted.

Reine held out her hand. "Would you care to audition, Everinne?"

Her eyes widened and the nerves she'd kept safely stowed away flared to life. "You mean tonight?"

Reine lifted one shoulder, then let it fall. "I don't see why not. There are no rehearsals at the Mystic Obscura. Our hoop dancers never have a set routine. They feel the music in their veins, in their souls, and allow the rhythm to guide them."

Everinne found herself smiling without even realizing it.

Losing herself to music while dancing on a hoop high above the rest of the world sounded like the perfect means of escape.

She glanced over at Jarek, who gave an encouraging nod.

"I'd love to audition tonight." Everinne accepted Reine's outstretched hand. "Lead the way."

* * *

Everinne followed Reine down a gilded spiral staircase, leaving Jarek behind. She guided her through a series of halls beneath the iridescent glass floor, so the walls reflected dozens of prisms. Other Mystic Obscura performers mingled in the rainbow-hued hallway, some of them smoking stigs and laughing quietly, decked in glittering fabrics embellished with jewels. Others, however, appeared more transfixed on their upcoming act. They paced list-lessly or lounged against the walls, their eyes glazed and out of focus.

Before Everinne could dwell on their strange, trance-like state, Reine swung open a door and led her inside.

"Wait right here." She threw one arm out, waving toward the opulent sofa on the opposite side of the lavish space. "I'll be back in just a moment."

She walked out, leaving Everinne alone to admire the dressing room that thrummed with activity.

The walls were papered with dark pink and gold scrollwork, and four vanities were set along one wall with glowing lights outlining each mirror. Jars of paint, pots of liner, lipsticks, powders, and glosses were scattered across the surface of each one. Piles of silk, lace, feathers, and tulle were tossed over a chaise, and the cloying scent of floral perfume hung in the air like a hazy cloud. An armoire stood in the corner, complete with velvet-lined drawers overflowing with necklaces, rings, and bracelets—all of them gleaming with precious gems. Six other females milled about the dressing room, applying the finishing touches to their makeup or adjusting their costumes, and not one of them spared her a glance.

Under normal circumstances, Everinne might've taken it as an insult.

But tonight, she was almost relieved.

Reine appeared again, pushing a rolling rack full of costumes into the room. She tapped the metal bar with the tip of her nail, eyeing Everinne once more. "These all look to be about your size. Take your pick and once you're changed, come find me upstairs, and I'll show you to your hoop."

She left the dressing room again, this time with a snap of her fingers, and four of the females followed her out.

Everinne didn't pay attention to the two who stayed behind, instead her gaze was drawn to the rack of costumes full of shimmering fabrics and exquisite accessories. She ran her fingers along the satins and silks, toyed idly with the beaded fringe and lace detailing. Since this was her audition, she knew she would have to choose something eye-catching, something that would leave the audience wanting more.

She opted for a bodysuit of sheer red satin with tiny crystals that covered *just* enough skin. Since it was sleeveless, she put on a pair of gloves that came up over her elbows and sheer thigh-high stockings with fire rubies dotting the back seam. Her hair was unruly, so she twisted it back into a simple braid, nothing compared to the elaborate styles some of the other females wore.

Stealing a hasty look in one of the mirrors, she shrugged.

Good enough.

"Oh, *milazk*," a female voice crooned. "You cannot go on stage without your face."

"Without my face?" Everinne turned and faced a female with vivid blue eyes and wild hot pink curls that hung loosely around her shoulders. Her pointy ears marked her as fae, and when she smiled, her dimples winked. She was dressed in a pale blue skirt that was shockingly short and embroidered with fine silver lace. The top she wore was the same color, but it was nothing more than a teensy corset, and the lace overlay reminded Everinne of intricate snowflakes.

"You want the audience to be able to see you underneath the lights." The female took Everinne's hand and ushered her to sit in a chair in front of one of the vanities. She gestured to the wide array of makeup scattered across its marble surface. "May I?"

"Um...yes." Everinne sat, praying to the goddess that she wouldn't end up wearing so much that she would have to scrape it off later before she went to bed. "Of course."

"Wonderful." The female instantly set to work, dabbing a rosy pink cream onto Everinne's cheeks. "I'm Aisling."

"Everinne." She closed her eyes as the fae named Aisling dusted gold powder onto her lids. Then she peeked one open.

"That's a lovely name." Aisling swirled a tiny brush with a thin tip into a pot of black liner and Everinne closed her eyes again. "Is tonight your first show?"

"More or less," Everinne murmured as Aisling slowly slid the brush along the length of her eyelids, fanning them out to a sharp point. "I'm auditioning."

Aisling laughed, low and sensual. The tempting sound of it caused Everinne's eyes to flutter open.

"No one auditions, Everinne." Aisling applied a tint to her lashes next, lengthening and curling them. Then she grabbed a lipstick, a fiery red shade with an opalescent sheen. "If you're performing, it means Reine already knows you'll be a perfect addition."

Those wretched nerves flickered inside of Everinne once more, but she crushed them. If she could swing from the chandeliers at the Grand Cru without giving a fuck about anyone or anything else, then she could certainly dance on a hoop. Her mind already knew the moves, her body would simply follow the music.

"There." Aisling spun her back toward the mirror. "What do you think?"

A gasp slipped from between her lips before she could stop it.

The reflection of the female gazing back at her was hardly recognizable. Oh, she knew she was looking at herself, those turquoise eyes with rings of gold around her pupils were a dead giveaway. But other than that, it looked as though she was wearing a mask. A striking mask of beauty that hid the painful magic inside her. It had been so long since she'd truly looked at herself in a mirror, since she'd been able to face the darkness inside of her. Now, here it was, staring back at her, beneath layers of powder and glitter.

A pretty little monster.

"Do you like it?" Aisling asked, an almost indiscernible tremble in her voice.

It jarred Everinne from the swirling torment of her thoughts. She looked up at Aisling and smiled. "Can you make me look like this every time?"

Aisling's husky laugh filled the dressing room once more. "I'd love nothing more."

She grabbed Everinne's hand and pulled her to her feet. "Come on, I'll take you up to Reine."

Then she leaned close and whispered. "You'll own the night, I just know it."

Everinne followed Aisling back through the radiant quarters below the menagerie. Together they climbed another spiral staircase, but this one didn't lead to the same place as before. Instead, it deposited them right below the base of the main stage.

Reine stood at the top of the stairs, waiting. When she caught sight of Everinne, her brows lifted with approval and a small smile tugged at the corner of her mouth.

Everinne approached her and Reine reached out to cup her cheek. "Captivating. Absolutely captivating."

Aisling squeezed her hand once, then disappeared back down the steps, and Reine helped her up onto the stage. Bronze gossamer curtains fell in a wide circle, obscuring her from the audience. She could see through them, but they could not see her. The scent of magic, heavy and dense like citrus and woods, hung in the air.

Glamour.

Reine snapped her fingers again, and this time a solid gold hoop appeared. She handed it to Everinne and as she slid her fingers around the cool metal, a thrill of exhilaration coursed through her. The spark of energy sent her blood rushing with anticipation, despite the goosebumps pebbling across her flesh.

"When you're ready to be lifted, call out *trivno.*" Reine looked to the ceiling, then back down at Everinne. "There are no levers, or safety nets, or ropes here. *Everything* is controlled by magic. So long as you don't let go of the hoop, you'll never fall."

Everinne didn't care if she looked like she'd just gotten her first taste of a kiss, she couldn't help the smile causing her heart to soar. She'd never been more ready, more prepared for anything in her life. She was *meant* to be here.

"Once you're in the air, the curtains will vanish. As soon as you hear the first chord of music, that's when you begin." Reine cocked her hip to the side, surveying Everinne for a final time. "Yes, I think you'll do just fine here. Welcome to the Mystic Obscura, Everinne."

Then she spun on one heel and headed down the stairs, vanishing beneath the stage completely.

The gold wash of lighting illuminating the audience dimmed, and their murmurs and laughter faded into a kind of revered silence.

Everinne didn't even hesitate. She settled herself onto the hoop, seating herself so her knees were pulled up and her arms fell to both sides.

"*Trivno.*"

At once, the hoop gradually lifted her into the air. Higher and higher, until she felt like she was floating. Like she could walk among the stars.

Full darkness fell in the theater, the glamoured curtains faded away, and a dazzling beam of ruby light fell upon Everinne.

She inhaled. Exhaled. Tilted her head up to the ceiling and arched her back, knowing she'd enraptured the entire room with her provocative position. She could feel the intense gaze of their eyes, the insatiable hunger of the mystical and fantastical grew with each passing second. All of them watching. Waiting. For her.

Strings hummed to life, there was the first tantalizing chord of a piano, and Everinne let the music take her.

Ten

A loud pounding noise echoed through Atlas's subconscious, dragging him from sleep.

He groaned, rolled onto his stomach, and yanked his pillow over his head. There was no way he drank nearly enough for him to be suffering from a hangover, yet the relentless thumping continued despite his best effort to drown it out.

Tossing the pillow aside, he rubbed his hands over his face and glared out the glass doors on the opposite wall. The sliver of the winter moon was high in the sky, its silver reflection glinting off his private pool like a moonlit faerie orb. If he had to guess, it was the middle of the night—the witching hour, as some liked to call it—and that damn thumping sounded again.

Some asshole was knocking on his bedroom door.

Muttering a stream of vulgar obscenities, Atlas threw off the comforter and rolled out of bed. He padded across the hardwood floor, scooping up a pair of discarded pants as he went. Tugging them on, he raked a hand through his hair and yanked open the bedroom door.

Caedian stood there, his fist raised, ready to knock again.

"Captain." Atlas leaned against the doorframe, crossing his arms over his bare chest. "If you've come to ask for your coin back after losing to me in Cups, I'm afraid you're going to be sorely disappointed."

Caedian straightened immediately, tucking both of his hands behind his back. His black shirt was rumpled, as though he, too, had been forced out of bed. But it was the look of disquiet shadowing his eyes that put Atlas on full alert. That, and he was fully armed with two swords at his waist and a leather band of daggers across his chest.

He instantly sobered, shoving off the door to have a word with his Captain of the Guard. "What is it?"

"You have two visitors waiting to speak with you, Your Highness." Caedian's gaze shifted to the hall, then back to Atlas.

"Two? At this hour?" Unease crawled along the back of Atlas's neck and down his spine. This wasn't the typical method amorous females usually used to sneak into his bed, so whoever was calling upon him likely had a very good, if not gravely important, reason.

"Who?" he demanded.

Caedian swallowed. "Valaina, Eldress of the Morvayne clan, and her mate, Davorin."

"Fuck."

He thought he'd have a little more time before having to deal with Khiran's disappearance, but apparently Valaina was in no mood to play games.

Atlas motioned for Caedian to step into the room, then shut the door soundly behind him to avoid any listening ears.

"Where are they?" he asked, putting on a fresh shirt from his closet and buttoning it quickly.

"In the reception room of your wing." Caedian handed him a pair of boots and Atlas pulled them on. "I feel I should inform you that they requested an audience with the kralv first and he denied them."

Lovely.

"I suppose I was their second-best option." Atlas stalked into the bathing suite, gargled mint water, then attempted to smooth his unruly hair. "They're alone?"

"I have four guards stationed outside of the reception room, just in case." Caedian opened the bedroom door, and they strode out into the dimly lit hall. "Each one is armed with a pure silver blade."

Pure silver, the only metal capable of incapacitating a vampire, should the need ever arise. As far as he knew, no one in his lifetime had actually managed to kill one. There were methods, of course. Cutting off their heads completely. Piercing their hearts with blades of silver or stakes of ash wood.

Atlas stalked down the length of the wing toward the reception room, each step intentional so the vampires would know he approached. "Have they made any demands?"

Caedian shook his head. "No, Your Highness. Only that they wish to speak with you."

Atlas nodded, muttering greetings to the four guards positioned outside of the room. Caedian stepped in front of him and opened the door. "His Imperial Highness, Prince Atlas Skye."

Shrugging off the pompous introduction, Atlas strolled into the room. He kept his manner easy and carefree—he would never be like his father, a hostile serpent waiting to strike.

He spotted Valaina first, her pale blonde hair piled on top of her head like a crown. She wore a gown of gray silk and ivory pearls that pooled around her like liquid smoke. Her eyes, a piercing pale blue, latched onto him and her red lips curved into a seductive smile. Atlas had been on the receiving end of those gracious lips more times than he could count, much to Davorin's revulsion. In Atlas's defense, he hadn't known she had a jealous mate at the time, and he was fairly certain the only reason he survived Davorin's wrath was because the vampire knew he couldn't kill the imperial prince without bringing death upon his entire clan.

Atlas's gaze flicked to Davorin.

He still looked ready to rip out Atlas's throat. His eyes were pitch black and his upper lip was curled into a sneer. The suit he wore was a perfect match to the gray of Valaina's gown, except there was a pin in the shape of a raven piercing the front pocket of his coat. The insignia of the Morvayne. Davorin bowed, reluctant, his dark hair falling in front of his scarred face. Not once did he take his eyes off Atlas.

"Evening, Valaina." Atlas inclined his head toward her mate. "Davorin."

"Your Highness." Valaina's voice always reminded him of silk and steel. Soft, yet cold. "We're so grateful you were able to meet with us on such short notice."

"As if I could ever refuse such a request from you." He could, but he wouldn't, not when it came to Khiran. "Please, sit."

He dropped into a high-back chair, resting his elbows on the arms of the seat. Valaina lowered herself onto the evergreen sofa across from him, smoothing away imaginary wrinkles from her gown, while Davorin remained standing.

Atlas stretched his legs out and laced his fingers together. "I take you're here because of Khiran."

Valaina's eyes widened, her thick lashes fluttering. "You already know?"

"My captain informed me a few hours ago." Atlas rolled his neck, trying to dislodge the tension settling there. "He also mentioned my father refused you."

She made a derisive noise. "It would seem the kralv was *indisposed*."

Meaning Oldrich was taking a whore to bed, further neglecting the chaos gradually unfolding throughout his kingdom. Interesting how it was perfectly acceptable for him to fuck a maid or lady of the court, but when Atlas did it, he was a disgrace to the crown.

He shook off the aggression simmering to a boil in his blood. Loosing a breath from the tightness of his lungs, he nodded toward Valaina. "Tell me what happened."

Valaina rubbed her lips together, squeezing her hands in her lap, and looked to Davorin.

He grunted, still full of loathing, but when he spoke, his voice was eerily calm. "Khiran never misses a mating ritual. When he failed to show up for this one, I sent a few members from our clan to track him down."

Davorin settled on the edge of the sofa next to Valaina, his shoulders dropping slightly in defeat. "They found nothing. Not a trace of him anywhere."

Atlas drummed his fingers on the arm of the chair, considering. He'd heard stories about the vampire mating rituals, how they begin as ceremonial events full of dark magic and rites of passage, then more or less descend into blood-sucking orgies. It seemed logical that Khiran wouldn't want to miss such an event, but there were plenty of other festivities to choose from if one knew where to look.

"You don't think there's a small chance he would've skipped this one and sought out pleasure in one of Starysa's parlors instead?" Atlas asked.

"Absolutely not." Valaina's words were clipped. Her lips were pinched together and the hands she'd folded so gracefully in her laps were clenched tightly, the knuckles white.

Atlas leaned forward, curious about the sudden change in her demeanor. "How can you be sure?"

Her pale gaze cut to him. "Because this mating ritual was for *him*."

Shit.

Well, that definitely changed things.

"The last time we saw Khiran, he was at the Mystic Obscura," Davorin supplied, rising from the sofa. He shoved his hands into the pockets of his suit pants and turned to stare out the window.

Dawn would be approaching soon.

Atlas could see the tension bunching in his shoulders. It wasn't the same as the loathing from before. No, this was concern. A tremor of fear.

"He's a patron there?" Atlas wasn't aware many of the vampires frequented the unique establishment. Considering what it cost to receive an invitation and gain entry, he didn't assume many vampires would be willing to give up a precious drop of blood. Then again, it had been some time since he'd ventured inside the Mystic Obscura. Perhaps he owed them a visit.

"Yes." Valaina sighed, fingering the strand of diamonds at her throat. "A very select few from our clan are, myself included. Khiran has always been fond of the ribbon dancers, you know, the ones who perform above the stage wrapped in streamers of silk?"

She waved one slender hand through the air, dismissive. "Anyway, I figured he wanted to get in one last fuck before he was mated to someone for an eternity...a pity not all of us were allowed such an opportunity."

From the corner, Davorin turned, a low growl emitting from the back of his throat. His fangs lengthened, sharpened to dagger-like points. But Valaina silenced him with a look so threatening, not even Atlas would want to cross her.

He bit back a smile, knowing full well her comment was directed at him, and the rude interruption of their activities by Davorin. But Atlas wasn't one to tempt fate twice, so he changed the subject. "Khiran possesses a rare type of blood magic, does he not?"

Valaina's gaze slid from her mate, back to him.

"Yes." She drew the word out slowly, with caution. "His blood can cure life-threatening wounds. It can rid a bloodstream of poison...he's saved many lives."

"And not just the lives of vampires," Davorin grunted, running his tongue along the point of his sharp fang.

"Really?" Atlas ignored his intimidation tactics, more intrigued by this new information. "And when he uses his blood to heal another, it doesn't turn them?"

"No." Valaina shook her head, morphing back into the prim Eldress of the Morvayne. "I imagine it has something to do with his maker."

Atlas leaned forward, resting one elbow on his knee, and running his thumb along his jaw. "Who's his maker?"

Davorin stomped back over to Valaina's side, pinning Atlas with a heated glare. "You have a lot of questions, Your Highness."

"The more I understand, the easier it will be to find out who has taken Khiran, and why." Atlas kept his focus on Valaina when he spoke, but he didn't miss the way Davorin bristled at the slight out of the corner of his eye.

"Khiran's maker is Lothaire, an ancient elder from the Stravoka clan." Valaina stole a quick look out the window before returning her attention to Atlas. Already the stars were winking out and a hue of violet was painting the sky. "He hails from the Northernlands."

It was Caedian who spoke next, stepping further into the reception room. The silver of his eyes was clouded with apprehension. "So, Elder Lothaire is still alive?"

Valaina's eyes flicked to Caedian, and those lips of hers lifted into a feminine smile. "Very much so, Captain Trivaris."

If Caedian wasn't careful, Davorin would be after him next.

"And why," Atlas asked, drawing Valaina's attention away from his captain, "do you think Lothaire has some effect on Khiran's blood?"

Valaina's seductive smile vanished. Her expression shifted to one of solemnity, she closed her eyes briefly, and when she opened them again, the icy blue burned like fire. "Because Lothaire is fae."

Atlas gaped at the Eldress.

He snapped his mouth shut, shared a fleeting look of "what the fuck" with Caedian whose face reflected the same shock and disbelief. Atlas pinched the bridge of his nose, replaying her words in his mind. "Let me make sure I'm following you. Lothaire...is a fae vampire?"

"Fae vampire. Vampire fae. It's all the same thing, really." Valaina shrugged, then held out her hand. Davorin clasped it readily, lifting her to her feet. "But yes, that is correct, Your Highness."

Atlas couldn't believe it. He didn't think such a thing was

possible. A *vampire fae*? Not in all his hundreds of years of study and education, of poring over lore and traditions, had he ever read about a faerie vampire. It was absurd. Worse, it was slightly terrifying. He imagined this Lothaire would be damn near unstoppable in terms of magic and strength.

"Will you help us find Khiran, Your Imperial Highness?" Valaina turned her alluring smile on him, but that charm had faded when Davorin threatened to cut off his cock. "He's incredibly important to our clan."

"I'll help in any way I can, Eldress." He stood, dipped his head in a show of respect, half listening, half thinking the disappearing immortals were becoming a more troublesome situation than he'd originally thought.

"Good." Valaina moved closer to Davorin, the nearness of her mate somehow amplifying her power. "Because if not, we will search for him on our own and kill anyone who stands in our way."

"I'd expect nothing less." Atlas flashed her one of his most devastating grins. "But there is no need for bloodshed...yet."

Valaina curtsied. Davorin bowed. And then they blurred from sight, disappearing into the night before the first rays of sunlight could catch them.

Atlas raked his hands through his hair, then spun to face Caedian. "A fucking vampire fae? Have you ever heard of such a thing?"

"No, Your Highness." Caedian worried his bottom lip, looking more than unsettled by the wealth of newly uncovered information. "Never."

"Bleeding skies. How does that even happen?" Atlas walked over to the long table on the far wall, where bottles of liquor and empty glasses waited patiently to be enjoyed. He poured a hefty amount of honeyfire for himself and then another for his captain. "It sounds like something out of one of the horror novels my mother used to read."

"Indeed, it does," Caedian agreed.

They clinked their glasses together.

"*Dravska.*"

Atlas nodded once. "*Dravska.*"

Caedian downed his shot, then replaced the small glass on the table. "I'm afraid I have more slightly unfortunate news for you, Your Highness."

The smoky sweet liquor burned Atlas's throat, doing little to ease the swell of agitation gnawing away at him. "Lovely. What now?"

"Per your orders, I sent a scouting group of my three best soldiers to track Everinne and keep an eye on her."

A sinking sensation seized Atlas's gut. The alcohol turned rancid and his heart dropped.

"What did they discover?" he asked, dreading the answer.

"The good news is, she found employment." Caedian shifted on his feet, uneasy. "The bad news is she's working at the Mystic Obscura."

"*What*?" Rage bubbled to the surface and his grip on the glass tightened until he thought it would shatter in his fist. "The Mystic Obscura is by invitation only, and the cost to get in is…"

Not something he would want her to pay. In this life or the next.

Fuck.

Atlas threw the glass against the far wall and it exploded, raining down like broken shards of ice. "How did she get in? How did she even find the place?"

It wasn't easily done. The Mystic Obscura was hidden behind a heavy wall of glamour. One had to already know where they were going to even get there.

Caedian's deep umber skin turned ashen. "That's where the bad news gets worse, Your Highness."

Great.

"Out with it, Captain," Atlas growled.

"She was brought there by Jarek Zima." Caedian's voice grew cold. Brittle. "The demon summoner."

"Fucking skies."

Atlas seethed. He'd *told* her to stay away from Jarek, trusted that she wouldn't be so fucking stupid. Fury ravaged him. He was pissed at her for being so mindlessly careless and furious with himself for not doing more to stop it. The Mystic Obscura was no place for her. Not to entertain, and certainly not to work. He knew firsthand what it was like inside those magical walls, he knew what they *did* behind those glamoured curtains.

Atlas stormed out of the reception room, heading for the far end of his wing. Opening one hand, he summoned a sleek black helmet. He would take his *arcanic volt*, the two-wheeled vehicle would get him to her apartment faster than even his wings.

"Your Highness!" Caedian called out after him. "Where are you going?"

"To talk some sense into Everinne." Atlas spared his captain a glance, his anger mounting with each passing second. "Before her brother finds out what she's done."

Eleven

Everinne was on a thrill-seeking high and decided she never wanted to come back down.

Dancing on the hoops at the Mystic Obscura had been all she ever wanted and more. She'd never felt more alive. More free. And best of all, for those fleeting moments when she'd been floating above the grand theater impressing the audience with visual delights, her violent magic had been all but forgotten.

Reine had seemed genuinely impressed, offering her a small purse of silver and gold coins for her performance with the promise of notes so long as Everinne continued to awe the patrons each time. It was the first time she'd been in possession of her own money, and she had to admit, the sense of independence was something she could get used to—maybe she should thank Veros for cutting her off.

She'd even made a new friend.

Aisling had been both welcoming and kind, and while Everinne had been appreciative of her friendly demeanor, a small part of her wondered how long it would last. She never kept friends past a few seasons. Eventually, she shoved them away, severing the relationship before it could fully take root to bloom and grow. She was a rot. A poison.

"So," Jarek drawled, "what did you think of the Mystic Obscura?"

He'd offered to drive her home after she performed, and now they were sitting in his arcane-powered vehicle, the gentle hum of magic filling Everinne's ears. His wasn't nearly as luxurious as Atlas's *valade*, but the two-seated vehicle was just as stylish, if not just as expensive.

She tipped her head back against the leather seat, a faint sigh slipping from between her lips. "Mesmerizing."

It was the only possible word to describe it.

Jarek faced her, draping one arm over the steering wheel. Darkness loomed, blanketing the city streets, but in the distance, the glow of dawn was just beginning to crest. His eyes fixated on her, warm like melted gold.

"Mesmerizing," he repeated, the corner of his mouth lifting. "Yeah. You were."

Everinne allowed his compliment to slide without acknowledging it. Jarek's flirtations hadn't gone unnoticed and had become slightly more obvious as the evening progressed, but Everinne found she was no longer in the mood for a one-night stand with him. She'd been intoxicated and pissed off the first night she wanted to take him home, but now she wasn't entirely sure about sharing her bed with a demon summoner.

Besides, if Veros found out, there was a good chance he'd kill her. Or ship her off to some other realm as punishment. He would never allow such blatant disrespect to stand.

"Reine is fabulous, too." She tugged on the exceedingly short hem of her dress. "I still can't believe she agreed to let me work five nights a week."

With that kind of money, she wouldn't have to ask Veros for anything ever again. She could buy her own clothing, her own shoes, and her own jewelry. She could stock her pantry with cakes and her cupboards with honeyfire if she wanted. Her sense of freedom knew no bounds.

"Thanks for the ride home." She reached for the door to make her getaway when Jarek snagged her wrist.

His cold fingers curled around her flesh, chilling her.

"Need me to walk you up?" His offer wasn't laced with charm or innuendo, but she denied him all the same.

"I'll be fine, thanks."

He released her arm, and she pushed open the door, then climbed out into the blustery night. "I'm going to have a drink then head to bed."

Jarek watched her a moment longer, his mouth lifting into a smile. "Fair enough. I'll see you tomorrow."

Everinne shivered. "Tomorrow?"

"Yeah." His grin widened, one brow arching. "At work."

She hadn't realized he worked at the Mystic Obscura as well. It never even occurred to her to ask him how he could even get into the exclusive parlor or how he knew Reine so well. She was really going to have to get better about that sort of thing.

"Right. Tomorrow." She flashed a friendly smile. "Goodnight."

"Night, Everinne."

Closing the door of his vehicle behind her, she darted up the front steps of her apartment building, her heels clicking noisily against the rough stone. Once inside, she avoided the lift and started up the seven flights of stairs, even though her legs were on fire from hoop dancing. Halfway up, her thighs were already shaking and her knees felt ready to give out. She paused to catch her breath, gripping the wooden railing before continuing her trek to the top floor. When she finally made it to her apartment, she shoved open the door and stumbled in, loosing a sigh of relief.

She let the door catch her weight as it closed, sagging against it.

If she was going to keep working at the Mystic Obscura and climbing all those stairs nightly, she was definitely going to have to improve her stamina.

Maybe she should start training...

But first, a shot of honeyfire, and then bed.

"Did you have fun tonight?" a low, masculine voice rumbled from the penetrating darkness of her apartment.

Everinne startled, her heart hammering against the tight wall of her chest, and her blood turned to ice.

She plastered herself against the door, a spike of terror running straight through her. With practiced ease, she slid her thumb along the band of her amethyst ring, a faint clicking sound echoing in the stillness as the blade sprung loose. Her eyes strained into the pitch of the kitchen, searching for something—an unfamiliar shadow, or the barest of movements. Anything to give her some idea of where the intruder was hiding.

"What do you want?" she demanded, slinking closer to where she knew the small round table was located. She kept her right hand coiled into a fist, ready to strike, while the other remained stretched out to her side, grabbing only air.

Fuck, why was it so dark in here?

And why in the stars weren't her candles illuminating? Usually, they flickered to life as soon as she walked through the door. She'd bought them from one of the witchy stores in the shopping district for that exact reason. She hated the dark.

"You should really learn to lock your door," the deep voice mused, his threatening whisper coming from her right.

At least, she thought that's where the voice came from.

Everinne turned in a slow circle, panic lodging in the back of her throat. She bit down on her bottom lip to keep it from trembling until the metallic tang of blood coated her tongue. Her breathing grew shallow, each breath becoming more difficult to control as the ruthless beast she kept caged inside of her slowly awoke.

Frenzied, brutal magic poured through her veins, primed for release. It slid from within her like a venomous serpent, coiling around her tightly, ready to strike. Sinister power crawled along her skin, stretching out in vicious tendrils on the hunt for its prey. Her thread of control wavered, then frayed, and her lungs hollowed out. Everinne squeezed her eyes shut, and the darkness she possessed sunk its vicious claws into her mind, beckoning her to surrender to her violent nature. It would be so easy to crush bones until there was nothing left but ash and dust. Easy and lovely. With a flick of her wrist, she could render a beating heart into a pulpy mess, inflicting a pain so torturous and devastating, her victim would beg for mercy. Until she finally granted it, by shattering their minds.

Her emotions fueled her magic, and the dread bubbling up inside her coaxed the fiend inside her to life.

Pain, it whispered.

She gritted her teeth and her eyes flew open. Shuddering, she desperately tried to restrain the terror slipping from her grasp.

Everinne swore her power leered at her. Mocked her.

She was touched by death.

"I can hear the erratic beating of your heart. Which can only mean one of two things." The voice wrapped around her like tempting silk, soft and seductive. "Either I frighten you..."

Warm breath coasted across her neck and she whirled, but no one was there. She sucked in a ragged gulp of air, fighting against only herself.

"Or?" she prompted, angling the blade of her ring, prepared to lash out.

"Or I excite you." Phantom fingertips grazed her waist.

Blind fury ricocheted through her.

"In your dreams, you cock-sucking bastard." Everinne lunged.

The attacker knocked her hand away and her balance faltered. Her heels slid against the hardwood floor, and she cried out. She stumbled backward, smacking her head against the wall as tiny stars danced before her eyes.

A strong arm snared both of her wrists, yanking them up over her head, pinning her in place. She struggled, thrashing against the assault, until two fingers hooked her chin, forcing her head up.

There was the click of a tongue.

"Attacking the imperial prince is a death sentence, Wildheart."

Everinne froze. Her heart dropped into the pit of her stomach and all at once, the scent of cedar layered with delicious citrus and a hint of spice consumed her.

"Atlas," she hissed, trying to free herself from his hold. His grip on her wrists only tightened. She peered up into the faceless dark, where she knew he towered above her, even with the extra height from her damned shoes. "What in the bleeding skies do you think you're doing?"

"I could ask the same of you," he fired back, that seductive voice of his fueled with venom.

"I *live* here." She sucked in another ragged breath. Damn it, his overwhelming scent was everywhere. Impossible to escape. Just like him. "I'm getting ready for bed and—"

"And flirting with a demon summoner?" he interjected. The contempt in his tone left her recoiling.

A single globe of fire spit and sparked from one of her candles, dousing half of him in shadows and the rest in a wash of warm light.

Atlas Skye stood over her and when she dared to meet his gaze, she couldn't look away. His dark blond hair was tousled, like he'd just rolled out of bed, and it hung in his face, concealing his eyes. But that didn't matter, she knew exactly what they looked like, she'd committed his face to memory long ago. Eyes that were golden like the sunrise kissing the top of the mountains, or warm green like a spring forest, depending on his mood. His prominent jawline was always shaven smooth, he'd inherited high cheekbones and dimples from his mother and full lips with a slight cleft in his chin from his father.

His dark brown pants hung low on his waist and his fitted shirt was tucked in, the top four buttons undone, revealing inches of golden skin and the snarl of the wolf tattooed on his chest.

It wasn't fair that someone so arrogant could be so damningly beautiful.

"Answer me," he demanded, blowing a lock of hair from his face so she could clearly see the fury burning in his eyes.

Everinne locked her spine into place, refusing to back down.

"I wasn't flirting with him," she ground out.

"No?" Atlas's jaw clenched, a vein along his neck pulsed. "Then how else did you find your way into the Mystic Obscura?"

Did he honestly think—that prick.

"I worked for it, Atlas." She arched off the wall, rolling her hips into him. "I *earned* it." If he truly thought so little of her, then she would let him believe it. "Is that what you wanted to hear, Your Radiance?"

She thoroughly expected him to jerk away from her, to release her in disgust. But instead, Atlas surprised her in the worst way imaginable.

He palmed her waist then nudged his leg between her thighs, pressing himself flush against her, diminishing every last shred of space. With his muscled leg wedging both of hers apart, the hem of her absurdly short dress rose even higher. The crystals hanging from the fabric tinkled in warning. Her breasts were squished against the solid wall of his chest, and on each ragged inhale, they threatened to pop free from the strapless confines of silver that barely covered them. His furious gaze dipped to where they swelled, and a different kind of heat banked there before his eyes traveled up her neck, pausing to linger on her lips.

Atlas's thumb traced a slow, lazy circle along her waist.

"You're bleeding," he murmured. Instantly, his jaw locked, his gaze darkening with the promise of vengeance. "Did he fucking hurt you?"

Everinne shook her head, breathless. Her heart refused to cease its incessant pounding, and her lung were entirely too compressed. Why did he always have this effect on her? She hated him, but more than anything, she hated what he did to her all those years ago.

He grabbed her chin once more to inspect the wound on her bottom lip. Faeries might not have fangs like vampires, but those two particular top teeth were sharper than most.

Atlas shifted closer, sending a jolt of heat straight to her core.

"He didn't hurt me." She swallowed hard as warmth spread through her, causing her toes to tingle, her belly to clench, and her nipples to harden. "I bit my own lip to..."

To keep it from trembling.

She would never admit he'd scared her.

Suddenly, he was lowering his mouth toward her.

Everinne held her breath and then Atlas's tongue slid across her bottom lip, swiping gently over the wound. Her entire body vibrated with desire, betraying her completely as she melted into him. His hand squeezed her waist, his fingers digging into her.

Atlas leaned back, just barely. He made a strange noise then, a feral sort of sound. The fusion of a growl and a groan.

When those eyes of his latched onto her, they were tainted with lust.

Alarm fired in the back of her mind, and she stiffened, refusing to allow herself to fall into one of his traps. She knew who he was, what he was, just as she was fully aware of the reputation he wore like a fucking crown.

"Don't you dare use your magic on me," she warned. She'd suffered through his torture once before, she would never do so again. She wriggled against him in an effort to break free, a useless endeavor, but she refused to give up.

"That's all you, Ever." His careless smile was a dagger to her heart. "I'm not using my magic on you. If I was, you would *know.*"

Right.

She would know. The feel of his magic was sheer ecstasy, the scent of it like amber and vanilla. Luscious and tempting.

"Let me go." Her tone lacked its usual conviction, instead her plea came out in a hushed breath. "Please."

"On one condition."

Everinne scowled up at him.

"You tell Veros where you're working." His grip on her wrists loosened, his hand fell away from her waist. "Before he hears it from someone else."

Now it was Everinne's turn to smirk. "You mean someone like you? Planning on running off and tattling to my big brother about how I'm being naughty?"

"You don't know the meaning of the word." Atlas's teeth scraped along his bottom lip and she tracked the movement. He released her arms, and she almost sighed in relief, dropping them to her sides. But then he gripped her hips instead, dragging her so close, she felt every *hard* inch of him. Including that distinctively large bulge straining against his pants.

Oh, gods.

She'd gone too far.

"But no, I won't be the one to tell him." He took the smallest step back, away from her. His dismissal was a slap in the face, the sting of it left her cheeks flushed with humiliation. "It's better if Veros hears it from you. Directly. Since you have a tendency to make his life an unnecessary living hell."

Bastard.

She shot a pointed look at his erection, of which he was not at all ashamed, then met his damning gaze. "Was there something else you needed, Your Radiance?"

"No." This time, his voice was hoarse.

"You've said that word a lot tonight." Everinne tilted her head, eyed him coolly. Now that she knew exactly what kind of effect she had on him, she was quite certain she could play his stupid little games.

"And yet, you never listen."

Beats of painful silence passed between them as they stared at each other. Watching, waiting to see what the other would do.

Everinne's gaze darted to his mouth, to the wolf tattooed across half of his chest, to where his dark gold locks fell around his pointed ears. All the while, his enchanting eyes trailed over every inch of her, igniting her like a flame without a spark.

Then suddenly, Atlas bent down, and she thought for sure he would kiss her. He was impossibly close, and even though she loathed him with every fiber of her being, she knew that if his lips touched hers...she would kiss him back. Her lashes fluttered, her breath hitched.

But instead, he tucked a strand of her dark hair back behind her ear, his mouth gently grazing the sensitive flesh of its tip.

She almost came undone, would've peeled out of her dress on the spot for him.

Goosebumps riddled her flesh.

He reached up, his fingers gently playing with the dagger earring dangling from her ear.

"Be careful, Everinne," he whispered. "Immortals are disappearing."

Disappointment snapped through her and she straightened, locking her knees, and silently vowing to never fall under his spell again.

"Aw," she sneered, shoving the pain splintering through her back into her pit of a soul where it belonged. "Are you worried about me?"

Atlas shook his head, and the rest of her candles flared to life, illuminating the kitchen. He snatched his black helmet off the table, then headed for the door. She watched him leave, prayed to the gods he'd never return, but then he stopped. Tossing a glance at her from over his shoulder, he muttered, "I always worry about you."

In the next moment, Atlas was gone.

And she was alone. Again.

Everinne stalked over to her near-empty cupboard and grabbed what remained of her honeyfire. She downed all of it, reveling in the burn, the way the sweetened smokey alcohol scoured her stomach. She told herself it was to keep the nightmares away, to temper the foul magic that tainted her blood. But this time, it was to numb the memories of her past. The ones she kept locked away in the icy fortress of her heart, from when she fancied herself in love with the Imperial Prince of Prava.

Twelve

E verinne's blood was an aphrodisiac on the tip of Atlas's tongue. Dark and sinful, just like her.

There was no sharp metallic tang—instead she tasted of stolen kisses during the witching hour, when the moon was full and high, and the rest of the world was still. She was silk sheets and seductive whispers, a midnight swim when the heat of summer hung thick in the air. That singular drop of her blood weakened him. Owned him. Consumed him. She was a complexity of everything he longed for in this life yet would forever be just out of his reach.

Atlas hit the accelerator on his *arcanic volt* and peeled away from the curb of Everinne's apartment. The arcane magic powering the vehicle thrummed beneath him and the two wheels shrieked against the rough cobblestone as he sped away. He flipped up his visor as the brisk air cooled his heated body. The steady hum of the engine crackled like kindling to a fire, shooting out silvery blue sparks from the back pipe in his wake. Gripping both handlebars, he cruised through the nearly empty streets of Starysa to clear his head.

To rid his thoughts of Everinne.

Yet she occupied every darkened corner of his mind.

When he had her pinned against that wall, his knee nestled between her thighs, he'd wanted nothing more than to rip off that dress and bury himself so deep inside her that he forgot his own name. He would've given his soul to run his tongue over the sweet swell of her breasts, to suck her nipple into his mouth until her knees weakened and she unraveled in his arms. Each breath she took set his blood on fire. He could picture her clearly—naked and tangled in his sheets, that mouth of hers cursing him while he used his cock, his tongue, his magic, to coax her to life.

He shifted on the leather seat of the *volt*, adjusting his aching erection.

It would be easy enough to find a willing female to help erase the desire coursing through him, though it wouldn't make a difference because he would only be imagining a pair of turquoise eyes with gold rings around the center and the lushest lips he'd ever seen.

But Everinne Auvyre was strictly forbidden.

Atlas had sworn to Veros that he would do everything within his power to keep her safe and protected, with the unspoken understanding that included keeping her out of his bed. Not only was she off limits as his best friend's sister, but she was also dangerous, capable of inflicting immeasurable amounts of pain. So long as her magic continued to control her, she was a risk. Simply being in her presence was like standing on the edge of a gaping chasm, waiting for a gust of wind to send him careening to his death. It didn't matter how badly he wanted her. She could come all over him one moment and kill him in the next.

He shook his head.

Definitely too much of a risk.

He rode along one of the winding roads that followed the outlying mountains of the city toward the scenic overlook situated on the highest peak. The overlook faced west, toward the Ladova Bay, where calm teal waters were home to the dozens of ships in port. The harbor itself curved like a crescent moon and was dotted with small wooden structures to house imports, fresh fish markets, and numerous stalls where local merchants sold their wares. Stable docks stretched out into the bay and behind Atlas, the early glow of dawn blanketed the city in a wash of gold. A breeze billowed up the cliffside, carrying with it the scent of the sea, briny with the faintest hint of magic.

He scanned the port, watching as sailors, traders, and vendors gradually opened the harbor for business. His gaze sought anything out of the ordinary, something that might give him a hint about the immortals who were disappearing from his kingdom. But then he caught sight of a vessel sailing across the smooth waves of the bay, preparing to dock. The hull stood out among the rest of the ships with its stern and bow curling like majestic vines, the polished wood glinting in the morning sunlight. Despite not having any sails, it propelled through the water with ease, and when the wind unfurled its burnt orange banners, Atlas smiled.

A black creature with three heads, each one similar to an eagle with golden beaks and skinny horns, was embellished upon the main banner. The body was like a dragon and covered in scales, and its feathered wings were reminiscent of a flame. It had been some time since Atlas had seen a *trechen*, and there was only one person he knew who sailed under the flag of such a magnificent beast.

Aran Ruhdneah, the High Prince of the Autumn Court of Faeven, had returned to Prava.

* * *

Atlas parked his *volt* on the docks and removed his helmet. Salt spray whipped through his hair on the stiff breeze, and he ran a hand through the thick strands, shoving it back from his face only to have it fall forward again. Bulky shadows lounged in the alley behind him, the glint of their swords unmistakable. Somehow, Caedian always knew where to find him. At least these guards weren't the pompous dickheads roaming the halls of the palace in their shiny black and gold leather armor. No, these were elite warriors who moved like wraiths in the night, hand-selected by Caedian to protect Atlas in case he couldn't be there to do it himself.

He glanced over his shoulder, nodding stiffly to one of the guards lurking between the buildings.

Another gust of cold wind swept off the bay and through the harbor, and he grit his teeth. If he had known he was going to be at the bay this early in the morning, he would've brought a coat, but instead he took the bite of chilly air in stride. He adjusted the rolled cuffs of his shirt, smoothing away any wrinkles, and strolled down the pier toward where the *Amshir* was docked.

Plank after plank unfolded from the right side of the hull, and the scent of orange blossom and cedarwood mingled with the brine of the sea. Crossing his arms and with a steady smirk on his face, Atlas peered up at the main deck.

A moment later, a fae male appeared, the echo of his boots striking the wooden deck pierced through the harbor's usual bustling noise. His pants were dark brown and stitched with gold thread. He wore a shirt the color of fire rubies and his topaz over-coat was embroidered with tiny autumn leaves on each shoulder. Red hair was pulled up into a knot on top of his head and around his neck hung a piece of leather adorned with beads. Dangling from the necklace was a compass, one Atlas knew always pointed back to the Autumn Court of Faeven, and attached to it was what looked like a piece of rosy pink glass.

Beyond him, two other males emerged from the below deck.

Atlas didn't recognize them, but anyone who sailed with Aran Ruhdneah wouldn't be a stranger for long.

Aran spotted him instantly and strode down the planks, the two males following his lead. He grinned, his emerald eyes crinkling at the corners, and fisted both hands on his waist.

"When I requested the royal treatment upon my arrival, I never expected to be welcomed by the Imperial Prince himself." Aran laughed, walking towards him. They gripped each other's forearms in greeting. Far too much time had passed since his last visit. "How are you, old friend?"

"Better than ever." Atlas released him and shoved his hands into his pockets, but the High Prince was anything but a fool.

Aran tilted his head, his smile vanishing. "Your eyes deceive you."

Atlas nodded once, returning the prince's knowing stare. "As do yours."

Ghosts of regret and despair haunted the prince's eyes. His shoulders dropped and he faltered, his mask of confidence slipping just slightly. "The war was..."

The war for Faeven had taken its toll upon the High Prince. Atlas had heard rumors from across the Gaelsong Sea of its atrocities. *Temny feya*—or dark fae, as Aran called them—had damn near decimated the legions of the Summer, Autumn, and Winter Courts. The casualties had been atrocious. They'd prevailed with the help of some allies, though there was one in particular Atlas wouldn't trust even if he was the last man on earth. Atlas wanted to send reinforcements to aid their cause, but Aran never asked, and though an explanation wasn't necessary, he knew why.

The kralv of Prava could not be trusted.

Now, the story was Aran had given up his throne and returned to the sea, leaving his sister to rule as the renowned Faerie Queen of Faeven.

Atlas would like to meet her someday, he imagined she was a sight to behold. In fact, he wouldn't mind taking a former warrior princess as a bride. Unfortunately for him, she already had a mate.

He lifted one hand. "Let's not discuss it here. Matters of woe and war are easier to talk about with a drink in our hands."

"I couldn't agree more." Aran stepped to the side, gesturing to the two males standing behind him.

They appeared to be brothers as their facial features were nearly identical. Dressed impeccably, they wore trim pants, buttoned shirts that appeared to have been dipped in stardust, and long coats with an embroidered eight-pointed star and twin crescent moons stitched onto the lapels. Whereas Aran's pointed ears were pierced with gold hoops, neither of these males had any visible piercings whatsoever. Each of them possessed prominent cheekbones, dimpled smiles, and hair so dark it almost looked blue. While their eyes were silver, one of them had a scar running down the left side of his face, from his eyebrow to his jaw. His eye in particular was most interesting. Where it should've been silver, like the other one, it looked to have been slashed with a streak of sapphire.

"Allow me to introduce you both to His Imperial Highness, Prince Atlas Skye." Aran nodded toward Atlas. "Your Highness, Lords Tovian and Nyxian Starstorm Celestine of Aeramere."

Lords of Aeramere. Fascinating.

"My lords, welcome to Starysa, the Golden City." Atlas extended his arm out behind him, to where the expanse of his kingdom rose in glittering buildings, rugged mountain peaks, and darkened forests.

Atlas turned, made eyes with one of the guards watching his every movement, and jerked his head toward his *arcanic volt*. "Tell the Captain we're headed to Novak's."

"To Novak's?" Aran chuckled, glancing up to the sky where the sun was barely cresting above the mountains in the distance. "Already?"

Atlas draped an arm around his shoulders and started walking toward the tavern in question. "I haven't slept and I'm starving."

"Novak's is an absolute dive, so be forewarned," Aran tossed back to Tovian and Nyxian, following behind them. "But they have the best spiced beef omelets around. And the best ale."

Tovian flashed a broad, easy smile. "Sounds like our kind of place."

Nyxian knocked his elbow into his brother's ribs, his answering grin was far more mischievous. "We're always up for an adventure."

"And a hell of a one it's been so far," Tovian laughed, running a hand through his seaswept hair.

"It's their first time sailing, first time leaving Aeramere actual-ly." Aran bent his head low to not be overheard. "But that's a story for another day."

"How long will you be gracing the streets of Starysa with your presence, my lord?" Atlas asked, smoothly changing the subject.

A wrinkle of concern marred Aran's brow. "Not long, I'm afraid. Just a few days to gather more supplies before we sail again."

"I see." Atlas sent him a knowing look, then dropped his voice to a whisper. "And does a particular witch know you're in town?"

Aran bristled, fiddling with the piece of sea glass dangling from his neck. "She does *not*. And I intend to keep it that way."

Ah. So he *was* still in love with her.

"Sure," Atlas drawled, letting his arm fall away as they trudged up the cobblestone path. "Just remember, word travels fast in the golden city."

"I'm aware." Aran's mouth pressed into a hard line, but a flicker of humor illuminated his eyes.

Atlas laughed, yanking open the door to Novak's. It groaned loudly, and he was instantly assaulted by the scent of stigs, fried eggs, and stale alcohol.

Propping it open with his foot, he bowed dramatically. "My lords of Faeven and Aeramere, who's ready for a drink?"

Thirteen

S leep for Everinne was fitful, if it could even be called such a thing. She tossed and turned most of the night, restless. While her dark magic lurked between her dreamless state, waiting to pounce, it was pushed to the furthest corners of her mind by the image of an annoyingly handsome prince.

No thanks to Atlas, her body was still humming, tingling from the sensations of feeling every inch of him crushed against every inch of her. Each time she closed her eyes, she could remember the way his mouth brushed featherlight against the tip of her ear. Or how he'd taken ahold of her hips and ground himself against her, ensuring she felt the way he strained for her. There'd been no mistaking the distinctive hardness of his erection while he had her pinned against the wall.

She rubbed her eyes and rolled over, facing the window of her bedroom where morning light spilled in and slanted across her bed.

It was a rare occasion she woke so early, but since sleep felt the need to evade her, she supposed she was left with no other choice.

Everinne groaned, threw the pile of blankets off her, and slid from her bed. She pulled on a pair of navy blue leather leggings and grabbed an icy blue sweater that slid dangerously low down one shoulder. She raked her fingers through her mass of tangled dark brown waves, grateful she'd scrubbed off her makeup from the previous night. If there was one thing she couldn't stand, it was leftover crusty eyeliner that made her look as though she'd just emerged from the threshold of the otherworld.

She wandered down the hall of her apartment toward the kitchen, following the incessant growling of her stomach, then paused. Last she checked, her cabinets were damn near bare. Instead of buying food like she was supposed to have done, she'd gotten distracted by Jarek and his invitation to the Mystic Obscura. Not that she regretted going with him, but she was terribly hungry, and the remorse from her previous decision meant she'd have to venture to the market. Again.

Sighing, she debated on grabbing her earnings from last night and venturing out to brave the crowds of patrons doing their daily shopping when a cream-colored card propped up on her kitchen table caught her eye. More enticing, however, was the glossy black wax seal depicting a wolf.

Her heart skittered and she snatched up the card, wondering what Atlas could have to say to her, if anything. She ran her thumb along the wax seal, silently debating. Maybe it was an apology for his actions, and if that was the case, she'd toss the damn thing in the trash. Or...maybe it was something else entirely.

She flipped it open and skimmed the contents, her face falling when she immediately recognized the tidy script.

Not Atlas.

Veros.

Her brother's neat handwriting glared up at her against the sturdy parchment.

I noticed your cabinets and pantry were still looking a bit empty. Join me at the palace as soon as you wake for a proper breakfast. There's an important matter I wish to discuss with you.

And before you throw my note into the garbage, I know how much you like fresh biscuits with honey.

Yours,

Veros

Damn. He knew her too well.

Biscuits and honey sounded positively divine.

But it was the "important matter" that made her hesitate. If Atlas told Veros she was working at the Mystic Obscura after promising to keep quiet, she would make him regret it. She would hold up her end of the bargain and tell Veros herself, but she would do it in her own time. Atlas hadn't mentioned *when* she needed to tell Veros, only that she *should*. And those were two entirely different things.

Then again, she wasn't sure she was ready to face him after their little interlude last night. She found herself staring at the table where his helmet had been sitting. She knew he had an *arcanic volt*, the sleek vehicle powered by arcane magic and streaks of blue spit out of the back pipe whenever he revved the engine. Most males dressed in leathers, from their pants to their jackets, when they rode them through Starysa's streets. But not Atlas. The few times she'd seen him ride his *volt*, he'd been wearing gray slacks, a white button-down shirt with the sleeves rolled to his elbows, along with a dark green embroidered vest and a knotted silk tie. Godsdamn if it wasn't one of the hottest things she'd witnessed in her life. As much as she didn't want to admit it, the image of him parked outside the palace dressed like that, with a pitch black helmet concealing his face, had taken up permanent residence in her mind.

The memory of it sent tingles of delicious warmth coursing through her.

When he'd flipped up the visor and his eyes met hers, she'd almost fucking melted on the spot. It had taken all her willpower to remember why she hated him, why she would never have anything to do with him, why she would never forgive him.

Fuck, she *had* to get him out of her head.

Hopefully, luck would be in her favor and Atlas wouldn't even be at the palace. It's not like he was ever up before the sun, anyway.

Deciding she was too hungry to care, she freshened up, tugged on a pair of sapphire high heels, and made her way to the palace.

She hired one of the many *valade* drivers to drop her off at the side entrance of the palace, where the guards knew her by name and where none of the snobbish elite cared to mingle. One of the guards ushered her in through the curving bronze gates, closing it soundly behind her, and Everinne gazed up at the staggering building.

It was set atop one of the higher hills in Starysa, overlooking the city and the Ladova Bay. Layers of sand-colored stone made up multiple levels of covered balconies, parapets, and glittering arched windows. Sweeping towers adorned with gilded spires stood prominently in the back, while dozens of curving staircases led to gardens overflowing with evergreen trees and lush flowers in varying shades of silver, navy, and white. Two expertly carved obsidian statues depicting Prava's famed black wolf were at the forefront of the grounds, their eyes crafted from molten silver. While on the outside the palace looked welcoming, dazzling even, Everinne knew that warm sentiment faded the moment one stepped foot through its ornate wooden doors.

The inside of the palace made her skin prickle with keen awareness.

Even when she walked through its excessive black and gold halls, it was as though she was always being watched. She swore that behind its daunting interior, the walls held secrets long forgotten by time.

She carefully made her way to the main dining hall, her heels clicking softly against the smooth marble. Veros, fairly predictable and always on time, would likely be waiting for her there.

"Everinne?" a gravelly male voice called from behind her.

Swallowing down the knot of apprehension clogging the back of her throat, she slowly faced Kralv Oldrich.

"I thought that was you." He stalked toward her, his ruddy cheeks already an indication that he'd had at least two pints of ale this morning. The kralv towered over her, his bulky stature crowding her personal space, and it took every ounce of willpower for her not to cringe and step away from him.

"Good morning, Your Imperial Majesty." She dipped into a quick, practiced curtsy.

"You're looking well." He angled his head, running his thumb and forefinger over his trim beard as he watched her. The stench of sour ale seeped from his pores, and she held her breath. "It's been some time since you've paid us a visit."

Because the last time she'd come to the palace, months ago, he'd indulged in too much alcohol and had gotten a little too handsy. When his rough, meaty hand had grazed her ass, Veros had nearly lost his damn mind. Atlas had been forced to bribe his father to retire early for the night with the promise a whore would be waiting in his bed.

Whether or not that was true, Everinne didn't know. Nor did she care. Though if it was, she pitied whatever woman had to spread her legs for this cocky prick.

She tucked her hands behind her back, clenching her fists. "I was just on my way to join my brother for breakfast."

"Excellent," he murmured, his glassy black eyes fixating on the dip of her sweater, where the swell of her breasts was clearly visible.

Gross.

Then the kralv reached out and patted her gently on the head like she was some kind of well-behaved pet. "Don't stay away too long, the court misses you."

Yeah.

Sure.

"Of course, Your Imperial Majesty." Everinne dipped her chin and sidled past him, wishing the walls of the corridor were slightly larger so she could afford to give him a wide berth.

As she headed to the dining room, she could feel the kralv's slimy gaze tracking the sway of her hips, and she bit her nails into her palms to keep from screaming.

Gods, that male was vile. Horridly disgusting.

She rounded the corner, finally reaching the safety of the dining hall, and one of the guards opened the door for her. Walking in, she spied Veros instantly. He was seated at the far end of the table, his timepiece in his palm. Magic throbbed in the air, the permeating scent of ink spilled across parchment, worn leather, and soft earth. Swirls of navy blue runes and alternating moon phases surrounded him. He lounged in his chair, scrolling and shifting through the runes with one finger, connecting the space of time and other realms. His power was far beyond her sense of comprehension, but it was entirely fascinating.

The things she would do...the things she would *change*, if only she could control time.

Everinne gently cleared her throat and Veros's head snapped up. Immediately, he clicked his timepiece closed, shoved it back into his pocket, his magic vanishing right along with it.

"Everinne." He adjusted the collar of his shirt, tugging on it lightly. He never liked to be caught off guard. "I didn't think you'd show up."

She crossed the floor to join him. "You sound surprised."

"I am." He stood, pulling out a chair for her. "Hungry?"

"Famished."

She lowered herself into the seat next to him at the end of the table, then filled her plate. She grabbed two biscuits, drizzling them with a hefty helping of honey, and snatched a dark chocolate and raspberry pastry from the platter in front of her. Veros slid her a glass of water as well as a steaming cup of coffee loaded with cream and sugar, and while he was acting as though nothing was wrong, there was a troubling line of worry across his brow.

They ate in companionable silence—Everinne devouring the

sweets on her plate first as Veros picked at what remained of his omelet.

Everinne licked a drop of chocolate off the tip of her finger. "Remind me to buy the ingredients to make these the next time I go to the market."

Veros's gaze slid to her, the corner of his mouth lifting into a mocking smile. "You know how to bake pastries?"

"It can't be that hard." She peeled away a section of the flaky crust, then popped it into her mouth. "I'm sure I can figure it out."

Veros chuckled and she couldn't recall the last time she actually heard him laugh, at least not in her presence. But then he turned in his seat to face her, all remnants of amusement fading away with his somber demeanor. His eyes, a mirror image of her own yet filled with cool precision, fixed on her.

"Everinne, there's something we need to discuss."

She scraped her teeth along her bottom lip, bracing for the inevitable lecture, when the noise of raucous voices echoed just outside the dining hall.

"What the..." Veros jumped out of his seat and positioned himself in front of her, one hand on the hilt of his sword. Always protecting.

She peered around him just as Atlas stumbled into the room, followed by three fae males she'd never seen before.

One of them had auburn hair pulled into a lopsided knot on top of his head. He was rather handsome, in a roguish kind of way, and wore jewel-toned clothing that reminded her of a seafaring captain. Like a faerie pirate. The other two males, however, were exceptionally well-dressed in trim suits, collared shirts, and carried themselves as though they were of noble birth. She supposed they were brothers, given their similar facial structures and unusual hair color. It wasn't quite black, but more of a deep blue, like the darkest part of the sea.

"Veros!" Atlas waved his hand and sauntered forward, but then his eyes landed on her, widening slightly. "Everinne."

He bowed and almost fell over.

Everinne stood, moving beside her brother. Every male gaze in the room, save for Veros, tracked her movement. She leaned close to him and whispered, "Is he drunk?"

Veros flicked his wrist, checking the timepiece he wore. "It appears that way."

"At this hour?"

His only response was to grumble in annoyance and shove his hands into the pocket of his pants.

"Aran, you remember my closest friend, Veros Auvyre?" Atlas clapped Veros on the shoulder soundly.

"Ah, yes. The Lord of Time." Aran, the redhead who seemed the least intoxicated of all of them, dipped his head in a show of respect. "We've met once or twice."

"I thought as much." Atlas gestured to her next, trying to maintain some sense of the proper decorum that was expected of him. "Then allow me to introduce you to his sister, Everinne Auvyre."

He nodded to the three males in front of her. "Ever, this is Aran Ruhdneah, High Prince of the Autumn Court of Faeven, and his companions, Lords Tovian and Nyxian Starstorm Celestine of Aeramere."

Aran tucked one arm in front of him and bowed. "It's an absolute pleasure."

Everinne preened, tossing her dark hair back behind her, and flashing her most brilliant smile. She could get used to being treated like one of the ladies of court. Perhaps she should show her face around the palace more often, after all.

"Nyxian, my lady." One of the fae brothers stepped forward and clasped her hand, pressing his lips to her knuckles.

Everinne forced herself not to stare at him, but he had the most startling eyes. They reminded her of pools of moonlight, except the left one had a vein of stunning blue slashing through it. He noticed her fascination and winked.

A flush bled into her cheeks when he released her.

Oh, that one was trouble.

The other brother, Tovian, captured her hand next. But instead of mimicking his brother's gesture, he flipped her palm up and planted a kiss on the inside of her wrist, keeping his dazzling silver eyes on her the entire time.

"My lady," he murmured softly.

Everinne damn near swooned.

They were *good*.

She knew nothing about Aeramere, had never even heard of it, but she was definitely certain of one thing—these two brothers knew their way around females. She had no doubt they were well-practiced in and out of the bedroom, but it was the way they carried themselves that left her a bit flustered. They were aristocratic yet dashing, graced with smooth manners, and impressive charm. Usually she was the one who was overly flirtatious, she was the one who tried to lure males into her bed, then kicked them out before the sun rose the next morning.

But Tovian and Nyxian didn't strike her as the kind of males looking for a quick fuck.

No, they were looking for *mates*.

She stole a glance at Veros to gauge his reaction. He'd been her protector for so many years, and he was incredibly wary of any males who showed interest in her. At least, the ones he knew about. But Veros wasn't looking in her direction. He was watching Atlas, who was staring at her.

The slightest tick feathered along his jaw. The golden-green of his eyes darkened, swirling with tempered rage. His muscles bunched, tense and flexed, and though his arms were by his sides, his hands were clenched into tightly coiled, white-knuckled fists. For a moment, she thought he was pissed at her for some unknown reason, but then she noticed how he cut down both of the brothers, Tovian in particular, with a look of warning.

Atlas wasn't mad at her, he was *jealous*.

Under any other circumstances, she would find envy a pitiful characteristic. Yet when displayed by Atlas, it caused some traitorous part inside of her heart to stir with warmth.

She shook off the uncomfortable sensation and adjusted her sweater, so it slid a little bit lower. Tovian's gaze sparked like shattered moonbeams.

"Will you be staying with us long, my lord?" she asked him, sidling a few inches closer to his side.

"Us?" Atlas ground the word out, and she ignored him.

"I'm afraid not, my lady." He tucked his hands behind his back, a lock of deep blue hair falling onto his forehead. "We sail in six days' time and then once more we will be out at sea."

How disappointing. "I bet you've had a number of adventures."

"Indeed." He bent his head close, the scent of aged bourbon, vanilla, and clove surrounding her. "I wish I was afforded the opportunity to tell you about them sometime."

Everinne grinned, a blush spreading to her cheeks. "I'd love that."

"Sounds like a brilliant idea," Atlas announced loudly. When he glanced her way again, his face was a mask of unexpected indifference. A chill had crept into his eyes. "My father is requiring me to host a ball in the hopes of finding a wife."

Wife.

The word sliced through Everinne like the blade of a honed sword, piercing her.

She didn't realize he was being forced to marry. Of course the kralv would pressure him to take a bride. Oldrich Skye kept a leash around Atlas's throat, bending his son to his will while threatening him if he dared to disobey an order.

Atlas turned away from her to face Aran. It was as though the topic at hand had sobered him in an instant. His rueful smile was gone. He straightened, his posture morphing from lackadaisical and carefree into that of a polished prince. "I imagine I can throw something together before the three of you set sail again. After all, it would give our Everinne a chance to dance with Lord Tovian."

Our Everinne?

What the fuck was that supposed to mean?

Veros clicked his tongue, crossing his arms over his chest. "Everinne doesn't participate in royal affairs."

But she would certainly be willing to change her mind, if a certain star-kissed lord was in attendance.

"Oh, I don't know, Veros," she crooned, fiddling with the collar of aquamarines around her neck in an effort to hold Tovian's attention. "I think I can make an exception."

Atlas took one lurching step toward her, but Veros tossed out his arm, halting him.

"A ball sounds like an excellent idea." Aran's lilting, mild voice slivered through the tension in the dining hall. "My lords, would you care to attend the prince's ball while he hunts for a wife?"

Nyxian laughed, his dimples flashing as he rocked back on his heels. "Sounds like exactly the type of party we'd attend back home."

Tovian's smile widened. Either he was completely oblivious to Atlas's simmering rage or he simply didn't care. "If it means I get to spend a few precious hours with Lady Everinne, then I can think of no better way to enjoy an evening."

"She's not a lady," Atlas muttered under his breath, his words clipped.

Everinne disregarded his cruel insult, choosing to focus instead on the flattery Lord Tovian Starstorm so graciously offered her. "And will you save me a dance, my lord?"

He captured her hand again, pressing another wickedly charming kiss right on the inside of her wrist. "I'll save every one of them for you."

Everinne tossed Atlas a careless look, then coated her voice with sickening sugar. "Prince Atlas?"

She could've sworn she heard his teeth grinding.

"Yes, Ever?" he asked, maintaining a cutthroat smile.

"When will you be hosting your ball?"

His jaw ticked and he inhaled sharply. "Three nights from now."

"Well, then." She slid her hand from Lord Tovian's grasp, letting her fingers link with his before releasing him. "I suppose I should go buy a dress."

Veros arched a brow and Atlas's mouth curved into a vile smirk.

Damn it.

She'd almost forgotten her promise to him. She was supposed to tell Veros about her new job at the Mystic Obscura.

Well, it was best to do it now and get it over with. Veros wouldn't dare berate or admonish her in front of royal guests.

"Don't worry, Veros. I've got it covered." She rose up on her toes and gave her brother a quick peck on the cheek. "I work at the Mystic Obscura now."

His jaw fell slack and his eyes widened. She may as well have told him she'd taken up a job removing her clothing for money at the Dancing Nymph.

Everinne slowly backed away. It was time to make her grand exit. "Well, this has been fun, but I promised Zoryana that I'd meet her for lunch before my next shift. It was so wonderful to meet all of you."

"Everinne..." Veros warned, moving toward her.

"My lords." She dropped into a quick curtsy. "Your Highnesses." She would have to run if she wanted to make it out of the palace alive.

"Ev—"

"See you in three nights!" she called over her shoulder, rudely cutting off her brother and hastening her steps.

As soon as she left the dining hall and was out of their sight, Everinne broke into a sprint. She had no doubt in her mind that Veros was furious with her, but she didn't particularly care to be reprimanded in front of three fae nobles. And certainly not Atlas.

The humiliation would be insufferable.

Chest heaving, she rushed down one of the corridors, her high heels slipping on the obsidian surface of the floor. Flinging her arms out for balance, she kept her pace, refusing to slow just in case Veros came after her. Knowing him, he had duties to the court first, but that wouldn't stop him from coming to find her the moment he got a chance. She shoved open the grand doors leading to the side entrance where she could safely hail a *valade* and make her way back to her apartment.

Everinne took a deep breath as the cold air slammed into her, cooling her burning lungs. Squinting into the bright morning light, she forced herself to walk at a normal pace. Even if the guards knew her, it would look incredibly suspicious if she was seen fleeing from the palace like she was being chased by the Wild Hunt. She waved at the guards as she passed and they nodded in return, not the least bit suspecting.

The gates groaned open, creaking against the strain of bronze and metal.

Almost there.

Without warning, a gust of wind sent her tumbling forward, and the sound of beating wings echoed in her ears.

She whipped around.

"What the—"

Everinne shrieked as Atlas collided into her. He snatched her into his arms then, shot into the cloudless blue sky.

Fourteen

"Atlas!" Everinne shouted, squirming in his hold. If she wasn't careful, she'd slip from his grip completely. "What the hell do you think you're doing? Put me down right now!"

He ignored her and tightened his grasp on her waist, pressing her into the heat of his body.

"ATLAS!"

"That's right, Ever," he whispered into her ear, his lips moving lightly across the amethyst studs piercing the pretty little pointed tip. "Scream my name again."

She fell silent and still, her lips parting slightly as she stared at him with those mesmerizing eyes.

He'd shocked her. Good.

At least that would shut her up for a minute.

His wings rippled and shifted through the stiff breeze as he flew with her over Starysa. Everinne had one arm around his neck while her other hand was fisted into the front of his shirt. Gray winter clouds sifted past them, the stiff breeze sending her dark hair fluttering in every direction. Her pale blue sweater slipped dangerously low down her shoulder, revealing the perfect swell of lightly tanned flesh hidden just beneath.

Atlas focused on catching the currents, instead of the way her body felt crushed against his own.

"Where are you taking me?" she finally asked.

"Home."

She huffed, her warm breath tickling the underside of his chin. "I could've gotten a ride myself."

"And I could've let you."

But fuck if his raging jealousy hadn't gotten the better of him. He had no idea why he went after her once she fled the dining hall. All he knew was that if Lord Tovian touched or kissed her one more time, he would set fire to the whole of his city.

"So, you chose to scoop me up into the air and fly me back so I could freeze to death?" Everinne snuggled closer, burying her face in his chest. "Sounds noble of you."

Atlas inhaled sharply, regretting his decision in the next moment. The delicious scent of her, warm caramel layered between rose and black currant, enveloped him. Heat spread through him, pinpricks of desire chasing the sensation. His jaw locked into place. This was Everinne. She was maddening. Infuriating. After that one fateful night where he'd humiliated her beyond all repair, he'd spent years avoiding her, frequenting parlors and venues where he knew she wouldn't dare step foot in the door. Only to have her in his arms two days in a fucking row.

Mother Goddess...curse him now.

"Do you really have to get married?" Her voice was muffled against his shirt.

Regret gnawed at him. "Yes."

"Mm." She peered up at him. "Pity that."

Annoyance fired through him, and he swooped down through the clouds until the rooftop of her apartment came into view. "It's not my choice."

He was being bent to his father's will. Again.

"I'm sure it's not."

Her fake smile caused his teeth to grind.

"I wouldn't imagine the prince of pleasure would be too happy about having to give up his most favorite activity."

Atlas grabbed her chin, forcing her face upward, his fingers digging into her flesh. "You don't know what you're talking about."

He wouldn't dare tell Everinne about the first time he took a lover, he wouldn't mention how that female was the one who snuck away from his bed before dawn broke. She told anyone who would listen about the size of his cock, the skill of his tongue, and how his magic rendered her useless after a night of seemingly endless orgasms. The next thing Atlas knew, females from all over the city were flocking to him like bees to honey, desperate for a chance to share his bed. At first he was cocky, thinking his looks and charm had something to do with their sudden interest. But what he thought was flattery soon became gross obsession coupled with vile lies. It was then his reputation had branded him. It was then he realized he would have to discard females before they could discard him.

"Oh, really?" Everinne jerked away from his grasp, her eyes full of turquoise fire, the gold in them sparking like flames. "So, you don't seek out a new female every week?"

He glared at her. "More like every night."

Her lips curled in disgust. "How lucky for them."

Now it was Atlas's turn to smile. "You sound jealous, Wildheart."

"Not as jealous as you when Lord Tovian took an interest in me," she spat, fueling his anger.

"Yeah, and you crawled toward his affection like a cat in heat," Atlas snapped. "Next time, just ask him to bend you over the table. It'd be far less shameful."

The sting of her hand against his cheek hit so hard, he almost dropped her.

She yanked her arm from around his neck, then bunched both of her hands into fists against his chest. "You fucking bastard."

"No." Atlas shook his head and dove between two buildings toward her apartment. "You don't get to act like your feelings are hurt. You don't get to call me a whore, then not expect any kind of backlash for your own behavior."

"You're forgetting one thing," Everinne muttered.

"And what's that?" he asked, more annoyed than he cared to admit.

But when she looked up at him again, there was an unfamiliar sheen in her eyes.

Fuck.

She was going to cry.

"I know you're not a whore, Atlas. Do you think I'm blind? Do you think I'm stupid? I know the reason you act the way you do, and it has nothing to do with your magic and everything to do with how your father, and everyone else for that matter, treats you." She bit her bottom lip, blinking hastily. "I said those things because I knew you could take it. Because that's what we do. I tease you about your sexual encounters and you scorn me about my rash and sometimes questionable decisions."

Her breath hitched, and by the time he landed on her balcony, she was scrambling to get out of his arms.

"But you..." She shook her head, tucking some dark, fallen waves behind one ear. "You wanted to hurt me. You intentionally wanted to make me feel devalued and worthless. So, congratulations, Your Imperial Highness. You succeeded."

Somehow, hearing his proper title instead of the more annoying one she gave him hurt more than any insult tossed his way. "Everinne, I—"

She held up one hand, backing away from him. Never before had she looked at him with such hate. Such contempt. "Don't waste your breath on me."

"Ever, I'm sorry. I didn't mean to—"

"Save your apologies for someone who cares." Then she disappeared into her apartment and slammed the glass door behind her so soundly that it rattled.

"Great work, Skye," Atlas mumbled to himself, his wings catching the breeze to take him back to the palace. "Now you're the prince of fuckups as well."

He landed in the gardens, preferring to avoid having a conversation with anyone, which made no difference to Caedian, who leaned against the far wall, watching him from beneath an overhang of frostbitten trees.

Furious with himself, Atlas stalked through the gardens, kicking loose stones and mumbling any number of vulgar obscenities. It was probably best for Everinne to continue to hate him, for them to despise the presence of one another. Anything else was far too complicated. Eventually, his pace slowed and his frustration ebbed, so he found himself wandering near the pond where bushes of wild roses bloomed. For as long as he could remember, they'd always been his mother's favorite. The petals changed with the seasons—soft pink in spring, vibrant turquoise in the summer, deep red in the autumn, and snowy white in the winter. Their scent was sweet, lightly floral and enchanting. Such a beautiful flower for such a beautiful soul.

He lowered himself onto one of the large gray stones near the water's edge and pulled the crumpled pack of stigs from his pocket. Sticking one between his lips, he sought his lighter next, and the blue flame flared to life.

Atlas inhaled, then blew out a puff of smoke. The smell of skullcap and passionflower floated around him, before it was replaced by the scent of inky papers, earth, and leather.

He took another drag of his stig, then asked, "What do you want, Auvyre?"

Veros strolled out from behind a row of evergreen bushes. "Care to tell me what all that was about?"

Atlas only stared at him in return.

"You know, the part where you were seething with jealousy because some fae lord swept my sister off her feet?" Veros reached up, plucking an evergreen leaf off one of the nearby trees. He twirled the tiny stem between his fingers, then let it fall to the ground. "And then when she left, you proceeded to go after her?"

Atlas took another drag of his stig, wishing the pounding ache between his temples would go away. His head was throbbing—he should've known better than to drink so early in the day. But he was definitely going to need a shot of honeyfire if he stood any chance of making it through this conversation.

"I'm pretty sure you were in the same room as me," he answered, unable to hide the bitterness seeping into his tone. "She practically threw herself at him."

Veros straightened, rolling his shoulders back. He adjusted the sleeves of his coat, flicking both of his wrists in unison. His tone was cooler than normal as he said, "With all due respect, Your Imperial Highness, my sister's behavior is none of your concern."

"It is when she's inside the walls of my palace," Atlas countered, pinching his stig between his thumb and forefinger, flicking away the ash.

Veros watched him with measured indifference, his face a mask of his emotions. The master of the hour was always calm. Always collected. "Eventually, Everinne will find a husband. And when she does, he'll be the one to take care of her and protect her."

The thought of Everinne with another male left Atlas strangely unsettled. He wasn't an idiot, he knew she preferred casual relationships. She took other males to her bed, just as Atlas often found females whose names he couldn't remember tangled in his sheets in the morning. But a husband was a permanent arrangement.

He snuffed out his stig, his gaze sliding to his boots, where he kicked a pebble into the rippling blue waters of the pond. "You want to see her married off, then?"

"Not exactly." Veros tucked his hands into his pockets, then rocked his heels back into the soft ground. "But if a dashing fae lord from another realm asks for her hand, I won't stand in her way."

A beat of heavy, burdensome silence passed between them.

"And neither will you," Veros added.

Atlas's head snapped up.

"He could be good for her, Atlas," Veros continued, walking slowly toward the edge of the pond where the waters lapped against blades of frozen grass. "He could take her away from this city, give her a life worth living. And make it so she doesn't have to work at the damned Mystic Obscura."

Atlas almost smiled, then thought better of it. If he hadn't been so fucking envious, he might've laughed when Everinne announced she was working at the Mystic Obscura then fled like her life depended on it.

"You know," he drawled, rising from the stone. "She wouldn't be working there if you hadn't cut off her financial lifeline."

"I'm aware." Veros shook his head and his shoulders bunched with tension. "But I also know that she would have continued down a path of self-destruction if I stood by and did nothing."

Out of all the shops and clubs to find employment in Starysa, she'd chosen the one place where the protection of the palace couldn't quite reach. The woman who owned the Mystic Obscura, Reine, was a witch with a penchant for the exceptional and occult. She could move between spaces like a wraith, create and alter illusions. Abilities that likely made operating the Mystic Obscura possible. Running an exclusive club by invitation only wasn't illegal by any means, but requiring a single drop of blood from the patrons to gain entry was unusual. But the Mystic Obscura had been operating without any complaints or problems for months now, so perhaps it was all in his head.

Still, anywhere that was shrouded in glamour set Atlas on edge.

"Maybe Lord Tovian can give Everinne what she needs," Veros said, dragging Atlas's attention back to the topic at hand.

"And what's that?" he muttered, doubtful the fae lord could offer her anything other than a title and fancy gowns.

"Peace, Atlas." Veros spread his arms wide. "Peace for her fractured soul and an understanding of her magic."

A stream of silent curses filtered through Atlas's mind. He could really go for that shot of honeyfire about now. "She doesn't even know him."

Veros smoothed a hand over his windblown hair, making sure not a strand was out of place, and the corner of his mouth lifted. "Then it's a good thing she has three days to fall in love."

Atlas's jaw went slack. "You can't be serious."

Veros shrugged, pulling his gold timepiece from his pocket. "Only time will tell. You could help speed up the process. Make it so they just so happen to end up in the same place on more than one occasion. I'm sure Aran would be willing to help."

"Sorry, Veros. I will not be Everinne's matchmaker." Nor could Atlas even believe that his friend was legitimately considering setting his sister up with some fae lord they just met. He shook his head, crossing his arms over his chest. "I have to find my own wife."

Otherwise, he'd be sent to the Rizenrok Forge.

"Atlas!" Oldrich's booming voice exploded from across the gardens.

Lovely.

This day was just getting better and better.

"Your Imperial Majesty." Veros bowed, but Oldrich stomped across the path, waving him off. His dark eyes were focused on Atlas.

"I hear you've already chosen a day for the ball." He stepped through a bed of snowdrops, crushing the delicate petals and obliterating the stems. "I must admit, I didn't think you'd be so quick to get a move on your engagement. But three days? I'm almost impressed."

Atlas schooled his expression into one of feigned disinterest. He shouldn't be surprised that his father already knew about the ball, the palace was *always* listening.

"Good work." Oldrich clapped him hard on the back, but to

Atlas's credit, he firmly held his ground. "It's about time you start taking your duty to this kingdom seriously."

Hardly.

More like it was done out of pure spite, no thanks to a certain female with spellbinding eyes.

"Right. Actually, since you're here, Father, I was hoping to discuss another matter." Atlas steeled his spine, knowing damn good and well he was about to face off with his father's wrath. "The Eldress of Morvayne paid me a visit last night."

Oldrich's wrinkled brow furrowed into a scowl. He puffed out his chest, his ruddy cheeks darkening with anger. "I have no time for those damned bloodsuckers and their petty grievances."

Gods, the kralv was a self-righteous dickhead. "I'd hardly call a missing member of their clan a petty grievance. In fact, Khiran is—"

"Enough!" Oldrich shouted, stepping so close, Atlas could see the spittle clinging to his beard as he spoke. "Now, you listen to me. Court and political dealings are none of your concern. If I want your advice, I'll ask for it. But until then, you do exactly as you're told. Find a wife, fill her with your seed, and leave ruling *my* kingdom to me."

His father spun away from him then, trudging back through the wilted flower bed, mumbling a stream of vile curses in his wake.

Blind fury radiated from Atlas. What he wouldn't give to crush the bastard's windpipe with his bare hands, to watch his black eyes bulge from their sockets until they damn near popped out.

Veros stood nearby, saying nothing.

He never judged Atlas. He'd witnessed him being on the receiving end of his father's outrage more times than either of them could count. That didn't make the encounter any less humiliating.

Veros flicked open his timepiece, staring down at the runes that whirred and spun. "You'll take it eventually."

Atlas spared him a glance. "Take what?"

Veros clicked the timepiece closed, then slid it back into his pocket. His gaze was steady and even when he said, "The crown."

Then he walked away.

Atlas stood in the garden as gray clouds rolled in from off the coast, blanketing the sky and blocking out the sun with the promise of freezing rain. He pulled out another stig and lit it, dropping down onto the round stone once more.

Perhaps Veros was right.

He would be kralv one day. Eventually.

But Atlas didn't know what he was dreading more...the future crown or his future queen.

Fifteen

"So, let me get this straight," Zoryana mused, her arm linked with Everinne's as they strolled through the shopping district, their heels clicking against the rough cobblestone. "The Mystic Obscura is as magical and fantastical as we thought, you met a fae lord with stars in his eyes, and you never want to speak to Prince Atlas again?"

"That's right."

Everinne bundled closer into Zoryana's side, bracing herself against the stiff breeze. Winter was steadily approaching the Golden City. It wouldn't be long before the first snowfall came, and with that, the impending dark. Already the sun was sinking earlier than the day before, painting the sky in brushstrokes of rose and ruby with wisps of burnished gold.

Everinne and Zoryana had just finished devouring sandwiches of meat and cheese at one of the local cafes where Everinne had divulged the past day's events. The only thing she hadn't mentioned was her run-in with Atlas in her apartment when he'd pinned her to the wall. She'd swallowed down that little secret with her second helping of apple cake and cinnamon frosting.

Zoryana shook her lush, spiraling curls back from her face, the wind flushing her cheeks. "I'm away from you for barely a day and you manage to live an entirely new life without me."

"Don't be ridiculous." Everinne patted her hand, dipping her chin as another chilly gust of air swept through the streets, biting through the fur of her coat. "I could never live without you."

Zoryana laughed but it was lighter than usual, not the full and decadent sound that was so familiar. A sigh escaped her and her steps slowed.

"I won't always be around, Everinne. One day, you're going to have to learn how to control your magic without relying on me to soothe your emotions."

Everinne stopped, faltering as they rounded the corner toward her apartment. "I don't *rely* on you."

Zoryana arched a singular dark brow.

"It's more like I just look to you for guidance." The lie left a foul taste in Everinne's mouth.

Before she met Zoryana, she'd been nothing but a shell. A lost, wandering soul tortured by the haunting memories of her past. With the exception of Veros and sometimes Atlas, Everinne made it a point to avoid any kind of relationship, friendly or otherwise. It was easier to be alone, to abstain from forming connections with anyone, to evade the emotions that sought to destroy her from the inside out. Fear and sorrow. Anger and panic. Whenever those sorts of feelings overwhelmed her, they roused the monstrous magic she kept hidden from the rest of the world.

Without friends—and as much as it broke her, without family —Everinne ensured she was never at risk of succumbing to those damning emotions of hers. The ones she felt so keenly.

Unfortunately, she'd deprived herself of happiness and love in the process.

Yet it was worth it, she reminded herself, to keep from harming anyone.

"I'm serious, Ever." Zoryana reached out, tucking a few

wayward strands of Everinne's dark hair behind her ear. "I can only take on so much before..."

"Before what?" Everinne asked.

Concern knitted across her forehead. She knew Zoryana could absorb the uncomfortable feelings of those around her, it was both an art and a discipline, but she never thought that perhaps Zoryana was left without an outlet to purge them from herself.

Zoryana adjusted the silk handbag dangling from her shoulder and her jade eyes shifted to the cobblestone path beneath their feet. "Before I can't help you anymore."

Everinne watched her friend closely, noting the way she idly fidgeted with the pearl button on her coat, the way she rubbed her burgundy painted lips together. No, there was something else there. Something Zoryana wasn't telling her.

"I don't understand." Everinne tilted her head, and her hair fell around her like a curtain of velvet. "What is it?"

Zoryana glanced hastily over her shoulder, then moved closer to avoid being overheard. When she spoke, her voice was hushed. "There's been some rumors in my coven. Talk of how immortals and other magical beings are disappearing in Prava."

Everinne nodded, remembering Atlas's warning from the other night. She'd jokingly asked if he was worried about her, but he hadn't returned a smile in jest.

Zoryana shivered then, though whether it was from the sun dipping beyond reach of the city streets or the more ominous matter at hand, Everinne couldn't be sure. "It's been suggested that we—that I—lie low for a while until the threat passes."

"I completely agree."

Zoryana's lashes fluttered back in shock. "You do?"

"Yes." Everinne placed her hands upon her shoulders. "You're my best friend, Zory. Of course I want to see you safe, especially if there's any truth in these rumors. And if that means we have to hide out in my apartment all day, eating lemon berry tarts and drinking honeyfire, then that's a sacrifice I'm willing to make."

Everinne grinned, and quite honestly couldn't imagine anything better.

But Zoryana's shoulders dropped, and a crestfallen, ghost of a smile graced her lips.

This time, Everinne's frown deepened. "What's wrong?"

Zoryana shrugged free, shaking her head slightly. She lifted her gaze to Everinne, and her eyes were filled with glimmers of remorse. "I'll be going into hiding by myself, Everinne."

Everinne blinked, her arms falling to her side. Surely she didn't intend to leave Prava, to leave her here...alone. Again. "But can't I—"

Zoryana lifted one hand, cutting her off. "The coven has made it clear that I'm to disassociate from you until they deem it safe for me to return to the city again."

It was as though a blade skewered with white-hot spikes had been driven right into Everinne's gut. She sucked in a harsh breath, struggling to process the words that left her blood rushing so loudly she could hardly hear herself think.

"Disassociate?" Everinne tossed back, and a gnawing sense of dread clawed up the back of her throat. "What, like we can't be friends anymore? Are they forbidding you to speak to me?"

A beat of tense silence passed between them, filled with everything Zoryana didn't say. When she never voiced the denial of the claim, Everinne's lungs seized tight, and the sting of unbidden tears left her sight blurry.

"You're too reckless, Everinne." Though Zoryana's tone was gentle, it was inflected with cemented accusation. "You make rash decisions with little to no regard for the consequences."

"That's not true." Her words fell flat, ringing in her ears with mocking ridicule. She knew she was hasty and inattentive, that her wild behavior usually ended with Veros attempting to drag her out of a mess of her own making. But hearing Zoryana voice such a truth shook the foundation of the protective wall Everinne had so carefully built around herself.

"Really?" Zoryana crossed her arms, cocking one hip to the

side. "Name a time when you weighed the good versus the bad before diving headfirst into a situation."

Everinne opened her mouth, then snapped it shut.

There had to be a time when she'd taken more care, she wasn't *always* impulsive.

"Think about it, Everinne." Zoryana's face softened and the line of disappointment crinkling her brow smoothed away. She reached out, gently cupping the side of Everinne's face. Her touch was warm, save for the cool press of the moonstone rings she wore against Everinne's cheek. "It's been seventeen years since you killed Callum. And not once have you tried to regain control of your magic since then. You let it own your thoughts and dreams. Your emotions feed it because you never use enough of your power to keep the magic inside of you satisfied."

Zoryana's hand fell away, and with it went Everinne's last scrap of composure.

"Oh, forgive me if I don't want to go around hurting people all day for practice." She bit the words off as a violent chill scraped down her spine.

"That's not what I meant, and you know it. There are other ways." Zoryana tilted her head, assessing her, and for the first time in the course of their friendship, Everinne felt the keen intensity of her disapproval. "You're just scared."

"Of course I'm scared!" Everinne shouted in a rasping whisper. She glanced beyond Zoryana, down the emptying streets of the shopping district, to where shadows lengthened. She could've sworn she saw someone lurking, watching, but there was only the shuffle of merchants and vendors as they closed up their carts for the day.

She returned her attention to her friend, unable to prevent the sliver of pain splintering through her.

"I killed a man I loved, Zory. I *loved* him. And I turned his mind to ash and dust. I watched him wither into nothing right in front of me." Everinne's chest heaved, her lungs suddenly too tight. Each breath was pinched while her heart hammered, despair crippling her resolve. She hadn't spoken those words out loud in years. "I *killed* him."

Zoryana shook her head, the dangling beaded earrings she wore glinting like droplets of moonlight. "He was a human, Ever. And he was *hunting* you."

The memory of what she'd done shattered Everinne's soul into a thousand broken fragments, weakening her. "A life is still a life."

Zoryana grabbed her hand and squeezed. "You own your magic, it doesn't own you."

But that was where Zoryana was wrong.

It was too late for Callum. Now, it was too late for Everinne as well. At least this way, she could save the one person she thought still cared about her.

Everinne pulled back, slipped her hand from Zoryana's grasp. "I'll see you around, Zory. Maybe."

Then she turned around and walked away, leaving her friend behind, uncertain if or when she'd ever see her again.

She walked the rest of the way to her apartment by herself, took her time trudging up the stairs. Zoryana may have been wrong about her magic, but she was right about so many other things. Everinne was scared. Terrified, even. Of the dark. Of her own magic. Of losing her only friend.

Oh sure, she could appear fearless in front of anyone, not giving a damn what anyone thought about her, whether or not she regretted her actions later. But alone, when it was just her and the murmurings of her mind, that was when the beast of despair seized her. Its mangled claws of misery sank deep into her subconscious, its constant grip of fear strangled her, choked her, subjecting her to the ruthless torment of her power.

Everinne stumbled through her front door as it swung shut behind her, concealing her from the rest of the world as the dark magic simmering beneath her surface awoke.

The power of pain purred its approval as she struggled to maintain control, to force herself to calm down. Volatile magic pulsed to life, preying on the turbulence of her emotions, on the erratic chaos of her mind.

"No." She pressed her fingers to her temples as she staggered down the hall to her bedroom, desperately trying to fight off the well of violent magic harboring within her. But the beast had already bared its fangs, pouring from her in a vengeful rush of agonizing pain. The tip of her shoe caught on one of the wooden beams and she tumbled forward, her knees cracked against the hard ground as threads of darkness swarmed her.

"No," she whispered again, panting as she toppled over, curling into herself. A rush of cold swept through her bones. Her body trembled, convulsed against the frigid chill that left her teeth chattering.

She could see him clearly then. Callum. Again, she witnessed the way his brown gaze bulged as her merciless retribution sought justice for the crime committed against her. She invaded him. Owned him. His bones snapped, his harrowing screams echoed as she inflicted the full wrath of her might upon him. Blood seeped from the corners of his eyes while she released her power, watching as he crumpled to the forest floor in a heap of ruination. With a twist of her wrist, she shattered his mind until there was nothing left. He sucked in a final garbled breath, his pulse ceasing to beat. Until he became an empty shell, just like her.

Whimpering softly, Everinne squeezed her eyes shut, and the nightmares descended upon her.

Sixteen

⟊⟊⟊

Atlas was lounging on the sofa in his study, his ankles kicked up on the table before him. He swirled the glass of honeyfire in his hand and stared at the cluttered mess of papers, pictures, and swatches of fabric strewn beneath his boots.

He was still stewing over everything that had happened the day before, his mood growing more bitter with each passing hour. In his mind, he continued to replay the way Lord Tovian had kissed the inside of Everinne's wrist and how she'd nearly melted into a puddle at his feet. But worse was the image of her fighting to hold back her tears after he so callously insulted her. Each time he closed his eyes, every time he *blinked*, all he saw was her face, and the pain he'd caused her.

Now, he was expected to sift through the preparations of hosting a ball.

He didn't give a fuck what it looked like. He didn't care what kind of food was served, or what sort of flowers would be arranged. It made no difference to him the songs that were played or if the theme was to his liking. The entire ordeal felt less like a means of finding a wife and more like a march to his own death.

Without warning, the door of his study burst open, and

Caedian darted into the room. His gray eyes were wild with a sheen of panic, but he snapped to attention immediately, tucking both of his hands behind his back.

Something about the look on his face set Atlas on edge, filled him with an unnatural sense of dread. He was on his feet in a second, his glass of honeyfire slipping from his grasp and shattering against the floor.

"What is it?"

"Your Imperial Highness, my soldiers have reported a disturbance at Everinne's apartment. Her place is crawling with shadows." Caedian's throat bobbed and a tiny bead of sweat slid down his temple. "I think she's in trouble."

"Fuck." Atlas swung his head towards the windows. The wind was fierce tonight, rattling the glass panes in their wooden sills. He could fly to her, but he'd be going against the currents. His wings would drag, and it would take longer to reach her apartment. "I'll take the *volt*."

Less than ten minutes later, the engine of his *arcanic volt* was revving through the streets of Starysa, spitting out flames of bright blue fire as he shifted the gears. He gripped the handlebars, cutting smoothly around the corners while darting in and around other vehicles crowding the uneven road. All the while, his thoughts ran through every possible worst-case scenario.

He never should've said such awful things to her.

He should've known it would send her into a spiral.

Atlas's *volt* skidded to a stop in front of her apartment tower, the wheels shrieking against the rough stone. He quickly shut it off and hopped down, powering up the steps to her apartment two at a time. With every floor, the beating of his heart increased, anxiety rushing through him and flooding his veins with ice.

Fucking skies, it was taking forever to get to her.

He wrenched open her door with so much force, he nearly ripped it clean off the hinges, and drew up to a sudden halt.

Shock held him in place as he stared at the mass of power billowing within the walls of her home. Silky black and shimmering violet shadows crawled over every surface in long, sinewy tendrils. They moved like mist, slow and intentional, twisting and curling, making it nearly impossible to see. The scent of her magic —midnight lilacs—permeated the air. Lovely yet lethal. Wisps of black entwined with violet rose before him like a sheer barricade. Some of the shadowy threads danced along his arm and cheek, as though inspecting him, then they gradually shifted to one side, allowing him to pass through.

Atlas took a cautious step into her kitchen. At least, he assumed it was still her kitchen.

"Everinne?" he called out softly so as to not startle her. "Everinne, where are you?"

He was met with no response.

Carefully, he closed the door behind him and ventured further into her home. He inhaled deeply, breathing through the heady fragrance of her magic, searching for the scent of *her*. He caught the faintest traces of warm caramel, rose, and black currant drifting from the back of the apartment.

Her room.

She was in her room.

Atlas moved carefully through her space, but in her bedroom, the strength of her magic seemed to magnify. He reached out blindly, feeling the cool touch of her power as it threaded between his fingers.

"Everinne?" He took another step when something purple glittered on the floorboards, catching his eye.

An amethyst ring.

Everinne's amethyst ring.

The one she always wore, still on her limp, outstretched hand.

"Shit!" Atlas rushed to her side, dropping onto his knees next to her. "Ever? Can you hear me?"

He smoothed back some strands of tangled hair from her face, cupping her cheeks with both of his hands, and turned her head toward him. Her eyes were closed and her lips were parted, but he thanked the gods that her skin was still warm to the touch. He watched as her chest rose and fell in deep, even breaths, felt the steady beating of her pulse in his own veins.

"Everinne, wake up." He brushed his thumb lightly back and forth across her jaw. "I need you to wake up now."

Still, she remained motionless.

Atlas raked a hand through his hair as uncertainty edged him toward desperation. There was only one thing he could do and know without a doubt it would work. He could only hope she'd be able to forgive him.

Gathering her into his arms, he gently nudged her sweater out of the way and placed his palm over her heart. He calmed his mind and summoned his magic, closing his eyes as it flowed from him and into her. Warmth ebbed and flowed between them, like the lulling waves of the sea always returning to kiss the shore. His blood heated as his magic tenderly caressed her soul, seeking the source of her power. Of her pain.

On a sharp inhale, he ventured into her mind, sliding into her dreams.

It was far quieter than he expected. There were no chaotic thoughts or broken sobs of anguish. Instead, he was greeted with a kind of melancholy, an almost unnatural stillness. But it was dark, a vast swath of endless pitch. Her magic pressed in on his own, surrounding him, almost curious in nature. Ribbons of midnight and violet twirled around fibers of emerald and gold— the origin of his power—weaving an intricate tapestry of pleasure and pain.

Through the delicate balance, a pair of turquoise eyes found his own.

Relief flooded him when he saw her, his breath catching as her fingers softly grazed the blend of colors and magic spanning between them.

"There you are." He took one guarded step toward her.

"Atlas?" Everinne's voice was almost ethereal, his name a song that fell from her lips. "What are you doing here?"

He kept his movements slow and methodical. He couldn't

risk scaring her, not when he almost had her within his reach. "I came for you."

She stared at him, lightly brushing the fibers of his power between her thumb and forefinger.

He shuddered in spite of himself.

When she didn't respond, he took another step. Close. He was so close to her now. "I'm here to bring you back."

"Back," she repeated, her forehead scrunching as though she didn't understand his intent.

"Yes." One more step. One more breath. "To bring you back home. With me."

"You shouldn't be here, Atlas. It's dangerous." Everinne shook her head, her dark brown waves tumbling around her bare shoulders. Sadness haunted her gaze and she sighed. "I'm dangerous."

No.

No, no.

He refused to leave her in the deepest recesses of her own mind, when he knew she wouldn't be able to find her way back by herself.

"I'm not afraid of you." He glanced around the lengthening shadows. "Or your magic."

She blinked in surprise. "You're not?"

"No, Everinne. I'm not." Atlas raised his arm, uncurling his fingers one at a time. "Take my hand."

She hesitated, scraping her teeth along her bottom lip. Her gaze remained focused on his outstretched hand and when she lifted her eyes to meet his, those captivating pools of turquoise ringed with gold held him spellbound. And he knew then he would go to the ends of the world for her.

"Come back, Wildheart."

Her hand reached for his own, hovering above his open palm.

"Come back with me." To me, he wanted to say.

Everinne placed her hand in his, interlacing their fingers together, and Atlas didn't waste a second. He pulled her flush against him, withdrawing his magic and bringing Everinne back with him.

She was still in his lap on the floor of her room, and he quickly moved his hand from her heart to her shoulder. The looming black and violet shadows receded, vanishing from sight as her power waned. He continued to stare down at her, holding his breath, silently counting each second until her lashes fluttered open.

She looked up at him with sleepy, hooded eyes. "Atlas?"

"Yes, Wildheart?"

"Thank you for coming to get me." Everinne relaxed against him, her body going pliant in his arms.

"You're welcome." His fingers idly toyed with a few fallen strands of her hair.

Her full lips pursed to one side. "I'm still mad at you."

Finally, Atlas grinned, pulling her into a sitting position. He pressed a featherlight kiss to her forehead. "I know."

A deep, almost devastating sigh escaped her.

"Zoryana told me she can't be seen with me anymore. She said she has to go into hiding and made it sound like she was going to leave the city. Perhaps even leave Prava." She dropped her head onto his shoulder. "I'm assuming it has to do with what you told me the other night, about immortals disappearing."

"It's likely," Atlas agreed. Zoryana was a notorious witch with the ability to absorb and harbor the emotions of those around her. Not only that, but her coven was one of the most powerful within Prava's borders. It would stand to reason that they would conceal themselves and seek refuge elsewhere, especially if the situation became more out of hand. "One of the vampires from Morvayne has gone missing, as well as a few other immortals. I'm afraid it's becoming a more serious matter than I originally thought and the kralv refuses to do anything about it."

Everinne sat up then, moving away so she faced him fully. Her sweater dipped low but he ignored it, forcing himself to look into her eyes instead.

"Should I be worried?"

"No. I—Veros and I won't let anything happen to you." Atlas ran his hand along the back of his neck, hoping she wouldn't implode with his next suggestion. "That being said, I know I can't change your mind about working at the Mystic Obscura..."

She instantly stiffened, planting both hands behind her on the hardwood floor. Her brows narrowed, but he continued before she could interject.

"But," he added quickly, "would you at least consider finding another form of employment? Preferably in a place not hidden away by a veil of glamour?"

Her nails tapped against the flooring, and she tilted her head so a tumble of dark waves fell around her. "I'll think about it. But the pay is good, and I need this job. Besides, I've only worked there one night. I need to stay for a few months to start. It won't look good if I bounce between jobs every couple of weeks."

Atlas didn't even care, a win was a win. "So, you'll consider it."

"I'll consider it." She pushed up from the ground and planted her hands on her hips. She peered out the window of her bedroom where twilight was bleeding across the sky like spilled ink. "But I have to get ready or I'm going to be late."

"Alright." Atlas stood, dusting his hands on his pants. "But I'm going with you."

She groaned then, rolling her eyes before pinning him with a hard stare. "And what will you do while I'm working?"

"The same thing I used to do when I frequented the place for a good time." Her gaze darkened and he smirked, leaning against the doorframe. "Sit in my suite with a carton of buttered rum popcorn and watch the show."

Everinne crossed her arms in a silent challenge. "Fine."

"Fine." He smiled again. "I'll give you a ride."

"Lovely," she muttered, stomping over to her closet and rummaging through it.

She pulled the door wide so it concealed her from view, and

the next thing he saw was the sweater she wore flying across the room. It missed the bed, landing on the floor near his feet, and Atlas bit the inside of his cheek. She draped a cropped black leather coat over her arm, then slowly eased back, peeking at him from the other side of the open door. All he could see were glimpses of bare skin and the tingling sensation of desire rippled through him.

"Atlas?"

He kicked one ankle over the other as he watched her study him. "Yes, Wildheart?"

She rubbed her lips together, then glanced hastily about her bedroom. Her gaze landed on the floor where she'd been unconscious in his arms only minutes before. "Are you going to tell Veros about...the nightmare?"

"No."

"You answered so fast this time." Everinne's lips curved, and she stepped out from behind the closet door in a pair of leggings and shiny red top covered in gold beads that showed off her toned stomach and the fullness of her breasts. She pulled on a thick coat, it stopped just below her waist, and then slipped her hands into the pockets. "Maybe you're getting good at keeping secrets after all."

Atlas nodded. "Maybe."

But this particular secret would be one he took to his grave. Because there had only been one possible explanation for Atlas to be able to slip into her mind, there was only one reason he could hear her thoughts and join her dreams. It was something he had suspected for a while now, something he'd known but had refused to admit, even to himself.

Everinne Auvyre was his mate.

Seventeen

E verinne stared at the *arcanic volt*, her lips tugging to one side.

She'd seen dozens of them zipping through the city, and she'd seen Atlas ride his own a handful of times, but that didn't stop the butterflies from fluttering in her stomach at the thought of riding one with him. The rider and passenger seats were black leather, and given their size, she would be pressed incredibly close to Atlas. Which was fine. Completely fine. One headlight in the front flashed bright silver while the one in the back burned red. A curved sheet of shiny black metal glowed where the arcane magic hummed, powering the two-wheeled vehicle to life. Small pegs stuck out from either side, where she assumed she was supposed to put her feet, and sparks of blue arcane fire shot from a cylinder tube in the rear.

It was fascinating yet oddly terrifying.

"Take this." Atlas glamoured her a helmet that matched the one he yanked on over his head. Whereas his was a matte black, hers was the color of crushed amethysts.

Everinne grasped the helmet with both hands, then crinkled her nose. "It'll ruin my hair."

Atlas glanced over at her, the helmet and visor concealing his face so only the tips of his ears were visible. "Just put it on, Ever."

She sighed, more dramatically than was necessary, but tugged the helmet on over her head. The visor covering her eyes tinted the world in a vibrant purple hue. Fussing with her hair, she attempted to adjust it and shove it back behind her ears, but the snug helmet made it impossible. Two straps dangled beneath her chin, and though she tried to clip them together, she couldn't quite line them up on her own.

"Here, let me help you." Collecting the straps from her, Atlas expertly snapped them in place, securing them for a perfect fit.

She stared up at him, silently longing to flip up his visor to catch a glimpse of his eyes. His knuckles grazed the underside of her jaw, and a heady zing of desire speared right through her. There was something devastatingly attractive about him and that damn helmet.

"There." He stepped back and slung one leg over the *volt*, then held out his hand to her. "Climb on."

"I've never ridden on one before." Everinne grasped his hand, carefully situating herself behind him.

She was absolutely right.

There was no shred of space between them, no clear definition of where he began and where she ended.

"It's easy." He raised his voice and revved the *volt*, the hum of it reverberating all the way to her bones. "Just hold on to me and you'll be fine."

Everinne did as she was instructed and wrapped both of her arms around Atlas's waist. The thrumming intensified, and when Atlas kicked up the stand with the back of his heel, she held onto him even tighter. In the next second, the *volt* darted forward and she squealed in delight.

Starysa became a dizzying blur of dazzling lights and beautiful colors, a painting smeared by the hands of motion. She stole quick glances, left and right, desperately trying to take it all in. The buildings and shops whirred past them, a late-night wonderland come to life, and she'd never witnessed anything more thrilling. The pulsing district of parlors and bars illuminated the streets in washes of vivid colors, and through the chaotic clusters of people and pounding music, Everinne spotted the Grand Cru.

On the back of Atlas's volt, it looked like a majestic palace with its mosaic windows and glass ceiling.

"Look!" She pointed as they streaked by its splendid visage, though she doubted he could hear her over the crush of music and magic. "Isn't it wonderful?"

She didn't know if Atlas responded, but he grabbed her wrist and linked her arm back around the security of his waist. Then he held her in place, steering the *volt* with one hand. Everinne tilted her head, resting it against his muscular back. She should've asked him for a ride years ago.

Unfortunately, the speed of the *volt* brought them to the Mystic Obscura much faster than Everinne anticipated and before she knew it, Atlas was parking outside of a dimly lit alley where a thick veil of glamour throbbed in the air. In one easy movement, he lifted her off the *volt*, keeping his hand protectively fastened to the small of her back.

Atlas flicked his wrist and their helmets vanished.

Everinne gaped up at him. "Seriously? Why didn't you just do that in the beginning?"

Mischief glinted in his eyes and he winked down at her. "It was more fun to watch you struggle."

Together they walked through the glamour, and the wisps of intense magic tickled her cheek yet pricked along her spine. They approached the back of the alley, where the door marked with whorls and runes kept the otherworldly festivities of the Mystic Obscura hidden away from the rest of the world.

Atlas reached for the handle but Everinne caught his arm. "You can just walk in?"

She knew Jarek could do the same, but it was different because he worked there. It seemed wrong that anyone who looked too closely could simply enter through the glamour and waltz inside the Mystic Obscura without being met by some kind of barrier.

"I told you, I'm a member." Atlas flipped his hand over and showed her his forefinger, where a tiny white scar marked his flesh. "The Mystic Obscura goes beyond the norms of exclusivity. Only those who received an invitation can open the door, but in order to do so, they also have to forfeit a drop of blood."

Everinne reared back. "What?"

"A drop of blood for access to an elite parlor boasting the finest exhibitions and the most extraordinary experiences. Seems like a small price to pay, doesn't it?" Atlas nodded toward the stone exterior, his gaze trailing from the door up to the highest point of the wall that lacked any windows. "Except our blood is imbued into the runes on this door. Granted, we can come and go as we please, but at what cost?"

Apprehension prickled the hairs along the back of Everinne's neck and goosebumps pebbled across her flesh. She rubbed a hand up and down her arm in an effort to rid herself of the troubling sensation.

"Blood magic?" Even she knew that sort of magic should never be trifled with. "Isn't it dangerous?"

"It can be." Atlas pulled open the door. "Yes."

She peeked around him, then hesitated, drawing back. "This can't be right."

Instead of billowing curtains of bronze silk that seemed to move and shift of their own accord, the entrance of the Mystic Obscura was draped in wide ribbons of black velvet that tumbled down from the high ceiling, diminishing the light. They crafted a new labyrinth, fluttering in time to the haunting strains of a distant, sinister melody. Ornate daggers with jeweled hilts were embroidered onto every panel with silver thread, each one different, like snowflakes falling from the sky. At their feet, a thick fog swirled, crawling along the floor and curling like bony skeletal fingers ready to pry her soul from her body.

Atlas nudged her forward, but Everinne dug her heels into the uneven cobblestone, wary. "It's not the same as it was last night."

"It changes based on Reine's mood." His tone was even and cool, unfettered despite the chilling welcome.

"You know Reine?" she asked, stepping slightly closer to his side.

"We've met once or twice."

Everinne glanced up sharply, one brow arched in silent question.

"Not like *that*," Atlas muttered, grabbing her hand. Then he tugged her into the Mystic Obscura.

He led her through the winding passage, but whereas Atlas was able to move with ease, Everinne found it difficult to keep up. The unusual mist thickened around her, making each step feel as though she was trying to wade through a bog of sludge. Dampness settled over her skin, harrowing and chilling. Warning fired through her as the mist intensified, choking her with the stench of dank air and decay. Her eyes watered and she stumbled forward, tripping as the opaque murk tangled around her limbs like bestial vines. Raw panic climbed up her throat, slowly awakening the dark magic lurking in her veins. Atlas's grip loosened, and her clammy hand slipped from his hold.

"Atlas!" she shrieked, gasping as the foul air tainted her lungs.

He spun around to face her, and the disturbing wall of fog evaporated.

"Hey, are you okay?"

Everinne launched herself into his arms. He caught her by the waist, pulling her close. She clutched his shirt, fisting the soft fabric with both hands. Gently, he brushed a fallen strand of hair from her face while his free hand slowly slid to her hip. "What's wrong?"

Everinne swallowed around the knot of fear lodged in the back of her throat. "The mist...it...it vanished."

His brows knit together in concern as he studied her. "It disappeared as soon as we walked inside, Ever."

Except it hadn't...not for her.

"Come on." He took her hand once more, lacing their fingers together. "The menagerie is right around this corner."

Once they were fully inside the Mystic Obscura, everything was exactly as Everinne remembered. The rows of velvet seating and sweeping balconies were brimming with Starysa's wealthiest patrons while patrons and performers alike roamed the lower level of the menagerie. An enchanting melody floated through the air, so sensual in sound, she could almost taste the flavor of it on her tongue—lush berries drizzled in dark chocolate. Pattering rain fell on the main stage where a male and female took the lead. They danced together, never breaking contact, as every slow twirl, spin, and dip showcased the torture of forbidden desire.

"Everinne." A cold, deep voice coasted past her ear and she shivered, turning around to find Jarek standing directly behind her.

His brown hair was a little more unkempt than usual, as though he'd raked his hands through it one too many times. He looked at her with those honey-colored eyes, except this time they appeared frosted, touched by ice. There was a snag near the collar of his black shirt where some of the fabric had begun to fray and a dark stain, like mud, along the hem of his pants. He cracked his knuckles, the skull rings he wore glinting in the low light.

Beside her, Atlas stiffened.

Everinne took in Jarek's roughened appearance and cocked her head to the side. Smirking, she asked, "Rough night?"

He ignored her question.

"I see you brought the prince as your guest for the evening." Jarek looked pointed at their joined hands.

Atlas's grip increased, squeezing her hand.

Jarek bowed obnoxiously low. "Your Imperial Highness."

Atlas merely inclined his head in acknowledgement, his gaze darkening.

The tension between the two males was pulled taut like a tightrope, ready to snap. This was not the same wave of jealousy she'd sensed from Atlas while flirting with Lord Tovian. No, this was something more potent and bitter. Hostile and ancient.

"Well..." Everinne glanced up at the two males staring off with one another. "I have to go get ready before I'm late."

Jarek offered his arm. "Do you need me to show you to the dressing rooms?"

She gave him a tight smile. "I can manage on my own."

At least, she would've been able to find her way if Atlas would let her go. He pulled her to his side, pointing up to where one of the balconies protruded from the center, higher than all the rest. Silken emerald curtains were tied back with gold cord, framing a gilded chair fit for a kralv. Or a prince.

"My suite is up there." He met her gaze in earnest, then released her hand. "If you need me, you'll know where to find me."

"Thank you, Your Radiance." She grinned when he gritted his teeth, then she turned on one heel, stalking off with purpose away from the glowering males. The floor beneath her feet shimmered with each step and she tried not to stare as she passed a pretty vampire dressed in a gown of sheer scarlet lace that was so snug, the intricate details looked painted on her ivory flesh. With a stig pinched between two of her fingers and a glass full of bubbly gold liquid in the other, her bell-like laughter only further entranced the gathering of mesmerized males surrounding her.

Not so long ago, Everinne held that kind of power.

She could waltz into a room and snare the wandering eye of every male in her general vicinity. But instead of merely enjoying the attention she craved, she was forced to work for it. Now, she danced on hoops and put the extent of her talents on display out of necessity. Eventually, she might grow weary of performing and maybe the excitement would fade with time.

But not tonight.

It took her slightly longer than she expected, but finally Everinne discovered the dressing room beneath the menagerie.

She shoved open the door and was instantly greeted by Aisling's wide and welcoming smile.

"Everinne!" Aisling pulled out a chair in front of one of the vanities. "Dress quickly, *milazk*, so I can do your makeup before your performance."

A blush crept into Everinne's cheeks.

"You don't have to, I was only joking about that last night." Everinne walked over to the racks of glittering fabrics to choose an outfit for the night. "I'm perfectly capable of putting on my own makeup."

"Nonsense." Aisling waved one hand through the air, the silver bangles on her wrists jingling with the movement. Her hot pink hair was twisted into a braid that fell over one shoulder, a few of the pieces pinned into place by charms shaped like snowflakes. She wore snug black leather pants, and the beads sewn onto her white bodice sparkled like moonlit snow. She tapped the back of the chair with her nails. "Besides, I've been here for so long, applying makeup has become an expression of art for me."

"So long?" Everinne asked, selecting a sapphire bodysuit. "The Mystic Obscura hasn't been in Prava for more than a few years."

"You're right, of course." Aisling's face shuttered, her cerulean eyes losing a hint of their previous light. "Forgive me, I don't know where my mind has been lately. I must've misspoken."

Everinne couldn't fault her. Working in a place like the Mystic Obscura, where exotic nights blurred into forgotten days, it seemed only natural that someone would simply lose track of time.

She switched out of her clothing and slipped into the body-suit. It crushed her breasts, shoving them upward, but the satin straps offered her security and would keep them in place while she was on the hoops. The lower half of the suit cut high up her thighs, and dozens of misshaped diamonds fell like fringe, tinkling with every movement. Again, Aisling worked her own kind of magic, fanning out the liner across the tops of Everinne's eyes and painting her lips a deep, cherry red. Everinne strapped on a pair of heels that looped around her ankles, and then her new friend was hustling her out the door, warning her not to be late.

She stepped out into the hall, glancing long enough behind her to catch Reine shuffling into one of the rooms further down the dimly lit corridor.

That was fine, Everinne had a better sense of direction now, and made her way back up the winding staircase to the grand stage easily enough. Except when she arrived, Reine was there waiting for her.

Everinne almost lost her footing and threw one arm out, grasping the railing for support. She looked behind her, back the way she came, then back up at Reine. "How did you..."

"How did I what?" Reine asked, tilting her head so that her pin straight hair fell like a curtain of rich brown silk.

Everinne blinked, shaking off the confusion. "I could've sworn I just saw you go into one of the rooms below the menagerie."

Reine laughed, and the golden spirals hanging from her ears slithered like tiny snakes. She placed one hand on her hip, then leaned against the bronze railing. "I wish I could be in two places at once. Sometimes I feel like I'm running around in circles here."

She clicked her tongue, her hooded eyes sliding to the vast audience. "Someone is always needing something."

"Running the Mystic Obscura must take a lot of effort." Everinne climbed the last few steps, preparing to go on stage. "I'm sure it's exhausting."

"You have no idea." Reine gestured to the stage, and the swath of glamour enveloped them both. "You remember the word?"

"Yes." Everinne nodded, catching sight of a smudge of red on the back of Reine's hand. "You've got something on your hand. Just there."

Reine glanced down sharply and sighed, smearing the streak of crimson away with her thumb. "Lipstick," she muttered.

"Unfortunately, not all of my performers are as talented with makeup application as Aisling."

Then she slid past Everinne, the train of her black velvet gown pooling around her like a midnight lake. A warm smile lifted her lips, and she nodded in encouragement. "You're up, Everinne."

The same solid gold hoop appeared before Everinne and she reached out, gripping it tightly with one hand. Magic coated her skin, a soothing comfort as the glamour rippled around the outer edges of the stage, waiting patiently for her.

"*Trivno.*"

At once, the hoop lifted into the air, suspending her high above the rows of balconies where the audience fixated upon whatever wonder awaited them beyond the shimmering veil of the stage. Somewhere out there, watching and seated upon a chair like a throne, was Atlas.

Nervous energy crackled through Everinne.

Just for tonight, she would dance for him.

Eighteen

tlas sat in his suite, his fingers tapping a haphazard rhythm against the glass of honeyfire, his gaze focused on the stage before him. At some point, a servant had entered with a container full of his favorite popcorn, but he'd left it on the side table, discarded and untouched. The warm lights of the chandelier dimmed, shrouding the balcony in darkness, and a singular beam of silver light reflected off the gossamer curtains of glamour. They shimmered as the first chords of music resonated through the Mystic Obscura, and then the magic fell away.

A golden hoop hovered from a dizzying height, and perched along its bottom curve was Everinne.

Atlas's heart stopped.

Fucking gods, she was beautiful.

Her outfit was as blue as the deepest part of the ocean, the tiny straps on her shoulders hardly looked strong enough to hold the bodice in place. It cinched her waist, cut incredibly high to reveal her shapely hips, and hundreds of diamonds spilled over her thighs. Waves of dark hair tumbled down her back with ribbons of sapphire satin twisted throughout. Thick liner fanned out from the corner of her eyes, giving them a smoky look, and her lips...damn, those lips. His thoughts were an incoherent mess, and he found himself debating whether he should remain in his suite or toss her over his shoulder and haul her to his bed. He didn't think he'd ever seen anything more magnetizing, more spellbinding, until she started to dance.

Everinne spun and twirled on the hoop like a ballerina waltzing on air. She was fluid and graceful, performing the splits and bending her body with subtle elegance. Her flexibility left Atlas's mouth dry, and he swallowed a gulp of honeyfire, wincing as the heat of it stole down the back of his throat. She hooked her knees onto the hoop and bent backwards, releasing it and stretching out her arms wide as though she was an offering. A gift to the gods.

If she could move like that on a hoop, there was no telling what she was capable of in the bedroom.

His cock thickened at the thought.

Atlas leaned forward, propping his elbows on the balcony's smooth ledge, slowly swirling his glass of honeyfire.

Dipping back, she gradually dragged one leg off the hoop, lengthening it in front of her. Gasps and murmurs of appreciation echoed through the audience, and when Everinne smiled, her turquoise eyes were on him.

Atlas drained his drink.

The sensual music crescendoed, signaling her act was drawing to a close as she swung, soaring on the hoop as applause ruptured around her. Atlas was fixated, enthralled, when the barest of movements down near the bottom of the stage caught his eye.

Jarek loitered near the bottom of the winding staircase and there was no mistaking the lascivious glint flashing in his eyes.

Atlas stood immediately, abandoning his suite.

Not today, demon summoner.

He would be the one taking Everinne home, not Jarek.

Atlas made his way to the menagerie, moving with speed and ignoring the calls of females who recognized him. He dodged their advances, heading directly toward the main stage, fully aware no one would dare stand in his way. Sometimes, being the imperial prince had its perks.

Heady magic coated the air as the glamour ensconced the stage once more, its ethereal veil concealing Everinne from view. She emerged a moment later, passing the next performer with a quick smile, and Atlas's lips twitched with a smug sense of satisfaction when she noticed him waiting for her first.

Jarek didn't miss the snub of her gaze and tossed a hasty glance over his shoulder to where Atlas stood. His eyes fired with indignation and simmering rage. The demon summoner forced an easy, carefree smile, but it was strained. Tainted with envy.

"Don't you belong in your suite, Your Imperial Highness?"

Atlas tucked in hands into his pockets as Everinne descended the stairs. "I prefer the view from here."

"Come on, Everinne. There's a party downstairs." Jarek tossed his arm around her shoulders, and Atlas knew it was only a matter of time until he had the demon summoner's blood on his hands. This time when Jarek grinned, it was a taunting sneer. "Performers only."

Atlas closed the distance between them in two strides, a silent challenge. "Where she goes, I go."

Jarek barked out a grating laugh. "What, are you her bodyguard now?"

"Where she goes," he repeated, the icy promise of death dripping from his tone. "I. Go."

Everinne's teeth sank into her bottom lip and she shimmied a bit, sliding out from under Jarek's hold.

"Actually, Jarek, I promised Prince Atlas we'd explore the menagerie for a while." She peered up at him, her sultry eyes imploring him to play along with her game. "Ready?"

He offered her his arm and she readily accepted, tucking her hand into the crook of his elbow. Atlas drew her to his side, his brows drawing together as Jarek glowered at them.

There was a pulse of dark power, like the chill of a thousand lost souls. It was almost imperceptible, the violent shift in the air, but it was just noticeable enough for Atlas to maneuver Everinne behind him. Jarek's hands fisted at his sides, the ruby eyes of the skull rings he wore glowing like fire. The demon summoner snarled, and a low growl rumbled through Atlas's chest. He bared his teeth in retaliation, arching one brow in a threat, daring Jarek to show the truth of his sinister nature.

"Got something to say, demon summoner?" Atlas taunted.

Jarek rolled his neck, his chest heaving. A vein bulged and throbbed at his temple. "You'll regret standing in my way."

Atlas scoffed, the corner of his mouth curling into a sneer. "We'll see about that."

He turned around, shuffling Everinne away from Jarek, guiding her through the throng of people milling about the menagerie.

"What was that all about?" she asked, her brows knitting together in a frown.

"I don't trust him." Atlas bit off the words, annoyed by her complete disregard for her own safety. She needed to pay more attention, to not be so oblivious to her surroundings.

"You mean you don't trust me."

Everinne released his arm and he spun, blocking her from walking away from him.

"Stop twisting my words. Sure, you can handle yourself in most situations." When she even knew a threat existed. He held up one finger. "But to be perfectly honest, I'd rather not take any chances when it comes to you."

She rolled her eyes, sliding past him to a display of treats behind a glass case. The gold tiers were filled with swirled lollipops, bags full of crystal gems which were nothing more than flavored sugar meant to look like diamonds, and an assortment of fizzy bursts. That particular candy had been his favorite as a child, he loved the way they popped and crackled on his tongue. He hadn't had those in years. Everinne's eyes widened, and she peeked up at him from beneath her long lashes.

"Will you buy me a lollipop?"

"I..." He blinked down at her. "What?"

"A lollipop, Atlas." She jerked her head towards the display, then spread her arms wide. "This outfit didn't come with pockets, so I don't exactly have any notes or coin on me."

He made the mistake of raking his gaze over her once more, admiring the swell of her breasts and the way strands of diamonds glittered along the high cut of the bodice, barely covering her ass. Hells, she barely had anything *on* her.

"Sure," he croaked out, and pulled a gold piece from his coat. He flipped it onto the counter. "One lollipop please. And some fizzy bursts."

The female behind the glass case handed Everinne a shiny pink lollipop with a smile, and she bounced on her toes, almost as giddy as a fae child on Winter Solstice morning.

"Mm, thank you." She popped the hard candy in her mouth, sucked on it, and Atlas almost died. Then she pulled it out slowly, her lips gliding over it with ease. "I'll pay you back."

Atlas swallowed, cramming the small paper bag of fizzy bursts into his pocket. "Unnecessary."

Her turquoise eyes snapped to him. "Why are you so angry?"

"I'm not angry."

She swirled the glassy lollipop over her tongue before pointing it in his direction. "Yeah, you are. Your jaw is clenched, your shoulders are bunched, and there's a vein on your neck that keeps throbbing like you're about to combust."

Everinne sucked the candy back into her mouth.

Fucking gods, if she twirled her tongue around that lollipop one more time—she did, and then licked her cherry red lips.

Atlas shoved his hands through his hair, blowing out a harsh breath. He stood there, barely able to breathe, and fighting with every last shred of his willpower to keep from touching her, while she licked a lollipop. And the only thing he could imagine was his cock in her mouth instead.

"So, now you're going to ignore me?" Her tongue slid over her lips again. "You know what your problem is, Atlas?"

"What?" he ground out.

"You forgot how to have fun."

She grabbed his hand and dragged him through the menagerie, tossing her half-finished lollipop into a waste bin, something he found himself grateful for, until she stopped in front of a wooden table lined with daggers. Most of the hilts were wrapped in leather, and the polished blades were sharpened to a fine point. Across from the table, the perfect distance for throwing, was a wheel with two binding leather straps attached to the top and bottom. The wheel itself was scored, littered with dozens of nicks from where the daggers had pierced the surface.

One of the shirtless fae males who always seemed to be loitering about the menagerie strolled over to them.

His gaze landed on Everinne. "Care for a spin?"

"No," Atlas spat at the same time Everinne let go of his hand and said, "Absolutely."

He reached for her but she dodged his grasp. "No way in hell, Ever."

She spared him a look, tossing her waves of dark hair over one shoulder.

"It'll be fine." She smirked up at the male who watched her with covetous eyes. "I bet you never miss, do you?"

He held out his hand, flashing a too-bright smile, and she accepted. "Never."

If Atlas could burn the whole place down, he would. Rage fired through him, fuming and seething beneath the surface of his skin. His jaw locked into place, his muscles tensed with fury. Everinne sauntered toward the wheel and while the male strapped her into place, all Atlas could think about was how easy it would be to launch a dagger into the bastard's neck. Envy clawed through him like a beast ready to rip his throat to shreds when he knelt between Everinne's spread legs, locking her onto the wheel.

Atlas's pulse thudded heavily, and with each beat, only one word echoed through the storm of his mind.

Mine. Mine. Mine.

All it had taken was for him to finally admit to himself that this female was his godsdamned mate, and the keen stab of possession, the primitive desire to own her, had left him untethered.

The fae male stalked back over to the table of daggers and reached for one.

Atlas's hand shot out, snatching the hilt of the blade. "Not a fucking chance."

If anyone was going to throw daggers at Everinne, it would be him.

"Suit yourself." The male shrugged, then paced across the floor back to the wheel. He reached up, grabbed one of the notches, and yanked it down hard.

The wheel started to spin, and Everinne became a blur of sapphire and diamonds. Her absurd laughter caused his ears to ring with panic.

Fuck, he was really going to do this.

"Five daggers," the male called out, then stepped away from the wheel. "Fire at will."

Atlas grabbed the first dagger, raising the weapon, poised to strike. He gripped the leather-wrapped hilt in his damp palm, clutching it tightly, watching as the wheel spun and the divide between her body and the slabs of wood became indistinct, more difficult to discern. He tuned out the obnoxious thunking noise the wheel made with each rotation, focusing instead on his breathing. Inhale. Hold. Exhale. Since his youth, he'd been trained to fight with both dagger and sword. To never miss. To aim true. His chest hollowed out, his blood cooled. He stared at the spinning wheel, finding his mark on the wood to spare Everinne's flesh.

He calmed his racing heart, pulled his arm back, tracked her gasping breath of air, and threw the dagger.

Thud.

Drowning out the sound of Everinne's wild laughter and squeals, he pinpointed her heartbeat, the rush of her breath, then repeated the process. Launching the daggers at the wheel, praying to the gods he hit his mark.

Each time, the dagger stuck deep into the wood.

The wheel started to slow, creaking and grinding. Turquoise eyes found him as he threw the last dagger toward her, striking the wood next to Everinne's head. Her cheeks were flushed, her smile more brilliant than he'd seen it in years, and all because the thrill of danger, of peril, was the one thing that made her feel alive.

His relief bled away, fueling his anger.

Atlas strode to the wheel and unhooked the leather straps binding her ankles, wrists, and waist to its worn surface. Her ragged, uneven breathing made him grit his teeth as she toppled, half dizzy and delirious, into his arms.

"See?" She beamed up at him. "I told you it would be fun."

"Shut the fuck up, Everinne." Atlas scooped her up and tossed her over his shoulder.

She fought him the whole way, kicking violently and thrashing in his hold. The words that fell from her mouth...he'd never heard such sordidly vile things. But he didn't let her go, despite her vicious protests and cruel threats. Her fists pounded against his back, certain to leave bruises, but he was sick of her shit. So, he smacked her ass once—hard—and smiled with his own kind of wicked satisfaction when she yelped and fell silent.

He strode toward the exit of the Mystic Obscura with her in tow, not caring about the onlookers who gaped and whispered as he passed.

Let them talk.

Atlas tossed her onto the back of his *volt*, glamoured her helmet and secured it snugly, then climbed on, adjusting his own helmet. He didn't even wait for her to wrap her arms around his waist. If she wanted to be so damned stubborn, then she'd learn the hard way what would happen if she chose not to hold on to him. Firing the engine, he revved it fast, sending bolts of blue fire streaming out the backend of the vehicle, then gunned it.

Everinne shrieked, her high-pitched scream barely audible over the blaring thrum of arcane magic. She threw her arms around him, clutching him, sinking her nails into his abdomen like the assault was some kind of vengeance.

All it did was send a spiral of arousal pumping through his blood.

He sped through the city, flying past buildings, shops, and parlors in a blinding blur of color. He steered the *volt* up the winding roads on the outskirts of the city until the gilded lights of Starysa were nothing more than twinkling lights in the distance. The overlook appeared before him, crowned in starlight, the beauty of the Ladova Bay stretching out in an endless sea of deep sapphire from the edge of the docks to the horizon beyond. Here, there was nothing but the chilling kiss of the wind, the gentle rustle of trees, and the soft crash of waves. The air was crisp, tangy with sea spray, and it soothed the irritation coursing through him.

Atlas dropped the kickstand of the *volt* and reached around behind him. He grabbed Everinne's thigh and waist, dragging her around to the front so she sat propped on his lap, straddling him. Goosebumps riddled her flesh, and he yanked off his coat, draping it around her bare shoulders. He flipped up his visor, then lifted hers as well, only to find a pair of turquoise eyes radiating with wrath, the gold around the center burning with the flame of a thousand suns.

"Don't ever," he sucked in a sharp, rasping breath, "make me do something like that again."

"I didn't make you *do* anything." She crossed her arms, glaring at him. "You could've let someone else throw the stupid daggers."

He rolled his neck in vexation, working out the kinks riddling his nerves like tightly coiled springs of tension. "As if I would."

"Oh right, because goddess forbid I do something fun

175

without you or Veros rushing in to rescue me." She scooted closer, inadvertently dragging her legs up the sides of his thighs. "Well, guess what, Your Radiance? I don't need saving."

"It was dangerous, Everinne!" He planted his hands on her waist, desperately trying not to shake some sense into her. "What if I had missed?"

"But you didn't," she countered.

"Gods," he groaned, tilting his head up to the blanket of night sky. "You're so fucking infuriating."

"And you've been an overprotective dick for days." She jabbed him in the chest with her finger. "What's your damn problem?"

"You!" he bellowed, hating the way she shrank back from him. It was almost impossible to draw breath around her, much less concentrate. "You're my problem, Ever. You've been my problem since the first time I saw you."

Careful, he warned himself.

"You're insolent, spiteful, and annoying as hell." His hands slid higher, the beaded fabric of her bodice rough against his palms. "Half the time you look at me like you want to slit my throat, and I'm quite certain you hate me."

"I do hate you." There was no conviction in her words, just a catch in her voice.

A sliver of awareness.

"But you've got a face that radiates fury, and even when you're scowling and spewing your constant loathing, all I want to do is kiss those fucking lips of yours until you forget how to speak." He stared into her eyes, searching for something he knew he'd never find. "I have wanted you for *years*. A lifetime. But I won't..."

Atlas tipped his head forward, so his helmet touched lightly against hers. "But I won't touch you, because you're off limits to me. I took a vow to Veros that I'd protect you from everyone."

Including himself.

That vow had carved out a piece of his heart.

Because he'd known then, even though he'd refused to admit

it, that he'd given her up. He'd given up his *mate* in a promise to his best friend, and in turn, he'd lost a part of his soul.

And there was nothing he could do about it.

A vow was a vow.

Everinne stared at him, and in her eyes he saw a glimpse of a world just out of his reach. Those pools of turquoise glittered in the glow of moonlight, the golden swirls drew him in, ready to drown him.

She leaned forward, reaching for the waistband of his pants. "Then let me touch you."

Nineteen

Everinne was the queen of bad decisions.

And taking the Prince of Prava's cock in her hand was definitely a bad decision.

After all, she hated him. Because eighteen years ago, he'd brought her to orgasm in a room full of nobles at the palace. To make matters worse, it had been her first one. Oh sure, she'd had sex with plenty of other males before, but none of them had ever delivered to the extent Atlas had. And the bastard hadn't even *touched* her.

That moment replayed in her mind—the way she sank back against the far wall of the parlor, her fingers curling into the draperies until she thought she'd tear them from the window. The way she cried out, gasping, unable to contain the waves of pleasure crashing into her so her toes curled and her knees softened. She'd been left panting, chest heaving, while raucous laughter echoed in her ears. Atlas hadn't even spared her a glance.

She'd been humiliated. Absolutely mortified.

The ridicule followed her around for months on end. She'd been teased relentlessly, called the prince of pleasure's whore. The stain of embarrassment had branded her. Anywhere she went, she was followed by smug, sidelong glances, or overly obnoxious jeers meant to insult her further. Females called her a pathetic harlot, males thought of her as an easy fuck. She spent many lonely days curled up in a chair on her balcony, watching the world pass by without her as Starysa's skies bled from sunrise to sunset.

But for weeks on end, at night when she was alone in her bed, she would replay the sensation of his magic pulsing through her. Over and over.

Gods, she'd never felt more alive.

Atlas had never apologized, and she'd never forgiven him.

Now it was her turn to be in control. She'd drag him over the edge, coax him until he was spent, then walk away and not look back.

Everinne slowly unbuttoned his pants, the bulge beneath the taut fabric thickening beneath her touch. With the final button undone, Atlas's cock sprang free.

More than ever, she wished she had that visor pulled over her eyes, because she knew without a doubt they betrayed her. He was far larger than she imagined, not that she tried to imagine the size of his shaft very often, but nothing could have prepared her for *that*. She half expected him to be pierced, at least according to the rumors she'd heard, but she was actually quite astonished to find him unadorned.

Atlas leaned back on the *volt*, propping his hands up on the seat behind him. "Something wrong, Wildheart?"

Her head snapped up, her blood thrumming beneath the intensity of his gaze. The helmet he wore obscured almost all of his face, only his eyes were visible. Those endless depths of green flecked with gold. They weren't mocking. They weren't even cocky. They were hungry.

"No." She choked the word out on a harsh whisper and reached for him, but he caught her by the wrist.

"Take off your ring."

There was a quiet demand in his tone, and a chill that had nothing to do with the cold breeze sent shivers racing down her spine. She wouldn't mind him telling her to take off other things as well. Her gaze dipped back down to where her hand hovered above his cock.

"The ring, Ever. Take it off." His thumb traced tiny, lazy circles along the inside of her wrist. "The last thing I want is for you to accidentally release the dagger hidden on the underside of that amethyst with my cock in your hands."

She unhooked the strap under her chin and took the helmet off, shaking out her waves of dark hair. Then she set it on the handlebars, the corner of her mouth curving as she bent forward. Meeting his gaze, she smirked. "Who says I'm going to use my hand?"

"Fuck," Atlas groaned as she twirled her tongue around the tip of his cock before taking him into her mouth.

Skies above, why was he so damn big?

Her lips glided over the smooth flesh, teasing and lightly scraping with her teeth as she took him a little deeper. She licked and sucked, sliding her hands beneath the waistband of his pants, her fingers exploring the carved muscle near his hips. Warmth pooled between her thighs, and she rubbed herself against the ridge of the seat, desperate for any kind of friction. She pulled back, tempted to slip her fingers into her own wet heat, when he fisted a hand in her hair, forcing her lower.

"All of it, Wildheart." He bit the words off, sucking in a ragged breath. "Every inch."

Everinne relaxed her jaw, and the head of his cock nudged the back of her throat. She hastily blinked, her eyes watering from the sheer bulk of him, hating and loving every minute of it. Hollowing out her cheeks, she sucked harder, practically drooling down the length of him.

"Everinne." Atlas ground out her name, his hips thrusting up, forcing her to meet his demand for more. He slid one finger between her breasts, snaring the beaded fabric of her bodice. "I want to rip this damn thing off of you."

She yanked her head back, freeing him from the confines of her mouth, and stared up at him. It was the only way for her to ensure he realized her intent. "I know you said you wouldn't touch me. But your magic can."

"It's not a good idea." He shook his head and shadows danced across his eyes. "Last time—"

"Last time is burned into my memory, Atlas." She sank her teeth into her bottom lip. "For *many* reasons."

His hand, still tangled in her hair, slid to the back of her neck, gently caressing. "Then you know I can't."

His voice was too soft. Almost pitying.

Everinne set her jaw, her spine stiffening as she pulled away. "Then I guess you can finish yourself."

"Gods, Ever." Atlas tightened his grip, just enough to send a thrill of pleasure ricocheting through her. "Please, don't stop."

She tilted her head, eyeing him coolly. "Then play fair."

His chest rose and fell with the beating of her heart. "Are you sure?"

Nodding once, she lowered her head, but he pressed two fingers under her chin, tilting her face back up. His eyes searched hers, looking for something she couldn't quite pinpoint. "Say it. I need you to say it."

"Use your magic on me, Atlas." She dug her nails into his hips. "Please."

His head rolled back. "Thank fuck."

The moment she took the full thickness of him back into her mouth, a thousand sensations stole into her, gathering her up in a haze of lust. That delicious scent of his magic, of amber and vanilla, infused her blood until he was all she needed to breathe. Her nipples hardened into painful peaks, scraping against the tight stretch of fabric binding her. She rocked her hips, sucking at him greedily while his power overtook her body. Phantom touches cupped her aching breasts, stroked her thighs, and delved into her throbbing core, applying the perfect amount of pressure to her clit.

A cry escaped her, but her gasp was garbled by Atlas's thickening cock. Each time she pulled him further into her mouth, it expanded in size.

Her eyes rolled back in her head, the tears she'd kept suppressed streaming down her cheeks, as his enlarging shaft speared her mouth.

His magic was a wraith, stealing into her, eliciting pleasure from every fiber of her being. She couldn't think, she couldn't focus. Her whimpers became moans and when his illusionary touch reached the most sensitive part of her core, curling inside of her, she lost control.

Everinne convulsed, tremors overtaking her. She spasmed, gripping his hips to keep from falling, and her name tore from his lips on a sky-shattering growl. They climaxed together in a devastating crush of desire—him whispering her name over and over as she swallowed every last drop of his spend.

Gradually, she eased off of him, and he reached out, wiping his thumb across her mouth. Clearing away any traces of their shared moment of longing. He adjusted himself, buttoned his pants, and save for the faint call of the sea and the howl of the wind, silence stretched between them like a gaping chasm. Atlas reached behind her, gently placed her helmet back on her head, and fastened the strap under her chin.

She told herself it was better this way. There'd been no kissing, no feigned intimacy. Simply a mutual need for release. Nothing more. Nothing less.

"Come on, Wildheart." He scooped her up, tucking her back behind him on the *volt*. "Let's get you back home before sunrise."

Everinne didn't have the heart to tell him she hated going home. Because it meant she would be alone. Like always. And though she tried not to read too much into it, she clung to him a little tighter on the ride back to her apartment, and he kept one hand comfortably on her thigh the whole way.

Twenty

A tlas's sleep was haunted by a pair of sparkling turquoise eyes and cherry red lips. Everinne had taken up permanent residency in his mind, and though he'd never actually seen her naked before, his subconscious imagined each dip and curve. Skin as smooth as satin. Full breasts with nipples that hardened to tiny peaks beneath the flick of his tongue. Long legs that wrapped around him and hips that flared, perfect for gripping while he surged into her. It had been some time since he'd awoken from a wet dream, not since his youth at least, but as soon as his eyes blinked open, all he could see was her mouth sucking on him the same way she'd done with that damn lollipop.

He groaned, rolling over, and slid from his bed.

What he needed was an ice-cold shower, anything to purge the lustful images of her from his mind.

An abrupt knock sounded outside his bedroom door, and before Atlas could tell whoever it was to piss off, Caedian barged into his chambers.

"Do you mind?" Atlas spread his arms wide, fully nude, his dick still partially erect. "I'm a little preoccupied at the moment."

Caedian snorted, shutting the door soundly behind him to avoid the wandering eyes of any passing maids. He leaned against the wardrobe, his gray eyes alight with mockery. "Nothing I haven't seen before, Your Imperial Highness. Besides, this can't wait."

Atlas grabbed one of the velvet throws from his bed and wrapped it snugly around his waist. A sinking feeling seized Atlas's gut. If Caedian couldn't spare him a few minutes of peace, then whatever news he was about to share was likely grim.

He inclined his head. "Report, then."

Instantly, Caedian shoved off the wardrobe, straightening. He widened his stance, tucking his hands behind his back. "There's been another disappearance, Your Highness. A young witchling by the name of Kestra Sephiran, from the Coven of the Scarlet Moon. She was last seen leaving Belladonna's Atelier in the shopping district of the city, and no one from the coven has heard from her since."

Shit.

Atlas shoved his hair back from his face. First it was fae. Then a vampire. Now a witch. If they weren't careful, Starysa would collapse into a state of unrest. Rebellions would rise, a siege would befall the palace, and war would come from within Prava's own borders. It was a risk they couldn't afford to take, and if Atlas had to guess, his father had already refused to offer any kind of assistance in the matter.

He pressed his thumb and middle finger to his temples, trying to ease the pounding ache forming there. "What of the witch's magic?"

Caedian tugged on the collar of his uniform, the stiff midnight fabric making him look uncomfortable in his own skin. "She's a siphon. She can drain magic from others and use their power for herself. Temporarily, of course, but it's still unusual. And it falls in line with Veros's theory."

"That's what I was afraid you'd say." Atlas roughed a hand over his face, considering. "We'll have to handle this without my father's knowledge. If he wants to continue to be an arrogant ass who doesn't realize the severity of the situation, then he can be the one who suffers when all hell breaks loose. But I refuse to stand by and do nothing. I won't let my kingdom fall under his disgraceful watch."

Caedian rolled his shoulders back and dipped his head in acknowledgement. "Orders, Your Imperial Highness."

"Arrange a meeting with Eldress Valaina of the Morvayne and High Priestess Rozalie of the Coven of the Scarlet Moon tonight. I want the day and location agreed upon by both of them, and as far away from the listening walls of the palace as possible." He paced the hardwood floors of his bedroom, knowing they would have to end this madness before they had an uprising on their hands. He didn't even want to think about the bloodbath that would ensue if fae, vampires, and witches fought against one another. Or worse, if they banded together and started slaughtering the mortals. "Have your soldiers stay vigilant. I'm not saying start an interrogation, but we need answers. Have them listen for any clues, I want them in the parlors, by the docks, in the shopping district. Anywhere and everywhere that might give us an indication of who or what is behind the disappearances."

Caedian bowed and a wrinkle of concern marred his brow. "Is there any chance...do you suppose the mortals could be the cause?"

Atlas gave a short, barking laugh. "Never."

Not that he didn't think them incapable, but they simply weren't strong enough. It would take a kind of poison, perhaps even something stronger, for a group of mortals to incapacitate an immortal. Not only that, but as far as he knew, they had no motive. However, that didn't mean they didn't know anything about the situation.

"On second thought," he muttered, "make inquiries with the mortals as well. I don't want to discount anything they might have heard."

"Yes, Your Imperial Highness." Caedian turned to go, then paused, a wry smile on his face. "Rumors through the guard claim you went to the overlook last night. And before you say it, where you go is always my business."

Atlas scoffed, refusing to feed into his captain's trap. "I need a shower."

"Heard you had a pretty female with you," Caedian continued, inspecting the cuffs of his uniform. He straightened the gold bands at his wrists. "I thought she was off limits?"

"She is," Atlas growled and pointed to the door. "Now, get out."

Caedian chuckled and ducked his head, strolling out of the room. "Don't forget, you're hosting a ball tomorrow night."

Right. The ball. Where that damn lord of stars would attempt to win Everinne's heart. And worse, Veros was going to allow it.

Teeming jealousy flooded his veins, filling him with a sense of incomprehensible dread. He would be forced to find a suitable wife from among Starysa's nobles, all the while watching as some other male pursued his mate. Anguish cut through him, like a dagger carving out his heart. Yet there was nothing to be done. He'd sworn an oath to Veros seventeen years ago, after Everinne killed the man she *thought* she loved, vowing then to help protect her after Callum's death sent her into a spiral of self-destruction. But there'd been a caveat. Veros had also insisted that Atlas keep his hands to himself. He didn't want his younger sister falling for the prince of pleasure, didn't want her yielding to his charms, or getting tangled up with someone who lusted after a new female every night.

Granted, Veros had never actually spoken those spiteful words, but his intent was implied.

Imperial prince or not, Atlas wasn't a good enough match for Everinne.

Frustrated with his current circumstances and pissed off with his former self, Atlas tossed aside the throw around his waist and yanked on a pair of pants.

He could shower later.

Right now, he needed to hit something.

* * *

Sweat slid down Atlas's spine and rolled down his forearms, freezing to his skin. The sun was hidden behind a wall of ominous gray, and the clouds were spitting out tiny daggers of ice. Despite the frosty temperature, he'd discarded his grossly damp shirt.

Unfortunately, it meant there was one less barrier between the sting of Caedian's blade and his flesh whenever he failed to dodge an advance.

The cut across his left shoulder burned as the fae magic of his blood slowly healed the wound, but it didn't make the injury any less of a disgrace. He was the prince, he'd been trained to handle a sword since he could walk, and already his Captain of the Guard had struck him twice. Both times Atlas had left himself open to attack.

"You seem a little agitated today," Caedian called out, his sword slashing through the air.

Atlas narrowly avoided the blow, the clang of their weapons reverberating down his arms. "I'm fine."

Caedian paced in a slow circle and Atlas matched him, his weapon raised. He moved with ease, an elite warrior well-versed in the art of stealth and sarcasm. "Maybe you need to get laid."

Atlas's gaze narrowed, his grip on the hilt of the sword tightening until his knuckles turned white. "Maybe you need to take a long walk off a short cliff."

His captain laughed, full and robust. "Is that the best you've got?"

This time Atlas lunged, determined to wipe that mocking smirk off his captain's face. Caedian side-stepped him, anticipating his next move. They clashed in a torrent of metal and strength, the force of one another's assault driving the other backward, the deafening clang of their blades cracking throughout the field like thunder.

Atlas blinked, sweat stinging his eyes, but he refused to falter. His muscles were on fire, burning from exertion. He ducked low and spun, twisting, and Caedian clicked his tongue in disappointment.

"Your footwork is sloppy. Your wrist is weak." Their swords met overhead and Caedian shoved him away. "And your form is slacking."

Atlas swung again, his blade slicing through the air. A clear miss.

Caedian's words hung between them, thick like the humidity of summer's hottest day. He tried to ignore them, then his father's demeaning voice scraped against his mind.

Quit now. Before you embarrass yourself further.

Atlas roared, launching his sword in a fury of loathing across the training field.

Magic slammed into Atlas, dragging the air from his lungs. Colors faded into muted blurs. Across from him, Caedian's eyes went wide, frozen in shock. Gilded threads unraveled around him, each one scored with runes and numerals. Showers of silver light rained down as he stood completely still, unable to move his body, his heart thudding loudly. The sound of it a low, dull thump like that of an archaic timepiece. The scent of worn leather, fresh earth, and ink upon aged parchment overwhelmed him, and his gaze tracked to the far side of the training field where Veros's arm was outstretched, controlling the hands of time.

He stepped forward, plucking the suspended sword out of the air—the very one whose blade had been aiming for Everinne's heart.

Atlas's stomach dropped.

He didn't know she was watching, he didn't realize she'd been standing there at all. He'd been so consumed with bitterness and resentment...he never would've thrown the damn thing if he thought she would be in harm's way. Veros had been his closest friend for 132 years, and this was the first time Atlas had ever witnessed him use his magic to save a life.

Veros inspected the sword, his gaze turning frosty when his eyes landed on Atlas. "Lose something?"

The stillness distorted his voice, making it sound as though he was everywhere at once.

In the next breath, the Lord of Time rescinded his magic, and Atlas stumbled forward, Caedian following suit.

"Shit." Atlas rushed toward them, wiping the sweat away from his brow with the back of his hand. "Everinne, are you alright?"

He skimmed her briefly, checking for any sign of injury. But even that was a mistake. She wore tight dark purple leather pants and glossy black boots laced up to her knees. Her silver sweater draped off both of her shoulders, the fibers somehow twinkling like crushed diamonds. She'd worn her hair up, twisted into a messy bun on the top of her head, and tiny pieces had fallen loose to frame her face. Her cheeks were flushed from the wind and her lips were painted a delectable color that reminded him of ripe berries.

"I'm sorry." He tore his gaze away from her and accepted the sword Veros held out to him. "Apologies, Veros."

The Lord of Time shifted his shoulders, tucking his hands behind his back. Always calm. Always collected. "You rarely let your temper get the best of you."

"It was my fault," Caedian piped up, taking the sword away and placing it back on the rack with the rest of the weapons. "I was goading him."

"It wasn't you." Atlas shook his head, shoving some longer waves of hair back from his face. He roughed a hand along his jaw, annoyed by his own lack of composure. "I was distracted."

Veros checked his golden timepiece, where magic still seemed to thrum and whir around its circular shape, then slipped it back into his pocket. "It's understandable. You've had a lot on your mind these past few days."

Atlas dared a look at Everinne, who boldly met his gaze without hesitation. "So, Ever...what are you doing here? It's not like you to grace us with your presence twice in one week."

Her brows narrowed slightly, and she crossed her arms,

cocking one hip to the side. The gold rings around her pupils flared with irritation. "Veros is taking me to find a dress. For your ball."

If she was attempting to provoke him, it was working.

"Right," he drawled, barricading his mind. The last thing he wanted to know was the truth of her thoughts, especially where he was concerned. Instead, he grinned at Veros. "Going shopping, then?"

The corner of Veros's mouth lifted into a smile, and he flicked his wrists, loosening the cuffs of his gray sweater. "So it would seem."

"It was *your* idea," Everinne countered, poking him roughly in the chest with her finger. "You're the one who said I needed something suitable to impress..."

Her voice trailed off and she bit her bottom lip, taking up a sudden interest in the cropped hem of her top, where a swatch of lightly tan skin was on display.

So. Veros was taking his sister shopping for a gown to help her catch Lord Tovian's eye. Not that she needed any help in the matter, but the idea of *his* mate being matched with anyone else fueled him with insurmountable fury.

Atlas ground his teeth together. The muscles along his shoulders and the back of his neck grew taut, tense with feral rage. He popped his jaw, desperately trying to hold himself back from reaching out and strangling Veros.

"We're going before my shift at the Mystic Obscura. And yes," she continued, waving a hand dismissively through the air so all the bracelets she wore jingled in unison, "I'm looking for another job. I might try to get a position at Belladonna's Atelier."

Atlas made a derisive sort of noise. A witch's bauble shop was better than the Mystic Obscura, though if he had things his way, Everinne wouldn't need to be looking for another job at all. She'd be living in his palace. Lounging in his arms. Sleeping in his bed.

"Come on, Ever." Veros guided her away from the training

field, nodding to Atlas on his way. "Let's go before the shops close for the night."

As they walked down one of the corridors, Atlas simply stood there, half hoping, half wishing, Everinne would turn around once. All he wanted was for her to cast a casual glance over her shoulder, maybe even flash one of those damning smirks. He told himself it would be enough.

But she didn't look back, and he didn't look away.

Deflated, he let out a shallow, painful breath.

Caedian strolled up next to him, dusting the dirt from his pants. He planted his hands on his hips, tracking Atlas's line of sight. Then he loosed a low whistle. "You're really going to stand by and let her marry some lord from another realm?"

Atlas sighed. Veros may as well have stuck a dagger in his back when he'd made that fucking vow. "I don't have a choice."

Twenty-One

Everinne changed out of her costume after her performance and pulled on a pair of black leggings that slung low across her hips and a snug, cropped red top with sheer sleeves. She'd just finished lacing up her boots when Reine breezed into the dressing room, a demure smile on her face.

"Another standing ovation tonight, Everinne." Reine folded her arms across her chest, her amber eyes sparking with appreciation. Her pin-straight, sleek brown hair was pushed back from her face with a band of jeweled fabric, showcasing her rich umber cheekbones that were dusted with gold. "The crowd seems quite pleased with you."

"Thank you." Everinne grabbed her coat from off the rack of clothing. "There's definitely something freeing about dancing on the hoops. I really love it."

"How wonderful of you to say so." Reine moved forward, her silken skirts swishing around her like a river of magenta. She slid a bronze dagger from her pocket, it was skinny enough to be a letter opener, but sharp enough to pierce flesh.

Everinne lurched backward, and Reine laughed, full and sensual.

"There's nothing to fear, *milazk.*" She flicked the small blade between her fingers. "I only need to collect a simple drop of blood."

"Blood," Everinne repeated, yanking on her coat, her gaze focused on the tip of the dagger. She clenched her hands into tight fists. Her mind reeled, snippets of her earlier conversation with Atlas flooded her thoughts, his warning prickling along the back of her neck. "What for?"

Blood magic was archaic, fabled for being dangerous, and those who used it, whether for good or ill will, were not to be trusted.

"It'll be imbued into the runes carved into the entrance of the Mystic Obscura." Reine spoke with such nonchalance, as though she was well-accustomed to asking those in her employ for their blood. "Once it's imbued, you'll be able to come and go as you please."

Everinne lifted her chin, refusing to believe such utter nonsense. "I can already enter any time I wish."

Reine tilted her head and arched a single brow. Her face remained impassive, her eyes empty and lacking their usual subdued warmth. "Can you though?"

"Yes, I—" Everinne fell silent, her argument leaving her tongue papery and dry.

No. Reine was right, not once had she entered the Mystic Obscura of her own accord. The first time, Jarek had been the one to open the door. Then Atlas. And tonight, Everinne had arrived early enough after shopping with Veros that she'd caught another performer walking in just ahead of her. The brown-eyed female had held open the door for her.

"It's common practice, you see, for all our performers and staff. An added measure of safety. Of precaution, if you will. We can't have just *anyone* walking into the menagerie." Reine studied her for a moment, then sighed, an air of disappointment surrounding her. "Of course, you can always say no."

Everinne opened her mouth to speak but Reine smoothly interrupted her. "But if that's the case, you shouldn't expect to return. I'll gladly pay you your wages and let you be on your way."

Uncertainty warred within her. She'd already promised Atlas and Veros she'd start looking for employment elsewhere, which she did plan to do...eventually. But she *loved* dancing in the air, she loved the way the music seemed to hum through her veins. She lived for the roaring applause, the hushed gasps, and the startling cries of shock whenever she performed some gravity-defying feat. For those few sacred moments, the world was hers alone.

It was only a drop of blood.

Harmless, really.

Besides, Atlas had done it as well. Not to mention the hundreds of other patrons currently milling about the menagerie upstairs.

Everinne hesitated, chewing on her bottom lip as tiny beads of sweat gathered in her palms. "Just a drop?"

Reine's crimson lips curved into a comforting smile. "A mere prick of the finger and nothing more."

Swallowing the knot of trepidation lodged in the back of her throat, Everinne held out her hand.

Reine was gentle, carefully holding Everinne's hand steady while the sharp point pierced her skin. Everinne winced against the sting. A tiny drop of crimson welled on the tip of her finger and Reine removed the dagger, angling it to collect the drop on the flat edge of the blade.

"There," she crooned, blowing lightly on the wound to ease some of the pain. "All done."

The small cut was already closing as the fae magic coursed through her, healing her quickly so there was only a tiny white scar left behind.

Everinne shoved her hands into the pockets of her coat, balling them into tight fists.

Reine glided toward the door of the dressing room, then paused, glancing back over her shoulder. "I'll see you tomorrow, yes?"

"Actually, I'm supposed to go to the ball tomorrow night." Everinne ducked her head, hoping it wasn't too late to ask for the night off. "I forgot to mention it to you earlier."

"Ah, yes. The ball where Prince Atlas will choose his bride." She shook her head, a tiny line crinkling across her smooth brow. "I couldn't imagine being forced to wed someone against my will, could you?"

Everinne shifted her weight. She'd been trying not to think about Atlas marrying anyone at all. Just like she'd been trying to shove every memory of him to the furthest corner of her mind, yet each time she blinked, she relived the images from last night over and over. More specifically, the way he looked with that damn helmet on, his eyes glazed with lust, and one hand gripping the back of her neck while he all but begged her to keep sucking his dick.

Heat flared across her cheeks as the blush crept up her neck.

Everinne cleared her throat and pressed her lips together. "No, I suppose I couldn't imagine that either. But how do you know he's being forced?"

She knew Atlas had to take a wife, he'd told her as much. But she highly doubted that little slice of information was common knowledge.

Reine's airy laughter filled the space once more. "Oh, *milazk*. Everyone knows His Imperial Highness would never get married unless his hand was being forced. He's the prince of pleasure. Even if he does find a wife tomorrow night, his loyalty to her will not hold fast. His eyes will wander, and he'll continue to slink from the beds of willing females."

She lifted one shoulder, her lips pursing. "After all, it's in his blood."

Reine sauntered out of the dressing room and as Everinne left the Mystic Obscura, Reine's words continued to follow her.

It's in his blood.

It seemed like such a careless and cruel thing to say, yet words always held a deeper meaning. A more complex context. Reine had collected a drop of Atlas's blood, and while she claimed it was strictly for the runes lining the entrance of the Mystic Obscura, that didn't mean she hadn't used it in some other manner. Atlas was the Prince of Prava, and a drop of his blood could be manipulated for spells and charms, or worse, exploitation. She'd heard rumors about the Marzena from Zoryana, a black market of sorts that once thrived in a network of long forgotten tunnels and passages beneath the Starysa's streets. Everinne imagined Atlas's blood would fetch a high price if such a market still existed.

Shivering, Everinne tugged her coat around her, bundling herself into the fur-lined leather. The walk home wasn't far, but with the frigid wind barreling into her, each step was a fight. Like walking through a strand of wet sand along the shore. She looked up at the night sky, disappointed to find the moon wasn't visible. Instead there was just a thick layer of silvery clouds. Tucking her chin to her chest, she gritted her teeth against the harsh slap of wind, until the noisy click of her boots against cobblestone was the only sound keeping her company.

A chill that had nothing to do with the cold slid its icy fingers down her spine.

She stilled, glancing around her.

Eerie swatches of darkness seemed to stare back at her. It was oddly quiet. There was no thump of music, no warped conversations flowing out of open doors and cracked windows, enticing people inside. Even the lanterns lining the cobblestone streets appeared to waver and fade, as though they would be snuffed out at any moment.

Wrong.

The word whispered to the forefront of her mind.

This was all wrong.

She hastened her pace, and even though there was no sound of footfalls echoing behind her, she couldn't erase the feeling of being followed. Of being tracked. Of being *hunted*.

That tiny voice inside of her pitched with panic.

Run!

Everinne ran. Her legs pumped as she bolted around the next corner, hoping to find someone, anyone, who might be willing to help her. But it was as though the whole of Starysa had been deserted. The penetrating darkness gained on her, closing the distance between them until she could feel the cold kiss of death along the back of her neck. Terror soared inside of her, awakening the callous magic that slithered through her veins as the threads of her control unraveled.

She opened her mouth to scream and was snatched by the hands of violence.

Her head slammed against a wall of hard stone, snapping back with such force, dizzying stars danced in front of her eyes and her vision blurred. Pain speared from the base of her neck, all the way down her spine. Gruff, muffled voices bounced off the dark alley, but she couldn't focus on the indistinct shapes of her attackers. Her arms were pinned over her head, and a knee had been shoved between her thighs, forcing them apart. Someone yanked her hair and she yelped, tears springing at the corner of her eyes, but she blinked, refusing to let them fall.

A face swam before her, the eyes too difficult to see in the thick shadows surrounding them, but a fracture of light high-lighted the scrape of scruff lining his jaw and the scar above his mouth. She struggled against his hold, but he only leaned in closer, pressing his full weight against her until the stone bit into her back and she thought her lungs would collapse.

He grabbed her cheeks, pinching, jerking her face up to him. "Well, well. If it isn't the fae who likes to drink and fuck. Looks like you've found yourself in a bit of a bind."

"Let me go." Everinne's voice was a harsh whisper, grating like nails scouring coarse brick. Her magic seethed, black and violet shadowy tendrils crawled from her fingertips like phantom hands of death.

"Or what?" he taunted, his mouth twisting into a crooked sneer.

Mocking laughter filled her ears, heightening the pulse of her anger.

"Or I'll kill you," she snapped, baring her teeth.

He chuckled mirthlessly. "I'd like to see it."

Then his mouth slashed across hers and he forced his slimy tongue between her lips. That same sardonic laughter raked through Everinne's mind, and she bit down, sinking her slightly sharp canines into his tongue, until the metallic tang of his blood filled her mouth.

The man screamed, ripping away from her. He threw her aside, scarlet pouring down his chin and neck. She stumbled forward and spat, then whipped around to face her attackers. Five figures loomed before her, large, beastly men, dressed in hooded cloaks. They thought they could take what they wanted from her, they thought they could berate her, *violate* her...and think they would live to tell the tale. But they were sadly mistaken. There would be no mercy tonight. Only death.

"Fucking bitch!" he roared, stalking toward her like predator to prey. "I'll slit your throat for that."

Everinne wiped the back of her hand across her mouth, and the power of torment inside her smiled. "You can try."

Dark magic lashed out like a feral, caged beast, tearing through the fraying tethers of Everinne's control. It consumed her being, sweeping through her like a storm of violence and chaos. Shadows of midnight and deep violet consumed the alley, devouring the space, slithering around two of the hooded men whose eyes had gone wide with panic. Even in the sickly, dim light, she could see the ghastly pallor of their terrified faces. Snarling, her magic speared each of them, splintering their bones, crushing their lungs. Blood moved like sludge through their veins, their garbled screams muffled by the pulse of power squeezing around their hearts.

Everinne could taste their pain, sweet and thick like honey.

She stretched one arm out, palm up, then slowly closed each of her fingers. Her shadows mimicked the motion, the sinewy phantoms sinking like claws into the frenzied minds of the two men. Apathetic and jaded, she watched their bodies contort and writhe as the agony she inflicted only increased.

She clenched her fist.

They crumpled to the ground, lifeless.

Three.

Three lives she'd taken so far. Callum, and these two males. And tonight, she would steal three more. But there was no regret. No remorse. She was numb on the inside, a vast well of emptiness. Perhaps in the morning she would feel guilt for her actions, or perhaps she would simply feel nothing at all. It made no difference to her. For now, survival was all that mattered, and if the only way to do so was through a lack of mercy and violence, then so be it.

Power hummed, lifting the hair from her shoulders, preparing to strike again, when a rough cloth was clamped over Everinne's nose and mouth.

She choked and gagged as the stench of damp woods and herbs flooded her senses. Alarm fired through her. Arms flailing, she struggled to fight, to escape, but her movements were sluggish and heavy. Her lungs burned for air as though she'd been shoved underwater.

Without warning, the world tilted, Everinne's body swayed, and everything went dark.

* * *

Flickering lights danced behind Everinne's eyelids, wavering in and out of focus to the pounding ache throbbing at her temples. She felt as though she'd been bashed upside the head with the hilt of a sword, the pain sending a wave of nausea roiling through her. Groaning, she clutched her stomach, sucking in a breath of air that smelled oddly yet sickeningly familiar. Sulfur and smoke. It triggered something in the back of her mind, almost like a warning, but her mind was swimming in a haze of delirium, and she couldn't tell if she was awake or still falling into oblivion.

HILLARY RAYMER

"Everinne." A subdued, masculine voice prodded at her.

Her head lolled to the side as she tried to peel her eyes open. She blinked in a desperate attempt to focus, but her vision was barely more than a smear of watercolors.

She knew she was seated on a sofa, or perhaps a chair. She couldn't be sure, but there was a soft cushion cradling her weakened body. The lights burned a little brighter and she squinted, gritting her teeth against the assault on her senses. A figure loomed over her, then crouched down, and Kralv Oldrich's face came into view.

Everinne startled, swallowing a yelp. She slid from the chair, her muscles spasming, as she fought to stop herself from tumbling toward the floor in front of the kralv.

He snared her by the shoulders, dragging her back upward, and repositioned her in the seat. "Easy, Everinne. The effect of wolfsbane takes some time to wear off. It will be a few hours yet before you regain full control of your body."

Hours?

How long had she been out?

Her bleary gaze slid around the room, gradually taking in her surroundings. The walls were all dark, papered with black satin scrollwork and gilded shelves housing a sparse, untouched collection of dust-laden books. A large desk was behind the kralv, its glossy surface free from any kind of clutter, as though it was rarely used. Sconces shaped like wolf heads with gaping jaws lined the walls, golden fire illuminating the eyes, giving the impression of ferocious beasts. There was only one window in the expanse of the room, and the thick, black draperies were pulled closed, revealing only a sliver of the outside.

From what Everinne could gather, which wasn't much, dawn was approaching.

The kralv stood, edging backward so he leaned the bulk of his weight upon the desk. He crossed his arms and angled his head, his dark brown hair with slashes of gray covering half of his face. "You're in quite a bit of trouble, Everinne."

"Trouble?" She swallowed around the word, her throat dry and scratchy like she'd slept with her mouth open.

Kralv Oldrich ran a thumb along his beard, his dark eyes narrowing slightly beneath two bushy brows. "Do you remember what happened?"

"Yes," she croaked. "I..."

Everinne's voice trailed off, the memory of only a few hours ago just out of her reach. She could vaguely remember her conversation with Reine, the prick of a dagger, and then...nothing. It was a bleak void of emptiness, and no matter how hard she grasped at the time that had been stolen from her, she couldn't recall anything after leaving the Mystic Obscura. The pressure in her head only amplified.

"Would you like me to remind you?" the kralv asked, arching a brow.

She winced. "Yes, Your Imperial Majesty."

"My guards were on patrol when they discovered you curled up in a ball in a dank alleyway, a few blocks away from the Mystic Obscura." He heaved his large frame off the desk, tucking his meaty hands behind his back. "They offered you assistance, an escort to return you safely back home, which you refused."

"But I—" She snapped her mouth shut when his gaze cut to her with cruel authority.

He inhaled deeply, his chest puffing out. "You then attacked them. Killing two."

"What?" Everinne shrieked. She slumped further into the chair, attempting to dig her heels into the black fur carpet to keep from sliding. But her legs simply would not work. "No. I would never."

Except she had, because on her right forearm, the vine tattoo had lengthened, and two more blood roses had appeared.

"Do try to be still, you're only making things worse." The kralv sighed with an air of disappointment, his expression almost pitying. "You're lucky they only chose to subdue you as opposed to using force, which would have been thoroughly warranted, I might add."

She rolled her head from side to side in a pathetic attempt to dispute the accusation. "Your Majesty, please. That can't be right...I wouldn't...couldn't. I have no such power."

"I have seen the bodies, Everinne. Or at least, what is left of them." He paced around the study, and she tracked him with her eyes until he disappeared from view, walking behind her. When he spoke again, his hard voice scraped past her cheek. "Do you know what the punishment is for killing a kralv's guard?"

She bit her bottom lip to keep it from quivering. "Lashings?"

He made a *tsk*ing noise and stalked back around to the desk, leaning one hip against it. Rolling the cuffs of his black shirt, he shook his head once. "If only it was that simple."

Everinne's breathing hollowed out. If it wasn't lashings, it must be something far worse.

"Under normal circumstances, there are usually two types of punishments, depending on the severity of the crime." Kralv Oldrich cracked his knuckles, the corners of his mouth lifting into a placating smile. "A permanent trip to Rizenrok Forge. Or death."

Dread slammed into her, and a tiny bead of sweat slid down her back.

"Now," he continued, his eyes roving over her, "you will have to be an exception to the rule. It would look rather shameful if the Lord of Time's sister was put to death or sent off to the mines, which is why I'm willing to offer you a deal. You've been keeping your magic a secret for a *very* long time, Everinne. It was wise of Veros to keep you hidden away. But someone of such power could prove to be quite useful to their kingdom."

Her heart squeezed in her chest, her lungs were too tight. "I don't understand."

"In exchange for my forgiveness and sparing your life, you will marry my son." He pushed off the desk once more, closing the distance between them. Snaring her chin, he lifted her face. "And once you are engaged, you will utilize your magic at my every request."

She tried to pull away, to escape his firm grasp, but the kralv only tightened his hold.

"You don't understand," she pleaded, tears springing to her eyes. "It's too dangerous, I can't control—"

"Oh, don't worry about that," he crooned, his sinister laugh ringing in her ears. "I control you now. Do as your kralv commands, or else."

Kralv Oldrich's magic exploded in a fit of tempered wrath. Its acrid stench of sulfur and smoke consumed her, stealing into her mind as he tore through her, bringing her worst fears to life. Visions swarmed her, awful images that left her trembling in terror with tears streaming down her cheeks—Veros being beaten and forced into submission, Atlas slogging through the mountains of the mine camp, battered and bleeding, and then Everinne, naked on her hands and knees, as a faceless man drove into her from behind while vicious laughter drowned out her screams.

A choking sob escaped her.

"That's right." The kralv's cold voice pierced the horrors breaking her. "If you refuse to accept my offer, you will become a pet to the kralv's guard. A toy for them to use and discard as they see fit. A proper repayment for the lives you so carelessly took."

Everinne squeezed her eyes shut, convulsing against the onslaught, but the fears the kralv enforced upon her did not ease.

"Do we have a deal?" he asked.

"Yes," Everinne rasped, opening her eyes to find the kralv staring down at her.

"Good. The ball is tonight. Make sure you dress the part." He slowly loosened the cuffs of his sleeves, his lips pressed into a firm line, and his magic finally ebbed. "One word, one breath about this arrangement to *anyone* and I will ensure the severity of every last one of your fears."

Then he snapped his fingers and Everinne was being hauled out of the chair, her limp body dragged from the study.

"Take her to one of the guest rooms and be discreet," Kralv Oldrich ordered. "Then send a maid to bathe her. She reeks of the street."

The guards removing her from the study muttered their assent, their voices echoing quietly from somewhere above her.

"Death-touched," one of them snarled.

"Can already imagine what they'll call her." The other chuckled as they lugged her out into the darkened hall. "The princess of pain."

But Everinne didn't hear them.

The only sound she could focus on was the shattering of her soul.

Twenty-Two

Atlas loosened the collar of his shirt, undoing the top two buttons. Beads of sweat slid down his spine, clinging to the fine fabric of his shirt, dampening it. The ballroom was stifling. The heat from the throng of dancing bodies had forced the palace staff to throw open the windows and doors, allowing the brisk night air to circulate through the crushing room. No one else seemed to notice the excessive heat, they were too busy grinding against one another to the blaring music pulsating through the space. The obsidian dance floor was packed with fae, vampires, witches, humans, and the like, all moving to the discordant beat of pumping music that set Atlas's teeth on edge.

Rolling the cuffs of his sleeves, he propped his forearms on the gilded balcony overlooking the ballroom.

It reminded him of the Grand Cru—red and blue lights swirled overhead, the beams crashing into one another, drowning the space in mesmerizing hues of purple. A band was positioned in the corner upon a structured stage where lights slanted across them, illuminating the vibrant paint smeared across their bodies and instruments. With every new song, paint rained down on them from above, and they played through the colorful mess, their smiles electric as slashes of pigment stained the air like a rainbow waterfall. There were cocktails filled with shimmery blue liquid topped with red cherries and pitchers overflowing with frothy ale. The females were covered in swirls of iridescent glitter, the males all coated in a light sheen of sweat.

His mother would be so disappointed.

Fucking skies, he was disappointed.

This was it.

This was where he was supposed to find a wife, and not just the beginnings of a sham courtship. He was expected to propose.

Atlas roughed a hand over his face, groaning at his prospects. Perhaps he should've made more of an effort when it came to throwing this damn ball. Then at least he could've ensured it wasn't like a loud, raging parlor in Starysa but an actual event where he could hear those around him talking. But no, he'd tossed that responsibility aside and was now forced to suffer through finding a bride in an atmosphere reminiscent of his current reputation.

Loud.

Chaotic.

Overly sexual.

Resigned to the fate his father chose for him, Atlas attempted to slacken his jaw, but it was locked tight. Most of the females in attendance who were available were pretty, beautiful even, but none of them were Ever. Their smiles all looked the same—practiced and feigned. All of them were well aware of his magic, they'd heard the rumors, likely fell victim to their own fantasies, and the gleam in their eyes made his skin crawl with unease. Atlas wanted to be more than someone's bragging rights. He didn't want to be seen as a trophy or prize, he didn't want to fucking *settle*. But his options were to be tossed into a sea of flesh-eating females and be eaten alive, or be sent to Rizenrok Forge, where the only one waiting to greet him would be death.

Atlas pinched the bridge of his nose with his thumb and forefinger, rubbing away the ache that had started to form. He shoved off the railing and turned around, only to find Caedian standing in the doorway with his arms crossed, effectively blocking the path to the staircase that would lead to the ballroom below.

His Captain of the Guard stood there, one ankle cocked over the other, a fierce line of disapproval set between his brows. In the wild flash of lights, Caedian's white hair reflected an array of colors, but his gray eyes darkened to slate in the play of shadows bouncing between them.

Shackled to his own misery, Atlas nodded toward the door. "Let's get this over with."

Caedian didn't budge. "You're making a mistake."

No shit.

Of that, Atlas was well aware. He flung his arms out to the side, letting his shoulders rise and fall. "What would you have me do?"

Caedian rolled his wrist, flipping his hand palm up in a mock gesture of contemplation. "You could start by telling her the truth."

"I already did," Atlas snapped, clenching his teeth so the ache in the center of his forehead spread to his temples and down to the back of his neck.

"Oh, really?" Caedian countered, one stark white brow arching. "When?"

"The overlook." Atlas shifted on his feet, anxiety gnawing at him, and his palms dampened. "I told her she was annoying and that I've wanted her since the first day I laid eyes on her."

"Wow," Caedian drawled, inspecting the hilt of the sword fastened to his waist. "That's quite the profession of love."

Atlas bit back a snarl. "Everinne is hardly the type to swoon over pretty words and bouquets of flowers."

"I don't know." Caedian's gaze flicked to him. "She fell hard enough when that lord of stars was kissing her wrist and showering her with compliments."

Damn it.

Lord Tovian had practically swept her off her feet. She'd

blushed and fluttered her lashes, enjoying every minute of his attention, and what had Atlas done in return? First, he'd scorned her for her behavior out of pure jealousy, then used his magic on her when she sucked his cock. Hardly chivalrous and not at all worthy of winning her heart. Even now, just imagining those lips of hers on his shaft sent a thrum of desire coursing through him. His blood heated, and he raked both of his hands through his disheveled hair, hating himself for giving in to her so quickly.

But it was more than just physical attraction on his behalf, it was a bone-deep longing, the kind that made him never want to be separated from her. All those days, all those years he'd spent avoiding her, had been nothing short of torture.

And that fucking mating bond...the one that sizzled and frayed whenever she was near, waiting to snap into place, wound itself into a knot inside of his chest, threatening to cleave his heart in half.

Atlas stalked toward the doorway, but Caedian held up one hand, halting him.

"I know you, Atlas. I've known you longer than you've known yourself. I've seen the way you look at her, taken note of that jealous streak that morphs into cold-blooded possession. I've seen such a shift before, almost intangible to the naked eye, yet clear if you recognize the signs." Caedian tilted his head, his gaze narrowing. "It's more than love, isn't it? She's your mate."

Atlas could only stare at him.

His mind emptied of all rational thought because someone else knew, someone else *realized* what was happening to him.

Thank fuck it was Caedian and not Veros.

"Choose her." Caedian's voice was quiet, yet the words rang in Atlas's head, echoing like warning bells.

"What?"

"Choose Everinne to be your wife."

He shook his head. "I can't, Veros will kill me."

Caedian smirked, unsheathing half of his sword so the blinding lights of the ballroom slashed across the blade in an array of colors. "He can try. Veros might be the Lord of Time, but you're the Prince of Prava, and I know where the line is drawn between friendship and duty."

Atlas tucked his hands behind his back and paced the small balcony, the click of his boots silent over the roar of music and voices reverberating through the ballroom. He ran his teeth along his bottom lip, a spear of apprehension piercing his gut. If he did this, if he chose Everinne, then there was a very real chance he would lose his best friend. Veros had made it perfectly clear he wanted Atlas to keep his hands to himself, to neither toy with her affections nor her heart. But Veros didn't know his sister occupied Atlas's every waking thought, that she haunted his dreams, that when Everinne was around, Atlas couldn't even fucking breathe.

She'd stolen his air. His heart. His soul.

And there wasn't a damn thing he could do about it.

Except...marry her.

Another thought rushed to the forefront of his mind, and in one second, his blood turned to ice. He stilled, glancing over at Caedian, who was still lounging against the door.

"Caed..." Atlas blew out a harsh breath. "She could refuse me."

He shrugged, as if such a thing was impossible. "Then you kiss her. She'll know with absolute certainty then."

Atlas dropped his head back, rolling it from side to side until his neck cracked. A kiss would be damning. Everinne would feel it, she would be able to sense the bond, she would know the moment it snapped into place. But that didn't mean she had to accept it. What if she didn't want him? She could deny him, deny their bond, and the suffering would be inescapable. For the rest of his days, whether it be centuries or an eternity, he would be tied to her.

Her heartbeat would pulse through his veins.

Anytime she drew breath, his lungs would fill.

He would share her dreams, her thoughts, her emotions. All of it. All of her. Forever.

And for him, there would never be another.

Caedian shoved off the door frame, adjusting slightly to allow Atlas the opportunity to pass.

"Listen, if you don't do this, if you choose someone else because you think you're unworthy of her, and because you're worried it might ruin your friendship with Veros, the regret will eat away at you like a disease." He paused, then added, "I'd rather die than be separated from my mate for an eternity."

Death would be welcomed, a long-awaited reprieve.

"I'm going to ask her." The words fell from Atlas's mouth before he could stop them, before he could take them back.

His mother's ring burned a hole in his pocket, and now he could only picture the sparkling teal sapphire on Everinne's finger.

"The fuck are you waiting for?" Caedian barked, jerking his head toward the swarming ballroom. "Go find her."

"Fine." Atlas tugged on the front of his dark green silk shirt, straightening it, then glared at his Captain of the Guard. "Bossy prick."

Caedian bent forward at the waist in a mocking bow and Atlas strode past him, descending the staircase, and was immediately swallowed by the sweltering perfumed air.

The overpowering scent of heady florals, mixed spices, and clean soap caused his eyes to burn. Normally during such a party, he might consider amplifying his magic, drawing every gaze in his direction with a careless smile, but right now, all he wanted to do was maneuver through the crowd of bodies undetected. He popped his collar and ducked his head, attempting to slide and squeeze by the dancers without being noticed, all while searching for some sign of Everinne. Curious hands trailed over his arms, caressed his stomach, and he gritted his teeth as he untangled himself from more than one bold female who dared to touch him as he passed.

He should threaten to run his blade through their wrists, then maybe that would teach them to keep their hands to themselves. He opened his mouth to imply just such a promise to a promiscuous little vamp who'd snared one finger into the waist-band of his pants, when he caught sight of Everinne standing next to a fae with vibrant pink hair.

Atlas removed the vampire's finger from his pants, but her pout turned to a scowl when he nudged her out of the way.

"Not tonight, *milazk*," he muttered, ignoring her protests. "Go find something else to suck."

She bared her fangs, a flash of white against crimson lips, but he paid her no attention. His gaze was trained on Everinne. Her dark hair was twisted high on top of her head into a lopsided bun, and she was fiddling with a necklace dripping with purplish-blue stones. A flurry of movement snagged Atlas's attention, and he watched as Aran Ruhdneah made his way toward Everinne from the other side of the room, his pirate-like swagger unmistakable. Those damned star lord brothers were following right on his heels. The younger one, Nyxian, looked as though he'd rather be anywhere else, but the older one, Tovian, had his eyes fixated on a female fae with turquoise eyes and amethyst studs piercing her ears. If Atlas was quick enough, he could cut them off and get to her first.

But a cold, familiar voice kept him frozen in place. "Looking for someone?"

Not now.

Not now.

Atlas's gaze slid to his right, where he found Veros watching him. A swath of dark hair fell across half of his face, and his eyes, a perfect match to Everinne's, were unblinking. He wore black pants and a crisp white shirt, a little formal given the raging party carrying on around them. Then again, the Lord of Time was always impeccably dressed, no matter the occasion. He swung the gold chain on his timepiece in a quick circle around his finger, then casually reversed the direction.

Atlas shoved his hands into his pockets to keep his composure, the last thing he wanted to do was get into a fight with Veros over Everinne. His gut twisted and an uncomfortable sinking sensation filled him with remorse about keeping his plans quiet. But when his fingers accidentally brushed across the small engraved box containing his mother's ring, his heart thundered, colliding against the stiff wall of his chest.

"Yeah." He sauntered closer to Veros, determined not to look over at Everinne, even though it was killing him. "I'm trying to find my future bride tonight, remember?"

Veros nodded, his expression one of cool, measured indifference. There was no sign of suspicion or accusation, but he watched Atlas's face with guarded interest all the same. "Any luck?"

"Not yet." Atlas rocked back onto his heels, feigning boredom. "But I've only just started looking."

He dared a glance over to where Everinne was last standing, only to discover she was no longer there.

Shit.

"Something wrong?" Veros asked, his dark brow quirked in question.

"No," Atlas answered smoothly, but his jaw locked and his nails bit into his palms. "Nothing."

Veros nodded once, tucking his timepiece into his pocket, then started to stroll away. "Enjoy yourself, Your Highness. I'm going to go find a drink. Preferably a strong one."

Atlas called out after him. "The least you can do is find one for me as well."

Veros paused, spinning back around to face him. The corner of his mouth ticked upward, but it wasn't quite a smile. More like an acknowledgement. "Needing some liquid courage tonight?"

"And then some," Atlas muttered. His mouth was dry, his tongue heavy, and he swallowed around the knot of panic clogging the back of his throat.

He tried not to think about the fact that he was stabbing his best friend in the back, that he was breaking the vow he had made. The mere thought of it turned his stomach, left his insides roiling with acid. He'd always prided himself on the friendship he shared with Veros, there was rarely a truth they didn't share with one another. Their loyalty ran deeper than blood, and there was not a damn thing Atlas wouldn't do for Veros, including putting his own life on the line. Just like he knew without a doubt, Veros would do the same for him.

But he clutched the small box hidden away in the pockets of his pants, and Atlas knew all of that was about to change.

Atlas saw Everinne a moment later, dancing with that damned lord of starlight. They were on the outskirts of the dance floor, not quite deep enough in the mix to be swallowed by the sea of bodies. His hands were on her waist, pulling her close, but the second he reached up and tucked a lock of hair behind her ear, letting his knuckles graze her cheek, Atlas's blood roared.

He was violence and wrath. Obsession and envy. The bond crackled and hissed, thrashing and reaching, ready to mark her, to bind her, to make her belong to him. All the while, one word continued to hum through his mind with vengeance until it matched the steady beating of his heart.

Mine.

Mine.

Mine.

Caedian was right.

Atlas had to choose Everinne, and he'd find a way to ensure she accepted him. Because if not, there was a good chance he was going to kill any other male who stood in the way.

Twenty-Three

L ord Tovian Starstorm was chivalrous, handsome, and damn near perfect.

Almost too perfect, if Everinne was being honest.

He danced with practiced ease, like he'd been doing it his whole life, spinning her out then dragging her back against him as the music pulsed and the colored lights slashed across their skin. His movements were elegant, more refined than the other males around them who were grinding their hips against the rears of their dance partners, and even when he held her close enough to feel the warmth of his breath tickle her ear, his hands never slid any lower than her hips. Every so often, however, his mouth would find the inside of her wrist and brush the lightest of kisses across her flesh. The gesture sent her stomach fluttering, but the cold stab of regret quickly followed.

She would have to break his heart.

Not that she imagined Lord Tovian was in love with her already, but it was clear by the broad, dimpled smile he'd maintained since pulling her into his arms that he had no intention of letting her go anytime soon.

It was a shame, really.

Everinne could imagine herself getting lost in a world of fancy gowns and dazzling balls, where all she was required to do was sip on sparkling drinks and look pretty for the duration of the night. Surely the vibe would be far different from the pounding beats and dizzying atmosphere of Starysa. She could absolutely get swept away in the ethereal wonder of another realm, fall in love and get married beneath a sky full of stars, and for once, perhaps, be at peace.

And she knew without question that Lord Tovian Starstorm would be the perfect husband.

For anyone else but her.

He spun her gently, his thumb coasting along her knuckles as they danced. "Who was that female you were speaking with before? The one with startling pink hair?"

"A friend of mine." She angled her head to look at him, seizing the opportunity to deflect. "Are you interested? I could introduce you."

Lord Tovian laughed, rich and decadent.

Everinne's knees wobbled.

"I was merely curious. High Prince Aran was asking after her, he swore she looked vaguely familiar. As though he'd seen her somewhere before." His starlit gaze dipped to her mouth. "There is only one female who has captured my interest tonight. And she is currently in my arms."

Oh, damn.

Awareness prickled along the back of her neck, causing the tiny hairs to stand on end. She tossed a fleeting look over her shoulder only to find Kralv Oldrich through the haze of bodies, his dark eyes fixated on her. His large, bulky frame stood out against the crowd, and he was flanked by guards dressed in black armor with gilded leather shoulder pieces. Heavy lines furrowed across his brow, and his mouth twisted into a sneer.

It was a silent threat.

A warning.

She was running out of time.

Everinne's stomach coiled into unforgiving knots. Tiny beads of sweat slid down her spine, clinging to her satin dress. She tried to swallow the rise of trepidation in the back of her throat, but her mouth was dry, like she'd been force fed spoonfuls of gritty sand. How was she going to tell Lord Tovian she could no longer enjoy his company? But worse, how was she going to convince Atlas to marry her?

"Are you quite well, my lady?" Lord Tovian's smile faded, concern clouding his silver gaze. "You are looking rather pale."

"It's nothing." She blew out a soft breath, her cheeks feeling flush. "I have a lot on my mind at the moment."

Like the fact that she'd been drugged and had her memory wiped, which was why she couldn't recall exactly what happened after she left the Mystic Obscura the other night. Or how she was being coerced into marrying her brother's best friend for reasons that were still unknown to her, but she imagined the kralv's plan was wicked at best, because somehow he'd discovered she possessed the power of inflicting pain, and nothing good could come from it.

Her breathing grew shallow.

Lord Tovian cupped her cheek, lifting her face to his own. His thumb grazed her cheek lightly, and icy dread pierced her lungs, causing her chest to tighten.

"Perhaps some fresh air may help?" he asked.

"No." She stumbled back, planting one hand on his chest when he attempted to steady her. "That is, no thank you, my lord. Besides, it's too cold outside and my dress will hardly keep me warm."

Everinne glanced down between them, hating that she'd been so careless in her choice of clothing.

She wore a black strapless dress that barely fell to the middle of her thighs. The bodice was snug and embroidered with glittering diamonds. The satin skirt flared like a tutu, twirling around her whenever she spun, and her spiked heels were studded with silver gems, which gave her the slimmest boost of confidence. But now, however, that false sense of fortitude was waning.

"I find your dress rather fetching." Lord Tovian's gaze skimmed the length of her, his eyes hovering on the swell of her breasts before darting to her face. "Though the style of gowns for ladies in Aeramere is vastly different. A bit more formal, if you will. I think you would enjoy House Celestine immensely."

"House Celestine," she repeated weakly. House Celestine. His home, in Aeramere. Hopefully, he couldn't hear the regret in her voice over the blasting music.

"Indeed." He clasped her hand in his own as the other slid to the small of her back, swaying her in time to the melodic rhythm. "I could take you to Moonfall Peaks where the stars fall from the sky like diamonds."

Were males from Aeramere always so painfully romantic?

Lord Tovian moved closer, a lock of dark blue hair falling in front of his face. He was devastatingly handsome with a strong jaw, cheekbones that could quite possibly cut glass, and if her hand on his chest earlier was any indication, the male was crafted from granite. She had to find a way to get away from him before it was too late, before she recklessly tumbled headfirst into his alluring charm and let him whisk her away to a land of stars.

His dimples winked and his smile softened. "I could show you the constellations, create one solely for you."

Everinne blinked, unable to break away from the intensity of his eyes. They reminded her of pools of liquid starlight. She sucked in a breath, inhaling the tempting scent of bourbon, vanilla, and clove. Her head spun, and she leaned into his embrace.

"You can create constellations?"

He grinned, easing back slightly. Releasing her hand, he cupped his palm between them.

"Now," he whispered, "watch."

Magic bloomed in his open hand, a subtle glow at first, then brighter as fiery orbs danced and swirled. Warmth spread through her as his magic illuminated the breath of space they shared, casting them both in a silvery glow. It was mesmerizing, the way he crafted stars from nothing more than a thought, the way he garnered control of something as vast as the night sky with barely a flick of his wrist. Everinne stared, awestruck, as iridescent stars bounced from the tips of his fingers to his wrist, before finally falling into place in the shape of a flower. Streaks of stardust connected each star to form the floral constellation, and then Lord Tovian did the unthinkable.

He plucked it out of the air, gently tucking it back behind her ear.

Sweet gods, this male was too much.

She looked up at him then, into those eyes of moonlight with flecks of shimmering blue, and a blade of panic pierced her.

Everinne stiffened.

She knew *that* look.

He was going to kiss her.

Lord Tovian lowered his head and again, she placed her hand upon the ridiculously hard wall of his chest, holding him back.

"I appreciate the thoughtful gift, my lord." Her fingers reached up absently to touch the flower-like constellation tucked into her hair. "And I would love nothing more than to visit Aeramere with you. But I'm afraid...my plans have recently changed."

"Changed?" His brow furrowed and he searched her face, looking for the answer she knew would break him. "How so?"

"I..." Everinne's heart was thundering now, so loud, she swore he could hear it. She loosed a shaky breath and stepped away from him, shoving her clammy hands behind her back. The words spilled from her before she could stop them. "I've recently become engaged."

She saw the exact moment his face fell, when understanding crashed into him. He shook his head to disguise the confusion and hurt, but it was too late.

"You..." Lord Tovian trailed off, and his brow pinched. His spine snapped straight, and he took a decided step back, the air between them cooling with his abrupt departure. "You are betrothed to another?"

Wonderful.

Now she sounded like a whore.

"I am, yes." Everinne caught sight of someone barreling his way through the crowd, heading directly for them. She would recognize that arrogant stride anywhere. Streaks of blue light shone brightly against his wavy, dark blond hair, and a pair of green eyes glinting with shards of furious gold were focused on her.

Atlas was stalking toward her.

And he looked pissed.

Her stomach flipped. Oh, gods. This was not going to end well.

"To who?" Lord Tovian asked, snaring her attention once more, his crestfallen expression morphing into one of displeasure.

"Him." Everinne's voice pitched, her chest heaved, and violent waves of nausea rippled through her as she reached out and grabbed Atlas's arm, pulling him toward her. She plastered a fake, too-bright smile on her face, and her voice trembled as she said, "I'm marrying the Prince of Prava."

She dared a quick look at Atlas, only to find him staring down at her, bewildered. He arched a brow.

Please, she begged silently, squeezing her eyes shut, *please go along with it.*

Without asking, Atlas slid an arm around her waist.

Her eyes flew open to find Lord Tovian watching her curiously. She couldn't bring herself to look at Atlas again, but she could feel the weight of his gaze upon her. Questioning.

"I see." Lord Tovian nodded once, and the flower constellation he'd tucked behind her ear crumbled into stardust, leaving a trail of pearlescent shimmering powder on her bare shoulder.

Everinne's heart tumbled into the acidic pit of her stomach and roiled with the bile brewing there.

"Forgive me, my lord." She ducked her head, shame coloring

her cheeks all the way to the tips of her ears. "It was quite unexpected."

"Indeed," Atlas muttered under his breath.

She wanted to apologize again, to explain to Lord Tovian that she didn't *really* want to marry Atlas, but she'd been left with no choice.

Atlas's grip on her waist tightened, his strong fingers digging into her hip with so much force, she nearly gasped.

"If you'd excuse us, Lord Tovian, I require a word with my future *bride*." Atlas practically spat out the word.

He didn't wait for Lord Tovian to respond, he didn't even give her a chance to say goodbye, he simply maneuvered her through the ballroom, toward one of the glass doors that led out onto the patio. He shoved it open, hauling her along behind him as she struggled to match his pace.

Cold air assaulted her, biting through the thin satin of her dress, and her teeth chattered so hard her head began to ache. She wrapped her arms around herself, shivering against the frigid night, her eyes focusing on anything but the angry prince towering above her. Carved stone statues of wolves were perched along the railing, looking out over the silent gardens of the palace. Wind sifted through the trees, stirring the remaining leaves, sending the petals of fading winter blossoms clinging to their last shred of life fluttering at her feet. Moonlight slipped between passing clouds, bouncing between her and Atlas in a play of shadow and silver light.

He folded his arms across his chest and another chill crept down her spine.

This time, she forced herself to look up at him.

"Explain yourself, Everinne." Atlas's gaze narrowed. "Now."

"I..." She hesitated, the truth would be a death sentence for them both. For Veros. "Lord Tovian was going to propose and I... I needed an out."

"So, you figured you'd claim me as your own?" Atlas

demanded, his chest expanding as he inhaled sharply. "Use me as an excuse for your own benefit?"

"Atlas, I panicked." She sank her teeth into her bottom lip, despising the way the lie rolled off her tongue. It left a foul taste in her mouth, bitter and lingering.

"You realize this cannot be undone." Atlas shifted closer, blocking the bite of the wind with his broad frame. He took her by the shoulders, gently letting his hands coast up and down her arms to warm her.

Oh, she knew.

Everinne bobbed a hasty nod. "I'm aware."

He cocked his head to the side, raking a hand through his already mussed hair. For a brief moment, uncertainty warred on his face, and he pulled back, shoving his hands into the pockets of his pants.

"So." Atlas studied her then, his gaze slowly traveling over every inch of her as though he was committing her, and this moment, to memory. "You agree to marry me?"

"Y-yes." Her voice was a scratchy, shaky whisper. She told herself it was because of the cold, but she knew it was for another reason entirely. Her life was unraveling before her, the loose string of her fate held tightly in Kralv Oldrich's large fist, and there was nothing she could do to stop it.

"Well, then." Atlas pulled a small wooden box from his pocket. "Better make it official."

Everinne felt faint. Her knees softened as though they would give out from under her at any moment. Blood rushed loudly in her ears, drowning out the music from the ballroom, until all she could hear was the erratic thumping of her own heart. Her chest was suddenly too tight, she couldn't get air into her lungs, and the cold fingers of control Kralv Oldrich now held over her wrapped around her throat and squeezed.

"Atlas..." Everinne's voice cracked, her refusal fading when he knelt before her and popped open the lid of the sleek wooden box.

Set in a cushion of scarlet velvet was a ring. A large oval sapphire gleamed in a setting of swirling gold. The stone's hue reminded her of the Ladova Bay, a radiant mix of dark green with a sheen of vivid blue. It was beautiful. Stunning.

And she didn't deserve it.

"This was my mother's favorite ring." Atlas's voice had gone quiet, wistful. He tilted his head back, looking up at the heavens where stars danced behind thin veils of clouds, and the crescent moon shone brightly, its dark side hidden from view. Starysa's skies were always enchanting at night, full of mystical wonder and magic. Then those eyes of his, those endless pools of soft green with flecks of simmering gold, were focused on her. "She told me once whoever I married would sparkle beneath the spellbound sky."

Moonlight washed over her.

The diamonds of her dress twinkled. The glitter she'd dusted on her shoulders before the ball glimmered softly.

Standing before him, Everinne sparkled.

Guilt swarmed her, and when Atlas took her hand, her nose tingled and she tried to blink away the threat of unbidden tears.

He brushed his thumb across her knuckles, and she let a single tear escape.

Just one.

Atlas watched it fall, then he whispered, "I suppose she always knew it would be you."

Twenty-Four

A tlas didn't know why he was so damn nervous. It was only Everinne, and besides, she'd been the one to announce that *she* was marrying *him*, not the other way around. He knew she didn't love him, and with the exception of their little interlude at the overlook the other night, he was fairly certain she still hated him. Which begged the question, why did she suddenly want to marry him? He didn't believe for one minute that it had anything to do with that damned Lord Tovian asking for her hand, mostly because if he had proposed and she intended to deny him, nothing would stop her. Everinne had no problem standing up for herself or telling off any male who stood in her way, and if she didn't want to be carried off on a cloud of stardust, she would tell Lord Tovian she wasn't interested without hesitation.

So, it had to be something else.

There must be another reason she'd so readily agreed to marry him, and Atlas wondered what kind of secrets she was keeping. He could delve into her mind, listen to her thoughts as though they were his own, but he'd been cautious around her, building the layers of a stone wall between them in an effort to shut her out. To ensure he didn't eavesdrop on her personal turmoil. Even now, her mind was a muted whirlwind of chaos, her churning emotions and thoughts threatening to destroy the barrier he'd carefully constructed, sending it crumbling into a pile of ash and debris.

When she looked at him, his heart strained.

Tonight, Everinne's façade of indifference fractured, the vivacity of her aura waned. Her turquoise eyes were still brimming with tears, the rings of gold around the center flaring brightly like captured prisms of sunlight. The brazen cloak of fearlessness she wore had slipped, revealing the death-touched fae who wandered without purpose. Standing before him with her bottom lip quivering, he saw the truth of her nature—a lost soul whose magic left her broken, yet whose fire could not be contained.

She was flames against his skin, burning him with a single look.

Atlas twisted his mother's ring between his fingers, worried that if he took too much longer, Everinne might change her mind.

When he spoke, he kept his voice soft. "Are you going to break me, Wildheart?"

Everinne blinked, worrying her bottom lip with her teeth. "Break you?"

His chest tightened to the point of pain, and he slid the ring onto her finger. The air hummed, vibrating with energy, and he shoved up from the ground, drawing her close. He linked their fingers together, then wrapped one hand around her waist.

The chill of the night whispered around them, but all Atlas could feel was the heat simmering between them, and the distance he'd forced between them for years slowly evaporated, fading into a distant memory like a mistake.

"Are you going to make me fall so deep into a sea of longing that I forget how to breathe when I'm near you? Until all I want to do is drown in you?" Atlas watched as her lips parted, as her breath hitched, siphoning away his resolve. "Will you break my heart and destroy my soul?"

Her gaze darkened, shadows slipping into the pools of

turquoise that haunted his dreams. She shook her head, tucking her chin down. "My magic..."

"Not your magic, Everinne." He placed two fingers under her chin, tilting her face up to him. "Will *you*?"

"A heart can only be broken if it's been given out of love." She squeezed her eyes shut, her brows pinching together in a pain he couldn't erase.

Atlas cupped her face then, running his thumb gently along the apple of her cheek. "And will you give me yours?"

Her eyes flew open, and it was then he saw the depth of her suffering, the emotions that plagued her. Loneliness. Despair. Regret. "I don't think I have one anymore."

"You do." Atlas had seen her heart. The pulse of it was a song, a series of melancholy chords, music that could only be heard by him. "You have a heart, Everinne. One day, it will belong to me. Until then, I will give you mine."

"Atlas..." Her bottom lip quivered again, drawing his gaze to her mouth.

"Take my heart, Everinne. All of it." His hand moved from her cheek to the back of her neck and lowered his head, unable to tear his gaze away from those full lips that seemed to beckon him. "For as long as you need, for as long as you breathe, it's yours."

One kiss.

All it would take was one kiss, one meeting of the lips, and then she would know. She would understand the degree of his need for her, because she would know she was his mate. He told himself it didn't matter, she could either accept or reject the bond, but at least she would *know*.

He inhaled the tempting scent of her—warm caramel fused with the decadence of rose and blackcurrant—and his pulse thudded loudly in his ears, his blood raced.

Her eyes fluttered closed, waiting for the moment their lips touched.

Everything he ever wanted, everything he tried to avoid, was finally within his reach.

"Get your fucking hands off my sister."

Veros's voice, heated with malice, cut through the night.

Atlas spun away from Everinne to face him, only to see Veros's fist right before it connected with his face.

Pain ricocheted through him as bone crunched, as Veros's knuckles slammed into the space right below his left eye. Off to his right, he heard Everinne scream. Midnight stars danced in front of Atlas's vision, and he staggered backward, blinking through the agony. He rolled his neck, regained his bearing in just enough time to see Veros readying another swing, but this time Atlas lunged forward, tackling his friend to the ground.

They collided against the cold stone in a crash of fists and grunts, exchanging blows like they had in their youth, when one of them lost a bet. Except this time, there was more at stake.

"Stop!" Everinne cried. "Veros, enough!"

But they ignored her pleas, grappling against one another, each of them taking well-placed swings. Atlas landed a swift punch to Veros's jaw, splitting his friend's lip open. Veros retaliated with a hit to his ribs, the cracking unmistakable. White hot pain speared through him as his blood rushed to heal the wounds. Vile curses escaped Atlas through gritted teeth, and he rammed his elbow upward, connecting with the underside of Veros's jaw. Spasms of agony seared him, but he fought through the throbbing aches, because this discomfort was nothing compared to what he'd already suffered. He would take each hit without a care and fire back with one of his own, because nothing, absolutely nothing, would cause him more torment than being separated from Everinne for a lifetime.

Then suddenly Veros was being ripped off him and Caedian was there, tossing the Lord of Time across the garden patio as though he weighed nothing more than a bag of sand.

"That's assault on the Imperial Prince, my lord." Caedian stood with his sword drawn, its tip aimed at Veros's throat. Gone were all traces of humor and friendship, and in their place was the cold-blooded resolution of an esteemed warrior. "Stand down. *Now.*"

Veros straightened, a line of rage creasing his forehead, cutting between narrowed brows. He ignored Caedian, the focus of his ruthless glare directed toward Atlas instead. His chest heaved, his busted knuckles fisting at his side. "You swore an oath to me."

Atlas stood, wiping the back of his hand across his mouth, and his flesh came away smeared crimson. "And I'll uphold it. I'll protect her."

Everinne stalked toward them, her hands planted on her hips. She stared her brother down, but he didn't so much as spare a glance in her direction. "Do not speak of me as though I'm not right here."

"Just not from yourself." Veros spat, his bloodied saliva staining the stone ground at his feet. The accusation was clear. "She deserves more. She deserves the world."

"I will give her the world! The sun and the moon. The sky and all of its stars. The petal of every flower, every drop of rain, every snowflake from winter's coldest months. I'll give her every damn mountain and the endless sea." Atlas threw his arms wide, anger heating his veins, causing his blood to boil. "I will give her everything!"

"And what of your loyalty?" Veros countered, stepping closer, then freezing in place as Caedian once again raised his weapon in a silent threat. "What of your fidelity? Will you remain faithful to her or—"

"Is that what this is about?" Atlas exploded, his fury engulfing the pain carving its way through him, cut open by the hurt of his friend's open condemnation. He'd grown accustomed to the reputation he held, to how others perceived him, but never in a thousand years would he have imagined Veros would make the same callous assertion. The betrayal stung deep. "You think I'll sneak off to have illicit affairs while she's sleeping in *my* bed?"

Veros's jaw locked. "I won't allow her to be another one of your conquests."

"I'm standing right here!" Everinne shouted, but her voice was drowned out by the hollow loathing of her brother's words.

"You don't think I'm worthy of her." Not a question, but a testament to the truth. Atlas nodded slowly, stepping back, the realization all too clear. "Is that it, Veros? My closest friend thinks the worst of me, just like every other fucking soul in this damned city. That my magic, the power I wield, is also the substance of my character. You think I'm a rake, a playboy prince, who's undeserving of his sister."

Veros's shoulders bunched, and a vein ticked along his temple. "She's fragile."

"I most certainly am not," Everinne huffed, her warm breath misting before her.

"Fragile. Such a curious choice of words, my lord." Atlas ran his thumb along his jawline, considering, his contempt palpable. "Fragile...yet you've sat back and watched her break, refusing to use your almighty magic to help her."

"The hands of time are not so easily altered." Veros bristled, crossing his arms over his chest. "You know I have boundaries. Limits."

Atlas scowled. "As do I."

"You humiliated her in a room full of people!" Veros erupted then, stalking so close that the sharpened edge of Caedian's extended sword bit into the skin of his flesh. "They called her your whore, Atlas. How do I know you won't hurt her again?"

"Because she's my fucking mate!" Atlas roared, the rein of his control snapping, leaving him full of untethered wrath.

But a tiny, barely audible gasp held him in check.

His gaze flicked to Everinne, who stared at him in utter horror. Eyes wide and round with fear, she looked at him as though he'd just professed to being a monster, a demon of the night, as opposed to confessing the truth that had damn near killed him every day. She stood frozen in place by the words he'd shouted out of desperation, and in the thaw of the aftermath, she ran. Fleeing. Her heels clicked against the patio as she tore into the gardens, vanishing into the night.

Atlas's shoulders sagged. He roughed a hand over his face, raked his fingers through his hair, then stared at his best friend. "She's my mate, Veros."

"I know." His words were a hoarse whisper. "Why do you think I made you take that vow?"

Atlas dragged his gaze back to Veros, and with the flames of anger now just dying embers, he realized it wasn't vexation that was harbored in his friend's hardened expression, but something more like fear. Vast and all-encompassing.

And it caused Atlas's blood to run cold.

"Because time," Veros ventured, "much like fate, is not always kind."

Fuck.

"Go after her." Veros sighed heavily in resignation, swiping at the blood streaking down his chin. "She won't listen to me, but she might listen to you."

Atlas didn't hesitate.

He turned without another word and ran.

Twenty-Five

E verinne sprinted through the palace gardens. She had no clue what direction she was going, no idea on how to escape, all she knew was that she had to get away. She had to put as much distance between herself and Atlas as possible.

A gust of cold wind slapped at her, stinging her skin. It tangled into her hair and sank into her bones, causing her muscles to tense and seize.

She stumbled blindly through a maze of flowering bushes and ornamental hedges, the pointy heels of her shoes sticking in the solid ground. With only slivers of moonlight to guide her, she barely avoided running right into a massive pond, dodging its grassy banks at the last second. She veered to the left, cutting across an uneven gravel path, desperately trying not to break her ankle in the process. All the while, Atlas's words continued to echo in her mind.

She's my mate.

Mate.

The word struck her, sending a reverberating chord of fear through her soul. She shook her head, willing the thought away as her eyes blurred. It couldn't be true. If it was, the leash Kralv Oldrich had placed around her neck would only tighten, squeezing the last of her resolve. He grasped her fate in the clutches of his fist, and she knew nothing would stop him from ensuring she upheld her end of the bargain. Her stomach tangled into unforgiving knots at what he might ask of her, of what he might force her to do.

A line of trees appeared before her, their thick, inky branches the perfect place to hide. She didn't think there was a small forest on the palace grounds, but at the moment she didn't care, because she heard Atlas in the distance, calling her name. She tossed a hasty glance over her shoulder just in time to see him running after her at full speed.

"Ever!" He lifted a hand as he rushed toward her. "Wait!"

Later.

She would talk to him about this later, after she had time to formulate a plan. It had been different when she'd agreed to marry him at Kralv Oldrich's demand, when she thought she was only protecting him and Veros. But if Atlas wasn't lying, if she was his mate, they would both suffer for it. The kralv was anything if not ruthless in his endeavors, and if he discovered she was fated to his son, he would use that knowledge to the best of his advantage to control them both.

And that was something she couldn't allow to happen.

No.

First, she had to figure out how to navigate the web she'd been caught in, then she would talk to Atlas. And no matter what, no matter the circumstances, she would deny being his mate. Even if it meant taking that heartbreaking slice of knowledge to her grave.

Everinne braced herself and darted into the trees, wincing as their low-lying limbs smacked at her, and the spindly evergreen branches snagged at her dress. She'd half expected the forest to be dense, that it would possibly go on forever and afford her the opportunity to get lost. But instead, she burst through the other side in seconds, the toes of her heels sliding against slick stone.

She glanced down, realizing her mistake all too late.

Throwing her arms out for balance, she grappled with the air to stop herself from falling, but her foot caught the ledge and she shrieked, right before toppling into a steaming pool. The force of her momentum plunged her beneath the surface, and she jolted in surprise as warm water sloshed over her, heating her frozen body.

She kicked through the water as a strong arm wrapped around her waist, hauling her upward with far more efficiency than she would have thought was possible.

Everinne broke through the surface, gasping and sputtering, blinking away the droplets of water that clung to her lashes. She shoved her soaked hair back from her face, chest heaving as she welcomed the reprieve of fresh air, only to find herself entangled in Atlas's arms.

His grip was firm and she struggled against him, trying to break free from his hold.

"I know how to swim, Atlas." She grabbed his forearms and shifted away from him. "Let me go."

"No." His fingers dug in and he pulled her closer. Golden strands of hair slanted across his forehead like wet silk, curling slightly at the nape of his neck. In the pale light, his eyes reminded her of the ethereal green of the Ladova Bay, the streaks of gold glinting like when the early morning sunlight hit the smooth waters. But his brows were drawn and his expression was stern. "Because the second I let you go, you'll run."

"I won't...I won't run away." But she couldn't handle him holding her, touching her. It awoke a ravenous kind of longing, one she didn't want to experience ever again.

"Please," she pleaded with him, her voice hoarse. "Let me go."

Atlas sighed, his breath misting before him. Reluctantly, he released her.

Everinne immediately tread backward, then stopped the moment his gaze narrowed. The skirt of her dress rode up, floating around her, and even though she doubted he could see anything below the surface, she made a failing effort to adjust the fabric all the same. She tugged the hem down and sank below the water once more.

Atlas grabbed her again, lifting her up.

"I've got it!" she shouted, smacking his hands away.

"Leave your damn dress alone or you'll end up drowning yourself." He raked a hand through his hair, the small curls now more pronounced than they were before. "Your modesty is of very little concern to me right now."

"Fine," she snapped, coasting her arms through the water and slowly moving her legs to stay afloat. Her dress fanned out around her, well above her hips, hovering in the ripples she made. She would bet anything he would be far more concerned about her modesty if he knew what she was wearing underneath—the tiny triangle of black lace covered very little and left absolutely nothing to the imagination.

For a moment, they watched each other. And then Everinne realized he wasn't doing anything to stay above the water.

"Are you..." She glanced down between them. "Are you just *standing* there?"

Atlas shrugged, dismissive. "Apparently I was blessed with height, among other things."

His insinuation was not lost on her and a flush crept into her cheeks.

Everinne dipped her head, blowing out a breath, releasing a stream of bubbles in the process.

Atlas's lips twitched.

"I know you're getting tired," he drawled, rolling his head from side to side as she forced herself not to watch the little rivulets of water glide down his rather kissable looking neck.

"I'm fine," she muttered.

He clicked his tongue, they both knew she was lying.

Everinne huffed out a breath, glancing around at her surroundings. "Whose pool is this, anyway?"

"Mine." He angled his head toward the other side of the pool, and she followed his direction with her gaze.

Sure enough, across a slate verandah furnished with lounge chairs were two ornate glass doors. Soft, glowing light illuminated the room within, highlighting a sumptuous four-poster bed topped with a plush blanket and an overabundance of pillows. Without warning, her mind instantly filled with images of Atlas, sprawled and naked, his beautifully chiseled body stretched out on what were most likely luxurious satin sheets. Almost as quickly as she imagined it, another picture infiltrated her thoughts. This time, however, she was in that lavish bed with him.

Kissing him.

Touching him.

Taking him.

Everinne's entire body heated, unbidden warmth pooling between her thighs, and she sucked in a ragged breath.

"Lovely." The word was a scrape across her tongue while she attempted to disguise her arousal. "I take it this is your sex pool, then. And how many females have you brought here?"

Not that she really wanted to know, the number would only pain her.

Atlas arched a brow at her contemptuous tone. "You'd be the first. Even if it was by accident."

Part of her didn't want to believe him, wanted to think he was only saying it just to appease her. But it was incredibly difficult to convince herself that he was lying.

She leaned her head back into the water, arching to ease some of the ache that caused her muscles to spasm and twinge. Her arms were burning, on fire from constantly rotating forward and backward. Her legs strained as she continued to kick lightly in an effort to not sink.

"Would you please quit being so stubborn and let me help you?" Atlas asked. "It won't look good if the future princess drowns on my watch."

Everinne's head snapped up.

In truth, she should probably just swim to the ledge and climb out of the pool completely. But it was so cold outside, and the water was so warm, and it would be so nice to not have to keep treading the damn water.

"Fine." She eyed him cautiously. "But only because I feel like my body is about to quit on me."

Atlas didn't need to be told twice. He snared her by the hips, his palms skimming the lace straps of her nearly useless undergarments, and if he recognized that she wore barely anything beneath her dress, he made no show of it. He gathered her close, so her legs straddled his waist, and as soon as she was in his arms, she went pliant. Limp and weary, she let him support the weight of her and let her hands come to rest against his chest.

An error, on her part.

Because now they were only inches apart, and she could clearly see the way his damp shirt clung to his broad shoulders, how it molded to his solid abdomen, how it felt like she was touching the body of a damn god. Her fingers itched to rove over him, to explore every solid inch, but she didn't dare move. In fact, her lungs compressed, and she all but forgot how to breathe.

"See?" Atlas murmured, his hands spreading ever so slightly, his fingers grazing her entirely bare bottom. "I'm not so terrible."

When Everinne spoke, her voice was a raspy whisper. "I never said you were."

"But you have before," he countered smoothly.

She couldn't meet his gaze, instead she stared at the ring on her finger. The one that had belonged to his mother. The large oval stone glinted a deep green, then a radiant blue in the play of intermittent moonbeams.

"So." He leaned forward, pressing his forehead to hers. "Are we going to talk about this?"

She shook her head, her wet hair clinging to her bare shoulders. "I don't believe you."

Atlas pulled back, his brows pinched together in a scowl. "What?"

"I'm not your mate, Atlas." The words were out of her mouth before she could stop them.

"The fuck you aren't, Everinne." His fingers molded to her, gripping her backside, clutching her flesh. "You want to know why I used my magic on you all those years ago? Because I couldn't escape your thoughts. I could hear them as clearly as my own, and I wanted you just as much, if not more, than you wanted me. I figured if I used my magic, just once, then I wouldn't be breaking my vow to Veros. I wouldn't have touched you."

He nipped at her bottom lip, tugging lightly. "Then you had to go and have an orgasm and those sounds you made that night... they're burned into my memory. I still get hard just thinking about them."

As if to prove a point, he rocked forward, rubbing his hardening length against her core. "Try again, Wildheart."

She fisted her hands against him. Wishes to falling stars and prayers to goddesses would no longer be enough to sway the path of her fate. "It can't be me."

"And why not?" he demanded.

Everinne hesitated. If Atlas was her mate, he would have access to her thoughts, to her feelings, and emotions. She would have to protect herself, protect him. She did her best to shield her mind from him, to keep him locked out. There was no way he could find out that Kralv Oldrich was behind this union, that his own father had threatened to harm him, to break him, with *her* magic.

If such a thing were to happen, she would never forgive herself.

She grasped hold of the only excuse she could find, the hurtful insult he'd thrown at her the night he discovered her swinging from the chandeliers in the Grand Cru.

"Because I'm broken." Lifting her gaze, she met the hurt, met the realization reflected at her in his eyes. "You said so yourself."

"We're all a little broken, Ever." His thumbs traced lazy circles along her lower hips, slowly sliding beneath the lace straps to stroke her flesh. "Sometimes, those broken pieces fit together to make something beautiful. Eventually, the sharp edges soften.

The cracks and fractures fuse together to form a more perfect whole."

Her nose began to tingle and her eyes filled, causing her vision to blur with the familiar sting of tears.

Atlas lowered his head.

"Don't," she whispered.

"Don't what?"

"Don't kiss me."

His mouth skated along her cheek. "Afraid of the truth?"

Everinne's bottom lip trembled, she was afraid of more than the truth. "I'm afraid of everything."

"Not anymore. Not with me." One hand moved to the small of her back, anchoring her against him. The other slid up her arm and around to the back of her neck. "Never again."

Then Atlas kissed her and Everinne's soul ignited. The world fell away in a wash of dizzying colors and muted sounds. His tongue slid along the seam of her lips, and she opened for him readily, gasping into his mouth as a magical thread thrumming with power stole around her heart, weaving an intricate yet intangible design. The bond snapped into place and she shuddered, throwing her arms around his neck as it sparked and hummed, as every part of him became every part of her.

Atlas was the beating of her heart.

The blood flowing through her veins.

The air in her lungs.

She'd fallen into the tempest of his existence.

Her pulse thudded wildly as he angled her head, deepening their kiss. It was a clash of teeth and tongue, of licking and tasting and longing. He thickened against her and she pushed her hips forward, not realizing how long she had craved this moment. It was as though she'd been walking through her life in a fog of frigid gloom. Always lost. Always alone. Suffering by the hands of her own magic, subjected to a place of darkness and despair. Where light could not reach, where there was nothing and no one. The pain of her own torment had ruled her, haunted her for years, forced her to live in a nightmare of her own making.

Until Atlas.

Until her *mate*.

"Tell me," he said as he planted kisses along the column of her throat. "Tell me I'm not your mate. Lie to me, Wildheart."

Everinne could tell the truth. She could steal this moment from fate, keep it harbored away and safely hidden, just as she'd done with her twisted magic. Except she hadn't been able to keep it a secret. Kralv Oldrich had discovered it, he'd discovered the monster lurking beneath the exterior of her tortured soul. And he would find out about Atlas, too. He would learn about their bond and wield it against her like a weapon. His magic allowed him to sense someone's greatest fear and use it against them, forcing them to bend and break beneath his will.

Loving Atlas Skye would be the biggest mistake of her life.

"I can't be your mate." She choked the words out. Shaking her head, she shoved away from him. "I...I reject the bond. I reject you."

If looks could indeed kill, Atlas would've sent her to her grave. The raw agony, the absolute *hurt* on his face was like nothing she had ever seen. His eyes darkened, and the newly formed bond between them strained, a convoluted hiss and snap as she tried to deny what could never be undone.

He stared at her, unmoving. "Liar."

She swam toward the edge of the pool, clutching her heart as she went. The pain was unbearable, like she'd been run through with a poisoned blade. Hoisting herself up, she dragged her legs over the ledge and climbed out of the pool. Cold air assaulted her, and she wrapped her arms around herself and turned back, only to find Atlas swimming toward her. With her teeth chattering, she faced him, willing herself to hold his furious glare.

"I will be your wife in name only." Everinne shivered, gripping her elbows with her hands as the cold beads of water slid down her skin, turning to droplets of ice.

He hauled himself out of the pool and she tried not to stare at the way his silky wet shirt clung to his broad shoulders, the way it molded to the solid wall of his chest and abdomen. And she definitely didn't notice how his pants slung low across his hips as he stalked in her direction.

"Name only?" he growled, snagging her by the chin, his fingers bruising. "So, you have no intention of sharing my bed?"

Everinne clamped her mouth shut. She didn't dare speak, fearful that if she tried, she would place them both in danger.

"And what if I told you my father anticipates an heir?" His thumb stroked the side of her cheek, and she willed herself not to lean into his touch. "That I'm expected to fill you with my seed until you're swollen with child?"

That sounded exactly like some vicious command the kralv would set upon Atlas. But she could not allow herself to be swayed.

"Then I would say you should look elsewhere." Her voice was quiet. Hollow and empty. Just like her.

Atlas barked out a cruel laugh, jerking back from her like he'd been stung. "Elsewhere? You think he'd appreciate me siring a bastard?"

Again, Everinne said nothing.

"And you..." He pointed an accusing finger in her direction. "You're saying you'd be fine if I fucked someone else while I'm married to you?"

The bond revolted and her stomach heaved. The mere thought of Atlas finding another female to warm his bed made a wave of nausea flow through her, but she was determined to stand her ground. She was doing this to save him. To save both of them.

Everinne lifted her chin and swallowed down the rise of bile scalding the back of her throat. "I don't care who you fuck as long as it's not me."

Atlas opened his mouth but she kept going, refusing to let him get a word in. If she wanted him to believe she was denying him and their bond, then she would have to make it hurt. "You're the prince of pleasure, Atlas. I wouldn't expect you to be faithful to me."

His nostrils flared.

His silence rattled in her ears, deafening, and she trembled beneath the fury in his gaze.

Atlas stomped toward the double doors of his bedroom and threw them open so the etched glass panels shattered.

Following in his stormy wake, she leapt over the shards of broken glass littering the ground and tiptoed into his room. He disappeared into the bathing suite and she inhaled, only to be greeted by the overwhelming scent of him, of fresh cedar, mouth-watering neroli, and tempting spice. Her lungs ached and her heart thundered as his volatile emotions crashed down the bond, wrecking her.

He emerged a moment later and threw a towel in her direction.

She barely caught it before it hit the ground.

Atlas's face was a mask of utter calm, devoid of any emotion. He rolled his shoulders back, his chest expanding with deep, measured breaths, and the bond fell silent.

His cold gaze flicked to the door leading to one of the halls. "Get out."

Frozen in place by fear or dread, she couldn't be sure, but Everinne didn't move.

"I am not asking." He jerked his head toward the door. "Get. Out."

She ducked her head, clutching the towel to her. Oh gods, it smelled just like him, too. Something inside of her snapped, breaking her. "Yes, Your Imperial Highness."

Everinne bolted from Atlas's quarters, unable to look at him as tears slid freely down her cheeks. All the emotions she hated, the ones she couldn't control, slammed into her. One after another. She felt herself slipping off the ledge as she sprinted down the dimly lit corridors, passing snickering servants and whispering halls. Panic. Heartbreak. Fear. They were all a violent landslide, careening toward her with unfathomable speed, ready to smother her into a suffocating abyss.

Broken sobs escaped her as she muffled her face with the towel, as the dark magic inside her yawned, awakening once more. Welcoming her despair.

No, no, no.

Her body convulsed as she fumbled blindly toward the bedroom the kralv kept for her, her vision blurring as hot tears streaked down her cheeks. She swiped at them hastily, her fingertips coming away smeared with kohl and stardust, a stark reminder she'd broken *two* hearts tonight. Remorse sank its claws into her, pierced her until the stab of its agony met bone, until she thought she would die from the emotional pain she'd inflicted upon Lord Tovian and Atlas. She'd hurt them both, cut them deeply, and this time, she had only herself to blame.

Not her magic.

Two guards were positioned outside of her bedroom, but neither of them spared her a glance as she approached. They did not look at her, did not speak to her, no doubt they were only there to ensure she followed Kralv Oldrich's explicit demands. They simply opened the door, let her stagger into the dimly lit room, then shut it soundly behind her.

Everinne dropped the towel.

She peeled out of her still dripping dress, letting it crumple to the ground at her feet in a heap of sodden material. Shadowy wisps of pitch black and deep violet slipped from her fingers, and she curled her hands into fists, pleading with the chaotic magic to stay silent. Kicking off her shoes, she trudged over to the glowing hearth, but each time her bare feet met the plush carpet, the steps felt like a steady march to her own death.

Naked and shivering, she stood before the fire in an attempt to warm her frozen body. But not even the heat of the flames could offer her any kind of comfort. Her chest rose and fell in uneven intervals as the darkness within her magnified, preying upon the weakness of her mind.

Please, she begged before turning away from the hearth and walking numbly over to the bed.

Not tonight.

She crawled on top of the velvet comforter, drawing her knees to her chest, curling into herself.

"Just for tonight," she whispered out loud and squeezed her eyes shut, the silent tears still spilling down her cheeks. "Please, leave me alone."

Everinne ran her thumb along the band of the engagement ring on her hand and waited.

Tendrils of her power cocooned around her, blanketing her in a swath of shadowy magic. And for the first time, the harrowing beast inside of her fell blessedly silent.

Twenty-Six

tlas slammed his fist into the wall.

He stared at the crumbling hole of smooth stone, flicking a glance at his bloodied knuckles. The pain was fleeting. He didn't even feel it.

Anger flowed through his veins, drawing upon a well of rage that continued to fill, a fathomless pit of darkness that only served to stoke his fury.

Damn Everinne. And damn her for denying him.

I reject the bond. I reject you.

Bullshit.

Her words replayed in his mind, her voice cutting through him like a blade of steel fresh from the forge. Hot. Searing. Rendering him utterly useless.

He stalked toward his wardrobe and yanked the door open, ripping it clean off its hinges. The carved wood splintered and cracked, and he tossed it to the side, discarding the slabs of oak without care. Grabbing a half-full bottle of honeyfire from the shelf, he tugged the cork out with his teeth and spat it onto the floor.

Atlas swallowed two hasty gulps of the alcohol, enjoying the way the smoky sweet flavor burned the back of his throat.

The audacity of her—telling him to fuck someone else while she wore his mother's ring, when she would soon be wearing his crown, bearing his last name. As if he would. So, she believed him to be no more worthy of his station than most of Prava, thought he had every intention of upholding his damning reputation once they married.

Fucking skies.

He gritted his teeth, dragging the bottle of liquor to his lips once again to pull another healthy swig.

Everinne had to be hiding something. A secret.

He wasn't stupid. He'd read her thoughts like a book when they were on the *volt* and she'd had his cock in her mouth. She wanted him then, was practically begging for him without having to say a word. Not only that, but he'd seen the way her turquoise eyes softened, then glowed when he professed to wanting to touch her. For *years*. Even tonight, when she ran away from him and fell into his pool, her thoughts had betrayed her. Not only was she lying to him, she was lying to herself. But she'd thrown a barrier around her mind, concealing her emotions and feelings, everything, from him.

It was infuriating.

Maddening.

Atlas raked a hand through his damp hair, shoving the loose blond curls back from his face. He knew he shouldn't do it, knew it would probably only make things worse between them, but he didn't care. He wanted her to fight with him. Wanted her to argue and seethe until the only thing left to do was kiss her just to shut her up. And Everinne would let him. Because he was her fucking mate.

He scoured the bond, blazing through it until he thought the thread binding them would fray and snap completely, severing them from one another.

But what he found gutted him. Left him empty with regret and despair.

The slow, steady beating of Everinne's heart answered his call. But her mind was quiet as broken breaths shuddered through her.

She was crying in her sleep.

He'd done that, he was the reason her tears fell in silence and there was no one there to wipe them away.

Cautiously, Atlas withdrew.

He swirled the decanter of honeyfire once, watching the golden liquid churn. He finished it off, draining the bottle until it was empty, drowning his frustrations and fury in a sea of smoky sweet alcohol. The warmth heated him and blurred his senses, but the flavor died on his tongue, tasting only of regret and poor choices.

Pulling his arm back, he launched the empty bottle, watching as it smashed against the opposite wall. Glass shattered, covering the floor of his bedroom like sharpened crystals.

Atlas swayed once, gripping his bedpost with one hand to keep himself steady. His gaze fixated on his bed where hazy images of a naked Everinne, wet with need and swollen from his kisses, infiltrated his drunken mind. He could imagine her tangled in his sheets, writhing beneath him, bouncing on top of him as he filled her. While his magic heightened every sensation, leaving her trembling with pleasure, and her eyes glazed with lust.

He blinked, and the fantasy evaporated.

His erection, however, did not.

He glanced up at the painting above his bed, the one of the lone wolf running through a dark forest, and he could've sworn the beast snarled.

"Don't judge me," Atlas muttered, stalking into his bathing suite.

Bending over the ivory sink, he turned on the gilded faucet and washed away the blood from his knuckles. He hissed out a breath as the cold water ran over the gashes. Despite the fact that the wounds were already closing, the sting was still fresh. He splashed some water on his face, raking it through his drying hair, then dared to look in the mirror.

His mother's eyes stared back at him, green and gold but lacking her warmth.

Her kindness.

He wasn't sure what he expected to see or hoped to find, but the only thing there was the reflection of an image he'd created on his own. A prince of pleasure. A male who abandoned beds before daybreak because he couldn't remember the name of the female sleeping next to him. Who left a trail of broken hearts and vicious rumors in his wake. Whose magic drew out the best—and worst —in every female who spread their legs for him. Sometimes his power was too much. Too potent. He'd lost track of the number of times he'd been bitten, clawed, scratched, and hit right before bringing one of them to climax. All of that, and he hadn't even lifted a finger. Had barely touched them. It drove them mad with lust, so they were crazed and consumed by it. One female, a witch if he remembered correctly, had grabbed his dick with her pointy nails and tried to force him inside of her. When Atlas pulled back and refused, she'd punched him square in the jaw.

He hadn't used his magic on anyone since then.

Until Everinne.

Fucking Everinne, with her perfect mouth, perfect hips, perfect breasts, perfect everything.

Atlas glared at himself in the mirror.

She saw the same thing as everyone else when she looked at him.

A prince unworthy of the crown on his head, who was barred from court politics by his own father, whose entire life had been relegated to drinking and fucking.

Atlas cocked his arm back and punched the mirror.

It shattered, sending hundreds of pieces scattering like broken diamonds. Blood poured between his busted knuckles, sliding down the back of his hand to his wrist. He was pretty sure a couple chunks of glass were embedded in his skin, but he didn't care.

He staggered backward, kicking aside bits of debris, and

ripped off part of his shirt. He tore the hem of the fine fabric, the loud shred of it echoing in his ears, then clumsily bandaged his hand. Crimson seeped through the silk as he tied it off in a makeshift knot. Perhaps a shower would help him feel better. The new wound on his hand would heal eventually, but as he turned to head toward the granite shower stall, he lost his balance.

The back of his heel caught the clawfoot tub and he toppled backward, throwing his arms out to catch himself.

Were he sober, he might have been able to recover.

But the honeyfire inhibited his reactions, the bathing suite tilted on its axis, and Atlas landed in the tub.

His head smacked the porcelain ledge, sending ricochets of pain down his neck and spine. Black and violet stars danced before his eyes, and he winced as the throbbing ache pierced his temples. With one leg dangling over the curving ledge, he gritted his teeth and grappled with the side of the tub to try to find purchase, but his elbow knocked over a bottle of bath soap, spilling the fragrant contents all over his lap.

"Fucking skies," he mumbled, his bleary gaze struggling to focus on the mess he made while his head continued to pulse and spin.

Heaving out a breath, Atlas tilted his head back and gave up.

"Fuck it." He closed his eyes, ready for the swift blackout that would soon follow. "I'll just sleep here."

* * *

Atlas was on a boat drifting out to sea.

The waters were turbulent, rocking him back and forth, even though the skies were clear. His gut clenched and seized, the honeyfire sloshing around in his stomach like an acidic wave of bad choices. The vessel continued to sway, tossing him from side to side so bile burned in the back of his throat while his head felt as though someone had bashed it in with the hilt of a sword.

He clenched his jaw and inhaled deeply, breathing in the scent of the sea and something else, something vaguely familiar. Voices sounded from behind him. Perhaps they were going to push him overboard and let him drown. He deserved no less than to sink to the bottom of the ocean and spend an eternity in a watery grave.

Again the waves surged and he swayed on his feet, gripping the rail.

Admittedly, he wasn't ready to die just yet.

Why the fuck was he on a boat, anyway?

And who was steering the damn thing?

A swell of ice-cold water fell from the skies and Atlas lurched forward. He coughed, choked, and hacked his way into a state of consciousness. His stomach roiled and his head swam with dizziness as he slowly blinked open his eyes. He was soaked to the bone with soapy bubbles frothing on his pants and one leg flung out over the edge of a tub.

Ah, so not a boat then.

Atlas groaned, sinking down further into the tub. Hazy light spilled into the bathing suite from the framed window, making it nearly impossible to discern the time of day. There was a painful twinge in his neck, his head still ached like he'd been smashed with a brick, and his mouth tasted like old parchment soaked in alcohol.

"Rise and shine, Your Highness." Caedian's gruff voice sounded overhead as he hoisted Atlas out of the tub and hauled him to his feet. Atlas stumbled once, then squeezed one eye shut, trying to focus on his captain's face. Caedian's smooth brow narrowed and his mouth pulled to the side. "Care to explain what happened in here?"

"Fuck off," Atlas grumbled as he ambled toward the sink, pieces of glass crunching beneath his boots. Bubbles slid down his pants and he very much looked like he'd pissed himself. "What did you do? Dump a bucket of water on my head?"

Caedian scoffed. "Thought I might need more than one."

"Might have had better luck if you simply tossed me into the Ladova Bay," Atlas countered, scowling.

"And leave you to drown because of your own foolish indulgences?" His captain barked out a laugh. "Unlikely."

"I see your talk with Everinne went well."

Atlas swung his head in the direction of the other voice, instantly regretting the action. But he saw Veros lounging against the door frame with his arms crossed, a look of mild amusement dancing across his usually somber expression.

"You should be thrilled." Atlas turned on the faucet and hastily brushed his teeth. He washed his face until his fingers were numb from the frigid water. Then he pointed in Veros's direction. "She rejected me."

Veros blanched, his brows lifting slightly. "I honestly didn't think she would."

"Then apparently you don't know your sister as well as you think you do." Grabbing a towel, he scrubbed it over his face and disheveled hair. At least for now, with the mirror busted, he wouldn't have to face his own reflection.

"Everinne claimed she would be my wife in name only, and that I could fuck whoever I want." He tossed the towel aside. "As if I would."

To this, Veros said nothing. Atlas kept his mouth shut while his friend and captain helped him change his clothing. He kicked off the soapy pants and shrugged out of the wet shirt, discarding it on the floor. Though why they felt the need to make him wear proper royal attire was beyond him. They forced him into a pair of black pressed pants with freshly polished boots, a crisp shirt of deep evergreen, and a dark brown vest embroidered with golden threads. At some point, Maxim entered the room and deposited a silver tray filled with a basket of buttery rolls and a steaming cup of tea that smelled faintly of mud and brewed herbs. Since his poor valet had been relieved of his usual duties by both the Lord of Time and the Captain of the Guard, he set to cleaning the disaster left behind from Atlas's drunken rage.

Guilt swarmed him.

His bedchamber was freezing, no thanks to the fact that he'd shattered the glass door leading to his verandah last night. Two walls were in a state of disrepair from his fist, the stench of alcohol hung heavy in the room, and the bathing suite was covered in glass and drops of blood.

"Thank you, Maxim." Atlas grabbed a roll and shoved half of it into his mouth, hoping the bread would soak up some of the honeyfire still churning in his gut. "I apologize for the mess I've created."

Maxim just hummed in response. "I've seen far worse, my prince."

Of that, Atlas had no doubt. His valet was once a great warrior. He reached for the tea next, already knowing what would come.

He glared into the cup of sludge, and while he was grateful for the palace healers and their numerous remedies, he wished this particular one looked a little bit less like the muck scraped off the bottom of his boot. It didn't help matters that it tasted of wet dirt and moldy herbs, either.

His lip curled. "I hate this stuff."

"Unfortunately for you, Your Highness"—Caedian clapped him loudly on the back—"there's no faster way to cure a nasty hangover."

Atlas gulped the murky contents down, then quickly bit off another hunk of bread to get the foul taste out of his mouth. "Can't you just let me go back to sleep?"

"Not a chance." Caedian's gaze slid to where Maxim was sweeping up the remains of the glass door. The sky was the hue of gold and burnt orange. "You slept most of the day away in a drunken stupor and now you have a meeting."

Atlas ran a hand through his rumpled hair, and the messy curls fell into his face. "What meeting?"

Veros cleared his throat. "The one with Eldress Valaina of Morvayne and High Priestess Rozalie of the Coven of the Scarlet Moon."

"You know," Caedian ventured, adjusting the silver leather cuffs on his wrists, "the one you requested as soon as possible."

He arched one white, prominent brow.

Shit.

He was supposed to meet with the Eldress and the High Priestess to discuss the vanishing immortals, but he'd been so caught up with the announcement of his rather abrupt betrothal to Everinne that he'd completely forgotten. Not only was he trying to recover from a self-inflicted hangover, but he wasn't at all prepared for a discussion with two of the highest-ranking members of Prava's society. They would expect him to have a plan, they would demand answers, and he had neither to give them.

"That's today?" Atlas pressed his fingers to his temples, massaging slowly, grateful the pounding ache in his head was already beginning to ease.

"Tonight, yes," Caedian confirmed.

Atlas's gaze slid to Veros. "Are you coming, too?"

The Lord of Time gave a small bow. "If you'd like for me to be there, then I will."

Atlas nodded slowly. He supposed he should ask Everinne to join him, but if he was being honest with himself, he wasn't sure he wanted to see her. Didn't know if he would even be able to face her. Not so long as she continued to deny him and reject their bond. And after he'd kicked her out of his chambers last night, he wouldn't be at all surprised if she didn't want to see him either. There was a good chance his father already knew about their premarital falling out, Atlas hadn't gone to any great lengths to disguise his anger, and every servant and guard Everinne had passed in the halls once she fled his room had likely witnessed her outpouring of tears.

Knowing Oldrich, he'd likely force them to marry sooner rather than later to avoid any chance of scandal. Or escape. The last thing the kralv would want was his reputation smeared by the announcement of a sham engagement, especially one that tied his already scorned son to a female of no noble rank or birthright.

Perhaps this was the kralv's way of inflicting yet another form of punishment upon him.

Either way, Atlas knew he would have to reconcile with Everinne at some point, lest the kralv see fit to make their lives even more of a living hell.

He roughed his knuckles, now fully healed, along the jaw. "Where is Everinne?"

Veros shifted his weight from one foot to the other, and Atlas couldn't recall a time he'd seen his friend so uncomfortable in his own skin. He rubbed the back of his neck with one hand and looked at his boots. "I expected to find her here with you."

Atlas gave a short, humorless laugh. "She's not in her room?"

"I have my team tracking her every movement, Your Highness." Caedian stepped forward, rolled his shoulders, then tucked his hands behind his back. "They followed her out of the palace this morning."

"And she hasn't returned?" Atlas asked.

"Not yet."

"Where was she headed?"

Caedian rocked back onto his heels and stole a glance at Veros. "Northeast, toward the Deszvila Forest."

Atlas's gut clenched, seized with worry. The forest was not safe for anyone. It was more than stories and folklore that haunted the wicked wood, it was a desperate kind of darkness. A ravenous evil. He knew she made careless decisions, but for Everinne to walk into the forest alone with the winter night steadily approaching, that was damn near a death sentence.

"If she has not left on her own by the time the sun sets," Atlas ordered, his tone tainted with warning, "have them go in after her."

He blew out a low breath. Either that, or he would go in and bring her back himself.

Caedian nodded sharply. "Yes, Your Highness."

"Captain?" Veros leaned against the far wall near Atlas's closet, with his arms folded across his chest. Despite the fact that his features remained smooth and unruffled, his shoulders were taut with tension. "Might I have a word with the imperial prince?"

Caedian cocked a brow. "That depends, my lord. Are you planning on attacking His Highness again?"

Veros shoved off the wall and lifted both hands in surrender. "Only if he hits me first."

"Fine." Caedian motioned between the two of them, and the corner of his mouth tugged upward. "But the next time you two brawl, I want to place bets before I'm forced to draw my sword."

He bowed once, then left the room, closing the door soundly behind him.

Atlas popped the collar of his shirt and gave himself a hasty once-over in the floor to ceiling mirror of gilded branches that stood opposite of his bed. "What's on your mind, Veros?"

"I want to know why you proposed to Everinne."

Atlas whipped around to face him. "I didn't."

Confusion clouded the turquoise of Veros's eyes and he frowned. "What?"

"She claimed she was marrying me before I even had the chance to get down on one knee." Atlas shrugged, spreading his hands wide. "I only gave her my mother's ring after the fact."

Veros remained silent for a few moments, then he shoved his hands into his pockets and tilted his head. "You don't find that at all—"

"Suspicious?" Atlas interjected. "Fuck yes, I do. I know damn well she wasn't agreeing to marry me just to get away from that lord of starlight."

"No, I imagine not." He smoothed a few strands of dark brown hair back from his face, tucking them behind his ear. "Nor does it make sense for her to want to marry you, then deny the bond."

Atlas blew out a harsh breath and grabbed another bottle of honeyfire from his wardrobe. "I'll drink to that."

"The hell you will." Veros swiftly plucked it out of his hand. "You need a clear head when you meet with Eldress Valaina and High Priestess Rozalie."

"If I must." Atlas rolled his neck, wincing when it cracked loudly. He pulled open one of the drawers and rummaged through it, finding a crumpled pack of stigs. Flipping the top open, he plucked one out and stuck it between his lips. "Speaking of, have there been any more disappearances?"

"Not yet," Veros muttered. He reached into his pocket and pulled out a lighter. The brilliant blue flame sparked as Veros lit the stig for him, then he snapped it shut and returned it to his pocket.

"Yet..." Atlas repeated, hating the way the word sounded, like an omen. A promising threat of worse things to come. He took a drag of the stig and wisps of floral minty smoke floated in front of him. "You think there will be more?"

Veros turned slowly and faced him. His face was somber as he said, "I think this is only the beginning."

Somehow, hearing Veros utter those words caused tendrils of dread to curl around Atlas. They coated his skin like ice and the hairs along the back of his neck stood on end.

This particular sensation was far worse than the word *yet*.

If Veros's fears were true, then they would need to go beyond the docks, the parlors, and the city for more information. They would need to venture deeper into the underdark of the world below the gilded rooftops of the Golden City.

Atlas stared at his friend and his chest tightened. "I must go to the Marzena."

"The Marzena?" Veros frowned, a line of concern crinkling across his brow. "You're serious?"

"Completely serious." Atlas blew out another puff of smoke.

The Marzena was a maze of damp tunnels and misleading paths located beneath Starysa's streets. It was the sort of place that was only whispered about in darkened alleys, where the dealings were as obscure as those who dwelled there. A market for the occult, where one could find anything from untraceable poisons to necklaces made from merrow scales to jars of still-beating hearts. Clandestine shops were cloaked in shadows, and the underground passages were perfect for trading the invaluable and obscene. The Marzena operated under its own set of rules, out of sight of Kralv Oldrich, who couldn't care less about its existence, and so the foulest of beings made it their domain. Warlocks, demon summoners, and any soul with a penchant for the wicked and cruel took up residence with their illegal wares, striking unbreakable bargains, and demanding payment in blood.

Atlas took another deep inhale of his stig, considering his next words carefully. "If these immortals with rare magic aren't just disappearing...if they're being stolen for sinister reasons, then I guarantee you someone in the Marzena knows something."

Veros nodded, rubbing his lips together. "Are you going to tell the Eldress and High Priestess of your plans?"

Atlas blew out a cloud of smoke and his shoulders fell. "My guess is they already have connections down there. If anything, we're a step behind."

"Damn." Veros slid his timepiece from his pocket, and the golden runes spun and whirred. He snapped it shut and met Atlas's gaze. "When do we go?"

"We?"

"No offense, Your Highness, but sometimes you're a little too cocky for your own good." The corner of Veros's mouth twitched into what could almost be considered a smile. "You'll need someone who knows how to negotiate and strike bargains...if necessary."

The words hung in the air between them, and it was then Atlas realized exactly what Veros was saying.

"You've been there before."

It was a statement of fact, not an accusation.

Veros nodded. "I have."

"When?"

"A story for another time." Veros nodded toward the door. If they didn't leave soon, they would be late for the meeting with Valaina and Rozalie. He reached for the handle, then paused without looking back. "She'll come around, you know."

Everinne.

"Maybe." Atlas rolled his stig between his fingers, the ember almost snuffed out. "She seems pretty adamant on denying the bond."

Veros turned and placed one hand on Atlas's shoulder. His face was solemn and his eyes piercing as he said, "I will only tell you this once, Atlas. Because you are my friend. And because she is my sister."

He drew in a steadying breath. "Everinne never does anything without a reason. She may be brash in her thoughts and make hasty decisions, but it is *always* for a reason. Trust me, her agreeing to marry you and then denying the bond between you both was not done without a purpose."

It wasn't exactly helpful, but it wasn't horrible advice either.

Everinne wanted to marry him for a *reason.*

She'd denied their mating bond for a *reason.*

All Atlas had to do was figure out why.

Unfortunately for him, nothing involving Everinne was ever easy.

Twenty-Seven

Everinne trekked east, toward the outskirts of Starysa, past the towering stone walls that protected the sprawling city's border. The gate was pulled open, its bars lined close enough together to prevent anyone from slipping between them, the tops of them fortified with lethal spikes. Two massive wolf statues were positioned on either side of the gate, carved from dark gray granite with veins of gold. They looked ready to pounce on anyone who dared to enter. Guards patrolled the top of the wall, armed with bows and arrows, and other weapons that were hidden just out of sight behind the rough battlements. Four of them stood near the gate, so still she wasn't even sure they were breathing. Their shiny armor of black and gold marked them as the kralv's watch, and though they said nothing as she passed, she could feel the intensity of their gazes watching her every move.

It wasn't often anyone used the gates, most made the port of the Ladova Bay their point of entry into the city. She would have to return before nightfall if she expected to get home without any trouble.

At least the weather was on her side.

For now, the skies were clear, but she kept her eyes on the

eastern horizon where a bank of heavy clouds toiled just beyond the mountains' highest peaks, carrying the promise of snow. The first snowfall in Starysa was considered a blessing by some ancient goddess whose name had long since been forgotten but was celebrated all the same by the lighting of a bonfire. Each year, the silver flames of faerie fire would burn until the Winter Solstice, then once the longest night finally arrived, the streets were filled with citizens dancing and drinking warm spiced wine until dawn. Already, the haunting evergreens of the Deszvila Forest seemed to beckon the impending frost. Those woods were full of impossibly thick trees whose branches stretched toward the sky like skeletal hands and were covered in coarse green and gold foliage. When snow fell, the branches hung low and heavy, blocking out any shred of sunlight, and delicately sharp icicles dangled from them like the open jaws of a winter monster.

Everinne dipped her chin, burying herself deeper into the warmth of her navy wool coat. Her sweater wasn't nearly enough to keep out the biting chill of the promised winter, but at least this time she'd grabbed her fur-lined maroon leggings to ward off some of the cold. She'd forgotten gloves, so she stuffed her hands into the pockets of her coat, ignoring the wind as it stung her cheeks and slapped her hair in her face.

She veered off the path leading out of the city, her boots crunching against the still-frozen ground, and hesitated.

Trepidation pricked along the back of her neck and her hands, raw and chilled from the cold, grew damp. She squeezed them into tight fists, her chest heaving with shaky breaths. The last time she walked into the wicked wood, she'd been delusional and fractured with heartbreak, yet Zoryana had ensured her safety. This time, however, Everinne had only herself for company, and no guarantees.

But she knew Zoryana was in the woods, knew she was hiding in the secluded hut, where the wards and charms would protect her from the dangers of the Deszvila Forest and Starysa alike.

Everinne had to apologize. She couldn't afford to lose her only friend.

The moment she stepped foot into the woods, the air shifted.

Ancient magic lived here, breathed here. The scent of white pine, ripe berries, and fresh earth surrounded her. Stories were told through the rustling of spindly leaves, memories of the forest's timeworn power carved into the gnarled trunks with whorls and runes, each one older and more riveting than the last. Everinne knew the dangers of this place, she'd caught glimpses of the rare *krázstra*, a reclusive fae bound to a singular tree, whose warm laughter lured the foolish deep into forest, where she ensnared them in her vines and forced them into unjust bargains. Everinne had heard the nightmarish stories of the *baukvist*, or fleshflayers—terrifying beings who ripped the skin from their victims and then wore it as their own—and how they were compelled to kill because the evil of their souls slowly ate away at each new layer of flesh until there was nothing but rot and bones. Perhaps worse than all of that, though, was the way the Deszvila Forest never appeared threatening to her, as though it recognized her.

Like calls to like.

Of course a deadly forest would welcome the one who was touched by death.

Everinne sighed, and her breath puffed before her as she ventured deeper into the woods.

She hadn't stepped foot in the forest in years, not since Zoryana brought her to the Coven of the Scarlet Moon to recover after Everinne killed Callum.

Callum.

Callum, with his kind brown eyes and plain brown hair, with his slightly crooked nose and alarmingly handsome smile.

The image of him had yet to fade from Everinne's mind, despite the passing years.

She'd met Callum at the Grand Cru, they'd danced all night, and though she'd brought him back to her place, he was gone by the time she woke the following morning. It had been disappointing, of course, and while it wasn't the first time a male had slipped from her bed before dawn, the insult still stung. She figured she'd never see him again.

But Callum kept appearing, at the market while she was shopping, at the harbor when she was admiring the ships from other lands, and Everinne had started to wonder if fate had finally played her hand. She'd fallen for him so hard and so fast, found herself drawn in by his easy demeanor and how he made her laugh, and for a few treasured moments in his arms, she didn't feel like one of those monsters in the forest.

Until the night he tried to kill her.

Everinne could still remember his hateful words, the venomous loathing that spewed from his mouth. It was like he'd waited for the perfect timing, had been whittling away at her defenses in preparation to strike her down. She would never forget the feeling of his hand wrapped around her throat, squeezing with the intent to crush, to strangle as the weight of his body pinned her to her bed. Nor would she be able to erase the image of his blade glinting through the night, arcing overhead, aiming right for her heart.

She'd shattered his mind, destroyed him in a breath.

Her magic flowed from her in a torrent and slammed into him, all vengeance and fury. His back bowed, his head snapped back. Blood dripped from his eyes in tears of crimson, his mouth wrenched open in a soundless scream as his veins turned black, and she poured every last measure of violence, of hatred into him, so the pain he felt was excruciating. So he contorted, withered, then died.

A deserving death, especially for him.

Everinne had never understood why Callum had taken so long to attack, why he'd kissed her and fucked her all while wanting to end her life. For some reason, he'd set his mark upon her, and she'd never found out why.

Oh well, she supposed it no longer mattered.

Callum was dead.

And Everinne had spent a month in the Deszvila Forest with Zoryana, protected by the sacred sanctuary of the Coven of the Scarlet Moon. There she stayed with the witches as she attempted to heal her broken heart, as she struggled to come to terms with what she'd done. Recovery had been long, as she had never truly been able to forget about that fateful night. The memories haunted her still, terrorizing her in the form of nightmares and wayward power.

With her hands tucked into the pockets of her coat, she ran her thumb along the underside of her engagement ring and let her thoughts drift to Atlas.

She'd shut her mind off from him this morning after she'd sensed him probing at her thoughts last night. If he wanted to know where she was or who she was with, he could ask her himself. But she wasn't going to make it easy for him. She curled her hands into small fists as she approached the rundown cottage. The roof was barely thatched, and plumes of gray smoke curled out of a crumbling stone chimney, filling the air with the scent of peat and cinnamon. Stormy gray shutters hung from broken hinges, each of them groaning and creaking as the gusting wind threatened to silence them forever. From the outside, the cottage appeared as though it was ready to cave in upon itself and fall apart, but the inside was something else altogether.

It was warm and cozy with multiple bedrooms and comfortable furnishings. Zoryana had never explained how the cottage was glamoured by fae magic deep within the woods, and Everinne had known better than to ask.

She climbed up the front stoop and lifted one hand to knock when the door swung open and High Priestess Rozalie, Zoryana's mother, appeared.

Her hair was a rich brown like Zoryana's, but instead of spiral curls, Rozalie's was straight and chopped short to her chin. She wore a cape of velvet that swirled at her feet like smoke, and her long gown spilled around her in layers like burgundy wine, complete with a crawling ivy of black lace. Rozalie shared her bronze skin tone with Zoryana, as well as her nose, and though their eyes were different shapes, they were the same brilliant jade green.

And right now, those eyes were focused directly on Everinne.

A tiny line furrowed across Rozalie's brow, and she glanced out into the darkening forest.

"Everinne." She shifted, moving so she partially barricaded the entrance of the cottage with her body and the door. "You should not be here."

"I know." Everinne worried her bottom lip, flexing her frozen fingers within her pockets in an effort to keep the blood flowing. Wind whistled through the treetops, so the branches shuddered and moaned. "I was hoping to speak with Zoryana one more time before…"

Before she was no longer allowed to see her only friend.

She swallowed a lump around the words she couldn't say.

Rozalie tilted her head, her plum-colored lips pressing into one another. It wasn't exactly a smile, more like a look of pity. "Zoryana is not here."

Everinne's stomach bottomed out, and her breathing grew shallow. "She's already left?"

"She is safe." The High Priestess fiddled with the silver necklaces she wore around her neck, where charms representing the triple moon jingled together. "Safe from anyone or anything that wishes her harm."

Safe from me, Everinne wanted to say, but she kept those thoughts to herself.

And yet, beneath the layers of burning peat and cinnamon, the wind carried with it sage and juniper, the scent of Zoryana's magic when she absorbed grief or remorse. Everinne's skin tingled.

Rozalie was lying.

"Of course, I understand." Everinne nodded, attempting to

peek around the stoic matriarch of witches. "If you see her, would you please pass along a message from me?"

Rozalie inclined her head, waving one hand through the air for Everinne to continue.

"Tell Zoryana I love her and I'm sorry for the awful things that were said between us." The smell of sage and juniper strengthened, soothing Everinne. "And that if she wishes to reach me upon her return to Prava...she will find me at the palace."

Rozalie's dark brow arched in question. "The palace?"

"I am..." She sucked in a breath and her lungs ached. The bond she had rejected was still there, pulsing softly, connecting her to another soul. "I'm to be married to Prince Atlas."

There was a flicker of interest in Rozalie's bright green eyes. "A most impressive union. I did not realize you and the prince were so fond of one another."

Everinne ducked her head, and her curtain of dark hair billowed in the stiff breeze, hiding her face. "Neither did I."

The lie was weak but she held her ground, slowly lifting her gaze to find the High Priestess watching her intently. Rozalie pursed her lips, considering, then slid two fingers beneath Everinne's chin and gently tilted her face upward.

"Are you pleased by this arrangement?" she asked quietly.

No. Yes.

Kralv Oldrich had blackmailed her into marrying Atlas after discovering the power she wielded, and there was no telling what he would demand of her. Worse, she couldn't risk exposing the bond that had formed between herself and Atlas. If the kralv found out about it, he would use such information to his advantage, ensuring he inflicted as much harm to both of them as possible.

When Everinne failed to respond, Rozalie spoke again, her features softened, and her hand fell away. "Sometimes, the mind tells us lies in an effort to console the heart. We try to reason with logic in order to understand our desires, to make sense of our fate."

Rozalie leaned her weight against the door frame, and the old wood creaked loudly. "But even the moon holds secrets of her own, she too has a dark side. Yet it is not something to fear, but rather embrace."

"Embrace," Everinne repeated, not entirely sure how Rozalie's witchy moon logic applied to her. "It is not easy to embrace the unknown."

"Of course not, darling. The tapestry of the universe is woven by threads of beating hearts, thousands of souls, and archaic magic long since forgotten by those who still breathe." Rozalie cupped Everinne's cheek, the green of her eyes sparkling like mystic seafire. "You wander lost in this world, unable to see the truth of your purpose."

Everinne stiffened. She had no purpose, at least none that could be looked upon as anything other than a curse. It could not be seen as favorable by any gods or goddesses to be born with the power of pain coursing through one's veins. Though Rozalie's touch was warm, the air was suddenly sharp and cold, just like Everinne's tone.

"I am touched by death."

"No, my sweet child of the moon. You are *blessed* by death." Rozalie ran her thumb along the apple of Everinne's cheek, tracing a crescent moon with two uneven lines and a swirl beneath it. "You've been chosen by the moon goddess herself to wield her wild darkness. A strand to forge the grand design between the skies, the stars, and the realms of life. That power within you is an awakening, a reckoning. And you are its one true master, not your fear."

Everinne wanted to believe the high priestess, she wanted to place her trust in the witch and accept her destined path, to regard this moon goddess as a trusted deity. But she knew nothing of covens or the old ways. Instead, her prayers and pleas were thrown into the wind without tradition or ritual, hoping to catch the attention of any god or goddess that might listen.

"How can you be sure?" Everinne asked, her voice far less steady than she had planned.

Rozalie gave a small, non-committal laugh. "Only the Azoura, the three sisters of fate, know all with absolute certainty."

"Mm." Everinne knew nothing about the sisters of fate, though given the way Rozalie spoke of them in such high esteem, she could only assume they were powerful within their own right. Her gaze flicked to the sky, where sparse patches of indigo were barely visible between the tangled branched and feathered leaves. "I should return to the city before I am missed."

Rozalie dipped her chin, her plum-colored lips lifting at the corners. "As you do. Blessed tidings, Everinne Auvyre."

"Blessed tidings." Everinne pulled the hood of her coat over her head to block the wind, and set off, heading away from the lonely cottage in the woods and back toward the city that was so often more frightening than the forest.

She retraced her steps, treading carefully over worn paths that ended abruptly, and past hollowed trunks that seemed to watch her as she walked by them. Her breath puffed before her in a fine mist, the temperature dipping as the inky tendrils of night stretched across the sky. The trees were eerily silent, for there was no birdsong in these wicked woods, no scurrying of woodland creatures, no sign of life save for the creatures of darkness that already dwelled within the Deszvila Forest.

A ripple of unease caused her skin to pebble, and it had nothing to do with the biting wind nipping her cheeks and nose.

She tossed a hasty glance over her shoulder, half expecting to see one of the *baukvist* lurking in the shadows, tracking her every movement, ready to flay the flesh from her bones. But there was nothing there, just an unnatural fog that settled along the forest floor, slinking about as though it held secrets of its own. Gnarled vines curled around the carved trunks of the massively thick trees, slithering and coiling like venomous serpents. The bitter breeze stung her cheeks and scraped past her ears, carrying the coarse whispers of alluring voices, each one an ancient summons. But

Everinne didn't dare look back. When she finally emerged from the dense line of trees and the worn dirt path leading back to Starysa came into view, the canopy of branches shuddered then sighed, though whether it was one of relief or mourning she could not be sure, for the touch of death was no longer in its grasp.

Everinne's footfalls fell steadily on the earth, matching the even beating of her pulse. She replayed her conversation with Rozalie in her head and without warning, her thoughts drifted to Atlas. A spear of agony sliced through her, its blade of torment threatening to sever the bond in half. She clamped one hand over her mouth to keep from gasping, as the pain was wretchedly keen. Part of her wondered if he was still furious with her, she'd wounded him deeply. Despite her harsh words and outright denial, the connection between their souls remained in place. Soft and featherlight, her heart gently caressed the bond. Her hands trembled in hesitation and she clenched them into fists, burrowing herself deeper into her coat. His name echoed through her mind.

"Atlas."

For a moment, there was only silence.

And then...

"Yes, Wildheart?"

The deep rumbling of his voice left her breathless.

Everinne shook her head. Hot tears pricked at the corner of her eyes and she sniffled. *"Nothing."*

Twenty-Eight

A tlas's soul ached.

It didn't matter if he was still furious at Everinne for rejecting him, for denying the bond, because it was there, bleeding from him to her, binding them. He'd heard her whisper his name as keenly as if her lips had brushed his ear, and the sound of her voice in his mind did something to him, left him filled with a deep, insatiable kind of longing. For years, *years*, he'd known she was fated to be his, to belong to him, and he'd suffered in agonizing silence. He'd lost himself to surface level pleasure, pretending the next lover would be good enough, seeing Everinne's face every time he shared the bed of another female. He watched as she danced a waltz with death, slipping further from his grasp with each reckless twirl, and now that the truth was finally splayed open between them, Everinne had struck him where it hurt the most.

There would be time later to convince her to come to her senses, to have her accept him as her mate.

Right now, he had to figure out why immortals with rare magic were vanishing, and who was taking them.

Caedian had chosen the Dancing Nymph as their meeting point with Rozalie and Valaina. While the parlor was ideal for its secluded seating arrangements behind veils of glamour, moody lighting, and a panache for the discreet, Atlas wished his Captain of the Guard had picked a place where he wasn't so famously known.

Atlas had spent more than his fair of time tucked away inside the numerous dancing rooms of the parlor, drinking and fucking his way into a mediocre oblivion. No sooner had they arrived than he was swarmed by half-naked females, each one vying for his attention and whispering lustful promises as he passed them.

Caedian guided him to one of the back rooms of the pleasure hall, where sheer draperies of scarlet and gold swirled like silky mist, framed with black beaded curtains. Music floated between rooms and the winding halls, a low, melodic cadence highlighted by sensual moans. The scent of heady floral perfume lingered in the air, coupled with the minty smoke of freshly lit stigs and expensive alcohol. Gilded floors reflected warm faerie fire from ornately shaped lanterns lining the walls, casting flickering shadows and glimpses of golden light.

A shimmering ward was cast over the far back room of the Dancing Nymph, its gossamer façade impenetrable by sight, allowing those within to speak freely, their voices muffled and unrecognizable to anyone outside of the magical barrier.

Atlas walked through it, with Caedian on his heels, and a tingling sensation floated over him. His skin prickled and the hairs along the back of his neck stood on end as he moved through the layers of enchantment. It was like wading through a river of honey, thick and warm, smelling heavily of citrusy woods.

Inside the room, Veros was already waiting for them. He lounged in an ebony chair, his elbow propped on the cushions, his legs stretched out before him. The Lord of Time was dressed in his court finery—sleek black pants tailored with gold thread, a crisp white button-down shirt, and he twirled the chain of his timepiece around his finger, spinning it through the air. Rozalie was there as well, perched on a crimson sofa that seemed to curve like a wave. The High Priestess watched Atlas carefully as he entered, her sharp green gaze narrowing slightly before she inclined her head in acknowledgement. Valaina was there as well, sprawled on a pile of silk floor pillows, with Davorin standing watch right behind her. His arms were crossed and his mouth was pulled into a harsh scowl, as though he'd rather be anywhere else than in the company of a fae and a witch.

"I assume there's no need for introductions or pleasantries." Atlas discarded his winter coat, tossing it over the back of a chair embroidered with red roses. He rolled the cuffs of his sleeves, meeting the knowing gaze of every soul in the room. "Let's discuss what we know so far."

"Immortals are disappearing." Davorin canted his head to one side, the hue of golden light playing off his deep umber skin. One side of his head was shaved smooth, the rest of his hair falling in long, intricately woven twists to his shoulders. He huffed out a breath of frustration. "And Kralv Oldrich is doing nothing to stop it."

"Exactly. Which is why I'm here." Atlas rolled his neck once, then dropped into the embroidered chair, motioning for Caedian to step forward. "Captain, how many immortals have gone missing?"

Caedian stood at attention, tucking his hands behind his back. "In the course of the past six months, twelve immortals in total. Two vampires, three witches, and seven fae."

He cleared his throat, glancing down at his polished boots. "And those are only the ones whose absences have been noticed and reported."

"There could be more?" Rozalie asked, twisting the large onyx ring she wore around her finger.

"Yes, High Priestess." Caedian nodded firmly, his broad shoulders expanding with tension. "There very well could be many more. Especially when you consider the trooping and solitary fae. Not only that, but we don't know if these disappearances are localized to Prava, or if they are more widespread."

Widespread, meaning other kingdoms and realms...something Atlas hadn't even considered.

"Lord Veros and I were discussing the matter, and one rather distinguishable conclusion has been drawn." Atlas shifted in his seat, leaning his weight to one side. "All of these immortals have something in common."

Davorin scoffed. "Unlikely."

"Hush, Dav darling," Valaina admonished with a wave of her slender hand. "Let the prince speak."

Davorin glowered, his piercing gold eyes narrowing.

Atlas ignored him. "They each possess a rare magic or power."

At that, Davorin seemed to waver on his feet. He rocked back slightly, then squeezed his eyes shut. The vampire's mouth pulled into a hard line, and when he opened his eyes once more, his gaze dipped to where Valaina sat up from the cushions, her long nails sinking into the plush fabric. Her pale blonde hair was piled high on her head, woven into delicate braids and wispy curls. Rubies dangled from her ears and neck like drops of blood, and when she spoke, the lushness of her voice was replaced by a sharpened edge.

"This is terribly distressing." The blue of her eyes grew colder. "More so than I originally imagined."

"Indeed," Rozalie agreed. Though her hands were folded gently in her lap, Atlas took note of the way her knuckles whitened, of the way she gripped her fingers so tightly, he thought she'd snap her own bones. "Your Imperial Highness, if what you and Lord Veros speak is the truth, then these immortals aren't simply disappearing."

Apprehension carved into Atlas's gut, hollowing him out.

Rozalie swallowed, the golden bronze of her cheeks fading slightly. "They're being hunted."

Fuck.

Atlas raked a hand through his hair, shoving the curls back from his face. That singular word haunted him, spread through him like a plague. He stole a glance at Veros, and though his closest friend maintained an expression of calm neutrality, it was his eyes that gave him away. They were a storm of worry, clouded with swells of panic and dread. Atlas hated that he didn't realize it sooner, because the memory that was troubling the Lord of Time was the very same one that tormented him the most.

Everinne had been hunted once.

She'd almost lost her life.

"This should come as no surprise to any of us." Valaina held out her hand to Davorin, and he swiftly pulled her to her feet, his arm wrapping snugly around her waist, their fluid movements blurred around the edges. She rubbed her painted red lips together once. Twice. "They have existed for centuries. Vampire hunters. Witch hunters. Fae hunters. And they've all always had something in common as well."

"Human," Davorin ground the word out as rage rolled off him, flooding the space with tension. "The hunters are always human."

"Wait a minute." Atlas lifted one hand, leveling the fuming vampire with a look of malice. "We cannot just assume the humans, or mortals dwelling within the city limits of Starysa in general, are the ones to blame for this."

"And why not?" Davorin growled, his fangs lengthening. "They've done it before."

A valid point.

The man who hunted Everinne was a human.

Still, doubt prodded at the back of Atlas's mind.

"What motive would they have?" Veros asked, drumming his finger idly along the arm of his chair. Strands of dark hair fell in front of his face, concealing his eyes, but it did nothing to hide his growing disdain for the male vampire. "They are treated as equals here in Prava. They would have no reason to suddenly start ambushing immortals and making off with them in the middle of the night."

"Not only that," Caedian interjected, moving closer to stand by Atlas's chair. "But the humans who live in Starysa specifically aren't exactly educated in magic. They know nothing of our true capabilities, of our raw nature. If they are behind this, and I think the chances of that are incredibly slim, then someone of significant power would have to be the one calling the shots. And the bounty would have to be of great value."

"My dear Captain," Valaina crooned, her smile one of pure seduction laced with poison. "I think you are underestimating the workings of the human mind."

"No offense, Eldress Valaina, but I have fought in many battles, alongside and against mortals. They either believe what they read in books to be truth, or they blindly, if not willingly, accept what someone else tells them." Caedian's gray gaze flicked to where the charmed ward flickered, where shadows passed and laughter ebbed, where the scent of mortal blood mingled with the perfumed air. "Much like wolves, humans work in packs, and there is *always* a leader. Whoever is behind this must be of magical lineage."

Rozalie's brows pinched together, and she studied Caedian with an air of hesitation. "How can you be so certain?"

"Because the mortals have no justification." Veros stood abruptly and shoved his timepiece into his pocket. Annoyance sparked in the rumble of his voice. "No purpose or cause. There's been no discourse, no unrest. What reason would they have to seek some kind of vengeance against immortals?"

Rozalie toyed with the many necklaces she wore, the clinking of metal echoing softly. "Everything comes with a price, my lord. Especially magic."

"That sounds rather ominous," Valaina mused, pursing her deep red lips together.

"And telling," Atlas countered, pinning the High Priestess with a look. "What do you know, Rozalie?"

She seemed unperturbed by the scrutiny of his glare, but her shoulders stiffened all the same. "There are...rumors."

Atlas gestured, spreading both hands wide, waiting for her to elaborate.

Rozalie stood slowly, smoothing her burgundy and lace skirts.

"As you know, the Coven of the Scarlet Moon ventures to the Marzena for certain goods. Herbs, spells, crystals—"

"Get on with it, witch," Davorin interjected.

"Hold your tongue, bloodsucker," Atlas spat, his fists clenching. "Rozalie is a High Priestess, and while you may bed the Eldress of your clan, you are nothing in terms of rank."

Davorin hissed. His eyes darkened to a shade of melted gold and his fangs elongated further, glinting like tiny white daggers. Caedian reached for the hilt of his sword, preparing to withdraw it, but Valaina glided between them in a flurry of silk and malice.

"Enough, Davorin," she admonished, smacking him soundly upon the shoulder.

Atlas redirected his attention to Rozalie, but he felt the burning intensity of Veros's gaze upon him. If anything, her mention of the Marzena was all the confirmation he needed that they would have to venture to the underdark. "Your dealings in the Marzena are your own, High Priestess. Please continue."

"The hollow streets of the Marzena whisper of a dark power. One that seeks to restore what was lost." Again, Rozalie fidgeted with her necklaces, this time clutching the silver one where a pendant shaped like the triple moon hung low. "The Azoura consider it an ill-fated omen."

"What sort of dark power? An entity?" Veros kept his face guarded, but there was an undercurrent of trepidation lurking in the depths of his eyes. He reached into his pocket, clenching the timepiece in his hand. "A force outside our realm?"

"I could not say for certain, my lord. The Scarlet Moon does not loiter in the harrowing alleys of the Marzena." She lifted her chin, the shafts of spilled light and languid shadows hardening the lines of her smooth face. "Even witches know better than to linger for too long amiss the necrotic and vile."

Atlas glanced over at Veros and gave him a solemn nod.

They would go to the Marzena sooner rather than later.

"Keep the members of your coven and clan safe at all costs, but make sure they are all constantly aware of their surroundings." Atlas addressed them as a whole, ensuring they understood the urgency of the matter at hand. If immortals were being hunted, the situation was going to become far more dire. "We must listen for any information possible and never discount where it may come from, whether that be the Marzena, the docks, the parlors, or even the damned Mystic Obscura."

"I despise that place." Rozalie recoiled, her lips curling into a sneer. "I refuse to give any establishment a drop of my blood just for entry."

Atlas winced.

If only he'd been so adamant in denying such a sinister request.

"A few members of our clan have done so, and though they admire the entertainment, they've recently claimed the quality of performers has been rather lackluster." Valaina peered up at Davorin, snapping her fingers. "Though there is that one they all seem to obsess over. Which one was it again?"

Davorin plucked her hand out of the air and brushed a kiss across her knuckles. "The hoop dancer, *milazk.*"

Atlas faltered.

"Hoop dancer," he repeated numbly. "What does she look like?"

"I hear she's absolutely stunning," Valaina gushed, her frosty blue eyes warming with delight. "Positively ravishing."

"She's fae." Davorin nodded and scraped his fangs along his bottom lip, crimson bleeding into the gold of his eyes. "Long, wavy hair. Dark like the wicked woods, easy to grab a fistful. Eyes the color of the Ladova Bay. Slender, elegant neck."

Atlas damn near exploded. "That's Everinne."

His Everinne.

Davorin looked like he couldn't wait to sink his fangs, and possibly something else, right into her.

"Everinne?" Valaina whipped around to face Atlas, her lashes fluttering back in shock. "As in the future Princess of Prava?"

When his mouth fell open to deflect, she offered an innocent lift of her shoulders. "Rumors spread fast in the Golden City, Your Highness."

"What's your future wife doing working at the Mystic Obscura?" Davorin asked, his brows lifting in silent challenge.

"It was a mistake." His gaze cut to Veros. "A lapse in judgement. She's going to quit as soon as we're wed."

Whether she wanted to or not.

Valaina stared at him, and though she was usually rather pale, right now it looked as though death had her by the neck and was refusing to let go. "Atlas, darling. It will not be so easy. Everinne won't be able to just walk away. Not from the Mystic Obscura, and certainly not from Reine."

His gut turned acidic. There was something ominous about the way Valaina spoke, something that filled him with a sensation he had not felt in many years.

Fear.

"What do you mean?" he demanded, alarm needling its way down his spine.

Davorin shook his head once. "There's no way out."

"Those who work at the Mystic Obscura never leave." Valaina's expression softened into one of sympathy, and her eyes shone with regret. "If Everinne has given them her blood, she belongs to them."

Atlas's heart lurched. Bile scalded the back of his throat. "How do you know this?"

Valaina shared a look with Davorin, squeezed his arm, and when she glanced back at Atlas, her face was solemn. "Reine told us."

Fucking skies.

There had to be a way to get her out, to break her free from the Mystic Obscura's clutches. This was all Jarek's fault. That damned demon summoner had lured her in, appealed to her reckless nature, then snared her in his web of deceit. Worse, if they had a single drop of her blood, they would *know* what she was capable of, they would know about her power. Atlas clenched his fists, his nails biting into his palms. If they used her for her magic, if they harmed her in any way, he would kill them all.

Atlas pushed up from his chair, pacing. He shoved his hands through his hair, his boots clicking soundly against the hardwood of the room. "There has to be something I can do."

He wouldn't leave her there. Not with Jarek. Not with Reine. Not with any of them.

"There is only one way." Valaina's voice was too soft, too quiet. He barely heard her over the erratic beating of his own fucking heart.

"Name it," he growled. "Whatever the price, I'll pay it."

The light in Valaina's eyes dimmed as she said, "If you want to get Everinne out, you'll have to bargain for her life."

Twenty-Nine

Everinne danced upon the hoop high above the stage of the Mystic Obscura. She let it cradle her like the moon as she balanced with pointed toes and outstretched arms. She arched her back, stretching her legs into the opposite direction as the tips of her fingers grazed the glamoured, barren tree limbs reaching for her. Magic rippled through her as she spun and twirled, moving like a wraith above the skeletal branches. Dramatic chords of an evocative harmony pulsed all around her, tempting her to perform one harrowing feat after another, pushing her to risk more with each perilous act.

Reine's chosen theme for the Mystic Obscura closely resembled that of the Deszvila Forest, so similar that it left Everinne's palms clammy and her stomach tangled in unforgiving knots. Her stage was encircled with spindly trees that groaned and swayed in time to the chilling cadence of music. Though it was nothing more than a complex use of glamour, she felt the scrape and snare of the prickly branches on her thighs and arms with every pass. Below her, the menagerie was designed to look like a labyrinth of darkened woods, a forest that shifted to close off and reveal different paths, leaving those who wandered in search of revelry to become disoriented and confused. Free-flowing fountains gurgled with blood red wine and ominous silver faerie fire rained upon the tiered seating and balconies like beams of fractured moonlight. Female performers were dressed as dryads and forest sprites, wearing little more than swaths of fur or glittering leaves to lure unsuspecting patrons into sordid bargains. The males stalked about, taking on the appearance of the gangly *baukvist*—they wore fabric in varying shades that clung to their muscular frames, embellished with fire rubies and onyx to appear like bloodied, decaying flesh.

The entire atmosphere left Everinne unsettled.

It made her skin crawl to see so many revel in the lore of the wicked wood.

Not long ago, the hoops had been like home to her. She loved to feel like she was dancing in the night sky, weightless and free. Performing had been its own kind of high. On the hoops she wasn't death touched, she wasn't the sister of the Lord of Time, she wasn't Everinne...the reckless fae who made careless decisions and drowned herself in alcohol to avoid her nightmares. She was simply a fae with no name, whose mesmerizing talent held onlookers captive. But the air of the Mystic Obscura had changed, it was charged with a kind of threatening energy, one that left her feeling exposed and unsteady. Even the audience seemed more feral. Instead of gasps of awe and applause, she could hear their lewd calls and shouts demanding more from her over the hypnotic thrum of the music.

Everinne had never been so glad to finish a routine in her life.

Worse, she didn't ever want to do it again. She wanted to go home.

She quickened her pace as she navigated the lower level of the Mystic Obscura, aiming for the dressing rooms. The sooner she changed into her clothing, the sooner she could leave this place and never look back. Yanking open the door of the dressing room, she bolted inside, closing it soundly behind her.

A few other dancers startled at her abrupt entrance, and while they offered her polite smiles, their conversation easily returned to elusive whispers of confidence.

Everinne considered grabbing her clothing and just walking out, when she spied a shock of pink hair in the far corner of the room.

"Aisling!" She hurried over to her only other friend. "There you are. I haven't seen you since you left the ball."

"Oh, I should apologize for my hasty departure." Aisling stood from the chair in front of the vanity and planted a kiss on each of Everinne's cheeks. "Reine required my assistance back here, something about needing help with runes and charms."

Everinne opened her mouth to ask about the runes and charms, to maybe see if she could unearth some more information, but Aisling continued speaking, giving her no time to interject.

"What do you think of my new costume?" she asked, doing a little twirl. "I feel like the rhinestones and pearls give it just the right amount of sparkle."

Aisling looked like a snow princess in the best possible way. Frosty pink blush was dusted on the apples of her cheeks and her cerulean eyes were lined heavily with kohl. The sleeves of her bodice were shimmering white lace and bejeweled with crystal beads. Pearls dotted her low neckline and waist, where layers of pristine satin fell to her thighs, embellished with wisps of gossamer. Her hair was piled high into an ornate bun and some of the vibrant pink was threaded with strands of snowy white. The crowning touch was a silver tiara shaped like mountains that twinkled like stardust on top of her head.

"It's beautiful." Everinne admired her, canting her head to the side. "I've noticed you like the wintry, frostbitten looks."

"Winter is in my blood." An emotion banked deep in her eyes, and she hid it away before Everinne could discern its meaning. She grabbed her shoulders and gave them a gentle squeeze. "But tell me about you. Is it true you're engaged to the Prince of Prava?"

"Yes." Everinne lifted her hand to show off the ring and the teal sapphire glinted in the low light of the dressing room. "It all happened rather quickly."

"I didn't even know you were courting him!" Aisling squealed, then lowered her voice as the other performers glanced over at them, curiosity drawn all over their painted faces. "Have you set a date?"

"Not yet." Everinne scraped her teeth along her bottom lip, ignoring Aisling's first comment. "Though I imagine we'll marry sooner rather than later. The kralv has made his sentiments known, he's eager for his son to sire an heir. Once I'm pregnant, I'll be cast aside. The prince will have no use for me, and we both know his reputation precedes him."

The words were out of her mouth before she could stop them. No sooner had she spoken, than she regretted it. Especially since she already claimed she would be his wife in name only. It had been a callous, wretched thing to say. If anything, she knew Atlas would be faithful to her, he'd proclaimed as much himself. But she couldn't help but wonder if the fear of him choosing to bed others was more deeply ingrained within her, like it was wedged between what she knew to be true and her own lack of self-worth.

"Ever." Aisling's smile faded and a line of concern crinkled its way across her brow. She shot a glance toward the other performers who were filing out of the dressing room. "If you don't want to marry the prince, you can say no. Nothing is binding you to him. If you don't want to go through with this, just say no."

"I can't." Everinne sucked in a shallow breath. She couldn't walk away from this engagement, not without facing the kralv's wrath. And as much as she wanted to tell Aisling that she was bound to Atlas, that he was her *mate*, she kept silent. "I have no choice."

Aisling frowned, planting both hands on her hips. "What do you mean?"

"It's done. I'm marrying Prince Atlas." Everinne shook her

head, struggling with the laces of her corset. The sleek black ribbons slipped through her fingers, the bodice suddenly so snug, she couldn't quite catch her breath. "And honestly, it couldn't come soon enough. He doesn't want me to work here anymore and after tonight, I'm not sure I would want to stay."

The light in Aisling's eyes dimmed, snuffed out completely. "You plan to...leave?"

"I'm not sure I have much of a choice in the matter." That seemed to be the way of her life as of late. She pressed her fingertips to her temples to alleviate some of the pressure building there. "I'll be a princess, and I highly doubt it will go over very well to have a royal working at one of Starysa's exclusive parlors."

"No, I suppose that would be frowned upon indeed." Aisling grabbed a rose-colored pot from the vanity and applied a thin layer of shimmery gloss to her lips. Rubbing them together, she turned back to Everinne. "Um, tell me, did you give Reine a drop of your blood?"

Everinne shifted her weight, uncomfortable in her own skin. Again, she tugged on the laces of her corset to loosen them, but they only seemed to squeeze her waist tighter, until she thought her ribs would crack.

"Unfortunately." The word left her on a breathless rasp.

"Oh. Oh, I see." Aisling fiddled with her silver diamond earrings that dangled like dancing snowflakes. "That might make things more complicated."

Everinne paused, eyeing her friend.

Aisling looked anxious and ill at ease. Her worried blue gaze darted from the door of the dressing room to the racks of glittering costumes, then back again. She twisted the hem of her white satin skirt, threading the fine fabric between her fingers until it wrinkled.

"Complicated, how?" Everinne asked cautiously, not entirely sure she wanted to hear the answer.

Aisling sighed, the weight of whatever she was about to say

expelling from her in a heavy rush of air. "The blood is binding, Everinne."

Everinne's heart lodged in the back of her throat. "Binding?"

"Yes. When she takes a drop of your blood, she imbues it into the runes marking the entrance of the Mystic Obscura. But... there's a catch. It's different for performers as opposed to the patrons who want only to be entertained." Aisling closed the distance between them and took Everinne's hands, linking their fingers together. "Our blood binds us to the Mystic Obscura. To Reine."

Everinne's stomach lurched, dread roiled within her like a pit of acidic despair. Her palms became cool and damp, and she clutched Aisling's hands tighter. "For how long?"

The pretty rose hue coloring Aisling's cheeks waned. "Forever."

Bile scalded the back of Everinne's throat, she should have listened to Atlas, to Veros, but before she could respond, the door of the dressing room groaned open. She half expected it to be Reine, but it was Jarek who stood there instead, and his honey-colored eyes were zeroed in on her.

He wore a steel gray overcoat that fell around him like churning storm clouds and a black ribbed sweater that hugged his muscular frame. His pants were trim and tucked into polished boots with silver chains that clinked together as he stepped into the dressing room. He'd slicked back his brown hair so it swept away from his face, and his jaw was clenched so severely, Everinne swore she could strike a match against his cut jawline and it would ignite. Skull rings still adorned his fingers, but she didn't miss the way his hands fisted at his side before he quickly relaxed them. His gaze flicked toward Aisling, and he jerked his head to the open door.

"I require a word with Everinne." His voice was cold, lacking its usual charm, and it was as though his very presence leached all the warmth from the room.

A shiver of trepidation trekked down Everinne's spine, and

though she held onto Aisling's hands firmly, her friend pulled herself from her grasp.

"Of course, Jarek." Aisling ducked her head and shuffled past him, like she was trying to make herself as small as possible to avoid any more of his notice. "I was just leaving."

Jarek waited until she left, until the door clicked closed behind her, before he spoke. He tucked his hands behind his back, leveling her with a penetrating stare. "I'm glad I caught you. I wanted to offer my congratulations."

Everinne found that very difficult to believe.

"Thank you, but if you'd excuse me, I need to change." She forced a practiced smile, hoping she wouldn't give herself away. The last thing she wanted was for him to have the upper hand, for him to know his company left her tense, radiating with apprehension.

"I quite like what you're wearing now," he drawled, his gaze slowly raking over her.

He tracked the midnight satin bodice that was intolerably snug, seeming to admire the way it shoved up her breasts and cinched her waist to the point of pain. His eyes dipped lower, to the high cut of the bodysuit that put her hips on full display, then to the sheer, diamond-studded stockings that clung to her upper thighs. She fought back the urge to squirm beneath his lingering assessment, wishing she'd chosen to wear boots instead of absurdly high heels, as they would be much easier to run in if she found herself needing to escape.

The urge to flee was growing increasingly stronger with each passing second.

Jarek strode over to the vanity and propped himself against its cluttered edge, folding his arms across his broad chest. The skull rings he wore twinkled in the glowing lights above him.

"So, the Prince of Prava," he mused, running his tongue along his teeth. "I never would have pegged you for the blond royal type."

Everinne stiffened, locking her spine and rolling her shoulders back. "I don't have a type."

"Don't you though?" He angled his head as he considered her, one dark brow raising in question.

"You fancy males who walk with an air of danger, whose very kiss could mean life or death. Isn't that the sort that usually draws your eye?" Jarek shoved off the vanity and strode closer, and it took every ounce of her willpower not to step away from him. "Prince Atlas pined over you for years, but his loyalty to your brother held him back. And Callum...well, he lusted after his faerie prize, even though he was sworn to slay you. So, perhaps that was where I went wrong by moving too quickly. I should have chased you first."

Everinne swallowed her shock, and a spike of fear lanced straight through her heart. Alarm pebbled her skin with goose-bumps, and she suppressed a shudder. Her magic snarled at the threat and she wrapped her arms around herself, grasping at the fraying fibers of her control. She could not lose herself to her power here, not in front of Jarek. It was bad enough Kralv Oldrich intended to wield her as a weapon for his own devices, and the last thing she wanted to do was fall prey to another male's desire to command her. She had no idea how Jarek knew about Callum, but she would not give him the satisfaction of realizing he'd taken her by surprise. Nor would she display any outward panic, no matter how unsettled his words left her.

He inhaled deeply, as if trying to pinpoint her scent. "Is that it? Would the pretty Everinne Auvyre prefer to be hunted?"

Her heartbeat quickened.

"I don't know what you're talking about." She attempted to dismiss his claims with casual indifference, but her voice wavered, shaking her confidence.

Jarek loomed over her, and he grazed her cheek with his knuckles, the metal of the skull rings he wore chilling her skin. "Pity you chose him over me. We could have been so good together."

"My choices are my own," she muttered, even if they were forced upon her.

"So they are." The corner of his mouth curved in a wicked half smile. "Come with me to the afterparty tonight."

"I'm afraid I'm needed at the palace. Atlas is expecting my return." Everinne turned away in search of her clothing. There was no time to change. She needed to grab everything and go, otherwise she might not ever get out. "My absence will be noticed."

Cold fingers gripped the back of her neck and she froze, panic rushing over her in crashing waves. Dark magic prodded at her mind, seeking entry. It assaulted her, pinning her in place, and her head snapped backward. Screams and pleas for mercy echoed in her ears, the sound of a thousand lost souls. She winced, squeezing her eyes shut, as a whimper escaped her and the pungent scent of ash and brimstone overwhelmed her senses.

"You mistake me, *milazk.*" Jarek kept his hand planted firmly in place, refusing to release her. He applied more pressure, until his fingers were bruising, forcing her to look up into his face where she finally saw the truth of his power. His eyes burned with the flames of an inferno and his flesh thinned to reveal the monster lurking beneath the disguise. A vile and wicked demon summoner. His evil grin sharpened and Everinne's knees almost gave out from under her. "I am not asking."

* * *

The chilling grip of Jarek's fingers remained firmly clamped around the back of Everinne's neck as he guided her out of the dressing room and into the dimly lit, shimmering halls beneath the Mystic Obscura. Instead of returning to the menagerie, however, it seemed as though he was taking her to another lower level altogether.

Gradually, the smooth corridor gave way to a damp tunnel of crumbling brick. The gleaming lights of bronze sconces were replaced with makeshift torches fastened to the walls, the flames of faerie fire burning a violent red. They descended a winding stairwell of uneven stone, each step taking her further into a convoluted maze of underground passages. The air was cool yet thick, like walking through a dense layer of fog in the Deszvila Forest, coating her skin like the touch of death.

Her magic pulsed through her veins, harbored yet restless, as though it was waiting for something. It was the first time in years Everinne could sense the monstrous power inside her awaken without being subjected to the turmoil of her emotions. For once she was calm, if not slightly unnerved, and though her deadly magic stirred to life, it did not riot or seek to escape her control. The darkness she possessed seemed to prowl, like it was on the hunt, and her fingers tingled in response. She coiled her hands into fists, taking in her increasingly daunting surroundings, and whispered words of pleading tranquility through her mind in an effort to quell the rising angst.

"Where is this afterparty, exactly?" she asked, her harsh whisper echoing off the cavernous walls surrounding them.

Jarek barely spared her a glance. "It's in the Marzena."

Everinne dug her heels into the stone and drew up short. "What?"

His answering chuckle did little to alleviate her growing dread. He looked over at her then, and the slashes of red fire-light illuminated the sharp planes of his face, making him appear possessed. His sadistic smile reminded her of a story she'd heard as a child, about a bloodthirsty demon who used his charm to lure heedless maidens into the wicked woods of Prava, where he tempted them with promises of everlasting beauty and immortality if they swore to give their virtue to him. Some were willing, some were not, but he took them either way, claiming the young females as his own. It was said that during whatever carnal act he forced upon them, he sank his fangs into their breast and drained them of their blood. Once his spend was inside the maidens, their skin turned a charred crimson, their hair fell in stringy clumps, and they were doomed to wander the forest for an eternity as nothing more than the husk of a lost soul.

Zolvost, the Demon of Lust, is what everyone called him, and his creations were *deszlings*.

The first time Everinne ever heard that story, she vowed to never give herself to a demon, no matter what promises they made.

Jarek applied more pressure to her neck, his nails biting against her soft flesh, urging her forward. "Don't tell me you're afraid?"

"I'm not afraid," Everinne scoffed, forging her spine into steel. At least not of the Marzena. "I'm just wary."

Because she knew if she ventured into the Marzena with him, she might not ever be found.

Zoryana had been there before a handful of times with her mother, Rozalie, and the accounts she'd given Everinne were both intriguing and frightening. The Marzena was filled with shops of the cryptic, a place where one could sell secrets in exchange for goods or wares both mystical and diabolic in nature. It was a market for the unfamiliar, the bizarre, and eccentric—not once had Everinne imagined it would also house taverns and parlors, but that was exactly what she discovered.

Doors were built into the side of archaic brick walls, some of them carved with runes or words in other languages Everinne couldn't read or decipher. Panes of glass were crushed between cave openings and held in place with bronze bars. They were grimy and decorated with cobwebs, making it almost impossible to see what lay beyond the murky windows. Dozens of people loitered in the dank tunnels—witches, fae, and vampires alike—most of them smoking stigs, sipping drinks, and speaking in hushed tones. She felt their eyes latch onto her as she passed, appraising her like she was ripe for the picking, and despite her better judgment, she inched closer to Jarek's side.

"Never been down here before, have you?" Jarek murmured,

pausing in front of a nondescript door engraved with whorls and jagged runes.

"I can't say I've ever had the need, it's like a whole other..." Everinne's voice trailed off as Jarek knocked on the door and the design of the runes glowed an ethereal blue color.

"World?" he suggested and pulled the door wide. "You could say that."

His hand released her neck and moved to the small of her back, ushering her into a cramped alcove where wraith-like arms sifted in the shadows, reaching from the dank, arching walls to grab her. Phantom fingertips skimmed her hips and abdomen, the frozen tendrils curling around her throat and tangling in her hair. She smacked at them, panic building and bubbling inside her as the icy ribbons of death grabbed at her thighs.

"Keep walking." Jarek nudged her toward a hollow exit where a glow of amber light flickered, as though it might sputter out at any moment. "If you stop moving, they'll steal your soul."

She snorted, her lip curling. "What, like you?"

"I don't steal souls, Ever." He snared her wrist and dragged her into the golden wash of amber light. "I sell them."

Her mouth fell open in horror as he dragged her further into a room where the crush of bodies was overwhelming. Stagnant air tainted with the stench of mildew, sweat, and cheap alcohol assaulted her, caused her head to spin and her pulse to pound. There was music, but it was a low, dull thumping kind of sound, and could barely be heard over the cacophony of voices resonating up into the vaulted ceiling. A rickety bar was shoved against the far corner, made from uneven hardwood planks and a slab of black marble. Lanterns of cold iron swung overhead from rusty chains, and the lethal metallic odor sent a tremor of awareness skittering down her spine.

Not safe. The words blared in the back of her mind.

This place was not safe.

She needed to leave. Immediately.

But Jarek's grip on her wrist was like a clamp of cold iron. Powerful and deadly.

Everywhere she looked, she was met with more of the same—people dressed in varying shades of black—some wore long dresses, others were in skin-tight pants and tops that barely covered their breasts. The males were in pants, many of them without shirts, their muscled bodies glinting with the sheen of sweat. They moved and swayed in tandem, shouting over one another as they lost themselves to the hypnotic beat of music she couldn't quite hear.

"Drink up." Jarek shoved a glass into her hands, and she frowned at the gold-colored substance.

"What is it?" she asked, sniffing. It smelled of whiskey and herbs, not at all appealing. Not to mention the glass was dingy and looked as though it had never been washed.

"Drink first," he ordered, tilting the cup to her mouth. "Questions later."

Everinne intended to only take a small sip, but then Jarek grabbed the bottom of the glass and lifted it, forcing the tepid contents down her throat. She winced and choked the alcohol down, hating the way it spilled from the corner of her mouth to her chin. It burned like whiskey, but tasted of pine, rotten berries, and dirt. Swallowing hard, Everinne knocked his hand away and jerked backward.

"What the hell was that for?" she rasped, wishing she had a glass of water to wash the foul contents out of her mouth.

"Questions later," he repeated, sliding his thumb along her bottom lip. Jarek's eyes glowed with demonic power, the honey-gold of them streaked with tiny veins of black. "Dance with me."

"No." She shook her head. "I don't think that's a good idea."

Already, tiny beads of sweat gathered at the nape of her neck and slid down her spine. The alcohol had settled in the pit of her gut, where it sloshed and soured her stomach. Excessive warmth spread through her, as though her entire body was engulfed in white-hot flames, likely the result of whatever drink Jarek had given her. She blinked, and the world swirled into a blend of misshapen forms and muted colors.

"You're not married yet, Everinne. One dance won't hurt." Jarek was closer now, looming over her. She listed to one side, and he caught her by her waist. "Besides, do you remember who you're marrying? I highly doubt Prince Atlas is sitting at home in his palace waiting for you to return. He earned his reputation for a reason."

"No...that's not, that's not the real Atlas." Everinne frowned, trying to focus on Jarek's face, but it was blurry, and a wave of nausea swept through her. "I know him."

"Sure you do." He hauled her against him, fisting his hand against her lower back, and tugged.

The laces of her corset pulled tight, and she stumbled into him, gasping for air. He yanked harder and the bones lining the bodice dug into her ribs, crushing her lungs. She thrashed against him, tried to fight him off, but her movements were slow and sluggish, like slogging through a mountain of wet sand. Heat bled into her cheeks, and she sucked in a labored breath. Again, she twisted, attempting to claw her way out of his hold, when something stung her shoulder.

Everinne screamed.

Hot pain seared her skin, so intense that her vision went black, and for a moment, she thought she would pass out. Ash and brimstone clogged her senses, making it impossible to breathe. Jarek released her then, smirking as she stumbled away from him. Her knees nearly gave out and she staggered backward, trying desperately not to trip over her own feet. Dazed, she veered through the crowd of people dancing and shouting, her inability to remain upright increasing with every passing second. Her mind was muddled, full of incoherent musings and disoriented thoughts as she was jostled and groped, trying to find her way out.

There was a swell of movement behind her, and she pitched forward, slamming right into a solid wall.

She threw her hands up, recognizing cool satin beneath her palms.

Not a wall then, but a chest.

"So...s-sorry." Everinne's knees weakened, and she thought the floor might fall out from under her until a strong hand wrapped around her arm.

"Easy there," a masculine voice sounded from somewhere above her.

Above? Was she on the ground? She could no longer tell the difference. She craned her neck back, blinking rapidly to see who, or what, had caught her this time. Cast half in shadows, she peered up and spied a handsome face, long twists of midnight hair, and the flash of fangs.

Perfect.

A vampire.

"I know you." His velvety voice seemed to be everywhere at once, like a distant echo.

Everinne tried to shake her head, but her whole body moved, and bile scalded the back of her throat. She was going to be sick.

"Yes, I do," said the vampire. "You dance at the Mystic Obscura. I've seen you there. But you're also engaged to the Prince of Prava, are you not?"

Prince. Atlas. Home.

"Atlas." She managed to get his name out in one long, sluggish sound.

Her knees softened and her head lolled to the side. Each breath was a fight. She swore she was burning, that she'd been devoured by riotous flames, but her teeth were chattering and her hands were like ice.

The vampire took hold of her other arm. "What in the bleeding skies are you doing here?"

"Please," she croaked, her voice hoarse. Her tongue felt thick and papery. "I need...home."

"Yeah, I'd say so." He braced her elbow with his hand. "Come on, I'll get you back to the palace."

"What's..." Her eyelids continued to droop until she wasn't sure she could keep them open any longer. "Name?"

"You can call me Davorin."

She repeated his name in her mind, but it came out all wrong, slurred together and unintelligible. "Dav...vrrrin"

"Don't hurt yourself," he grumbled. He wrapped one arm around her waist, then scooped her off her feet. "Hold on to me and don't let go."

Everinne clutched at the satin of his shirt, slumping against his chest. She squeezed her eyes shut as the world swirled around her in a haze of colors. Frigid air and the rush of power surrounded her, cryptic and dark, and then there was nothing at all.

Thirty

"Where the fuck is she?" Atlas demanded, stalking about his study like a caged beast, ready to rip through the bars enclosing him. He slammed both of his hands on his desk, sending notes and pieces of parchment scattering to the floor. "Everinne should be back by now."

He was furious with himself. With everyone. He'd been unkind to her two nights before, when he'd thrown a towel at her and sent her from his chambers. But damn it, she'd pissed him off. Left him infuriated. He knew she'd been lying about the bond, he knew she could feel it, yet she'd seen fit to deny it, anyway. If he'd been more rational at the time, if he'd managed to control his temper, he would've seen right through the impenetrable wall she'd constructed around herself. He would have realized she was trying to push him away on purpose, but he still didn't understand why.

His gaze flicked to the timepiece ticking steady against the far wall, its bronze hands creeping closer to the early morning hour.

"The guards are searching all of Prava for her, Your Highness." Caedian straightened, tucking his hands behind her back. "They tracked her into the Deszvila Forest and then back to the city. But she went into the Mystic Obscura and never came back out."

Atlas ground his teeth together, clenching his jaw so tightly, a painful ache throbbed at his temples, beating in time to his chaotic heart. "Something is wrong. This isn't like her."

"This is exactly like her," Veros stated from where he sat in a high-back brown leather chair. His elbow was propped on the rounded arm, and he had one ankle kicked up, resting upon his knee. He gestured vaguely, his hand swiveling through the space between them. "She hates this palace. She hates me. She hates you. Why would she want to come back?"

Veros's chest rose and fell with a heavy sigh. "This is all my fault."

"It's not your burden to bear, Veros. If anything, this is my doing. I told her to get out, perhaps she took me at my word." Atlas raked his hands through his hair, turning to the window behind him where hues of pink and orange streaked across the eastern sky, pushing back the fading night. Beyond the city walls, the tops of ancient evergreens were set against a backdrop of cold, snow-capped mountains. "Why would she go to the woods first?"

"My guess is she wished to see Zoryana," Veros muttered, his voice tainted with remorse. "Many of the witches have fled Starysa to escape the possibility of being hunted."

Hunted.

Atlas always hated that word.

"If Everinne is still in the Mystic Obscura, then I have to find a way to get her out." Atlas spun back to face Veros and Caedian and gripped the edge of the desk, his nails biting into the glossy hardwood. "And if what Valaina said is true, then I have to free Everinne from Reine's hold. There's no more time to waste."

"We need a plan, Atlas." Veros was attempting to reason with him, but it was futile. They both already knew what must be done. "You can't just walk into the Mystic Obscura and—"

Two heavy thuds sounded against the door of the study, like someone was trying to kick it open.

Atlas lifted one hand. "Caed, answer the door. Be mindful of who is on the other side."

Caedian nodded sharply and strode to the door. He opened it a crack before yanking it the rest of the way, and when he stepped back, Atlas's heart dropped.

One of his guards stood framed in the doorway, and in his arms was Everinne.

She was limp and pale, likely unconscious given the way her head lolled back, and her lips were a terrifying shade of purple. Her skin was mottled with what could be mistaken for bruises. The discolored splotches were everywhere, slowly spreading like ink through her veins, creating webs that crawled over her neck, legs, and breasts.

Atlas rushed toward the guard and collected her into his arms. Her body sagged against him, her breathing was labored, and the beating of her heart was much too slow. He glanced over at the guard. "What happened to her?"

"I think she's drunk, Your Imperial Highness." But the guard's voice quivered, as though he didn't quite believe it.

Atlas inhaled deeply, breathing in the faint scent of alcohol. But there was something else. It lingered beneath the layers of sweat and damp air. Suffocating ash. Acrid brimstone. The stench of a demon summoner.

Jarek.

Rage flooded Atlas's veins, boiling his blood. If that bastard had harmed her, if he had so much as touched a single hair on her head, Atlas would end his life. His gaze raked over her, and it was then he saw it, the tender flesh of her shoulder was raw and pink, as though she'd been burned. The impression resembled the shape of a skull, and the slightest whiff of metal still carried on her skin. That fucking prick had marked her with cold iron. He'd *branded* her.

"Where did you find her?" Atlas asked, his tone laced with venom.

"I didn't, Your Imperial Highness." The guard's back snapped straight and he stood at attention. "She was delivered."

"What, like a package?" Caedian spat, fury radiating from him.

The guard ducked his head, shame coloring his cheeks. "Davorin of the Morvayne vampire clan dropped her off only a few moments ago. He said he found her in the Marzena and that I should bring her to His Highness immediately. He also apologized for not being able to bring her to you himself..." The guard nodded behind them toward the window. "The sun, you see."

"Thank you," Atlas mumbled, then moved quickly through the connecting doors that led to his bedchamber, with Veros and Caedian on his heels.

He carefully laid Everinne onto his bed and she slumped against the plush mattress, unmoving.

"Caedian, fetch a healer at once," Atlas commanded, pulling a small dagger from the inside of his boot. "Whatever is in her system, it is more than just alcohol."

"Yes, Your Highness." Caedian bowed then bolted from the room, his retreating footfalls echoing in the stillness of the morning.

Veros leaned over from the other side of the bed, pressing the back of his hand to Everinne's forehead, and then her cheek. "She's feverish."

"I know. Open the verandah doors."

Veros did as he was instructed, flipping the latch and wrenching them open wide. A gust of frozen winter air flooded Atlas's chambers. The fire in the hearth wavered and sputtered, and goosebumps pebbled all over Everinne's flesh, but she did not stir.

Atlas looked at his friend, leveling him with a hard stare. "If you have any qualms about seeing your sister naked, look away now."

He aimed the dagger at her bodice.

Veros lurched forward, grabbing his wrist. "What are you doing?"

"I'm going to cut her clothing off of her, it will be much faster than dealing with all the laces on the back of her corset." Atlas pulled his hand free, then slid the sharpened edge of the blade under the thick fabric and set to work. "If we don't get her out of this damned bodice, the poison will fester."

All the color leached from Veros's face. "Poison?"

"She was drugged. I've seen it before." Atlas bit the words out as the ripping of satin and snapping of the bone lining filled the space between them. "Now, either help me or don't, the choice is yours."

Veros helped.

He tugged on the satin ribbons, loosening them so Atlas could saw through the dense boning of Everinne's corset. Veros's movements were frantic as he yanked and tugged, tossing the scraps onto the floor to free his sister from the constraints of her costume. When Atlas tore the rest of the bodice from her, Veros averted his gaze, carefully unstrapping the heels she wore, and setting them aside. When Everinne was left in nothing but black stockings covered in tiny diamonds, Veros walked away completely, going to stand by the open verandah doors, his back to Atlas.

He slumped against the solid frame, his shoulders sagging in defeat.

A moment later, the door to Atlas's bedchambers burst open and Caedian strode in with a healer right behind him. Caedian stumbled to a halt, his eyes widening in both horror and shock at the sight of Everinne sprawled on the bed, and he instantly turned back around, forcing the healer to maneuver around him.

"Thank the gods," Atlas mumbled at the sight of Franseza.

She was one of the elders and had worked for the Korvny fae for well over a century. Her thinning raven hair was pulled back into a bun at the nape of her neck and deep-set lines showcasing her age wrinkled around her mouth and the corners of her gold eyes. She smelled of dried herbs and lemon balm, and long beaded earrings drooped from her pointy ears. Franseza bustled around to the side of the bed, wiping her aged hands on the tan apron that was smeared with stains from her latest remedy.

"Franseza," Atlas pleaded, his voice strained as his gaze skimmed the tiny threads of blackened veins littering Everinne's body. "Can you help her?"

"Don't worry, Your Imperial Highness." Franseza cupped Everinne's cheek, her thumb tracing her chin as she moved her head from side to side. "I can save the future princess."

"But?" Veros prompted from the opposite wall, still refusing to face them. He stood with his arms stretched out to either side, his hands gripping the door frame, like he was trying to breathe in the whole of the night to keep from losing control.

"But it will not be pleasant." Franseza rummaged through the leather pouch knotted around her waist, pulling out a cup, a bundle of herbs, as well as a mortar and pestle. "She's ingested a dangerous amount of blood ash. I'm honestly surprised she's not yet dead. Usually, blood ash is used as a means of sedation in small doses and is virtually untraceable. But when taken in extreme amounts, the toxin rots the blood. Whoever gave her such a copious amount either intended to knock her out cold or force her into an eternal slumber."

Atlas's hands curled into fists at his side. He knew exactly who was responsible. The minute he saw Jarek again, he would slit his throat. But right now, he had more important things to worry about, like making sure Everinne survived.

"What's the treatment?" Caedian asked. He rubbed one hand along the back of his neck and had taken a keen interest in his boots.

"That's the unpleasant part, I'm afraid." Franseza slipped a small tool from one of her pockets. The end was crafted from rose quartz, swirling and bulbous, with another crystal fused to its base. It was slender and hollow, tapering off toward its sharp tip. "I'll need to siphon the toxins from her blood."

Atlas swallowed the lump of anxiety lodged in the back of her throat. "Is it safe?"

"Safe, yes. But you may want to hold her down. The siphoning can be quite painful, especially give the amount flowing through her bloodstream."

He reached for Everinne, then hesitated, unsure of where to grab her or where to hold on. "I...I don't know what to do."

Franseza motioned toward the headboard with a flippant wave of her hand. "Climb up behind her on the bed. Keep a firm grasp of her waist and make sure her arms stay in place by her sides." The healer stole a look at Caedian. "Captain, if you could please secure her legs."

Caedian stiffened, his gaze darting to Atlas for approval.

He nodded once.

Caedian scooped his hands under Everinne's arms, slowly lifting her from the bed as Atlas climbed up to situate himself behind her. He hated the way her hair hung limp, the way her head dropped and rolled like a doll. Once he was seated with his legs stretched out along both sides of the bed, Caedian heaved her backward, laying her down gently against Atlas's torso. He locked his arms around her, pinning her against him, and sweltering heat radiated from her. She was like touching fire.

"Got her?" Caedian asked.

Again, all Atlas could do was nod.

His captain moved to the foot of the bed, linking one arm under her calves while the other reached over her shins. Then he lowered his chest, ensuring the weight of his upper body kept her firmly in place.

Franseza pinched the siphoning device between her fingers and met Atlas's worried stare. "Remember, Your Imperial Highness. Hold her tightly."

Atlas leaned back, clutching Everinne to him. "I won't let her go."

Franseza used the dagger-like tip of the siphon and pierced

Everinne's hip, slowly drawing out small amounts of thick, black ooze.

At first, Everinne didn't move, but on the second extraction, Atlas heard the faintest whimper slip from between her lips. Then she flinched, and Caedian grunted as her legs began to jerk and kick. Tension sent her arching off Atlas, and he tightened his hold, his forearms wrapping around her like rods of steel. Spasms ricocheted through her, and the sniffles of agony morphed into broken, choking sobs. Everinne thrashed, her disjointed movements becoming more violent with each withdrawal of the blood ash from her veins. Her eyes remained closed, severe pain etched into the beautiful planes of her face, and then she screamed.

Fucking gods, her *scream*.

His blood, once blistering hot with fury, ran ice cold with fear. He'd never heard her scream like that before, and he prayed to any god or goddess that he'd never have to hear it again. The sound of it, the keening shrill that escaped her, was like a spear of affliction straight through his heart. It gutted him, slashing through him, leaving him full of crushing despair. The bond between them roared to life, hissing and snapping, fueling him with the urge to save and the desire to protect, to never allow anyone or anything to harm her again.

"Almost done, *milazk*," Franseza crooned softly. "Almost done."

Tears stained Everinne's cheeks as she screamed again.

"Fuck!" Veros shouted, shoving his hands through his hair. "I...I can't..."

"Go!" Atlas jerked his head towards the verandah, to the sunrise beyond. "Just go. I'll find you when it's over."

Veros stormed out into the early morning light, disappearing as Everinne's hoarse cries ebbed and she collapsed against Atlas's chest, her body cool and pliant. There was no more fever. No more streaks of darkness flooding her veins. No more poison.

"There, there." Franseza soothed her, humming softly as she continued to heal.

She swiped her finger over the incision in Everinne's hip, coating it with a creamy white balm that reminded Atlas of wildflowers and honey. Then she sifted the dried herbs between her palms, dumping them into the mortar, then grinding them to a fine powder with the pestle. She popped off the cork of a large vial filled with some green-colored substance, the consistency of it similar to watery mud, and mixed the ingredients together.

Atlas slumped against the support of the headboard, cradling Everinne tightly, refusing to let her go.

Caedian eased up, releasing her completely, and swiped the back of his hand along his forehead. His face was flushed and there was a sheen of sweat on his brow. But it was the look in his eyes that was the most telling. The gray was haunted with shadows, and the deep umber of his skin was ashen. For even an elite warrior, seasoned in battle and blood, had never witnessed anything so harrowing. Either that, or Everinne's screams had dragged up a profusion of memories that Caedian would rather forget.

"Now, she needs to rest. She may be fitful, and it is likely she'll be disoriented when she awakens." Franseza packed up her tools and supplies, placed the mortar on the nightstand by the bed, then shuffled toward the door. "Best to keep her calm and make sure she drinks the healing brew, every last drop, as she'll be in a fair amount of discomfort."

Atlas barely heard her.

He couldn't hear anything except for the steady beating of Everinne's heart and the soft breaths she released with every exhale.

"We'll see that she does," Caedian confirmed, gathering one of the silk sheets and pulling it up to cover Everinne's mostly bare body. "Thank you."

Franseza dropped into a bob of a curtsy, her old bones creaking like weathered branches. "Let me know if you require anything else, Your Highness."

With that, the healer left. Caedian closed the door behind her, leaning against it, his head falling back against the solid wood. He roughed one hand over his face.

"I'm sorry, Atlas. I failed you." His lips pressed together in a hard line. "I failed both of you."

"No. This isn't your fault. Your soldiers can't access the Mystic Obscura because we forbade them from giving up a drop of their blood." Atlas adjusted his legs, drawing up his knees on either side of Everinne's sleeping form. "I should have forbidden her from going there as soon as I found out."

Caedian gave a short laugh tainted with sorrow. "That only would've emboldened her, my prince. I do not imagine she is one to take orders from you. Or anyone, for that matter."

"No." Atlas reached down, smoothing some of her hair back from her face, tucking it behind the delicate pointed tip of her ear, his finger grazing the amethyst studs she wore. "She thinks the rules don't apply to her."

"How did she end up in the Marzena, anyway?" Caedian asked, his gaze narrowing.

Anger simmered through Atlas's veins. "Jarek Zima."

"The demon summoner?" His captain shoved off the door and moved closer, his voice lowering. "You're certain?"

"I smelled him on her." Atlas's lip curled and he lightly touched Everinne's shoulder, where the imprint of a skull ring had faded to a milky white color against her skin. "He fucking branded her."

Caedian's jaw locked and he inhaled, taking a deep, stabilizing breath. Leave it to the Captain of the Guard to remain sensible when Atlas was ready to explode. "But if Everinne never left the Mystic Obscura, then how did Jarek get her to the Marzena without my scouts detecting her?"

"I don't know," Atlas muttered. If Jarek took Everinne to the Marzena without ever leaving the Mystic Obscura, then that could only mean one thing. "There must be an entrance to the Marzena from somewhere inside the Mystic Obscura."

"If there is," Caedian rolled his shoulders back, determination hardening his face, "we'll find it."

He stayed for a few more moments, then headed for the door. "I will go find Lord Veros and report that Everinne is recovering." Caedian reached for the handle, then paused, lowering his head.

"Fucking skies, Your Highness." His voice was hollow. "Her screams."

"I know." Atlas would never be able to erase them from his mind. He would hear them in his sleep, they would be the creation of his every nightmare come to life. When he spoke again, his voice was quiet. "Jarek will pay for this. With his life."

When Caedian left, Atlas sank lower into the cushioned mattress, anchoring Everinne against his chest. She shivered once, then rolled onto her side, snuggling into him, one hand curled beneath her chin while the other was splayed across his abdomen. He breathed her in, the sweet scent of caramel between layers of rose and blackcurrant as familiar to him as his own soul.

He leaned back against the pillow, his arms wrapped around her like a shield of protection.

Atlas swore to himself right then, he would get her out of the Mystic Obscura and as far away from Jarek Zima as possible. He would bargain with Reine for her life.

No matter the cost.

Thirty-One

Everinne was dead.

At least, she felt like she was dead, for there was no other explanation for the pain splintering through her head, or the weary ache in her bones. She'd expected more from the afterlife, for the death of the fae led to one of three places—Maghmell, the eternal paradise, the Ether, a realm in between worlds for wandering souls, or the Sluagh, a fiery pit of devastation for the most wicked of their kind. Yet for Everinne, there was only bleak nothingness. She was adrift in a fathomless sea, alone in a state of delirium.

Tears pricked at the corner of her eyes, and she hastily blinked them away.

Everyone was lost to her. Veros. Zoryana. Atlas.

Oh gods, Atlas.

With his beautiful golden green eyes and dazzling smile. She missed the way his dark blond curls fell across his forehead, the way he always knew just what to say to piss her off, the way he looked at her like she was his only reason for surviving. For breathing. But she'd said such awful things to him, she'd purposely tried to break his heart, to keep him at arm's length to protect them both from his father. Now, she would never get the chance to apologize. To beg for his forgiveness for lying, for refusing him. To tell him she...

A choking cry escaped her, and something warm brushed her cheek, her neck.

Perhaps she was not dead after all.

Her blood continued to pump through her veins and her heart was still beating despite the fact that she felt like she'd fallen from a cliff and broken every bone in her body. But there was something else, something familiar. A gentle tug, a kind of longing tethered to her subconscious.

She grabbed for that strand and pulled, yanking hard, and a soothing, masculine voice filled her mind.

"I've got you, Wildheart...I've got you."

Understanding crashed into her, and she whimpered. She knew that voice, recognized it in the deepest part of her soul as belonging to her. *Atlas.* He was the one who would drag her from the oblivion of her agonizing slumber, and it was not some imaginary rope she'd tugged upon in the hopes of waking, but the mating bond tying her to him. The one she'd denied.

Her heart splintered but she ignored it, breathing in the scent of fresh cedar, delicious neroli, and tempting spice. Atlas's scent. She clung to it, to him. He was her lifeline, her anchor, and she let him carry her back through the fog of endlessness to where she belonged...in his arms.

"Atlas," she murmured, her lashes fluttering slowly as she tried to open her eyes, but it was as though they'd been sealed shut for centuries.

"Right here." His palm coasted over her bare shoulder.

Everinne sighed, focusing on the rise and fall of his chest where her head was resting, the solid wall of his abdomen where her fingers carefully explored the firm ridges. Sweet stars, he was exquisite, all chiseled muscle and overpowering strength, every inch of him the most decadent form of temptation. Of course, she would never tell him as much. The last thing she wanted to do was boost his already overinflated ego.

Atlas chuckled darkly, the rumble of it melting into her bones. "Too late for that, Wildheart."

This time, her eyes popped open.

Her gaze drifted around the room, taking note of the way late afternoon sunlight spilled in through the open patio doors in shafts of gold. Just beyond them was a pool, the very same one she'd accidentally fallen into two nights prior. Which meant she'd somehow found her way into Atlas's bed, even though she'd sworn to herself she'd stay away. Her cheek was pressed against his soft shirt, her arms wrapped around his body, and given the cool sensation of silk against her bare skin, she already knew what she would find.

Everinne glanced down.

Her breasts were nestled against his waist, and she had one leg thrown over the top of his, the stretch of lace skimming her thigh just visible beneath the wrinkled sheets. Atlas, however, was fully clothed.

She lurched upright, instantly regretting the action. Her mind swam, her temples pounded against the abrupt movement, and a wave of nausea crawled from her stomach to the back of her throat. She grasped the silk bed linens with one hand, trying to keep the dizziness at bay, while her other hand reached blindly, catching Atlas's thigh. Her nails sank into the fabric of his pants as she tried to keep from fainting.

"Atlas." Her voice was low and raspy. "I don't feel very well."

"Don't move." He reached over and grabbed a cup of something off the nightstand. Easing one arm around her to keep her stable, he lifted the cup to her lips. "Drink this, you'll feel better."

She sniffed the muddled contents and bit back on the urge to gag. The stench was unbearable, it reminded her of stale water and dried mud. "It smells horrid."

"I know." He tilted it closer, his hand sliding to her hip to keep her in place. "But trust me, you need it."

Everinne met his pleading gaze and winced, swallowing down the vile concoction. It tasted as rancid as it looked, like someone had taken the slimy film of a bog and mixed it with putrid herbs, then labeled it as a remedy. As much as she hated to admit it, already the ache in her head was easing, and muscles and bones no longer felt as though they'd been buried beneath the weight of a boulder.

"Water, please," she croaked. "If you have some."

He replaced the empty cup on the nightstand, then grabbed a tall glass filled with what she prayed was actual water and not some clear healing potion. He offered it to her and she took a hesitant sip.

The refreshing taste of plain water with a hint of mint coated her tongue, and she gulped the rest of it down.

"Easy." Atlas pried the glass from her hands and set it aside. "You don't want to upset your stomach any further."

She nodded to appease him, but the water had cooled her throat and her mouth no longer felt like parchment drenched in paste. She debated on climbing out of bed to put some distance between them, but she didn't quite trust her legs yet to hold her up. There was a very good chance her knees would give out and she'd end up on the floor, in a far worse predicament than the one she already found herself in.

Everinne dared a glance at Atlas.

He was sitting up in the bed, his legs straddling either side of her, a few loose waves falling over one eye. His fingers tempted their luck, grazing over her hip in slow, languid movements. He stared at her in the silence, their hearts fused to the same rhythm, and when a gust of winter wind swept through the room, she couldn't keep herself from shivering. Goosebumps flooded her skin, and her nipples hardened to tiny peaks, drawing his attention. Despite the chill, she caught fire beneath the heat of lust banking in his gaze.

At least she knew that even when she was on the brink of death, he still found her desirable.

His eyes darkened, the green melding into the gold like a

sunset sinking beyond an evergreen forest. "I will always desire you."

She squirmed then shifted, tucking her legs under her so she sat upon her knees, and wrapped her arms around her chest. Her tongue darted out, wetting her bottom lip, and he tracked the movement. But he was an expert at reading body language, it was ingrained in him, a product of his sexual magic. So, Atlas eased back against the mound of pillows, planting his hands on his thighs as though purposefully trying to keep himself from touching her.

Keeping one hand clutched to her chest, Everinne raked a hand through her messy, tangled hair, so the strands fell haphazardly around her shoulders. "Where are my clothes?"

He arched a brow. "That's your first question?"

"Yes." She mimicked his expression. "Considering I'm naked in your bed, with only my stockings on, I think my question is fair enough."

Atlas's jaw popped and he tucked his hands behind his head, his look of bemusement morphing into hardened disdain. "Are you insinuating something, Everinne?"

"What?" Her mouth fell open in shock, not realizing he'd misinterpret her words as an accusation. "No! Of course not. I know you would never, that is...I don't—"

He jerked his head to the left. "Over there."

She leaned, peering over the edge of the bed to discover scraps of her bodice and frayed ribbons littering the floor of his room. "What happened?"

"I cut them off you."

Everinne had no idea what to make of that, or why he'd felt the need to destroy the costume, but she was somehow oddly grateful for it.

"Well," she huffed. "Good riddance. It was nearly impossible to breathe in that damn thing. But now I have nothing to wear."

"Does being naked in front of me make you uncomfortable?" he asked, and her gaze darted back to him. But there was no amusement in his tone, no inflections of ridicule. His eyes were fixated on her face, watching her with an intensity that sent a spear of heat straight to her core.

"Not uncomfortable, no." She squeezed her thighs together. "But it's strange to have a conversation with someone who is fully clothed when the other is not."

Atlas sat up and started unbuttoning his shirt. She watched, holding her breath as more of his golden skin was revealed to her, as the raging wolf tattooed across the left side of his chest was on full display, as every inch of sinewy muscle was showcased for her viewing pleasure. Her eyes wandered over the corded veins on his forearms, where another wolf tattoo marked his flesh. She stared at his chest as he flexed, then he removed his shirt completely, and her gaze wandering to his decidedly cut abdomen. She'd seen him shirtless before, but this was different. She wanted to know what his skin felt like under the palms of her hands. She wanted to trace the lines of his tattoos with her fingertips, then her tongue. Everinne knew what his mouth tasted like, what his cock tasted like, and she would bet anything the rest of him was just as delicious.

Goddess above, if he stripped right now, if he took off one more layer of clothing, there was no way she would survive.

She would absolutely perish.

Atlas groaned, adjusting his hips, his shirt fisted tightly in one hand.

It was only then she saw the large bulge straining against his pants.

"I swear to the gods, Ever." His voice scraped the air between them as he draped his shirt over her shoulders, helping her put it on. "If you don't get your thoughts under control, I will fuck you right here, and I won't stop until you can no longer think at all."

His words left her breathless, aching for him.

Wetness pooled at her center and he inhaled deeply, his nostrils flaring as he took in the scent of her arousal. He clenched his jaw, his knuckles grazing her breasts as he reached between them, fastening a single button, the one just below her navel. He slipped his hands beneath the hem of the shirt and he grabbed her thighs, spreading them. Her breath hitched as he jerked her forward, settling her on his lap, where his stiff erection created the most inviting friction. She looped her arms around his neck, drawing him closer, grinding herself against his hardened length.

Atlas gripped her ass and squeezed. "Tell me what you remember."

Her mouth opened then snapped shut. "What?"

"About last night. Tell me what you remember."

"But I...I thought we were going to—"

"Going to what, Wildheart?" The corner of his mouth lifted into a cruel smirk. "Last I checked, you denied me as your mate and claimed you would be my wife in name only."

He bent forward, lowering his mouth to the hollow of her throat. Her head fell back as he swiped his tongue along the column of her neck, leaving a blazing trail of heat up to her ear. His hands drifted to her hips, floating up to her sides where he idly swiped his thumbs back and forth, just beneath the underside of her breasts. She arched into his touch and then he whispered, "Unless something has changed?"

Her head snapped up. "Nothing has changed."

"Really?" His smile didn't falter. Power emanated from him, dark and seductive, so the bond they shared vibrated with overwhelming sensations of lust and longing. His magic teased her nipples into sensitive peaks, caused her breasts to grow heavy with need, and she writhed in his hold as ripples of pleasure centered around her clit.

"Because from where I'm sitting," he crooned as she ground herself against him, "it looks as though you're a little wet for me."

"Let me make one thing perfectly clear, Atlas Skye." Everinne tangled her fingers into his hair, dragging his face close to hers so the tips of their noses touched. "I am *always* wet for you."

A feral kind of noise escaped him then, it reverberated through his chest like a fierce roar.

He hooked an arm around her waist and flipped them over, so she was flat on her back and he was positioned above her, between her thighs. He snared her wrists over her head, and with his other hand, he grabbed the side of her face. Not punishing but demanding all the same. His thumb skated across her lips.

"Say it again," he growled.

"I'm always—"

"No." He shook his head once, his eyes swimming with an emotion she couldn't quite place. "My name. Say it."

"Atlas Skye." She whispered his name into the space between them.

Again he groaned, a cavernous sound that had her legs falling open as his mouth devoured hers in a hungry kiss. Their lips met, slashing across one another as their tongues meshed in a fierce tempo, both of them ravenous for each other. Teeth scraped and bit, she felt the sting of his sharp incisors, and he swallowed her moan, taking everything she gave him.

"You have no idea what you do to me. What you've done to me...for *years*." Atlas ran his hand from her face to her neck to her waist. He lowered his mouth to her, sucking her skin through the silk of his shirt she wore. The wet fabric fused to her flesh, and she lifted her hips, rolling them against his protruding erection. Atlas lifted his head, planting kisses between the valley of her breasts.

She struggled against his grasp, wanting nothing more than to wrap her arms around him and bring him closer to her, but Atlas held firm, refusing to release her.

"Seeing you here, in my bed, in my shirt, and in these fucking stockings..." He gripped her thigh, running his fingers beneath the fine layer of lace. "You torture me, Ever. You are pure torture."

Everinne locked her legs around him, digging her heels into the small of his back, shielding her thoughts. She knew what would happen if the kralv found out they were mates, but she was also no fool. If she refused Atlas's bed, the kralv would undoubtedly grow suspicious, and make her suffer for that as well. Not only that, but the thought of Atlas with anyone else filled her with immeasurable rage. She was damned either way.

Better to be damned and pleasured than damned and miserable.

The need building between her legs became nearly unbearable. His magic coursed through her, intensifying with every heartbeat. It flowed through her veins, heating her blood, sending bolts of sensual lightning straight to her core. Her muscles spasmed, then clenched, the impending orgasm growing like a rogue wave, threatening to drown her in a sea of oblivion. Just when she thought she couldn't take anymore, when she thought she would unravel if he didn't touch her, Atlas dropped his head once more, popped off the button so his shirt fell open around her, and sank his teeth into the top of her right breast.

He bit her.

Hard.

Release crashed into her, pulling her into an undercurrent of ecstasy, until she broke through the surface, trembling and gasping.

"Atlas." She choked out his name on a broken sob.

"Again," he demanded, moving above her so her gaze met the wild green of his eyes.

"Atlas," she begged. "Please."

"Please, what?"

"Please, let me touch you."

He hovered over her a moment longer, drinking her in, then finally let go of her wrists. She instantly reached for him, but he eased back onto his knees, trailing one hand down her stomach, then lower to where the apex of her thighs was still swollen and wet. The pad of his fingertip grazed her tingling flesh, and she nearly jolted out of the bed.

"You can touch me on one condition."

She nodded, willing to agree to anything he asked of her, eager to feel him. Taste him. Own him. Exactly as he had done to her.

"When you marry me, you will share my bed." Atlas stroked

her clit and she whimpered, longing to take him in her hands. "Once you're my wife, your heart, your soul, and your body belong to *me.*"

"Yes," she panted, angling her hips toward him in a silent plea for more. She knew what he was asking of her, what he was demanding of her. Just as she knew that once she agreed to his terms, once she accepted him as her mate, there would be no going back. Nothing could undo it, nothing could break it, not even death. The bond they shared would span an eternity, bleeding from one existence to the next, through the rise and fall of worlds, a thread of devotion woven through centuries.

Atlas stretched out alongside her, propping his elbow up on the pillows while his free hand moved between her legs. He kissed her cheek. Her neck. The tip of her ear.

"Tell me you're mine," he whispered.

His magic pooled in the palm of his hand as he cupped her, and another surge of ecstasy bloomed, centering at the apex of her thighs. It swirled and teased, delving inside of her, flowing through her until every inch of her body trembled with devastating bliss. His power was like a wraith, stealing over her, invisible caresses setting the entirety of her skin aflame. She rolled onto her side, pressing her hands to his bare chest while she rubbed herself against his rough palm. Another burst of seductive pleasure throbbed around her clit and she gasped, scraping her nails down his abdomen, her fingers finding the buttons of his pants.

"I'm yours," she murmured into the hollow of his throat. "I will always be yours."

Everinne made quick work of the buttons, nearly sighing in relief once the fullness of his cock sprang free. She glanced down, her mouth watering at the sight of him. It was a pity there was only one, for she could think of nothing better than to have him buried inside of her while she also took him into her mouth, if only such a thing were possible.

His groan was thunderous, a storm of burning need.

"Bleeding skies, Ever." Atlas flipped them over, anchoring her above him. The green of his eyes was dark with crazed hunger as she crawled down the length of his muscled body, seating herself on his large thighs. "Trust if I had two cocks, I would fuck your mouth and your wet little cunt until you couldn't remember your own name."

"I wouldn't need to remember my name. Only yours." She gripped his length, working him gently, and his eyes rolled to the wooden ceiling above them.

"Unfortunately," he ground the word out and tucked both of his hands behind his head. "This is the best I've got."

Warmth tickled her fingers, and she stared as he enlarged in her grasp. His erection lengthened, thickened, throbbed with wicked power. She gaped in shock, in utter awe of his impressive display. She could've sworn she noticed a similar sensation when she'd taken him in her mouth at the overlook, but it had been nothing like this...this was something beyond even her wildest of fantasies.

Her gaze darted back up to his eyes, which were now glinting with amusement.

"How?" she asked.

"Sex fae." Atlas grinned, his dimples winking. "Remember?"

She snapped her mouth shut.

"Make me come, Everinne," Atlas taunted, his smirk widening.

"But it...you won't fit," she countered, suddenly doubting her own sexual prowess.

He chuckled, settling back against the mountain of pillows. "Oh, I'll fit. But you won't be riding my cock tonight."

Her brows furrowed. She thought he wanted her, thought he wanted to take all of her. Completely. "Why not?"

"Because the first time we have sex, I won't be using any magic. It will be me, only me, who will make you writhe with need. Who will make you come so hard, you'll be begging for me again before you've even recovered."

Everinne pursed her lips together and scowled. "You're so arrogant."

"But you love me for it," he countered, winking playfully.

She would not dwell on the word he just said, for it hadn't seemed to bother him in the least. That was something she would contemplate later, when she couldn't escape the analyzing chaos of her thoughts.

"Show me what you've got, Wildheart," he murmured as tendrils of his magic slipped into her wet heat with promises of that ever-elusive release. "Make me come, or your next orgasm will remain just out of reach."

She whimpered, biting her bottom lip. "You wouldn't dare."

Atlas ran his tongue along his teeth. "Try me."

Staring down at the ridiculous size of his shaft, she decided to do the one thing she knew would bring him to his haughty knees.

"Whatever you say, Your Radiance."

Everinne splayed her body over his lower half, resting her forearms comfortably on his hips. If he were his normal size, it might not work, but the Prince of Prava had decided to show off and she had every intention of making him pay—in the most torturous way. Fitting his cock snugly between her breasts, she lowered her mouth to his tip and sucked.

Thirty-Two

A tlas nearly lost his damn mind.

His knuckles gripped the edge of the bed, if anything, to keep himself from taking a fistful of Everinne's hair and shoving his cock all the way down her throat. He itched to grab her, to prove his touch was a thousand times better than his magic. He watched in silence as his shaft disappeared between her dark pink lips, as her cheeks hollowed each time she drew him deeper into her mouth. Her dark brown hair tumbled down her shoulders, tickling his legs, and it took every shred of self-control not to jut his hips to see how much more she could take.

He'd expected a hand job, but seeing his cock sandwiched between her two perfectly round breasts while she teased him with her tongue, swirling and sucking on his cock like a damn lollipop, drove him mad with lust. Her nails dug into his skin, the bite of pain a welcome sensation. Every so often she used her teeth, scraping lightly, applying just enough pressure to shove him closer to the edge. Not like he wasn't ready to empty himself already. One touch from her, one look, and he went tumbling headfirst off a cliff of insatiable desire. That was the kind of effect she had on him, the power she held over him.

Atlas cast his magic out in provocative currents, each potent crest of pleasure acutely focused on Everinne. Her lashes fluttered closed, and she moaned around his length, squirming, struggling to stay in control. He magnified every sensation, coaxing her orgasm to life. Tendrils of incandescent gold spilled from his fingers, wrapping around her nipples and wrists like gilded ropes, snaring around her thighs and spreading them wide. Her eyes flew open, and his power surged, spearing into her slickness with fervent thrusts.

His balls tightened, tension coiling through his muscles when Everinne took him deeper into her warm mouth. Bleeding skies, she was intoxicating. A goddess in the flesh, crafted by the beautiful dark. He would gladly fall into her, wander blindly into the eternal pitch of her volatile magic, if it meant he would never lose her. Spasms ripped through him and his hips jerked as she quivered on the brink of destruction. He erupted then, the release all-consuming. She sucked and swallowed hard, draining him as his cock slipped from between her lips and she cried out his name on a broken sob.

Everinne collapsed, spent from the whims of gratifying bliss.

He reached down, scooped his hands under her arms, and hauled her against him.

"Next time," he murmured into her hair, brushing a few of the soft strands back from her forehead, "I'm going to taste you with my tongue and fill you with my cock."

Everinne smiled against his cheek, nipping the lobe of his ear. "If I let you."

She shivered then, rolling off him and curling into his side, pulling his shirt around her.

"Are you cold?" he asked, tugging the discarded fur comforter over them.

Goosebumps pebbled her flesh but she shook her head, her cheek resting against his chest. "Pleasantly warm."

Outside, the sun was already sinking behind a dense layer of clouds, its fading rays cutting between the gray, pillow-like formations. They drifted across the sky, low and heavy, a promise of snow.

He stroked her hair with one hand, marveling at the way the strands slid through his fingers like silk. It was too easy to enjoy this, to like the way she was sprawled across him, to imagine this was how it would always be between them. He could get used to spending hours with her in bed, locked away from the rest of the world, pretending no one else even existed. For over half a century, Atlas had wanted Everinne. He'd pined for her. Ached for her. Longed for her. The moment Veros brought her to the palace, saving her from that village that was devoured by forest and night, Atlas had known she was destined for him. Now, here she was with only a handful of sunsets left until they vowed their lives to each other, and he couldn't help feeling that it was all a mistake. Like she was sand slipping through his fingers and no matter how hard he tried, he'd never be able to hold on to her, or their bond, forever.

A breath shuddered out of Everinne and when she spoke, her words lured him back to the present, to all the unknowns they had yet to face. "I had just finished my performance at the Mystic Obscura, and when I went to leave for the night, to come back here, Jarek was there. He..."

Atlas's lungs pinched tight.

"He, what?" he forced out, holding back the bite of rage in his tone.

"He made me go with him to an afterparty in the Marzena. But it was wrong, the whole night seemed off somehow. At the Mystic Obscura, the audience was loud and unruly, nothing at all like it's been other nights when I've danced." She laid her hands flat against his chest, resting her chin there to look up at him. "And the Marzena...I've never seen anything like it. It's odd, and peculiar, and—"

"No." He wasn't going to let her finish that sentence. "There is nothing thrilling or interesting about the Marzena, Ever. It's dangerous."

Which was something she always craved, despite her better judgment.

"I know it's dangerous. Or at least, I realized that quickly enough." Her teeth snagged on her bottom lip, gnawing slightly. When her turquoise eyes lifted to his face, they were shadowed with worry. "Atlas, I only had one drink. But it must have been strong because I can barely remember anything else."

Again, his blood churned, boiling at the memory of her limp and unconscious in the guard's arms. He cupped her cheek, determined to keep his touch gentle, even though he wanted to rip out Jarek's throat with his bare hands.

"He drugged you, Everinne." His voice was rough, like he'd swallowed a blade of ice, and he couldn't stand the way her eyes widened in shock. "That's why you can't remember. You weren't drunk. You were drugged."

She scrambled to a sitting position in the bed, tucking her legs under her and fastening his shirt around her in an effort to conceal her body, as though the truth of last night had somehow left her more exposed, more vulnerable, than she realized. "Why would he drug me?"

Atlas wasn't going to answer that question. No fucking way. Because he already knew where his mind went, and it involved dark alleys, muffled screams, and the worst kind of assault. He shifted, propping himself up against the headboard of the bed. This was the sort of conversation he didn't want to have with her, the kind he'd dreaded since she started her downward spiral into the world of nightlife highs filled with easy alcohol and mindless sex.

"Jarek didn't just drug you." He nodded toward her left shoulder, where his shirt hung low to reveal her lightly tanned skin and the faint outline of a skull scarred her flesh. "He marked you."

Atlas's jaw popped.

He should have been the one to mark her. To brand her. Whether with his teeth, his hands, or his tongue, it made no difference. He wanted everyone to know she belonged to him. His gaze slid to the wolf tattooed across his forearm, to the vine of blood roses swirling around her wrist, and an idea took form in the back of his mind.

"What the fuck is his problem? First he drugged me, then he stamped my shoulder with his ring." Everinne ran her finger along the skull and a scowl marred her brow. "I'm going to kill him for this."

Atlas's lips twitched.

There was the Everinne he knew and loved.

Loved.

A lump of unwanted emotion swelled in the back of his throat, and he swallowed it down. He couldn't love her, not really. Her heart was too wild. Her affection was too fleeting. It was one thing to be bonded, to be fated, but love could not be gained from compulsion. It couldn't be coerced or demanded. It had to be earned, given freely and unconditionally. As far as Atlas knew, Everinne had only loved once in her life—the fae hunter, Callum —and in the end, she'd killed him. After that, she'd closed off her heart to anyone else. It was like an iron fortress, impenetrable from the outside, frozen on the inside.

He knew, because he'd seen it. He'd witnessed it that day he'd brought her back from the chaotic destruction of her own mind.

"There was someone else," she mumbled, fiddling with the open buttons, like she was trying to grasp pieces of her memory. "Someone recognized me. A vampire."

Atlas nodded, training his gaze on her face, refusing to look where the swell of her breasts strained against the white linen of his shirt. He cleared his throat. "Davorin."

He would have to thank the vampire. Truth be told, if Davorin hadn't found Everinne and returned her to the palace, there was no way of knowing what Jarek would have done to her. Once Atlas offered his gratitude, then he would ask Davorin what exactly he was doing in the Marzena, given the current climate.

"Yes. Davorin." Everinne tugged his shirt back over her shoulder, then tilted her head so her tumble of dark hair cascaded around her. "I asked for his help. But after that..." Her eyes were vacant for a moment, empty, and she shook her head once. "There's nothing after that. Until now. Until you."

"It doesn't matter." He wanted to reach for her, to pull her into his lap, but he knew if he tried, somehow that would only drive her further away from him. "You're safe now."

"But I'm not," she countered, her eyes flashing so the gold rings around the center flared hot and bright. "I'm not safe at all. Not anymore. I should've stayed away from him. I should have listened to you. To Veros."

Everinne raked both hands through her hair, then clutched the back of her neck. A tremor of frustration skated down the bond, its growing presence shrouding the rise of panic that caused her heart to race.

"I gave Reine a drop of my blood. My blood, Atlas. She's going to know, if she doesn't already, she will soon enough. That's probably why Jarek is after me anyway, they must know what I'm capable of. Why else would he drug and mark me?"

She clasped her palms together and shoved them in her lap, staring down as swirls of inky black and violet spilled from her fingers. The scent of midnight lilacs hung heavy in the air as she clenched her fists together, as her death-touched magic filled her with dread.

"She told me. Aisling told me I wouldn't be able to leave. I won't be able to get away from the Mystic Obscura." Everinne pressed her lips in a hard line and squeezed her eyes shut, pain etching across her usually smooth brow. Her magic amplified, the stretches of darkness unfurling like a caged beast. "I'm trapped."

"You are not trapped. Look at me." Atlas grabbed her and pulled her onto his lap. He cupped both sides of her face with his hands and lowered his forehead to hers. "Everinne Auvyre. Look. At. Me."

Her eyes flew open and locked onto his, drawing him into their stunning depths. It was as though someone had taken the beauty of the Ladova Bay, with its turquoise waters, and fractured it with sunlight. He wanted to dive in, to drown in her forever.

"Breathe with me." He stroked her cheeks in slow, measured movements, leaning in so her chest rose and fell in time to his, even and steady.

Then he slid into her mind, sneaking past the barrier of her innermost thoughts, determined to soothe her turmoil.

"*You control your magic, Wildheart.*"

Astonishment registered in her gaze, and then her lashes fluttered closed. She wove her arms around his neck, her lips brushing back and forth across his own, taking his every breath as though it belonged to her. Breathing him in, melting into him as the bond thrummed and warmed.

"*You control it,*" he repeated. "*Only you.*"

"*But what if I can't?*" Her voice was like music in his mind, a decadent cadence, the melody of his soul. "*What if it's too much?*"

Atlas dropped his hands from her cheeks, guiding them slowly to her waist. His fingers slipped beneath the shirt, his rough palms molding to her hips. "*Then I will be right here. Take whatever you need from me. I won't let you fall, Ever.*"

She sighed then eased back, breaking their almost kiss. "You say that now."

"What is that supposed to mean?" His grip on her tightened but she didn't seem to notice. Her arms were still draped around his neck, her knees nestled against the outside of his thighs as she straddled him, completely nude save for his shirt and those fucking stockings.

He hardened beneath her, and she rolled her hips against him. His pants were still unbuttoned, and the heat of her cunt pulsed against him, her slickness coating him with each little rock of her hips.

"It means," she hummed, her tongue swiping along his bottom lip, "that eventually I'll fall. You'll see. I'll push you away like I do everyone. You won't try to catch me, because you'll think

I can save myself. It's a kind of self-destruction. But it doesn't matter, because I'll fall all the same."

Her eyes finally opened again, and she pressed her mouth to his in a soft kiss. "And when I do, there will be nothing left."

She lifted slowly, rising over him, positioning herself directly above his erection. One good thrust of the hips and he'd be buried inside her. Gods, he was so fucking ready for her. He'd planned on waiting, figured he would finally take her on their wedding night, but right now she was so wet and willing, and if she wanted him, then who the fuck was he to deny her? Her nails dug into his shoulders, clutching him like he was an anchor and she was in danger of drifting out to sea. Her breathing hitched, coming in ragged pants, and he wasn't even inside her yet.

He bit back a grin.

The sweet noises she made turned him into an arrogant prick and he reveled in it.

Everinne lowered herself an inch, just barely enough for the tip of his cock to feel the slick warmth of her cunt, and then she froze.

"I can't."

She crawled off him, and his head slammed back against the headboard, a groan of despair erupting from some feral part of him. His balls ached. His cock throbbed to the point of pain, and he gripped it with one hand, squeezing firmly to relieve some pressure.

Bleeding skies, he wanted to die.

Everinne lurched off the bed, tugging his shirt around her, and folding her arms across her chest. "This was a mistake."

Atlas buttoned his pants and stood, stalking around the bed. She backtracked quickly, retreating from him until she was pressed against the nearest wall between the verandah and the bathing suite. Her chin was raised, but he didn't miss the way she tried to suppress the shiver when he slammed his hands against the wall, effectively blocking her path.

"Then take off your ring," he demanded quietly, searching

through the confusion plaguing her face. "If this was such a mistake, give my mother's ring back to me, and go tell my father you've changed your mind."

"That's not fair. You know I can't do that." She wet her bottom lip with her tongue, and he hated himself for tracking it, for being unable to tear his gaze from her lush mouth. "He'll punish me for it. He'll punish both of us."

An emotion flickered in her eyes and she banked it, but not before he felt it tug the bond, so hard he thought it would pull his heart from his chest. His lungs nearly collapsed.

Fear.

But not fear of him.

Fear of Oldrich.

What the fuck did his father do to her?

"I inflict pain, Atlas." She huffed out a breath, shaking her head slightly. "Blessing or curse, it doesn't matter. My power is one of pure agony, death even, and I can't control it."

"Can't? Or won't?" He stared down at her, but she ducked her head, refusing to meet his gaze. Her curtain of dark hair kept her face safely from view. "When was the last time you tried to use your magic without your emotions getting the best of you?"

"It doesn't matter." Her voice was barely a whisper between them.

"Yes, it does. You know what happens to a fae when they don't use their magic. You know the power ends up consuming them, drives them into a state of madness." Atlas tried again, gentler this time. "You cannot hide from that which is yours by blood."

Another faint tremor of fear bled through the bond they shared.

Carefully, he slid two fingers beneath her chin, lifting her face. "I will not let you fall."

Tears welled in her eyes, shimmering like diamonds. "My soul is broken."

"I don't care." Atlas moved closer and let his lips lightly brush her temple. "I want your broken everything. Broken heart. Broken soul. I want your darkness. Your pain. Your nightmares and dreams. Just as much as I want your smiles. And your laughter. I want every piece of you, Ever. Always."

"Skies above." She sniffled, crossing her arms so her breasts nearly popped out of his shirt, and he forced himself to meet her glassy eyes. "Since when did you become so smooth and perfect with words?"

Atlas grinned and kissed her soundly on the mouth, enjoying the little noise of surprise she made, liking it even more when she arched into him.

"I've always been smooth and perfect with words, Wildheart," he crooned against her mouth. "You just weren't listening."

Thirty-Three

A tlas walked the gardens alone.

Everinne wanted to stay in his room and soak in his tub, and he figured she could use some time alone because if he stayed a minute longer, he would've had her bent over the bed, the sink, or any fucking surface he could find until he was so deep inside of her, she forgot how to breathe.

He pushed a hand through the messy curls of his hair and loosed a harsh breath, the frigid air misting before him. Outside the palace, the world was covered in a fine layer of frost. It kissed the trees with their bare limbs, the petals of every winter-blooming flower, and even the lake was covered in crackling sheets of ice that spread like spider webs across its smooth surface. Had it been any other evening, Atlas likely would've thrown on an overcoat to ward off the chill, but his skin was on fire, set aflame for a fae with eyes that reminded him of ethereal crystalline waters.

The winter wind bit through the soft fibers of his navy sweater, and he shoved his hands into his pockets, his boots crunching lightly against the solid earth. He wandered closer to the pond, one of his favorite places to sit and be when the world was too much, when the politics of court and the rumors surrounding his magic and reputation often got the best of him.

Here on some large, misshapen stones where waves lapped against a shallow shore, he could silence the doubts, the questions, the disparaging remarks that tainted his soul and blemished his character.

But tonight, nothing could quiet the murmurs of the wicked wood.

Atlas's gaze drifted beyond the stone wall border of Starysa, to where heavy gray clouds blotted out slices of rising moonlight and the trees of the Deszvila Forest shuddered and moaned. Their dense branches creaked, their evergreen points jutting up like daggers from beyond the border. Within the walls of Starysa's reach, the trees were barren, their jewel-hued leaves had fallen with the arrival of winter's first breath. They were dormant, lying in wait until the arrival of spring. But the woods beyond, they never rested. They breathed with the shifting of the wind, stealing over the landscape of Prava, beckoning the dark, archaic magic that thrived within the forest to life.

He dropped onto one of the oversized stones, resting his elbows upon his knees. Despite the onset of winter and the harrowing woods that seemed to watch with cunning restlessness, Atlas attempted to clear his mind.

Yet his thoughts would not settle.

He would have to go to the Marzena before any other immortals disappeared. Unfortunately, he had no idea what the fuck he was looking for, other than maybe some back-alley rumor, or the possibility that one of the tainted souls who dwelled beneath the city knew something. It would be impossible to go around and interrogate everyone who made the Marzena their home, but if the Mystic Obscura did in fact have an entrance to the Marzena below its menagerie, then that seemed like the best place to start. It didn't escape Atlas's notice that Khiran, the missing vampire from Valaina's clan, was last seen at the favored parlor, and with their increasing collection of blood samples it was all too coincidental for Reine to have direct access to the occult market of the Marzena.

And now, with Everinne ensnared in their clutches, he had to find a way to get her as far away from there as possible. If Reine or Jarek discovered Everinne's magic, if they knew what she was capable of doing...

Reine was a witch, without a doubt she could find some nefarious use for Everinne. But Jarek...if a demon summoner got his hands on a fae who could inflict pain, suffering, and death—the possibilities were endless and grim.

Atlas pulled a pack of stigs from his pocket, slipping one between his lips, and flicked the lighter with his thumb. Fire sparked to life from the slim glass container filled with swirling magic. He inhaled, breathing in the floral, minty flavor. Blowing out a puff of smoke, he rolled his head back and stared up at the swath of thick clouds that stretched across the sky like a gray velvet blanket. A tiny scrap of white lace, a lone snowflake crafted from frost, cascaded down from the starless heavens, carrying with it the scent of worn leather, fresh earth, and ink-scrawled parchment.

"The first snowfall," Veros mused, stepping from the path of patterned stone and closer to the pond's edge. His hands were tucked in his pockets and his gaze was focused on the flakes that were slowly tumbling from the wintry sky. "They'll light the bonfire tonight."

Atlas nodded, shoving up from his sitting position to stand. Zemni Boheme was thought to take place to celebrate the first snowfall of winter, a blessing of some forgotten goddess. The bonfire burned silver until the Winter Solstice, to celebrate the passing of the longest night, a promise of spring's eventual arrival. But Atlas knew the real reason for the fire wasn't to bide the darkening nights until the passing of the Winter Solstice, but to keep the forest at bay. To keep it from creeping ever closer, to keep it from swallowing Starysa until there was nothing left but rubble and bones.

"I imagine the lighting will be a great time." Atlas rocked back on his heels and drew in another pull from his stig. He blew the smoke out so it curled around the dancing snowflakes. "Kralv Oldrich has much to celebrate. He'll throw an elaborate festival for the coming winter and host a stupidly lavish wedding while his citizens face an increasingly dangerous and unknown threat."

"I was only implying we might be able to garner some more information." Veros angled his head, one dark brow arching. "Faerie wine loosens lips."

Atlas considered his friend, it wasn't a bad idea at all. "Loose lips spill secrets."

"Exactly." Veros inhaled sharply and tucked his hands behind his back, his shoulders stiffening. "Caedian informed me that Everinne is well."

"Quite well." All Veros had to know was that Atlas had helped bring his sister back from the brink of death. He definitely didn't need to know anything else that happened afterward, all of which was grounds for Veros to murder him. Atlas rolled the stig to the corner of his mouth and roughed one hand along the back of his neck. "Though I am sorry you had to see her like that."

Veros's jaw tightened, and he glanced down at where a thin layer of snow was beginning to gather, his dark hair falling in front of his face. "All that matters is she's alive."

His voice was quiet and there was an edge to his tone, one Atlas hadn't heard in a number of years. Veros spoke as though he'd walked through time, as though the hours he held in the palm of his hand were gradually ticking closer to some cataclysmic event, one that would change the destinies woven by fate. With his head bowed, he glanced over at Atlas, and the turquoise of his eyes dimmed, the gold bleeding into them like tiny rivers of melted metal.

"I need to talk to you, Veros." Atlas took one last drag of his stig, then let it fall to the ground and crushed it beneath his boot. "About Everinne."

Veros threw both of his hands up in the air and stepped back. "If it involves any kind of intimate dealings, I don't want to hear it."

"It's not that." He would die of mortification first. Shifting his weight from one foot to the other, he met his best friend's intensifying gaze. "You were there, you heard what Valaina said about the Mystic Obscura. And as you've already pointed out, I'm not the best at striking deals."

Atlas liked to think his reasoning for always getting roped into shitty bargains was because of his hot temper and lack of patience, though he knew it had more to do with the fact that his father locked him out of court dealings. He lacked experience with negotiation, and if he didn't end up wrangled into some duplicitous deal, then he usually got what he wanted for one reason only.

His looks and his magic, both of which, when snared into bargains, left an unsavory taste in his mouth.

"Do you want me to bargain for you?" Veros asked, his head snapping up. "Because I will. She's my sister and the whole reason she's stuck working at that damn parlor is my fault. I will gladly—"

"No, I'll do it. I'll make the deal myself. You're the Master of the Hour, the Lord of Time, you have too much to offer." Atlas, on the other hand, could walk into the Mystic Obscura, strike an accord with Reine, and walk out practically unscathed. He was a fae prince with nothing to lose. He was an embarrassment to the crown, his father hated him, and if all he had to give up was his sex magic, then so be it. To him, it would be an invisible weight lifted from his shoulders. One less burden to bear. "All I need to know is what to expect. What I may have to offer or give up in exchange for Everinne's life."

Veros's teeth skated across his bottom lip as a line of concentration formed across his brow. "Reine is a witch, but she has no allegiance to the Coven of the Scarlet Moon. There is no way of telling what she might ask of you in return for Ever's freedom."

He swallowed, plucked his own stig from the front pocket of his coat, and lit it, his focus on the icy blue flame of the lighter before he snuffed it out completely. Veros inhaled deeply, blew out a stream of smoke, and said, "If she lets her go at all."

Something cold sank into Atlas's chest, like the frozen fingers of dread captured his heart and squeezed. The seizing ache spread through him, carving his lungs until they were hollow, scouring his gut until it rolled with acid and bile.

"You think she won't?" Atlas asked, apprehension causing his palms to slick with sweat. He never considered the possibility that Reine wouldn't release Everinne from the Mystic Obscura at all.

"I don't know." Veros pinched the stig between his fingers then flicked it once, sending a tiny clump of ash scattering across the freshly fallen snow. "Reine has a drop of her blood. If she figures out what Everinne can do, that her magic is dark and turbulent, that she lacks the control necessary to wield it with restraint and command...then Everinne herself could become the bargaining chip."

"Reine would sell her off to the highest bidder." A shudder of unease streaked down Atlas's spine. The alarm he tried to quell coursed through him, heightening his awareness. "To someone like my father."

Never before had Atlas known such an all-consuming rage. The bond roared at the thought, the urge to protect her, to destroy and ravage, to wreck and ruin anything that dared threaten her with harm swallowed him whole. The invisible strand of power tethering him to Everinne sliced through his muscles, ripped through his bones, peeling back every layer of his defenses until it secured his soul to hers. Her gasp echoed through his mind as he reached for her, as the mating bond captured her beating heart, so her breath, her thoughts, every aspect of her being, belonged to him. Atlas didn't relent, he grasped the thread binding them and wove it into the deepest layer of his soul, through his very aura, until he knew without a doubt that he could follow her to the ends of the earth, to realms not their own, and no matter what, he would *always* find her.

"Or worse," Veros muttered, tossing his stig to the ground, watching as the ember died and hissed in the veil of snow.

"Who could possibly be worse?" As far as Atlas was

concerned, his father ranked fairly high among the most despicable and abhorrent males in all of Prava. In all of Aedran, if he was being honest.

There was no one worse than Kralv Oldrich Skye.

But Veros met him with a long look, one that spoke of hushed rumors, forgotten vices, and terrors unseen. "Whoever is hunting the immortals."

"Fucking skies." Damn Veros and his infuriating talent for always knowing the exact wrong thing to say. It didn't matter if he was right, but his gift for pissing Atlas off usually happened at the most inopportune moments, when it was quite possibly the last thing he wanted to hear.

"Thanks, like I didn't need more of a reason to worry about Everinne's safety." Atlas rolled his eyes to the evening sky. The moon was haloed behind a wall of clouds, its silver glow barely visible as snow swirled down in heavy clumps. "My father is bad enough. But a fae hunter?"

Atlas's muscles pulled taut at the thought. He'd almost lost Ever to a hunter once before. He wasn't going to allow it to happen again. Veros might be the Lord of Time, but even Atlas knew every hour that passed was an hour wasted. Time was grains of sand, and he could do nothing but watch as it continued to slip through his fingers. Eventually, it would run out.

"I have to speak with Reine."

He turned around and started for the path that would lead him back to the palace when Veros stepped directly in his way, lifting one hand to stop him.

"Not tonight. You know damn well that if you don't show up to the bonfire of Zemni Boheme, *with* Everinne, your father will make you pay for it." Veros stepped closer, leveling Atlas with a glare that harbored death. "Oldrich will make you *both* pay for it. Every action you take from now on will have a direct impact on my sister's life. Don't forget it."

Again, Veros spoke the truth.

Oldrich had a sick love for doling out punishment through

violence and verbal assault. His fondness for disparaging comments and remarks are what kept every servant in the entirety of the palace silent for fear of his wrath. His magic allowed him to know the depths of someone's greatest fear, and he used their terror to his advantage, a prized weakness to keep him in control. His threats knew no bounds, his ability to grant nightmarish circumstances were limitless. He possessed the horrible ability to show his victims through visions in their minds exactly how they would suffer if they chose to disobey him.

Atlas's greatest fear was once worrying he would never amount to anything. That he was worthless, that his entire existence amounted to little more than a good fuck with pretty eyes. It was bad enough his father had shunned him from all palace dealings. When his mother was alive, he'd at least had a seat at the table. He'd been willing to accept that he wouldn't ever be enough—he hadn't been blessed with fire, or frost, or shadows. His power was one of a sexual nature. It was laughable. Demeaning. So, he'd owned it. Flaunted it. Forged it into a fucking weapon. Until there wasn't a single fear left inside of him for his father to expose.

Except for maybe spiders.

Atrocious little creatures.

Still, he would rather face an army of spiders than see Everinne hurt or in danger.

Everinne.

If Oldrich realized she was his weakness, that Atlas feared for her safety above all else, that her love was the one thing he feared being denied, there would be no end to his torment.

"Fine. I'll attend the lighting of Zemni Boheme with Everinne." Atlas held out his hand, watching in silence as the tiny flakes melted against the warmth of his palm. "But tomorrow, I must go speak with Reine."

Veros nodded once, and the sound of thundering footfalls echoed through the stillness of the gardens. Someone was running. Toward them.

Atlas caught Caedian's scent on the cold breeze, it swept in through the swirling snow—aged oak and musk. Then his Captain of the Guard halted before him, his disheveled white hair blown back from his face, his pale eyes alight with urgency.

"Your Imperial Highness." Caedian's breath misted before him and he locked his arms by his side.

Atlas was immediately on edge by his formal demeanor. "What is it?"

Caedian's hesitant gaze cut to Veros, then returned to him. "There's been another disappearance."

"Who?" Atlas asked.

His captain's throat worked, and he clenched his fists twice, a tell of warring confidence. "It's not good, Your Highness, she—"

"Who?" he demanded.

Caedian straightened. "Zoryana Daleth."

Oh, fuck.

"Zoryana?" Veros choked out, his brows pulling into a deep scowl. "As in Zory, Everinne's best friend?"

"The very one." Caedian nodded and leaned closer. In the haze of shrouded moonlight, his gray eyes glowed against the jeweled umber of his skin. His voice was hushed when he said, "As in High Priestess Rozalie's daughter."

Fucking skies.

Atlas thought the situation was bad before, but he'd been sorely mistaken. It had just gotten a thousand times worse. When Ever found out Zoryana was missing, there would be no consoling her, no stopping her. She would become completely irrational, her decisions would deteriorate from borderline unsafe to damn near treacherous.

"Does she know?" Atlas directed his question to Caedian, praying to the stars and skies that he already knew the answer. "Does Everinne know?"

"No, my prince. Not yet." Caedian lowered his head, bowing slightly. He reached into the front pocket of his long coat and pulled out a letter, then handed it to Atlas. "I was informed a few moments ago by one of the lower-ranking priestesses of the Scarlet Moon, who delivered this for you."

Atlas accepted the crisp piece of parchment. It was sealed with scarlet wax and imprinted with an image of a moon. His title and name were scripted across the front in scrawling, hurried penmanship. He folded the letter and tucked it into the back pocket of his pants. There would be time to read Rozalie's words later.

He started for the palace. "I must tell Everinne."

"Wait." Veros reached out and grabbed his shoulder. The look on his face reflected a plea, but also a warning. "Zoryana was the only one who could help Everinne control her magic. She absorbed Ever's emotions when they became too temperamental. If you tell her now, especially after last night and everything she endured with Jarek, there's a good chance she'll fall apart. We could lose her completely."

"We're already losing her, Veros." Atlas shook his head, pulling away from his friend's hold. "We thought we were protecting her by keeping her magic a secret, by letting her stumble down this detrimental path of despair. You've seen what she's done to herself, the dangers she willingly runs into headfirst without thinking, all because she's been trying to hide for so long."

He paced in a small circle, the understanding of so many years of neglect crushing his heart beneath a stone of guilt.

"We've nearly killed her." He stilled, sucking in a harsh breath, welcoming the freezing air into his lungs. "Are you aware she's not using her magic *at all*? That's she's letting it fester. That it only slips out in moments of emotional turmoil, or when she feels like the entirety of the world is caving in on her? No wonder she has nightmares and drinks herself into oblivion, she's driving herself mad."

"We'll bring her back." A look of resolution passed over Veros's face, and his jaw clenched in hardened determination. He rolled his shoulders back, the movement jerky and snapping with tension. "She already walks the line between control and chaos, we just have to bring her back. She needs confidence in her abilities, and reassurance that her power, her magic, is more than simply a death sentence."

Veros's gaze flicked to the timepiece in his hands.

"Perhaps that's something I should have given her long ago." He shoved it back into his pocket, then held up one finger. "A day. Just give it one day before you tell her about Zory. Then we'll approach her together, because you know as well as I do there will be no rest until she's found."

Atlas roughed a hand over his face. "I don't have a good feeling about this."

Caedian cleared his throat. "I hate to be the bearer of bad news..."

"Are you serious right now?" Atlas whirled on him, the new layer of snow crunching lightly beneath his boots. "How much worse can it possibly get?"

Veros cocked his head to the side, pinning him with a look of utter contempt. "Do not tempt the gods, Atlas."

"Quite a bit worse, I'm afraid." Caedian stole a glance over his shoulder, scanning their surroundings for any sign of movement, ensuring the whispering walls of the palace could not overhear whatever he was about to say next. "If we don't figure out who is hunting the immortals, it's only a matter of time before the Coven of the Scarlet Moon and the Morvayne take matters into their own hands."

He moved closer, ducking his head, and when he spoke, his voice was a hollow scrape against the howl of the wind. "Already there are whispers that the woods are awakening."

As if they could hear, the thick trees beyond the walls of Starysa groaned and creaked, their branches bending and snapping like the angry jaws of a feral beast.

A glint of apprehension reflected in Caedian's eyes as he locked onto the tops of the trees set against a backdrop of jagged mountains. His fingers twitched by his side, his hand hovering above the hilt of his sword, prepared to draw his weapon. A muscle feathered in his jaw and then he blinked, but the strain he harbored in his rigid frame did not ease. He remained tightly wound, ready to attack, his body primed with anticipation for a fight.

"The docks by the Ladova Bay are swarming with rumors," he continued, leaning back, eyeing the long shadows reaching across the gardens. "They could be overheard in every tavern and back alley, some of the hearsay was spoken in code, like a secret. Already there have been claims of the dryad's alluring laughter, the sailors at port swear she calls to them. And the hungry growl of the *baukvist* looms closer."

"This can't be happening. Not again." Not so soon.

Atlas raked both of his hands through his loose curls, sending bits of snow flying around him, clinging to his sweater and boots.

The last time the Deszvila Forest awoke, it was recorded in the histories as the Reaping, for never before had the outcome been so grim and plagued with death. The walls surrounding the city were reinforced and held against the wood's dark advances, but the madness of the forest still found its way into Starysa's secure and fortified borders.

Mortals were sacrificed on altars of quartz, their eyes gouged out, their bodies flayed open, their flesh given as gifts to the *baukvist* to keep them away from the city's gates. Vampires were overtaken by bloodlust, their cravings intensified with each new moon, their thirst growing more insatiable with every breaking dawn. They drained their victims dry, until their skin sagged from their bones, until they were merely empty shells of humanity. Not dead, yet not alive. Many took their own lives—their decaying bodies littered the streets for days.

Witches turned into frantic heretics, spouting off spells and charms to keep away the lurking evil. They smudged the city with bundles of sage, performed lulling musical chants during the witching hour, and wove necklaces of rowan berries. They hung bows of bundled ash wood over the doors of Starysa and engraved runes into the hardwood with their fingernails. Many of them,

Rozalie included, abandoned their homes in the wicked wood, seeking refuge in apartments above shops and below in cellars, taking shelter in the Marzena in hopes that the vile ancient magic would fail to snuff them out.

The fae survived as well, but they were not unscathed. Magic was torn from them, stolen from their souls in the pitch of night. It was so vile, so heinous of an act, that those who suffered from it keened in despair, and bound themselves in iron. If they were in possession of wings, they were ripped from their backs, carving a wound so deep the blood would continue to seep. Not even the healing properties of their magic were enough to save them.

When the wicked wood awoke, the world went dark.

Atlas lifted his gaze to Veros, searching his friend's face for something, any sign that they weren't meant to endure another Reaping.

"Tell me it isn't true." Atlas's plea was quiet, a coarse appeal to the gods. To the fates. To the skies. "Tell me time favors us."

Veros was still.

He didn't move. He didn't breathe. His face was lacking all expression, a plane of even neutrality, as it so often was when discussing the nature of his magic.

But there was a shift, the gold ring around his pupils dimmed.

And Atlas knew. "We can't catch a fucking break."

"One thing at a time, Your Highness." Caedian clamped his hand firmly upon Atlas's shoulder and squeezed. "One battle at a time. One breath at a time."

Right.

Except Atlas exhaled slowly, his breath misting before him in the winter's chill, and he suddenly wasn't sure if he'd ever be able to breathe again.

Thirty-Four

Everinne didn't want to crawl from the delicious comfort of Atlas's bed, but the thought of soaking in his luxurious gilded clawfoot porcelain tub was far too tempting to ignore.

The lights in the bathing suite were dimmed, most of the floating fire orbs had been snuffed out. Only a handful of half-melted candles remained, their tiny flames flickering and burning, emitting a soft, ethereal glow. A maid had been kind enough to bring her an assortment of oils, milks, and satchels of dried flowers for her enjoyment, and Everinne had chosen to soak in a fragrant milk bath that smelled of sweet cream and berries with velvety rose petals sprinkled upon its opaque surface. The steaming water molded against her skin, drawing out the exhaustion, soothing her aching muscles and tired bones.

She slid lower, melting into the curving back of the tub, so her breasts were covered. Then her neck. Until finally it reached her chin.

Everinne held her breath, closed her eyes, and sank under the water.

Her heartbeat echoed quietly in her ears, a calming thump

coupled with the easy coursing of her blood, like a midnight river's song. She melted into the calming bath, slowly coasting her hands along the side of the tub to grip its rounded edge, but she did not pull herself up. She waited. Until her chest tingled and her lungs tightened, until her magic stirred in warning, churning with disquiet at her defiance.

Rozalie's words drifted through her mind.

You are blessed by death.

If only there was a way Everinne could prove to herself that she was in control of her magic, not the other way around.

But she'd tucked her power away, she'd hidden it, refusing to use it at all after she'd shattered Callum's mind. It had been so easy, like snapping her fingers or plucking the petals of a rose. She hadn't even had to think about it or force it. She could still see his face in her mind. His handsome features chiseled with loathing and disgust, as though he couldn't bear to even look upon her. She thought about all the times he'd kissed her, about all the times she'd taken him inside her, and wondered how difficult it must have been for him to not slay her then. If he thought about slitting her throat when his lips were discovering hers. If he considered driving a blade through her heart while he pumped himself into her over and over. Even now, she could recall the night he'd attempted to end her life. One moment, Callum had been alive, his blade aimed to strike her down, and in the next breath, he'd been dead.

Breath.

Everinne needed air.

She heaved herself upward, crashing through the surface of the water, and gasped. Smoothing her wet hair back from her face, she stole another greedy breath.

In the adjoining bedroom, a door groaned open and footfalls shuffled against the hardwood floor. The maid had finally returned with her robe. Everinne had considered requesting some clothing as well, but if she planned on spending the remainder of the evening in Atlas's room, then only a robe would suffice.

Hopefully she grabbed one of fur and not silk, as there was a distinctive chill in the air.

"You can just leave it on the bed," Everinne called as she pulled the cord connected to the drain. "I'll be out in just a moment."

She stood, creamy rivulets of milky water gliding down her body, each droplet softening her skin. Damp rose petals clung to her stomach and thighs, and she wrung out her hair, twisting the dark locks over one shoulder. A shiver crawled along her spine and she shuddered, wrapping her arms around herself.

A flare of annoyance caused her brow to wrinkle in frustration. She'd forgotten to grab a towel.

The door to the bathing suite creaked and Everinne spun, bath water splashing around her calves.

"Oh, I said you could—"

The words died on the tip of her tongue, and her voice failed her. The stain of humiliation scalded her cheeks as she turned to find Kralv Oldrich standing in the doorway with her black fur robe draped over his arm. His large frame crowded the bathing suite, and his fingers, the ones capable of breaking a neck, stroked the fur lining her robe. A crown of obsidian branches dipped in gold was set atop his head, where his graying brown hair was swept back from his face. He was dressed in varying shades of black, while threads of gold trimmed his broad shoulders, and a wolf head was embroidered onto the lapel of his sleek coat. Thick brows were drawn over piercing black eyes, they were cold and empty, much like his heart, and skimmed her appearance from head to toe.

Everinne froze, covering her breasts with her left arm and clamping her right hand between her legs in a pitiful attempt to shield herself from his view.

Kralv Oldrich cocked his head to one side, roughing his knuckles over his short beard. "Is that any way to greet your kralv?"

"I…" Embarrassment heated her and she winced, ducking her head. "Forgive me, Your Imperial Majesty."

Everinne curtsied in the tub, naked and ashamed, her body trembling as goosebumps pebbled her flesh beneath his harsh stare.

He stepped further into the bathing suite, his polished boots clicking against the gleaming tile floor. "I find myself in need of your services."

The kralv reached out and plucked a rose petal from the top of her breast, crushing it between his fingers until it shriveled into a mottled lump.

It took every ounce of self-control for Everinne not to rear away from him. He was the kralv, and it made no difference if he was uncouth and repulsive. He could just as easily have her whipped or put to death for disobeying his orders…or worse.

Kralv Oldrich scoffed, tossing her robe at her.

She caught it quickly, clutching it to her bare body.

"Your magic, Everinne." He jerked his head toward the bedroom behind him. "Dress immediately. Your clothing is on the bed. There is a guard positioned just outside the main door, he will escort you to the dungeon."

Her nails dug into the fur robe, and she eyed the kralv with trepidation. "Dungeon?"

He'd made no mention of sending her to the dungeon.

Kralv Oldrich laughed, a brusque, dissonant sound. "Surely you don't expect me to have you torture my captives in the throne room, do you?"

Torture.

He was going to use her to torture people.

Nausea roiled in her stomach, leaving her queasy as the acidic pit scoured the back of her throat with bile. She swallowed the burning dread down and released a shallow breath.

What had she done by agreeing to this monster's terms?

As though sensing her unease, the kralv pounced upon her hesitation.

"You're not having second thoughts, are you?" he asked, the stench of his magic unfurling.

"No, Your Imperial Majesty." Everinne shook her head, but it was too late. "Of course not."

"Good. Because I'm sure you remember what awaits you if you refuse my demands."

The bathing suite was clogged with the acrid stench of sulfur and smoke. His power prodded at her thoughts, infiltrating her defenses, thieving its way into the darkest corner of her mind where it grasped her greatest fears and dragged them to the forefront, leaving her raw and exposed. She fought the intrusion, giving up the broken, sharp pieces of her, showing him exactly what he wanted to see. Weakness in her inability to control her death magic. Fragility of the heart, like it would fracture under the slightest pressure. But the bond remained secure, safely tucked away behind the layers of her own inner turmoil. She crafted a false terror to disguise the imprint Atlas had left upon her soul, a painful lie to ensure the thread binding them together was undetected by Kralv Oldrich's wretched power of extracting fear.

Horrific visions plagued her, inescapable illusions of what she would be forced to endure if she failed to heed the kralv's orders.

His heinous chuckle assaulted her ears. "So many fears."

Everinne let him believe it. As long as Kralv Oldrich couldn't reach the bond, then he couldn't reach Atlas. He wouldn't be able to use his own son as a weapon, and Atlas would be safe.

As quickly as his demented power seized her, it receded, withdrawing like the claws of a falcon.

"It certainly didn't take you long to find your way into my son's bed." Kralv Oldrich's lip curled in disgust as he turned to leave. "Though it's in his nature to be...rather convincing."

For once, Everinne kept her mouth shut.

She didn't want to give the kralv any kind of fuel he could use against her, especially not in relation to the prince. Instead, she steeled her spine, refusing to cower even as she clung to the robe barely covering her body.

"Fifteen minutes, Everinne." His tone dripped with warning and vile promises. "Don't be late."

The moment the kralv left Atlas's quarters and the door closed soundly behind him, Everinne lurched from the tub and staggered out into the empty room. Stacked on the bed were her favorite black leather leggings, a violet sweater threaded with silver, and a pair of boots with crystal-studded buckles.

Hardly the type of clothing one might choose for an interrogation.

If anything, it looked as though the kralv had snatched her clothing right out of the maid's hands with the intention to catch Everinne vulnerable and unaware.

She dressed quickly, berating herself all the while.

Her gaze snagged on the ring Atlas had given her, the teal gem glinted like the mesmerizing sea caught during the golden hour.

A twinge tugged on her heart.

She had to find a way out of this mess. It was too late to go back on her word. She would have to marry him, and a tiny, insignificant part of her was all too excited to commit to that part of the bargain. But dealing with the kralv, allowing him to use her to abuse and torture—she shook her head, clearing away the sickening thoughts of what he might make her do. She would have to be stronger, she would have to find a way to control her magic, to wield dark power like a goddess of the moon, just as Rozalie had said. To make it worse, Aisling had made it sound as though she'd never be free of the Mystic Obscura, and if there was one thing Everinne hated, it was the feeling of being trapped. Giving Reine a drop of her blood had been a wretched mistake with damning consequences.

Her impulsive and hasty behavior had finally caught up to her and now it felt as though she was tumbling into one horrible decision after another, like she was dangling from a cliff over a treacherous ocean and losing her grip. The rock was crumbling away beneath her fingers. The angry sea was ready to drag her under, to drown her beneath the swell of its lashing waves. One wrong move, and she'd fall to her death.

Escape.

The word whispered through her mind, like the wind sifting through the barren branches of a winter forest.

Escape from the Mystic Obscura.

Escape from Kralv Oldrich's clutches.

Everinne had to escape.

* * *

Everinne yanked open the door of Atlas's bedchambers and smacked right into the hard chest of one of the palace guards.

He grunted loudly, then scowled down at her, his voice gruff as he said, "This way."

The guard stalked down the hall at a clipped pace and Everinne followed, tossing haphazard glances over her shoulder. Though it was only the two of them, she couldn't shake the sensation that she was being watched. Or perhaps it was simply the walls of the palace, the menacing black obsidian that mirrored not only her reflection but also crawling shadows, skeletal hands, and wraiths that seemed caught between worlds.

Everinne stumbled to a halt, drawing up short behind the guard who'd stopped in front of a smooth wall with no obvious signs of a door. There were no handles or hinges, just a stretch of endless, glossy black. Like an impenetrable looming darkness, it obscured the pale light from the sconces hanging behind them, the faerie fire dwindling to nothing more than a sputtering spark. She stole a glance at the guard, who didn't seem at all bothered by the fact that he was standing before an empty wall. But then he lifted one arm and pressed his palm against the polished surface.

"Don't blink," he muttered, his voice barely a scraping whisper.

Her mouth fell open to question his warning, when her gaze

was suddenly pulled back to the wall, where her concerned reflection stared back at her.

Except it was no longer her reflection at all.

Where her eyes should have been, there were empty, hollow sockets, and trails of blood oozing down her cheeks and chin. Her face was gaunt, as though the muscle had been carved away until there was nothing left but a thin layer of flesh and bone. The clothing she wore was shredded, sagging off her wasted body, and only a few scraggly pieces of hair protruded from her scabbed, bald head. The rest had fallen out completely. Demonic hands with curving, talon-like nails wrapped around her throat, the cries and wails of a thousand tortured souls exploded in her mind, and Everinne swallowed her scream.

The guard chuckled. "Fear not, princess of pain. It's only glamour."

She stared in horror, gasping, as the piercing black wall glimmered and morphed, shifting to reveal an arching passageway of cold, damp stone.

"Helps to deter any unwanted visitors," he explained, nudging her further into the cramped cave-like tunnel.

Though there were no stairs, Everinne knew they were descending deeper underground. Cold air seeped from the tightly packed archways of stone, chilling her skin with each step against the solid, uneven ground. Bronze fixtures were anchored into the crumbling rock, where spitting midnight flames cast the corridor in an unusual, silvery glow. The mouth of the passage widened, spilling open into a dimly lit space, and the utterly foul stench that assaulted Everinne's nose was her first clue they'd reached the dungeon.

She coughed once, then gagged, dragging her sweater over half of her face in an effort to block out the disgusting smell. It reeked of stale blood, urine, and the lingering stink of sweat and soiled clothing. Rusted lanterns hung low from the cavernous ceiling, the black flames casting half the dungeon in darkness, the other half in that same eerie light. There was a steady dripping sound, a slow and methodical *plop...plop...plop...* that Everinne hoped was only a leak of maybe rainwater or some other known substance and not the noise of blood splattering against the ground.

Every so often there was a groan of despair or a muffled, choking sound, and she tried not to recoil at the atrocity of her surroundings.

She dared a few glances into the cells as she kept a close pace behind the guard, where crooked bars were shoved between slabs of gray rock, where all that stared back at her was the impregnable dark, so all-encompassing she swore the chill of its breath caressed her cheek as she passed.

Kralv Oldrich came into view then, cloaked in black and gold, a look of smug superiority etched into the severe lines of his face. He stood next to a cell, twirling the keys on one finger so they clinked together noisily, and for the briefest of moments, Everinne hesitated.

Did he plan to lock her in the cell with the prisoner? And what if said prisoner was actually dangerous? What if they weren't feeble and innocent, but actually someone whose very existence was threatening? She'd made the assumption that the kralv would use her to do harm against those who did not deserve it, but she didn't think about the possibility that she'd be pressured to torture a criminal. Perhaps they had killed in cold blood...exactly as she had done to Callum.

Perhaps they'd harmed a child.

Her steps faltered as she neared the cell. She sucked in a breath, cringing as she inhaled the revolting air, and prepared to face whatever sort of vile being the kralv held captive.

A faint skittering kind of noise grated against stone.

What if whoever she was supposed to use her magic against was none of those things?

What if it was—"A snow fox?"

Confusion plagued Everinne as she peered into the cell and frowned at the little creature. Its pristine white fur glinted like moonlight in the wavering darkness, though its small paws were muddied and brown. It darted back and forth across the cell, snarling and yipping, quite a bit wilder than she'd ever witnessed. Usually snow foxes were placid, if not clever and cautious. Though she supposed she'd be slightly ferocious too if she was locked in a cell with no way out.

The fox scurried to a far corner, curled itself up into a ball of fluffy fur, and its cerulean eyes locked onto Everinne.

"What's a snow fox doing in Prava?" she asked, more to herself than anyone else. The fox tilted its head, its tiny black nose sniffing the air. "They haven't been seen in years."

"Exactly. How bright you are, Ever." The kralv's voice jarred her, and she glanced over to realize he was standing right beside her. He inserted the key into the lock but didn't turn it, his gaze focused on the snow fox. Kralv Oldrich smiled then, but it was malicious, laced with a kind of odious evil. "A snow fox in Prava. Practically unheard of, and yet this one was caught slinking around the palace grounds near the healer's quarters. Why do you suppose that is?"

Everinne's gaze slid cautiously to the kralv. There was no mockery in his eyes, no condemnation. He was asking a serious question, expecting a serious response.

"Um..." She scraped her teeth along her bottom lip, considering. There was only one plausible reason a fox of any kind would be discovered by a healer's dwelling. "The herbs?"

"Perhaps." He unlocked the cell, and it groaned open, swinging wide. The fox's fur stood on end as it lurched back onto its rear haunches. "However, I have reason to believe this little fox is a shifter."

A shifter.

Trooping and solitary fae were not altogether rare, but much like the snow fox, they did not always exist in Prava. They were exclusive of other realms, made their homes in places where archaic power thrived, where they could be connected and bound to the earth and seasons, where the magic was *good*.

Not deadly.

Everinne eyed the fox carefully, noting the way its tail twitched, how its vivid blue eyes seemed too keen. "You think this fox is a solitary fae."

It was not so much a question as a statement, but the kralv obliged her observation.

"Indeed."

"How can you tell?"

Kralv Oldrich snapped his meaty fingers and the guard who'd led her into the dungeon stepped into the cell. He pulled a length of chains from his pocket and tossed it at the fox.

Everinne clamped one hand over her mouth as the poor little creature spasmed, as it attempted to climb up the wall, its claws not nearly strong enough to support its weight.

"You see, a normal snow fox would have no reaction to cold iron." Oldrich tapped the brass key against the bars of the cell, and the loud clang caused Everinne to grind her teeth. "But a shifting fae, one of the fabled solitary, would recognize it as dangerous."

He stepped back then and inclined his head, gesturing for Everinne to enter the cell.

She couldn't get her feet to work, couldn't get herself to move. It was like she was rooted in place, torn between right and wrong, knowing her hand was about to be forced. Clenching her fists at her side, she glared up at the kralv.

"What exactly do you want me to do?"

She wished she had never asked.

"Draw it out." He stroked his beard in contemplation, but it wasn't enough to disguise the way his lip curled. It couldn't mask the cruel delight gleaming within the darkness of his eyes. "Make this fae show the truth of its nature, force it into its fair form."

Everinne paled, all the blood draining from her face.

"What?" Beads of sweat licked the back of her neck, and she scrubbed her damp palms against the leather of her pants. She must have misheard. Surely the kralv wasn't expecting her to do something so ruthless, so unforgiving. "I...I don't know how."

He didn't even spare her a glance, his predatory gaze was so focused on the cowering snow fox. "Force the fae to shift, Everinne."

His arm shot out and he grabbed her by the nape of the neck, his fingers digging into her skin.

She shrieked in surprise as she pitched forward, and the kralv shoved her into the cell.

"*Now*," he demanded.

"Okay!" She straightened, cautiously taking one step toward the panting snow fox huddled into a grimy corner.

Everinne's mouth ran dry and a breath wheezed out of her. She attempted to swallow the knot of dread clogging the back of her throat, but it felt as though she was choking on sand and ash. Never before had she forced a faerie to shift, she didn't even know how such a thing was done, but she could only imagine the ramifications of compelling such a feat would be extreme. Lifting both hands, she carefully approached the snow fox, offering a tight-lipped smile to prove that she meant no harm.

They both knew it was a lie.

Everinne in her heart, where it constricted in agony.

The fox in its eyes, where shadows of fear haunted the brilliant blue.

She funneled her magic out slowly, tentatively, the scent of midnight lilacs permeating the air. The power of pain fell from her fingertips, silent and invisible, as it flowed from her into the fox. There was a yelp, a howl, as her magic pushed deeper. Further. Inky tendrils of violet and stormy black spilled from her open palms, pierced the cerulean blue of the fox's eyes, absorbing all the color. Everinne winced, squeezing her eyes shut as the touch of death delved into the fae's soul, moving through blood and bones, seeking the thread of wild, feral magic.

Strands of power scoured the beating heart, dragged its nails along the tenacious mind of the solitary fae. Still, Everinne continued to search, holding fast to her grip of control as strains of suffering continued to prod at the fox, weakening its resolve.

There was a shudder, the faintest glimpse, as though a veil of gossamer had been thrown over a singular fiber of magic. It pulsed with the power of runic tomes, of an eternal winter, of slumbering death by a frostbitten kiss. Everinne's power seized the sparkling thread and yanked, pulling it taut. She cried out as screams echoed in the dungeon, each one more chilling than the last. Her lungs caved, body trembling until she thought her knees would give out from under her while she peeled away layer after layer of glamour. A tear slipped from the corner of Everinne's eye as the fae's fair form was finally revealed, as the ability to shift was ripped and torn, left to mend with only the blood that bound it.

Everinne let go.

She gathered her magic, held it close, wrapping her arms tightly around herself as though that would somehow erase the torment she had inflicted.

Each breath she stole was shallow. The cruelty, the absolute viciousness of what she'd done, was cemented in the back of her mind, branding her as death touched. For now, not even just the walls of the palace would talk. Rumors of her insidious nature would spread, she would be forever marked with harsh judgement, so even the wicked trees of the forest would shiver whenever the wind whispered her name. All would think she'd committed such acts voluntarily, without coercion, because if she told one soul about her bargain with the kralv, his wrath would come down upon her.

And Atlas.

And Veros.

Everinne cringed, and gradually blinked open her eyes.

Crumpled against the far wall of the cell, was a fae whose clothing looked painfully familiar—a winter white bodice studded with pearls and lace, a wrinkled skirt of silk, and sheer stockings embellished with diamond snowflakes that sprinkled down her legs. Striking pink hair tumbled around her bare shoulders and down her back. Cerulean eyes framed with dark lashes stared empty and vacant, the only sign of life the horribly slow rise and fall of her chest.

Everinne's heart splintered.

"Aisling?" Her voice cracked as she stared down at her motionless friend. Regret bloomed in her chest, causing the ache there to magnify.

"You know this fae?" Kralv Oldrich asked, stepping into the cell for a closer look at Aisling.

Shit.

Lie.

She had to lie.

"No. Not really." She could still protect Aisling, could still find some way to keep her safe. It wasn't too late. Even after what she'd done, it wasn't too late. "We just work together at the Mystic Obscura."

"Interesting," he murmured, bending down. He pressed the back of his hand to Aisling's cheek and Everinne stiffened, her nails biting into her palms.

"She needs a healer, Your Imperial Majesty." Everinne couldn't tear her gaze away from Aisling, from the way she looked like each breath would be her last. "I...I don't know what kind of effect my magic will have on her and—"

"Yes, yes." He stood, waving a hand through the air, dismissing her. "Take the death fae back upstairs. It's snowing now, and I'm sure she will be missed."

"But what about Aisling?" Everinne asked as the guard snatched her arm and hauled her out of the cell.

The kralv's mouth pulled to one side. "You needn't worry about her."

"You don't understand!" She struggled against the guard's grip, desperate to keep Aisling out of the kralv's clutches. "If she doesn't show up at the Mystic Obscura, they'll hunt her down."

Aisling would be safer with Reine than she would with Kralv Oldrich.

Everinne jerked away from the guard once more. "She's bound by blood to—"

He was in her face before she could step back.

"You know not of what you speak." Kralv Oldrich grabbed her jaw, his large fingers digging into the hollow of her cheeks. He squeezed, applying just enough pressure that tears sprang to her eyes. "Now, shut your mouth before I seal it for you."

With one powerful thrust, he launched her backward into the guard's iron-like hold.

"Return her to the prince's quarters." The kralv stepped out of the cell and slammed it closed, so the bars clanked loudly, echoing through the dungeon. With one vehement look at Everinne, he shoved the keys into the pocket of his black coat and walked off in the other direction.

She said nothing as the guard led her back to the upper levels of the palace. Heavy silence lingered, muffling her footfalls, quieting her breathing, its dense presence damn near suffocating. No matter how hard she tried, she couldn't erase the image of Aisling, broken and battered, from her mind. And she couldn't free herself from the gravity of what she'd done, it burned through her bloodstream like a poison.

Or maybe she was the poison.

Everinne raked her hands through her hair, remorse twisting in her stomach like a serrated knife.

The guard swung open the door to Atlas's bedroom and she walked in, flinching as he closed it soundly behind her.

She inhaled, struggling to catch her breath as her heart pounded.

Without warning, a large mass of feathers and stone collided into her, sending her careening backward into the wall. Something cushioned the back of her head as the world tilted, and when she blinked her surroundings back into focus, she saw Atlas.

He'd barricaded her against the wall of his room, pinning her in place. His black and gold-dipped wings were stretched behind him, one hand was tucked behind her head, the other was fastened to her waist. His brows were drawn into a pinched scowl, his chest heaved against her own, and the golden green of his eyes was cold with rage.

He was furious and she had no idea why, but it didn't matter. Because at least his anger was familiar. At least his scent was comforting, it melded with her own in soothing, intoxicating layers. And because at least, for once, she finally wasn't alone.

"Where the fuck have you been?" Atlas demanded, glaring down at her.

And Everinne almost cried.

Thirty-Five

"Atlas."

There was a tremor in Everinne's voice, a waver that set Atlas's nerves on edge, and then she did the unthinkable. She wrapped her arms around his waist and buried her face in his chest.

Atlas stilled.

His Everinne wasn't soft. She wasn't an abundance of spring flowers or afternoon garden walks. She was wildfire, she was stolen kisses during the witching hour and dark satin sheets. Yet in this moment, she was somehow delicate. Like the fragile petals of a late blooming rose right before the first frost.

Atlas eased back, his wings vanishing, and he carefully stroked a hand down her hair.

"Hey," he murmured when she didn't lift her face to his. "What's wrong? Why are you—"

His question died on the tip of his tongue as the assault on his senses fully registered. The smell hit him first. Musty rot, stagnant air, the metallic tang of stale blood.

The dungeon.

Acid roiled in his stomach and his blood froze, stopping his heart as an all too familiar underlying stench taunted him. Sulfur and smoke. The reek of his father.

If that prick hurt her, if he touched her, if he even looked at her the wrong way, Atlas vowed right then and there that he would kill him. Blood or not.

Atlas grabbed Everinne's shoulders, and this time her head fell back when she looked up at him. He saw it in her eyes first, the shadowy threads of fear mixing with the pools of turquoise and ribbons of gold. Her breathing was even, but there was the faintest hitch, as though she'd been trying to keep it under control. And he didn't miss the way she bit her bottom lip to keep it from trembling.

"What did he do to you?" Atlas demanded, searching her face for the answers he sought.

Her eyes widened, the shadows in them expanding. "I…"

"Don't fucking lie to me, and don't you dare cover for that bastard." His hands skated up over her shoulders to her neck, where his thumbs gently grazed the smooth line of her perfect jaw. "Traces of his stench linger in your hair. And I can smell the stink of the dungeon as well. So, I am going to ask one more time, what did he do to you?"

That bottom lip of hers quivered again, but the lie fell from her with ease. "Nothing."

He inhaled slowly, stealing a calming breath, then reached for the bond between them. He could envision the luminous thread, imagine how it moved like shimmery ribbons of silk between his fingers as he twirled it, wove it, gradually tugging her closer to him. Everinne gasped then, barely even audible over the beating of her heart, but the sound of it caused his blood to hum. She shivered against him while he soothed and caressed the strand of fate binding them, as he eased the haunting darkness from her eyes.

Her hands found his arms and held, lashes fluttering as her gaze fastened to his mouth.

"Tell me," he whispered.

A tiny frown formed between her brows. "I can't."

"Yes, you can."

"Atlas, you don't understand." She shook her head and tried to pull away from him, but he held her slender neck with both hands, and a sigh of frustration escaped her. "I can't tell you. I can never tell you."

His temper boiled, scalding him from the inside out. "Why the fuck not?"

He would not tolerate secrets between them. Not if she was to be his wife, and certainly not since she'd acknowledged him as her mate. If his snake of a father had anything to do with this, if he'd threatened Everinne or forced her into any kind of unjust bargain, Atlas would shove his finest blade down Oldrich's throat.

Without warning, Everinne's voice, sultry and pleading, infiltrated his thoughts.

"Because he'll hurt you. He'll hurt me. He'll hurt Veros." The promise of tears clung to her lower lashes, but they did not fall. She rubbed her lips together once, tightening her grip on his arms. *"He will cause pain and suffering to everyone I love, and he'll use me to do it."*

Love.

Atlas filed that word away for later.

He stared at her, absorbing her earnest expression, the way her plea for him to understand echoed through his mind. He slid two fingers beneath her chin, tilting her face up just slightly, tracing the full curve of her lips with his eyes. Her quick intake of breath was exactly what he'd been hoping to find.

"That's why," he muttered quietly. His other hand fell away from her neck, moving to her waist instead to pull her closer so every breath of space was occupied by the press of their bodies against one another. "That's why you refused me the night of the ball. Why you so adamantly denied the bond even though you knew it to be true."

A single tear slipped free from the corner of her eye, proof of her reasoning.

Of course.

It was all so damn clear now, he'd been a fool not to realize it sooner.

"You don't want him to know." Atlas's hand cupped the side of her face, and he lowered his head so his nose grazed her ear where the amethyst studs sparkled. He feathered a few kisses along her ear, all the way to the tip, and she melted into him. "Were you trying to protect me, Wildheart?"

She huffed in annoyance and he grinned. "I was trying to protect everyone. Not just you."

"But maybe especially me?" he countered smoothly.

"Atlas." Everinne smacked him soundly on the chest, rearing back. "This isn't a game. It's more dangerous than you could ever think."

His smile vanished. "Ask me if I care."

She crossed her arms, a line of concern wedging its way across her brow, and her eyes flashed in agitation. That plump bottom lip stuck out again, and she wet it. Her sulking was definitely not having the desired effect.

"If he hurts you, I'll never forgive myself."

"And if he hurts you," Atlas growled, snaring her pouty lip with his teeth until she yelped, arching into him, "I'll end his fucking life."

His mouth slashed across hers in a hungry kiss, his tongue seeking entry along the seam of her lips. She opened for him willingly, let him taste and explore and claim. Everinne went pliant in his arms, her lush body molding against his like she was made for him, like she'd been crafted from the very temptation of nightfall itself. She was the blur between worlds, when the sun was at its weakest but the moon was not yet high, she was the rise of dusk. The twilight hour.

She sighed into his mouth, filling his lungs with warm caramel, dark roses, and blackcurrant. Her scent teased his tongue, and he wanted to unravel every layer of her.

"I need your help," she murmured, breaking their kiss.

"Anything." Atlas would give her the world. "Whatever you need."

She met his gaze and held. "My friend is in the dungeon. I need to get her out."

"Okay." He'd already decided right then he would never deny her, he would give until his heart gave out, bleed for her until all that remained of him was bones and ash. No matter what she asked of him, he would oblige, and she would always know she could depend on him.

Everinne blinked, her mouth falling open slightly. "You didn't even think about it."

The corner of his mouth curved into a smile. "I didn't have to, I will never refuse you."

Whatever concern or wariness still warring inside her faded away. Her features softened, and the bond warmed, securing snugly around his heart.

"You must understand," Everinne said quietly, a glimmer of hope rising in her voice, "we're not just freeing her from the dungeon, but the Mystic Obscura as well."

A needle of apprehension prodded at Atlas's spine. Blood magic was tricky, it could be tracked and traced. "If she's given Reine a drop of her blood, there is nowhere we can take her that she will be safe."

Everinne's brow arched, her mouth tugged to one side in a smart little smirk, and her eyes glittered with mischief. *That* look. Atlas had seen that look a thousand times before. Wild and spirited, it was the same one she wore whenever she indulged in reckless decisions, when all warning of caution and care were lost to her.

"There's one place she can go." Everinne held up her finger like she was about to spill a coveted secret. "But we'll need Veros's help."

The Astralplane.

Veros was the only one who could access the magical plane between worlds, he was the only one who could walk between space and time. It was guarded by wards that had been in place since the fall of the Ancient Ones, its archaic charms some of the most complex. And Veros alone could move through them.

Atlas captured Everinne's chin. "I have a mind to leave you there as well until all of this is over."

She rolled her sparkling eyes. "As if I would listen to you."

Atlas couldn't help it, he kissed her soundly on the mouth once more.

Her fingers fisted into his shirt, and she reluctantly pulled away. "So, you'll help me get her out?"

"Of course." His gaze slid to the glass doors leading out to the verandah where the snow continued to fall. "We'll miss the lighting of the bonfire."

They both knew what it might mean if they failed to make an appearance at the Zemni Boheme.

"It's worth the risk." Everinne shrugged then, but there was tension in her movements, and her back pulled taut against his palm. "Perhaps your father will forgive us if he thinks you were putting your talents to good use."

Atlas bent down and nipped her ear. "I have other talents."

"Oh, really?" She drew the last syllable out so it thrummed in her throat and he pressed his mouth to her pulse, pleased when it jumped against his touch.

"Yes. Perhaps I'll show you sometime." He grabbed her hand and kissed each one of her knuckles. "Let's go find Veros. Then we can save your friend."

Everinne rose on her toes and Atlas sealed his promise with a kiss.

* * *

"Stealing into the dungeon? This is a fucking terrible idea." Veros roughed a hand over his face and shot Atlas with a pointed look. "I can't believe she talked you into this."

"Veros," Everinne sighed, exasperation dripping from her tone as they walked down the slick stone pathway that led to the dungeon, each step taking them deeper underground.

Glowing black flames of faerie fire sputtered from warped sconces that looked like they would fall off the walls at any moment. The air was frigid, an unnatural kind of chill that settled deep into one's bones, and Everinne sidled closer to Atlas's side, grasping his hand in her own.

He linked their fingers together and squeezed in silent reassurance.

Veros craned his neck, glancing back at them, suspicion hiding in the depths of his eyes that were so much like his sister's. "What exactly am I needed for again?"

Atlas smacked him on the back with his free hand, offering a carefree smile. "It's a secret."

Veros frowned, the time lord hated secrets and loathed surprises even more.

He was going to be pissed when he discovered why they were bringing him along on their dungeon escapade.

"Besides," Atlas added as an afterthought, "you didn't have to agree."

"That's right." A smug kind of satisfaction pulled at the corners of Everinne's mouth. "You could have told me no."

Now it was Veros's turn to roll his eyes. His scowl deepened as he muttered, "As if I would."

But then he drew up short and Everinne's smile faded.

The mouth of the dungeon opened before them. Damp and dimly lit, the narrow passage they stood within emptied into a cramped hall with darkened cells on all sides. Bronze bars were jammed between the floor and ceiling, locking the inhabitants into a cage filled with beds made from straw, rough-hewn blankets, and tin plates with meager servings of days-old food.

Other than a few groans of agony and the incoherent mutterings coming from the shadows, the dungeon was eerily silent.

Veros took a cautious step forward. "Why are there no guards down here?"

"There's no need for them." Atlas followed, drawing Everinne in close. "Not when the glamour keeps most away."

"Yeah," Veros grunted, raking a hand through his dark hair. "That was one hell of a party trick."

The glamoured wall disguising the entrance to the dungeon had been put in place by Atlas's father. The kralv wanted it as terrifying as possible, to deter the need for guards as he deemed them better suited elsewhere—like protecting the border of Starysa from the Deszvila Forest. Kralv Oldrich had paid in gold for the tainted magic from the Marzena, monetary notes hadn't made a difference when it came to obtaining a demonic glamour. The wall served its purpose well enough, though. There were stories about some who'd tried to enter the dungeon, whether on purpose or by accident, and had died from fear.

Atlas expected nothing less from his father.

So long as one was not afraid, the glamour would ease, allowing them entry into the dungeon.

He let Everinne tug him along, hating how she was already familiar with the dungeon's layout. It made his skin crawl and his stomach twist knowing she'd been down here, knowing she'd been subjected to his father's harsh behavior.

She stumbled to a stop, and he nearly plowed into her, hooking an arm swiftly around her waist to keep her from toppling forward.

"There." Everinne disentangled himself from his arms and rushed toward a cell. She grabbed the bars and peered inside, tossing a fleeting, desperate look over her shoulder. "She's in here."

If it was at all possible, Veros's glower deepened. He crossed his arms over his chest and cocked a brow, his lack of compassion palpable. "She?"

"My friend." The look Everinne sent her brother was nothing short of desperation. "Aisling."

Atlas might have considered scolding Veros for being so heartless about the matter, but he couldn't manage to tear his gaze away from the body curled on the grimy stone floor.

Aisling, the fae in question, hadn't moved. In fact, if it weren't for the faint rise and fall of her chest, Atlas would've thought she was dead. She looked like a snowflake, covered in shiny white pearls and lace, but the hem of her skirt was now soiled. Her shoes were missing, and though she was wearing sparkly stockings, the sheer fabric wasn't nearly enough to keep her warm. The flesh of her lips was a pale shade of blue, and waves of hot pink hair fell around her, shielding most of her face from view. Every so often she blinked, yet the vivid blue of her eyes was cold and empty. Lifeless.

"What happened to her?" Atlas asked, stepping closer to the cell.

Everinne's throat worked as she swallowed. "Something... awful. Which is why we have to get her out of here. She can't stay in the dungeon, and she can't go back to the Mystic Obscura."

Veros tucked his hands into his pockets as he sauntered forward, his eyes never leaving the female who was curled into herself like a fae child on the ground. His jaw popped. "Do you have the key?"

"No. I've got something better." Everinne reached down and plucked a slender, silver pin studded with crystals from her boot. Then she set to work on picking the lock.

"Why am I not surprised..." Veros grumbled, but worry clouded his eyes, and he gnawed his lip as he rocked back onto his heels.

The lock snapped and Everinne pushed the gate wide so the bars creaked angrily. She heaved it open and gestured toward her brother. "Veros?"

He balked. "You expect me to take her? Was this your plan all along?"

"You're the only one who can hide her." She rushed to her friend's side, kneeling next to her. Everinne smoothed Aisling's brilliant pink hair back from her face, pressing the back of her palm to her pallid cheek. Her brows knit in concern. "The Astralplane is untouchable to anyone but you."

"Let me get this straight." Veros stepped into the cell, heaving a breath of displeasure. "Not only do you want me to steal your friend from the dungeon, but you also want me to break her blood contract with the Mystic Obscura and bring her to the Astralplane?"

"Veros, please," Everinne pleaded, and Atlas stepped in.

"Remember what we discussed." He shot a pointed look at his friend. Not so long ago, Veros was troubled by the fact that he wasn't there for Everinne, that he didn't offer her the love and support she so desperately needed. "She needs your help, Veros. They both do."

He hesitated for only a moment before pulling his timepiece out of his pocket. The runes whirred and spun in a kaleidoscope of swirling colors before he clicked it closed, shoving the timepiece back into his pocket.

"Fine," he conceded. His face was a mask of stoic calm, once more the unemotional Lord of Time. "But you must understand, Everinne, by taking her to the Astralplane, I am directly changing her fate."

Whether or not Veros's decision to help them would have a favorable or adverse effect on him and the use of his magic remained to be seen.

"Maybe you were meant to be here with us, in this moment." A wistful smile played at the corner of Everinne's lips. "Maybe you're part of her fate."

"Time grants no favors, Ever." Veros's calm façade did not change. He bent down low and easily scooped the nearly unconscious female into his arms. Her head lolled against his shoulder, her arms hung limp in his hold. "Not without asking for something in return."

Everinne nodded and stood, closing the cell door behind them. "I understand."

"I hope so." Veros shifted Aisling's weight and her eyes fluttered closed. "What did you say her name was again?"

"Aisling."

He grunted. "Of course it is."

Then Veros stepped back, carrying a sleeping Aisling in his arms. Atlas reached out and pulled Everinne to his side as the ticking of timepieces and the whispering rush of a thousand voices filled the dungeon. Veros's magic amplified, blurred swirls of colors swept around him in a sphere, streaks of suns, moons, and stars not of their realm revolved in a dozen different directions. Power rippled and flowed as distorted images of mountains, trees, oceans, and other worlds billowed in and out of focus. Veros stood in the center, and both he and Aisling seemed illuminated from within, as though they glowed with the magic of time. In one final burst of energy, Veros and Aisling disappeared, and all that was left in their wake was the scent of worn leather, fresh earth, and spilled ink on aged parchment.

Everinne let out a breath and leaned into Atlas. He draped an arm around her shoulder, and she grabbed ahold of his hand, holding tight.

"Come on." He guided her toward the steep path that would lead them out of the dungeon. "If we hurry, we can get to the bonfire and my father will be none the wiser."

And neither of them would have to suffer his unnecessary wrath.

"Thank you, Atlas." She spun into him, tangled her fingers in his loose, messy waves, and kissed him with such tenderness, she nearly shattered his heart.

"Mm." Atlas brushed his lips across hers. Once. Twice. "I could get used to your gratitude."

Everinne smiled, drowning him in those eyes of hers. Endless turquoise depths fanned with ribbons of gold. "And I could get used to your mouth."

Thirty-Six

There was something mystical about the first snowfall in Prava.

Even though the seemingly endless night was upon them and the skies were dark and heavy with clouds, streetlamps burning with golden light highlighted the cascading pieces of lace as they fell from the heavens. They twirled and danced, billowed in reckless abandon with the frigid wind, and Everinne tilted her head back, letting the flakes cling to her lashes and melt against her cheeks.

Gazing up in wonder, she stared at the halo of the moon, its silver light hazy and obscured. Not a single star in the sky could be seen, and for one breathless moment, it felt as though she was standing in the midst of a snow globe, with only stillness and the eternal beauty of winter around her.

Until the crackle of fire sparked to life and the logs of the bonfire to celebrate Zemni Boheme were set aflame. The pile of logs and wood chips were stoked, surrounded by slabs of black granite imbued with arcane magic to keep the fire going through the longest nights. Situated in the center of Starysa, it was guaranteed to burn bright enough until the first rosebud of spring. Not that it ever truly lasted that long, for eventually, the sun would take its time sinking across the western sky and the days would lengthen. The cold season, however, was when Prava was most vulnerable. In the winter, those who had been alive for hundreds of years held their breath, and prayed the woods continued their slumber.

A few musicians gathered near one of the empty fountains, their instruments striking evocative chords, blending into a haunting melody to welcome the upcoming Winter Solstice. The music stirred something inside of Everinne, its poignancy reminding her of evenings spent cuddled around a hearth, of soft voices and warm embraces, of stories of lore and songs of the season. A time, she thought with an ache in her heart, that was lost to her. Memories of her youth that were stolen by the wicked wood. The faces of her parents were a keepsake in her mind, locked away by time, by Veros, so she never forgot them. Yet, she could scarcely recall their voices. So, she'd relegated her mother to the tinkling of faerie bells and her father to the sound of rainfall against stone.

The heat of the silver flames fanned Everinne's face, drawing her back from the recess of her thoughts as warmth spread through the fur-lined coat she wore. She shifted her weight, boots crunching in the growing layer of snow, and though she was tempted to loop her arm through Atlas's, she thought better of it, shoving her hands into the pockets of her coat instead. She'd forgotten her gloves—again—and the biting cold was already nipping at her fingers, leaving the skin pink and chapped.

As if sensing her discomfort, Atlas draped an arm casually around her shoulders and pulled her close to him, the heat from his body far warmer than the fire blazing before them.

He slid two fingers under her chin, tilting her face up to him, the green and gold of his eyes more alluring than ever. They danced with the flames of the fire.

Her gaze flicked to his mouth, where his lips curved into a sensual smile, but then something just beyond his tall frame caught her eye. Against the play of light and shadow, through the hazy smoke, she saw Kralv Oldrich studying her. Watching her. Gauging her reactions to his son.

Atlas lowered his head and Everinne stiffened in his arms, her palms coming to rest on his chest in a poor attempt to push him away.

"Your father is watching," she warned, the words sharing the space between their minds.

Atlas's brow lifted. *"In that case..."*

He grabbed her throat, fingers digging into the back of her neck as he dragged her against him. She clutched at his arms as a spike of alarm pierced her spine, a strangled gasp barely escaping her when he increased the pressure, just enough to frighten her. Everinne's gaze snapped up and she found Atlas staring back at her, his eyes cold with unfamiliar cruelty. When he smiled, it was laced with malice, as though he'd donned a mask of deceit, morphing back into the character of the famed prince of pleasure.

"That's the thing about marriage, Everinne." Atlas spoke loudly, drawing the curious gaze of onlookers who lurked by the roaring fire. From beyond the silver gleam of flames, the kralv's dark eyes narrowed. "I can kiss you anytime I want."

His mouth crashed against hers in a brutal, punishing meeting of lips. He bit hard, nearly drawing blood, and then devoured her whimper of surprise. Curling her fingers into his coat, she held on tightly, gripping the thick fabric as his tongue lashed her own in angry strokes.

"Fight me." Despite his merciless kiss and the grip he held on her throat, his voice wove through her like ribbons of cool silk, soft and tempting.

Everinne shifted, tried to break free from him, but his mouth on hers was like drinking from a well of goddess-blessed water, and she was dying of thirst.

Atlas's answering chuckle caused heat to bloom low in her belly, sent shivers of longing shuddering down her spine so her nipples hardened to aching peaks, and a sigh of pleasure escaped her.

He slid his thumb lazily up the column of her throat. *"You'll have to do better than that if you want him to believe you don't love me."*

Everinne frowned and her eyes fluttered open.

Again, she caught Atlas staring at her, but it was different this time. Like he was daring her, challenging her. And she decided there was something delightfully sinful about kissing someone with her eyes open. Caught in the mesmerizing pull of the lusty green and gold of his gaze, she couldn't look away. Instead, Everinne scraped her teething along his bottom lip, tugging lightly.

"I never said I love you."

"Really?" He angled his head, deepening their kiss, and the featherlight brush of his fingers traced her jawline. *"So, it wasn't love when you sucked my cock while it was sandwiched between your breasts?"*

Shock slammed into her, and she shoved away from him then, shame coloring her cheeks at his crude dismissal of their shared intimacy.

"You bastard," she hissed, rearing back to slap that damning smirk and those stupidly adorable dimples right off his face.

But Atlas was faster.

He snagged her wrist midair and twisted, spinning her around so her back was pressed firmly against his chest, and she was pinned in his arms.

"Good girl," he whispered, his breath skating past her ear and across her cheek. "That was much more believable."

Sure enough, as much as she hated to admit it, he was right.

Past the spit of flames and curls of smoke, Everinne spied Kralv Oldrich. Shadows crawled up half of his face and the expression he wore was one of calculating interest. If she could make him believe she was merely going along with his plan, dancing for him like a puppet, then she would be able to keep Atlas safe. But if the kralv suspected for one moment that there was something between them, be it a mating bond or even something as simple as mutual affection, she would be putting both of them in danger.

Everinne schooled her face into frustration, giving the appearance of tempered rage, as though she'd rather be anywhere else than in Atlas's arms. But while she remained trapped against him, she carefully made note of their surroundings. The bonfire to celebrate Zemni Boheme was not nearly as lively as in years past. Not a single witch was present. Toward the outskirts of the center's square, just beyond the reach of firelight, a handful of vampires lurked in the shadows, lounging against the wall of an alley. There were a few fae scattered about, mostly in pairs or small groups, and none of them mingled with the humans who were present. In fact, the majority of the onlookers were mortal, and they clustered together like a flock of lambs, their eyes shifty, their movements restless.

It was their whispers, however, that gave Everinne pause.

"I hear they're being hunted, and that Kralv Oldrich is doing nothing to stop it."

Hunted.

Everinne's ears perked, and she listened closely to the conversation being discussed among a group of well-dressed mortals who looked as though they had money to burn and smelled as though they'd spent most of it at one of the city's parlors.

"That's terrible news for us." A woman with silky blonde hair shook her head. "Humans are almost always blamed for such atrocities."

"Do you think they'll come after us?" It was a man who spoke this time, his voice low and husky.

"I don't know, I hope not." The blonde moved closer to the group, and her paranoid whisper floated through the air. "But I heard the daughter of High Priestess Rozalie was missing, and that does not bode well."

Everinne's heart tumbled, dropping into the acidic pit of her stomach. Bile scalded the back of her throat. Certainly, she misheard. It was impossible, there was no way Zoryana was missing. She was safe, she was hiding in the Deszvila Forest. No one would dare go looking for her there. One moment, she was being cradled in Atlas's arms and the next she was ripping away from him, stalking toward the small gathering of humans.

"What did you say?" she asked, though it came out as more of a demand.

Her tone was all wrong, it was threatening, and the mortals reared back, glimmers of fright reflected in their wide-eyed gazes. Their fear was palpable and lingered heavily in the air.

She tried again, quieter this time, vaguely aware that Atlas was now standing right beside her, his hand gripping her wrist. "Please. Tell me what you know."

"You mean the disappearances." The blonde human shared a look of uncertainty with her company before she spoke, and when she did, her voice could barely be heard over the crackling of the bonfire. "The immortals are being hunted."

"Yes." Everinne nodded. "But you said something about the daughter of High Priestess Rozalie?"

Atlas's grip on her arm tightened.

"She's been taken. Or stolen." The human's face mirrored regret, confirming Everinne's fear. "But so have many others."

Everinne didn't care about any of the others.

She only cared about her best friend. About Zoryana.

Zory.

Not Zory.

"No, no," Everinne mumbled, turning away from the group of mortals so quickly the world tilted, and the colors of the night blurred. She stumbled forward, gasping as smoke filled her lungs, making it impossible to breathe. Her eyes burned and she swiped hastily at the tears streaming down her face. Everinne coughed, tried to wrench herself free from Atlas's hold, but he refused to release her.

She could hear him calling her name while she continued to lurch away from the bonfire, and though he held tightly to her wrist, he didn't try to stop her. He just kept pace as she staggered blindly into the night while the snow whipped around them, while the wind froze the tears on her cheeks. Her magic stretched, awakening the monstrosity inside of her. The power of death demanded payment and retribution. It sought vengeance as it clawed its way to the surface, ripping into her sense of self, snapping its angry jaws and tearing at her confidence and control like a raging beast.

Her chest heaved, lungs seizing with every ragged breath.

Zoryana was gone.

The cacophonous sound of pain, of death echoed through her mind. Loud, yet painfully silent.

Wisps of violet and ribbons of black poured from the tips of her fingers and Everinne clenched her hands into fists, until her nails bit into the chapped skin of her palms, until she drew pinpricks of her own blood. She clutched them to her chest as the violent power snaked around her heart, squeezing it in a vise-like grip, slashing it with blades of hot iron. It clouded her mind and battled her judgment, feeding off the swell of her storming emotions like a tempest of wrath.

Suddenly, Atlas was there.

He captured her face with both hands, warmth bleeding into her, his voice sharp and demanding when he said, "Look at me."

Everinne's eyes snapped to him.

Atlas's magic flowed into her, it shimmered down the bond like a gleaming sword of strength, defending her.

"You are in control." He leaned down and pressed his forehead to hers. His magic surged and the bond expanded, amplifying as he guided her out of the darkness. "Feel your power, Everinne. Own it. Rule it."

She swallowed hard, searching every gaping, cavernous part of herself. If she could summon it in the dungeon, then she could call it back, she could prohibit it from overtaking her once more. Shard by splintered shard, she collected every broken piece of herself, gradually piecing the shattered fragments back together until it resembled the reflection of her soul. Gazing into Atlas's eyes, she found clarity, but more than that, she found peace. With each breath, the agonizing pain subsided, the need to hurt, to destroy, ebbed. She gathered all the slivers of darkness, slowly plucking them from her heart. The veins of violet and black receded, her emotions calmed, and all the while there was an indistinct cadence, a sensual calling of familiarity that never left her. As though it had always been there.

As though he'd always been there.

"We'll get her back," Atlas murmured, his nose gently grazing hers.

His words struck her with a pang of despair. "You knew?"

Atlas leaned back, grasping both of her hands. The snow continued to fall, heavier now, so clumps of it gathered on his golden waves. "I knew, but I only just found out."

"And you weren't going to tell me?"

"Of course I was going to tell you," he pleaded, and she felt the distinctive tug of the bond, the aching strain of his heart for her. "But you'd just been drugged, Ever. I was trying to protect you, or at least give you time to recover from one traumatic event before informing you that your best friend had vanished."

Everinne knew he didn't mean to hurt her, she could feel it in the way the weight of his gaze settled upon her—it was brimming with an emotion she didn't want to recognize, that singular feeling that would make all of this so much more than a fated bond.

"I know." Her words were soft when she spoke. "I know you were trying to keep me safe. But I have to find Zoryana."

She turned to leave and Atlas's arm shot out, snagging her by the waist. "Where are you going?"

"There's only one place I can go if I want answers." Everinne's gaze drifted past the mighty stone walls that wrapped around Starysa, toward the forest blanketed in a dense layer of snow. "The wicked wood."

Thirty-Seven

A tlas followed Everinne to the Deszvila Forest.

No one stopped them from loitering in the shadows near the towering stone wall, and no one noticed when Atlas summoned his wings, scooped Everinne into his arms, and flew them over the other side. The main gates leading out of the city were already locked for the night, and though Atlas could've asked a guard to open them for him, he didn't want to draw any unwanted attention or raise any curious questions that could circulate back to his father.

It was bad enough he was already going to have to deal with a pissed-off Captain of the Guard, Atlas didn't want to face the kralv, too.

He landed on the other side of the wall, just along the forest's encroaching edge. The trees groaned in the wind, creaking like old aching bones, and the evergreen boughs, already heavy with snow, drooped low, reaching for the frozen ground like misshapen claws. Long shadows shifted between gnarled branches and with each gust of frosty air, the woods seemed to expand, to inhale, as though it was breathing in Atlas and Everinne's scent. The hairs at the base of his neck stood on end, a shiver of unease trekked down his spine, and though Everinne was already wiggling out of his arms, he wasn't at all keen to let go of her.

The forest was dangerous.

He knew the lore, he knew the stories born from the horrors of the wicked wood.

In all of his 148 years, only once had he dared to venture into the Deszvila Forest. That was on the night his mother died, and he'd stayed away from it ever since.

Just as he knew Everinne was familiar with those same stories, the ones intended to frighten and heed with caution. Yet she showed no signs of trepidation when she stepped away from him, warnings and vigilance meant nothing to her. She didn't fear the darkness because part of it lived within her. When the woods shuddered and yawned, stretching open in a deceitful welcome, Everinne walked right in.

But Atlas knew better.

He snared her by the hand, wincing when he realized her fingers were like ice. Interlocking their fingers together, he pulled her in close to his side. If they died in the wicked wood, it would be because some nightmarish creature attacked them and not from the temperature. Freezing to death wasn't exactly a noble way to die, and Atlas had long ago decided that upon his final sunset, he wouldn't go down without a fight.

So, he remained aware, his gaze darting from the carved trunks of the trees to the taunting branches to the impenetrable darkness that seemed to stare back at him.

He allowed Everinne to guide him, their boots crunching against the snow in perfect cadence together as they trekked deeper into the forest.

"Where are we going?" he asked, keeping his voice low.

Her shoulder brushed his and she tilted her head back, skimming the overhang of trees so dense, the snow could no longer fall through the thick branches.

"There's a hut just within the forest. Zoryana took me there after..." She squeezed his hand. "After Callum."

Just hearing her say that fucking hunter's name caused Atlas's blood to heat and boil. They never found out why he set his mark on Everinne, but that bastard human had tried to end her life. And in some sick, twisted way, Atlas supposed he'd succeeded. Everinne lashed out, she'd shattered Callum's mind, killed him, and in doing so, she'd become bound and trapped by her own magic. She saw herself as a monster. In death, Callum had filled her with doubt, sent her headfirst into a spiral of self-loathing and degradation. It was an absolute mindfuck, and she'd never fully recovered.

Atlas almost wished Everinne had kept him alive, that way he could have the privilege of killing Callum himself.

They continued on, passing ancient trees carved with whorls and runes, their roots buried deep beneath the solid ground, a source of archaic magic. Without the noise of their boots sinking into the snow, Atlas fixated on the lack of sound.

The blustery wind from before had fallen silent. The branches no longer trembled, and the forest held its undying breath.

It was nearly impossible to see anything, the pitch of night was suddenly thick like spilled ink, but he could just make out the outline of low-lying branches in the fading moonlight. Banking clouds continued to creep across the midnight sky and when they devoured the haze of the moon, the forest would be at its darkest.

Atlas steeled his nerve. He'd faced worse threats. "Do you think we'll find Zoryana there?"

"I'm hoping so." Everinne shivered, leaning into him as they walked. "It's a safe house."

Safe was not quite the word he would use. Not when they were being stalked by the wicked wood.

A scuffling noise echoed in his ears, a gnashing, a scrape of a sound between the space of their beating hearts and even breathing.

"Ever…" Atlas warned, but she stopped the moment he spoke her name.

"Gods, no." There was a twinge in her tone, a flicker of fear.

Atlas spun, prepared to face some unknown terror, and instead he found her staring at a rundown hut with a crumbling stone chimney. The thatched roof looked as though it was ready to cave in at any moment. Most of the windows had been broken, only jagged pieces of glass remained in the sills. Where the front door should have been, there was a gaping hole, and scattered about the stoop and forest floor were destroyed pieces of hardwood, remnants of what should've been the door. It appeared to have been ripped clean off the hinges, which meant whatever remained within the hut would only be in worse shape.

Everinne charged up uneven steps, determination firing her steps, but Atlas was faster. He grabbed her by the waist, plucked her off the derelict stoop, and planted her firmly on the ground behind him.

"You." He pointed a finger in her face. "Are *not* going in there. Not without me."

She knocked his hand away. "Zoryana is my friend. If—"

"Exactly," he fired back, snaring her wrist before she could smack at him again. "If *anything*, then I will be the one to see it first. We don't know what's in there."

He leaned in close, their breath misting and mingling, and stared into those turquoise pools of wonder where gold crested the surface. If there was one thing he would never get over, it was her eyes, the way they swam with a thousand emotions. Atlas pressed his mouth to the corner of her lips. "Let me go first, Wildheart. Let me do this for you."

She gave him the barest of imperceptible nods and then he was climbing the front stoop, cursing himself for not bringing a fucking sword, or at the very least, a dagger.

Atlas breached the entryway, blocking the entirety of it with his frame in case he needed to shield Everinne from anything. At first glance, he was grateful there were no bodies or blood, but there were definitely signs of a struggle.

What little furnishings remained were overturned, resembling chunks of wood for kindling as opposed to actual furniture. Curls of the oak flooring were lifted into ribbons, as though large claws had shredded the aged hardwood completely. Embers from a dying fire were scattered across the ground, their fading glow the only remnants of light. Stone walls were smeared with scorch marks shaped into unreadable symbols and even the iron stoker used for the hearth had been mauled and warped. The stench of ash and brimstone lingered in the air of the ravaged hut, the telltale reek of demonic magic.

His gut clenched, and bile burned the back of his throat.

There was only one person who could be responsible for this kind of wreckage.

Atlas ran his hand along the damp stone wall and his palm came away smeared with soot and an oily substance he didn't recognize. Rubbing his fingers together, he looked over at Everinne, who had finally joined him inside the hut.

She moved past him quietly, taking a slow turn about the ruined space, her gaze fixating on every mark, every piece of rubble, absorbing the full extent of the damage. He watched as she peered beneath broken slabs of furniture and rifled through the burnt remains of what should have been a kitchen, searching for clues, for any information that would lead her to Zoryana's whereabouts. But Atlas already knew they would unearth nothing here, they would only discover that which was meant to be found.

Evidence of the vile and demonic. The truly evil.

Another scent infiltrated the air, a gentler, floral smell. Midnight lilacs.

Everinne's magic stirred and she swiped at the silent tears sliding down her cheeks, wisps of violet and midnight spilling from the tips of her fingers. The beating of her heart thudded loudly in Atlas's ears and her chest heaved as her power awakened inside of her, cunning and ruthless, sending tremors of terror and dread down the bond. There were whispers of unease as well, and it was then he realized Everinne feared her power. Feared what she would do, what she would become if she stepped into it fully, if she embraced its strength.

When she sniffled and her breath hitched, he gradually coaxed her power back below the surface of her emotions.

"Think of your magic as a current in the ocean. There to guide you when you need it, but it is not the rogue wave that will drown you." He reached out, running one thumb beneath her eye to collect another fallen tear. "Who's in control?"

"Me." She sniffed again and loosed a shaky breath. Wrapping her arms around herself, she seemed to bury herself deeper within her fur coat, but then she lifted her chin in spite. "I am. I'm in control."

There was a waver in her voice, as though she didn't quite believe herself, but the rising tide of magic quelled.

Atlas lowered his head, brushed his lips across hers once. They were icy and cold, he needed to get her back to the palace. But not without a promise. "We'll find her, Ever. We'll find all of them."

A sigh escaped her but she nodded once, and when her gaze lifted to his, her eyes were hard with determination. Steadfast resolution.

And then the embers died.

A penetrating coldness sank deep into Atlas's bones, the fangs of frost biting all the way through his warming layers until even his blood froze. Everinne shivered in his arms and he gathered her close, his eyes straining against the slants of obscured moonlight trickling in through the door frame. Monstrous shadows lurked just beyond shattered windows, sulking like beasts of the night. The distinctive sound of gnashing teeth sent a shudder of apprehension racing down his spine. There was a scrape of claws against the outer stone wall of the hut, like nails being dragged across rough granite, the kind of noise that made Atlas lock his jaw. Again, he cursed himself for not bringing a fucking weapon.

The thatched roof creaked, and Atlas's gaze darted skyward. He tracked the movements, gripped Everinne tighter when bits of rock and debris tumbled down the hearth.

Fuck.

This was not good.

The fragments of moonlight vanished as a massive shadow took up residency where the door to the hut should have been, and dread curdled in Atlas's gut.

The *baukvist.*

He'd never seen them before, only ever heard the horrifying stories, but nothing could have prepared him for their grotesque appearance.

Two of them lurked in the door, their corpse-like bodies on full display. Elongated bones protruded from gray stretches of decaying skin pulled taut over rotten muscle. A foul, putrid stench, like that of an unearthed grave, hung heavy in the air. Thick and rancid. Beneath the thin layer of decomposing flesh, their corrupt hearts continued to beat, pulpy, malnourished organs that pumped black blood through their tainted veins. They possessed yellowed, curving claws instead of nails and where their eyes should have been, there was nothing but empty, bloodied sockets, as though they'd been gouged out long ago. Sharp, pointy teeth filled their gaping mouths and scarlet tongues, like that of a serpent, flickered out from between their papery lips, as though they were tasting the air.

Everinne jerked, her body spasming, and Atlas swiftly clamped one hand over her mouth.

"Don't scream," he pleaded through their bond. *"The baukvist have no sight. They rely solely upon scent and sound. Be very, very still."*

Her heart hammered in time to his, the erratic beating echoed in his ears like a ticking timepiece.

"Won't they smell us?" her voice cracked through his mind.

"Let's hope not."

The heat from her nervous breaths dampened his palm, and he carefully slid one arm around her waist, ensuring she was pulled flush against him—her back pressed firmly to his chest. It would be a painful escape. He'd only ever burst through a roof with his wings once before and he'd almost knocked himself unconscious. He'd been absolutely shit-faced and had only done it because Veros told him it was impossible, but nevertheless, he'd survived. So, shooting through a poorly thatched roof should be fairly easy, save for a few bumps and scratches.

Atlas's grip on Everinne tightened.

He was a second away from summoning his wings when he felt the prickle of frost along the back of his neck.

Fuck.

The windows.

Five searing claw tips pierced his shoulder, ripping through his coat, and then Everinne screamed. She was ripped from his arms a second later.

Atlas watched, helpless, as Everinne was dragged toward the window. She flailed and thrashed as one of the *baukvist* twisted her arm in a horrible angle and yanked her across the uneven floorboards. Her keen of agony fueled a fathomless rage, and Atlas grabbed the clawed hand tearing into his flesh, wrenching himself free from its spindly grasp.

He leapt across the splintered furnishings and reached for the iron stoker that had been mangled and contorted.

It wasn't the best weapon, but it would have to do.

The moment his fist closed around the rod of cold iron, his skin hissed and the stench of charred flesh filled his nose. He ignored the burning pain, didn't give a fuck if his entire hand melted off, he'd be damned if he was going to let that fleshflayer take his mate.

Atlas heaved the stoker behind his head, then slammed it down with a fury, severing the monster's arm. It yowled in agony, snapping its jaws and swinging aimlessly with its other gangly arm. Black blood spurted like sticky ooze from its hacked off member, sliding down the walls as it lurched away from the window. Its blood coated the oak floors like oil, staining them like spilled ink. Everinne toppled forward, clutching her arm to her chest, her eyes wide with fright.

Another *baukvist* appeared at the window where the other had fallen back. Claws tore through the roof as gaunt hands and arms reached between the sparse thatches of woven hay, grasping and clutching, desperate to flay the flesh from Atlas and Everinne's bones. The two by the door lumbered forward, their tongues lashing the air with each raspy growl.

They were surrounded.

Atlas grabbed Everinne's chin, forcing her to look into his eyes. "When I say run, you run."

"No." She shook her head violently, a line of determination creasing across her brow. "I'm not leaving you here."

He grinned. "I'll be right behind you."

"Atlas—"

"Stop arguing with me." He kissed her hard, knowing it would never be enough. "Just promise me you'll run."

Her mouth opened, then closed and he took her silence as acceptance.

His shoulder was on fire, his shirt stuck to his skin, the metallic tang of his own blood filling his nostrils as it slid down to his elbow. He grabbed the hilt of the stoker and raised it high— the skin of his palm was charred, the flesh melding to the cold iron, the pain white hot so beads of sweat formed along his brow. But he didn't care. He would only ever care about one thing.

Her.

Everinne.

Always.

Atlas charged toward the two *baukvist* staggering into the hut. He didn't spare Everinne a glance as he yelled, "Run!"

Thirty-Eight

Everinne hesitated.

"Now, Ever!"

Atlas's voice crashed through the bond, loud and demanding and full of urgency. She knew he was strong, knew he was more than capable of handling himself, but he was without a dagger or sword. He was armed with only an iron poker for the hearth, and though she was certain he could hold them off and stand his ground, he was simply far too outnumbered.

She stole one final look at him, watching as he swung the iron rod through the darkness like a blade of reckoning, piercing and gutting the *baukvist* with cutthroat accuracy, like he'd been born with a weapon in his hand. His movements were effortless and precise. Every jab, every slash met its mark. He was beautiful to behold, a warrior prince of Prava.

Only when something warm and thick splattered across her cheek and the bitter stench of rancid blood overwhelmed her did Everinne run.

She bolted for the door, crying out in anguish as the bond tugged fiercely on her heart, demanding she return to her mate's side. Each step away from the hut was a strain on her soul, the ache so keen and deep, she wasn't sure she'd ever be able to catch her breath again. She stumbled down the dilapidated stoop, tripping over the uneven stairs as she grappled with the air to remain upright. Frozen air burned her lungs as she rushed blindly into the forest, branches snared her hair, tangling in the loose tresses like the angry nails of a hag. Spindly tree limbs smacked at her face and clawed at her coat while gnarled, overgrown roots rose from the dead winter ground, determined to twist her ankles and slow her down.

The forest did not want her to leave.

Everinne dared a glance over her shoulder.

The hut was overrun with the *baukvist.* There were so many, she could no longer see the swooping thatched roof or the chimney. They crawled all over it, covering every inch with their spoiled flesh, elongated jaws, and beastly claws.

Fear lodged itself in the back of her throat and she screamed one name.

His name.

"ATLAS!"

But there was no response, only a horrid slurping noise, like a tongue sucking teeth, and a menacing growl.

Everinne didn't need to wait around to know that those flesh-flayers would soon find her. They would follow her scent and her scream, track her down like predator to prey. Again she started running, harder this time. Faster. Her legs pumped, spurring her through the forest as she fled, swatting at branches and avoiding the crooked roots that seemed determined to capture her. An overgrowth of bramble with thorny leaves clung to her fur coat, ripping and tearing it to shreds, biting through to her skin, until she was forced to abandon it completely. Her lungs burned, frozen from the wind and aching from each ragged breath. A stabbing pain pierced her ribcage and her muscles strained, throbbing with exhaustion.

Streaks of saltwater stained her cheeks.

She didn't know if it was sweat or tears.

She didn't care.

The toe of her boot struck a rock, and she catapulted forward. There was a twinge and then a definite crack as pain exploded through her ankle, rocketing up her leg.

A choking cry escaped her as her knees slammed into the solid earth and she attempted to break her fall. Her hands hit the cold dirt and she gasped, sucking in a breath as shooting spasms of agony pulsed from her ankle to her thigh. Her injured arm collapsed beneath her. Muck and filth soiled her clothing as she crawled, her nails digging into the ground for purchase, desperate to escape the clamor of gnashing teeth and raspy growls surrounding her. At some point, she'd been so consumed by running, by fleeing, that she'd lost her way. The path leading out of the Deszvila Forest had vanished, none of the trees looked familiar, and instead of being dumped out closer to the palace, she was now dragging herself uphill, clawing over uneven terrain. Her fingers were raw, bloodied, and bitten from the cold. A splitting ache was carving its way down her spine, her muscles felt like they might snap at any moment, and her bones were so weary, she thought they would turn to sand.

But all the while, Everinne's mind was focused on Atlas.

She repeated his name in her mind, whispered it like a prayer to the Mother Goddess as she fought for every inch of ground, as the murky haze of dawn infiltrated the snow-laden clouds.

Atlas.

Atlas.

Atlas.

Grasping a knobby bough from a nearby tree with both hands, Everinne heaved herself into a standing position. A peal of agony tore from her as nauseating pain splintered up her leg. Her vision swam with unshed tears, but she hastily blinked them away and swallowed down the rise of scalding bile in the back of her throat. She had to find her way back to Atlas. She had to get out of the forest. A broken ankle was nothing compared to having her flesh scraped from her bones.

Her gaze scanned her surroundings.

There was nothing but bleak forest for what seemed like an eternity.

Then she saw it. Through the dense branches weighed down by snow and the thick brush of evergreen leaves, there was a faint glow of foggy light.

A clearing.

Everinne winced and gritted her teeth as she hobbled and limped along the widening base of the hill. She must have been near the foothills of the mountains. Their jagged peaks were dusted with snow most of the year, and the whipping gales that cut between the faces and cliffs caused her teeth to rattle. Shivers wrecked her body as the forest thinned, the gusts of wind stung her cheeks and her eyes watered. She sniffed and ducked her head, wrapping her arms around her tightly and curling her frozen fingers into her threadbare sweater in a poor attempt to keep herself warm. Her breath came in icy, shallow pants and her heart sank, tumbling into the pit of her stomach as the forest spat her out into the clearing.

Except it wasn't a clearing at all.

It was a treacherous cliff, with sparse tufts of nearly dead grass sprouting up between smooth slabs of stone.

She thought she'd be safe here. She thought she could rest, maybe gather her thoughts and figure out a way to get back to Atlas. But stranded on the cliffside, she was vulnerable to the elements and exposed to danger. Perhaps she wasn't too high up, with any luck, she could climb down. Or at the very least, fall down, considering her ankle was utterly useless. Inching forward, she gingerly crept toward the ledge of the mighty cliff and peered over.

Her stomach dropped.

And so did her nerve.

Everinne teetered on the edge of oblivion.

Far below her, spanning a width as great as Starysa's city center, was a fathomless lake. If she were to jump, it would take an eternity before she plunged into its inky depths. The banks encircling it glistened like snowy diamonds, a few trees outlined its dark edges, the bare limbs draped with icicles and sprigs of frosty berries. Its surface was as smooth as glass, there were no ripples or waves, yet there was no reflection. Not the lurking forest or the majestic mountains. It was like gazing into a slab of obsidian and seeing nothing in return, just a great and vast emptiness.

A blast of wintry wind swept through the rising mountains, and she steeled her spine against the assault. The cold was violent and unforgiving, smacking her cheeks and tugging her hair. Her jaw ached from clenching it to keep her teeth from chattering, and her joints were stiff and sore from seizing against the brutal chill. But not even the slivers of early morning sunlight slanting through the mountain peaks would be enough to warm her, for already another ominous fringe of gray clouds hovered on the horizon, promising more snowfall.

She was lost. And alone.

Her heart strained for the one who spoke to her soul.

Atlas.

Warm, dank air pressed against the back of her neck, fluttering her hair, causing the skin to pebble.

Everinne froze, terror licking along her spine.

Something hot and sticky flicked the tip of her ear, then slid down her cheek to the curve of her throat, where it pulsed and fluttered...like it was tasting her. The barest of breaths slipped between her chapped lips and she suppressed a shudder, glancing down to catch the glimpse of a forked scarlet tongue as it laved across her flesh.

The stench of rot and fetid blood slammed into her.

Everinne shrieked.

She spun, all of her weight crushing her broken ankle, as she swung at the fleshflayer licking her. Another peal of agony wrenched from inside her.

The fleshflayer angled its head, its jaw falling open to reveal rows of tiny sharp teeth. A gurgling, gagging noise erupted from it, and Everinne reared back as its talon-like nails reached for her.

But when she stepped back, there was no more stone or ground to steady her, and her foot caught only air.

The *baukvist* lunged and she fell toward the bottomless lake, the freezing air rushing past her ears, her scream echoing through the mountains so they rumbled and quaked in fear for her.

She collided mid-air with something hard and warm, her body collapsing against the solid mass as she was cocooned in layers of fresh cedar, juicy neroli, and tempting spice. The bond flared, spearing her with comforting heat as it soothed the torturous ache buried deep within her heart.

"Atlas," Everinne choked out his name.

"Hold tight, Ever." He swept her into his arms, cradling her against his chest. "I've got you."

She shoved her wild hair back from her face as they soared, and when the misty glint of sunlight bounced off his loose golden curls and midnight wings, she got her first good look at him.

A sob stuck in the back of her throat.

Blood matted his hair to the side of his face and a gash ran from the corner of his left eye to his chin. The skin of his cheek was discolored where a bluish-purple bruise had formed. His coat was gone, scraps of his shirt stuck to his abdomen, fused by blood and grime. Claw marks mauled most of his flesh, especially across the wolf tattoo on his left chest and shoulder, as though the *baukvist* had tried to scratch the ink off his skin. His breathing was labored, each inhale a coarse wheeze, and she saw the horrid wound left behind on his ribs—one of the fleshflayer's claws had ripped him open, and a river of crimson trailed down to his hip.

There were so many injuries. And so much blood. Even with the magic of his fae blood, it could take days, perhaps longer, before he was fully healed.

She captured his face, gently cupping his cheeks, and her bottom lip quivered as she spoke. "You're hurt."

His gaze slid lazily to her. "You should see the other guys."

Everinne scowled. "That's not funny."

Atlas didn't even blink. "I'm not laughing."

She slid her arms around his neck, the tips of her fingers lightly grazing his feathered wings, and he groaned softly, pressing his forehead to hers. "Almost there."

She couldn't tell if his voice was hoarse from pain, exhaustion, or something else altogether. So, she blew out a soft breath, shivered into him, and held on as Atlas flew them back to Starysa.

By the time Atlas's verandah and pool came into view, Everinne's eyes were heavy with sleep, but it was his pallid and weak complexion that kept her awake. He looked worse than before, and though his grip on her never faltered, she knew he was drained. The wound from the fleshflayer continued to ooze blood, weakening him. His wings moved in a slow and steady rhythm, stretching and gliding as the sleek black feathers dipped in gold sliced through the bitter wind.

Atlas soared over the garden, then tucked his wings and swooped low between the lingering mist, clutching her to his chest.

"Hold your breath, Wildheart."

Everinne sucked in a gulp of air, curling into Atlas as he plunged them into the pool. Warm water surrounded her, rushing past her ears, soothing the chill that settled in her blood and the weeping ache of her body. The familiar pulse of Atlas's heart fell into cadence with her own, yet beyond the perpetual beating, there was something else. A feminine voice, lyrical and soft, called to her, the discordant words barely a whisper in a language Everinne didn't understand. The song was calming, like an atmospheric lullaby, slowly luring her to sleep.

A moment later, Atlas shot skyward, and they crashed through the surface of the pool, the eerily haunting voice fading like the remnants of the night.

Everinne gasped and sputtered, shoving her soaking hair back from her face as Atlas easily maneuvered them both through the steaming crystal waters. He looped an arm around her waist and used the other to cut through the pool, swimming toward the sloping, smooth ledge that gradually disappeared beneath the water's edge. He hauled them onto the shimmery gray stone veined with ribbons of silver and Everinne dropped onto her back, chest heaving, as Atlas collapsed beside her.

The heated, serene pool water covered most of her body, and tiny waves lapped near her shoulders, neck, and ears. Her uneven breaths puffed out before her in bursts of frosty mist, as curls of steam wafted across the pool like a marine layer rolling in from the Ladova Bay. The stabbing pain in her ankle subsided and she relaxed, a weightless sensation moving through her while she wiggled her fingers and toes to regain some feeling. Her leather leggings clung to her skin and the torn sweater floated in pieces around her, the violet fabric billowing in the small ripples. Beside her, Atlas groaned in discomfort, and she rolled onto her side to examine him.

Her lashes fluttered back in shock to find him mostly healed.

He was splayed on his back, his chest rising and falling in deep, even breaths. His color had returned, the golden tan of his skin suddenly vibrant and renewed. The slice running along his face had closed and was slowly fading, and the bruising beneath his eye was gone completely. Everinne rose over him, twisting her soaking hair back from her face. Though his eyes remained closed, there was a hard line creasing his brow, but she wasn't sure if it was one of discomfort or concentration. Gingerly, she dipped her hand below the water, the pads of her fingers gently grazing the horrible wound to his side. Her fingers feathered from his ribs to the dip of his hip, only to find the injury already mended.

Atlas snatched her wrist and she startled.

"You keep doing that," he murmured, eyes still closed, "and I'm going to return the favor."

Heat bloomed low in her belly, but she shook off the teasing sensation, focusing her attention on him.

"How?" Everinne asked, her gaze roving over his body. She cupped his cheek, carefully running her thumb just beneath his eye where the bruising had all but vanished. "Your injuries were so severe."

His eyes blinked open. There was something about the way he looked at her that set her nerves on edge and caused a knot of apprehension to tighten in her chest. His brows were drawn, giving him a look of severity, but his eyes were hauntingly sorrowful, full of secrets and remnants of pain.

"My pool isn't just for swimming." Atlas eased himself up, propping his weight on his elbows. "It's for healing."

Her hand fell away from his face, and she let her fingers drift through the warm water, realizing the sharp pain in her ankle had faded, her muscles no longer ached, and the weariness had all but bled from her bones. She was still exhausted, though she knew that was from lack of sleep and nothing else, but she didn't feel tired. Instead, there was a refreshing pulse of energy coursing through her, an invigorating burst of life that renewed her spirit.

She opened her mouth but Atlas spoke, answering her next question before she could ask it.

"It's imbued with my mother's magic." There was a layer of grief in his tone, one she never heard before, because neither of them ever discussed their tragic pasts. "She thought I would likely need it given my father's love of ruling with an iron fist."

His mother, Valentyna Skye, was renowned not only for her grace and beauty but also for her healing magic. The few times Everinne had met her, she'd been drawn to the kralvina's aura, for nothing shined brighter than a pure heart and soul. Her death was untimely and shrouded in mystery—no cause was determined despite Atlas's push for answers—and after, Atlas had been forced to live in the menacing shadow of his father. Kralv Oldrich was brutal, violent, and unkind. Though it was rumored he never raised a hand to his wife, it was said he spared his only son from no such torment. Everinne clearly remembered Veros telling her stories of the beatings Atlas suffered at his father's hands, most of it stemming from the kralv's utter disgust of Atlas's magic. Unfortunately, his abuse stemmed beyond just physical punishment. The kralv thoroughly enjoyed using his magic to get his way. His power allowed him to know and understand someone's deepest fear, and to use it against them for his own personal gain.

Bitter wind swept through the hedge of trees surrounding the pool, and Everinne shivered.

"Cold?" Atlas asked, sitting up and pulling her into his arms.

"I've been warmer."

"Let's remedy that, shall we?"

She barely had time to nod before he was picking her up and carrying her into the deep end of the pool. With each step, they sank lower into the water until she looped her arms around his neck and wrapped her legs around his waist to keep afloat. Tiny waves splashed between them and Atlas's hands skimmed down her back until both of his hands were cupping her bottom. His golden green gaze latched onto hers, hypnotic and tempting all at once. The heated pool continued to lull and soothe, until Everinne found herself leaning forward, resting her head on Atlas's shoulder while her mouth grazed the column of his throat.

"I'm sorry I almost got us skinned alive by the *baukvist*," she whispered into the warmth of his neck.

His answering chuckle reverberated through her, but then there was an immense stillness about him, and regret hung from his every word. "I'm sorry I didn't tell you about Zoryana the moment I found out."

Everinne nuzzled closer, clinging to him while she rolled through every possibility in her mind. The mortals at the bonfire had mentioned Zoryana was being hunted, which meant she hadn't just vanished or disappeared, but that she'd been captured. Or stolen. But the real question was who was behind it, as it had been years since hunters infiltrated the walls of Starysa. And if hunters were within the city, were they only hunting witches, or were they after others as well?

"All of us." Atlas quieted her mind by pressing a kiss to her temple. "Your thoughts are rather loud."

"All?" She leaned back and stared at him, taking in his somber expression, the way the teasing light in his eyes dimmed. "You mean fae, witches, and vampires?"

He nodded once. "And I'm afraid it's worse than that. The forest is awakening."

Everinne's stomach dropped, her heart slowly tumbling with it. Her teeth sank into her bottom lip and she shook her head, remorse clogging the back of her throat, making it impossible to breathe. If the forest was truly waking from its years-long slumber, then that meant Starysa was no longer safe, and it would once more have to stand against the ancient power of the Deszvila Forest. Perhaps they offended the Mother Goddess, or maybe they cursed the stars or cheated fate, for now it seemed as though every otherworldly entity had seen fit to punish them, to discipline all of Prava. Hunters were one thing, but the forest...the horrors of its last assault still haunted the hearts of those who survived it.

"We'll survive it again." Determination hardened Atlas's tone, and he slid his fingers through her wet hair, pulling her face close to his own. "No matter what comes at us. Be it the wrath of a goddess, the fury of the stars, or the sharpened point of fate's blade, we will endure it. Together."

"Atlas..." Her vision swam.

"No tears. Not yet. Only when you're sitting on my lap in that damn throne room with a crown upon your head as my kralvina. Then you can cry all you want." He wiped at the corner of her eyes where unshed tears clung to her lashes. "But for now, we will track down every last hunter. We'll stand against the wicked wood. And I swear on the souls of those before me, I will make whatever sacrifice necessary to keep you safe."

"Because for me," he whispered into the breath of space between them, "it has *always* been you."

Everinne's heart, once cold and shattered by unimaginable pain, tainted by her own magic, slowly began to mend. The broken shards softened. The desolate emptiness thawed, soothed by the bond as it expanded and amplified, restoring her soul. Maybe it was the warm waters of the pool imbued with Valentyna

Skye's magic, or maybe it was simply the fact that Everinne had found herself in Atlas Skye's arms, and maybe, just maybe, he'd been in love with her all along.

"Kiss me, Wildheart." Atlas brushed his lips across hers. "Kiss me like it's the last time."

She wove her arms around his neck and her lashes fluttered closed. When his mouth found hers, she inhaled, breathing his woodsy, spicy scent into her. She took every layer, fusing him into her blood, wrapping her essence around him, and vowing to never let go.

Once upon a time, Everinne fancied herself in love with the Imperial Prince of Prava, but their shared kiss told another story —the one where she'd never fallen out of love with him, the one where she knew he would belong to her for an eternity.

Thirty-Nine

A tlas faced off against Veros in the training grounds, the resounding clash of their swords was just enough to muffle their conversation. His feet moved swiftly over the frozen ground, and with every step he matched his friend's movements, his grip even, his strike sure. He opted for loose-fitting pants despite the winter chill in the air, and a trim sweater of soft wool for ease and accuracy. More than anything, however, he supposed he was grateful his wounds had healed in two days, and he was relieved there was only a scar from where that flesh-flayer had attempted to gouge out his intestines.

He circled Veros, keeping his pace slow and methodical, tossing a haphazard glance over his shoulder every so often.

Caedian stood just to the right of where they sparred, his arms folded over his chest while he lounged against one of the granite pillars, silently scrutinizing all of Atlas's mistakes. There was nothing his Captain of the Guard despised more than a pupil who refused to study. And while Atlas had been trained under Caedian for as long as he could remember, there were a few habits he'd refused to discard, and they set his captain's teeth on edge.

Conversing during battle, for one.

"Have you learned anything new?" Atlas asked, sparing

Caedian another glance as he dodged an attack from Veros. He knew it wasn't the best of circumstances, but at least this way, they lowered the chances of their discussion being carried back to the kralv. Out here on the training grounds, their voices would blend with the clang of metal, drown in the grunts of those fighting around them, and hopefully be lost to the howling wind.

"As a matter of fact I have." Caedian glowered, his gray eyes darkening with barely contained frustration. "While you were busy fighting for your life, nearly getting yourself *and* our future princess killed, I spoke with Eldress Valaina and Davorin."

Atlas locked his jaw and silently lunged into his next strike, which Veros easily dodged. Perhaps Caedian wasn't frustrated with him after all. Maybe he was straight up pissed. There was an edge of hostility to his tone, and it was quite obvious that he was still furious about Atlas following Everinne into the Deszvila Forest. It was unlikely he'd forgive him anytime soon, especially after going in without any kind of reinforcements.

"And?" Veros prompted, saving Atlas from having to pull the information from Caedian.

The captain cut him down with a look of pure menace.

"And," he drawled, shoving off the slate pillar, "Davorin confirmed our suspicions. There's an entrance that links the Marzena to the Mystic Obscura. Apparently Khiran visited a number of times."

Atlas considered this bit of knowledge. Khiran was the missing vampire whose blood could heal, whose bite never fully turned his victim. His type of power was rare, especially since his maker was a damn vampire fae—something that was almost unfathomable for the sole reason that faeries and vampires weren't exactly known to be anything more than cordial to one another. All that aside, Khiran had been one of the first well-known immortals to vanish and it was no small coincidence that the last place he was seen was the Mystic Obscura.

Veros swiped at him, the tip of his sword just licking Atlas's shoulder. The blade cut through the sweater and grazed his skin.

"You're distracted." Veros jabbed with his weapon again, and Atlas barely avoided the hit.

"I'm thinking," Atlas countered, tossing the hilt of his sword from one hand to the other, weighing it as he ran his tongue along his teeth.

He knew the hunting of immortals with rare magic and the Mystic Obscura had to be connected somehow. It was like he was staring at a puzzle, and there was only one piece missing, the one that would mesh the image together. He never should've trusted Reine.

Fucking blood magic.

"We're going to the Marzena," he announced, lowering his weapon. "Tonight."

"Giving up already, Your Imperial Highness?" Veros teased, twirling his sword with one hand. His dark hair fell in front of his eyes and tiny snowflakes started to fall from the graying heavens like a dusting of frost.

"No." Atlas sheathed his weapon, he would not be caught without again. "I'm merely saving my energy for whatever dangers await us in the Marzena."

He nodded toward Caedian, whose scowl only continued to deepen. "Make the necessary preparations. You're coming with us."

Caedian cocked his head to the side, his breath misting before him in an icy fog. "Why do I feel like you're trying to get rid of me?"

"I'm planning, because contrary to popular belief, I have every intention of ruling Prava one day. And since we're bringing Everinne along with us, I want to make every effort to ensure her safety." Atlas rounded on Veros then, pointing one finger in his direction. "And before you say anything, if you don't think she should come with us, then you can be the one to tell her she has to stay behind."

Veros lifted both hands in defeat and took a step back. "Point taken, Your Highness."

Atlas pinned Caedian with a look, quietly daring his captain to contradict him. He might be the prince of pleasure, he might smoke and drink and carouse into the early morning hours, but he was still the fucking prince. One day, he would wear the crown. One day, all of Prava would belong to him.

"Fine," Caedian grumbled, then raised one hand in warning. "But if you pull another stunt like you did the other night, trust you won't be able to take a piss without someone watching you."

Atlas smirked. "Fair enough."

Maybe his captain was coming around after all.

He waited until Caedian stalked off, until the door leading from the training grounds back to the palace slammed in his wake, before blowing out a long, low breath.

Veros raked a hand through his dark swath of hair, scattering bits of snow. Then he leveled Atlas with a look, one that spoke of raw emotion, one that requested the promise of necessary truths.

"How bad was it?" he asked, his gaze flicking to his boots before meeting Atlas's gaze and holding.

"Pretty fucking bad." Atlas rolled his neck, wincing when it cracked. Even though he was fully healed, his body felt as though he'd been slammed into the trunk of a tree, then tossed to the ground and left for dead. "And I'll be honest, for a minute, I didn't think I was going to make it out of that hut alive."

"And yet," Veros ventured, his voice barely above a whisper.

"And yet, I did. But I wasn't alone." Atlas stalked toward the overhang where two heavy workbenches were shoved together and a spread of practice weapons were at their disposal. He gripped the ledge of the wooden table and let his palms rest against its rough surface. Tension coiled between his shoulder blades, and he blew out another breath, his nails digging lightly into the grain as Veros appeared in his line of sight once more. "There was a wolf."

"A wolf?" Veros repeated.

"Yes." The image of the beast was clearly visible in his mind. Sleek black fur, eyes the color of slate, and vicious jaws capable of ripping muscles and crushing bones. Which was exactly what it did to the *baukvist*. Atlas had never seen a wolf of that size before, and the way it tore the fleshflayers to shreds, the way its piercing howl overpowered their screeches of pain, was like something out of a forgotten folktale. Yet what stuck in his mind the most was the way the wolf stared him down, like it *knew* him. "In fact, it was eerily similar to the painting of one hanging on my bedroom wall."

"The black wolf." Veros nodded slowly, setting his sword on the table, and shoving his hands into his pockets. He ran a hand through his hair, dusting away the half-melted flakes of snow. "Wolves have always been symbolic of Prava, they're commemorated throughout the whole palace. The black wolf, however, has always been the most elusive, yet he chose to help you in your time of need."

"Suppose I owe him a debt?" Atlas mused out loud, though after the wolf had ravaged the *baukvist*, he'd sauntered off into the forest without looking back.

"Perhaps." Veros angled his head and rubbed his knuckles along his jaw. "Perhaps not. Only time will tell."

Time. The only constant.

Atlas faced the training courtyard, where guards and soldiers were paired off, the falling snow slightly obscuring their shadowy outlines. He watched as they moved in expert form, precise and steady despite the gusting wind and thickening snowfall. His thoughts drifted from their mindful footwork to that of the Deszvila Forest, to when he'd told Everinne to run, to the moment he realized the threat was not to her life, but to his own.

Veros leaned against one of the benches and folded his arms over his chest. For a moment, he said nothing, and they stared at the training grounds in companionable silence. Atlas could hear his friend's mind working, and the weight of their next discussion weighed on him like a cloak of iron.

"There's something else," Veros finally said, kicking one ankle over the other. "Something you're not telling me."

"Yes." Atlas didn't even hesitate. He knew what concern continued to prod at the back of his mind, just like he knew that whatever he was about to admit would ultimately be his undoing. "The forest, the *baukvist*, none of it seemed threatened by Everinne. It was almost like...it recognized her. Or remembered her."

He shoved away from the benches and paced the stone floor, his gaze flicking to the courtyard every few minutes. "I don't know how to describe it, but when the fleshflayers arrived at the witch's hut, it was as though they wanted to take Everinne into the forest with them. Or were trying to keep her, maybe even protect her. Whereas they were blatantly trying to kill me."

"Like calls to like, Atlas." Veros's voice was hushed, a faint and distant whisper. His words hung hollow between them.

Atlas stilled and looked over at his friend, at the way Veros's face had become vacant once more. They way it always did when hours of time haunted him. "Your sister is not a fleshflayer."

"No, but she's death-touched. She wields a dark and dangerously powerful magic." Veros's turquoise eyes clouded like the late winter sky. "It could be the forest, and even the *baukvist*, can sense the power she possesses. I wouldn't be at all surprised if they considered her one of their own."

Like calls to like.

Atlas rolled the phrase around in his mind, yet it didn't sit well. For some reason he couldn't explain, it left him on edge. Disbelieving.

Everinne wasn't a monster. She wasn't a wicked creature of night or a ruthless fae who belonged in the forest's endless darkness. She wasn't sinister or malicious, she was the ultimate temptation. The utter divine. Everinne was the alluring yet devastating crush of pain and pleasure. It didn't matter if she was impulsive and fierce, because she was *good*. Her magic might be precarious, but Atlas had seen the darkest parts of her heart, he knew her mind, and she was a decadent disaster. Temperamental and uncontrollable, but he would gladly risk death if it meant surviving her storm.

Atlas met Veros's fixed stare. He spread his arms wide, helpless. "I love her."

Despite the admission, Veros's face remained impassive. "I'm aware."

It was a struggle to find words. He thought for sure Veros would punch him in the face this time. "I—"

"I've always known," Veros interrupted smoothly and the pinched line between his brows eased. "The only reason I asked you to take that vow, the only reason I wanted to keep the two of you apart, is because I have seen what awaits you both."

He looked away then, taking up a keen interest in his boots. "I am not a seer, Atlas. I don't hold fate in my hands. I can walk through time to the past, I can freeze the time of the present, and as for the future...what I see is only mere glimpses of events I cannot change. I don't know what has transpired to lead to those moments, I have no control over decisions and destinies."

Veros inhaled sharply and when his eyes found Atlas again, they were shadowed with an impending sense of doom. "This path, the one you've both chosen, will not be without hardship."

Atlas nodded once. "I understand."

Yet a harrowing unease was etched into every plane of Veros's face. Atlas knew he couldn't ask what he'd seen, what future he'd witnessed, but he wished there was a way. It would be far easier to be prepared if he knew what perils and hazards he and Everinne would face as opposed to the threat of the unknown.

"What of Everinne's friend?" he asked suddenly, determined to change the subject from the morose to the hopeful. "Aisling, was it?"

Unfortunately, his words plunged Veros into an even more somber and foul mood. "She...is not who we think."

"What do you mean?" Atlas lifted a careless shoulder. "We barely know anything about her."

"Exactly. We thought she was just some female who got

caught up in the exuberance of the Mystic Obscura. A friend of Everinne's. Maybe someone who needed to be saved from your father's dungeon." Veros rocked back onto his heels and pressed his lips into a firm, hard line. "That is not the case."

Wariness bled into Atlas, seizing his bones. "Who is she?"

He wasn't entirely sure he wanted to know the answer.

"Walk with me and I'll show you." Veros reached into his pocket and pulled out his timepiece, then flipped the gold lid open.

Runes of icy blue and numerals of gold exploded in a sphere of melted colors. Murmuring voices of the past, the present, and the future filled Atlas's head, their words indiscernible like the wind rustling through the leaves of a tree. Magic whirred and the world spun in a kaleidoscope, all of it drowned out by the precise and distinctive ticking of a hand that was never seen, of a bell that would never chime. The scent of worn leather, damp earth, and the splash of ink across weathered parchment hung heavily in the air.

Atlas's skin hummed and his lungs squeezed tight as he and Veros walked through time.

* * *

Veros had only ever taken Atlas through time once before. But that was long ago. Before either of them knew or understood the full extent of damage time-walking could cause.

It felt exactly the same as the first time he did it—dense magic coated his skin, the smell of it reminiscent of cedarwood and orange blossom. It was like wading through a river of honey, thick and impossible. Colors blurred around him like smeared watercolors, glimpses of other realms, other lives, other moments in time that were unfamiliar to him. Days spilled into nights, seasons mingled with no clear distinction as every breath was lengthened. There was no earth and no sky, yet with every step there was a shift in the air, a kind of crackling energy that heightened his awareness and caused his heart to hammer.

Beside him, Veros lifted his arm, keeping his hand coiled into a tight fist. Slowly, he opened his palm and spread his fingers apart. Magic emanated from him as golden light burst from a rift on the horizon where the colors wavered and trembled. Blinding rays poured from the fracture, cleaving the space in half, gently tearing a seam through the realms.

"Bleeding skies," Atlas muttered as he followed Veros into the Astralplane.

Veros caught him by the shoulder, holding him firmly in place as the brilliant beams of light ebbed and a vast field unfolded before them. Long blades of soft, emerald grass swayed in the warm breeze and pockets of wildflowers bloomed, their petals blossoming toward the sunlight. The sky was an endless stretch of crystalline blue, embellished with wispy clouds of white. In truth, the Astralplane was exactly how Atlas imagined Maghmell would look—it seemed fitting that the eternal paradise of the fae would be a place of ethereal beauty.

Yet it could not be, for Maghmell was not a world for the living, and seated upon one of the grassy hills with her knees drawn to her chest was the fae in question.

Her bright pink hair was woven into a plait threaded with strands of silvery white, and a cluster of pale yellow blossoms was tucked behind her pointy ear. She was dressed in a gown of deep navy satin, the sleeves were long and sheer, dotted with tiny sapphires, and ribbons of silver laced down her back. The wind ruffled her braid, pulling a few pieces of her hair loose, but she didn't stir. In fact, she didn't even blink. Her eyes, an interesting hue of blue, stared off into the distance, glazed and out of focus. And when a heavy sigh escaped her, it was dampened with weary emotion. Forlorn. Lost.

"If she's not just any fae," Atlas asked, his voice strained and hollow to his own ears. "Then who is she?"

Veros straightened, tucking his hands behind his back. "Your

Imperial Highness, this is Aisling Solasta, High Princess of the Winter Court of Faeven. Sister to High Prince Merrick Solasta and the late High Queen Ciara Solasta."

Atlas's mouth fell open and he quickly snapped it shut.

"What...the fuck." He whirled on Veros. "What was she doing in Prava? I highly doubt she was banished, at least not like Aran."

Aran, the High Prince of the Autumn Court, had been exiled from Faeven many moons ago and forced to live out the remainder of his days as a Dorai—one of the banished ones. At least until a fortunate turn of events involving his sister ended with his reinstatement.

But still, there was no possible way High Princess Aisling Solasta was Dorai.

"She vanished from Faeven during the Evernight War." Veros shoved his hands into the pockets of his pants, his gaze focused on the female whose eyes were now glossy with unshed tears. "Given her current situation, I would surmise she was likely abducted. It's possible she even had her memory stolen."

Atlas reared back in shock. "She doesn't remember anything?"

He couldn't imagine having the entirety of his life taken from him.

"Only her time at the Mystic Obscura and nothing else." An emotion banked deep in Veros's gaze, but then he blinked and it was gone. "She's barely spoken a word since I brought her here."

"What happened to her?" Atlas cleared his throat, lowering his voice in case the wind carried his words to the crestfallen faerie. "In my father's dungeon?"

Veros stiffened. His shoulders pulled back and he shifted on his feet, unease pulsing around him. Clearly uncomfortable, he swallowed once, then said, "Everinne happened. She used her magic to force Aisling to shift from a snow fox to her true form."

Atlas blinked, unable to register the words Veros had just spoken. "What? Everinne forced her to *shift*? No." He shook his head, unable to wrap his mind around the possibility. It was dangerous and too much of a risk, even for Everinne. Not only that, but it must have been traumatic for Aisling, if not excruciatingly painful. "That's impossible. Ever said Aisling was her friend, she wouldn't hurt her."

"Never on purpose, but if fear was used against her...if someone she loved was in jeopardy..." Veros's gaze slid to Atlas.

"Oldrich." Atlas spat out his father's name. "Of course he's behind this, I should've fucking known."

All at once, his heart dropped into his stomach and his gut clenched, as the realization slammed into him. "He knows. He knows about Everinne, about her magic. He'll use her to get exactly what he wants and if she doesn't bend to his will, he'll use me against her."

How could this have happened? They'd been so careful. They'd kept her magic secret for years and now his prick of a father had discovered it.

Veros's silence was the only confirmation he needed.

Atlas shoved his hands through his hair, dread building as he realized the bond was too quiet, nearly untraceable between worlds. He stole one final look at Aisling, shook his head, and faced Veros. "I have to go back. I have to get back to her."

Atlas vowed then and there that if his father touched a single hair on Everinne's head, he would stab him in the fucking heart and watch as the life bled from his eyes.

Forty

Everinne couldn't find Atlas anywhere.

As a matter of fact, she couldn't find Veros either.

The obsidian halls and unsettling rooms of Prava's opulent palace were oddly quiet. Usually brimming with back-handed compliments and idle social chatter, it appeared as though even most of the loitering nobles had abandoned Starysa's shining jewel in favor of other pursuits. Not that she could blame them. Everinne could only force a smile through mundane conversations for so long before she'd rather walk the entirety of the gardens in her most ill-fitting pair of heels.

Every so often she'd pass a pair of guards, and though they said nothing to her, she could feel the heat of their questioning gazes burning into her while she walked by them. Their stoic silence clashed with the decisive click of her boots along the obsidian floor. It was nearly impossible to move with stealth through the palace. Every time she took a step, she loudly announced her presence. Glossy black walls mirrored both her reflection and the darkened gold glow of firelight from gilded sconces. Though she knew it was impossible, it felt as though there were eyes behind the gleaming surfaces tracking her every movement. The thought alone made her skin crawl, and she tugged her sweater up over one shoulder even as it slipped down the other.

She glanced behind her, finding the long corridor empty, despite the murmur of indiscernible voices whispering past her ear.

Everinne *hated* the palace.

Were she crowned the kralvina, she would have it destroyed, burned to ash, then blessed with sage by the Coven of the Scarlet Moon before rebuilding something less...imposing.

She focused on the thread binding her to Atlas, plucking at it gently like the strings of a violin. It thrummed in response, melodic and pure, yet there was the slightest waver. As though she couldn't quite reach him.

Everinne twisted the ring on her finger, the one belonging to the late kralvina, Valentyna Skye. In the dimly lit corridor, the large stone glittered like the teal waves of the Ladova Bay. It was stunning, breathtaking really, and when Everinne lifted her gaze, she found her interest drawn to the row of arching windows where the frozen gardens had been kissed by winter. If she remembered correctly, Valentyna loved the gardens, and they were especially useful in terms of her healing magic. Right now, all the blossoms were decorated with frost, covering each petal with a layer of icy lace. Sprigs of berries burst from the elegantly shaped evergreens, the small lake surrounded by smooth large gray stones was frozen solid, and snowflakes danced down from the somber sky, coating the ground white.

Maybe Atlas was outside in the gardens.

Maybe he, too, needed to get out of the palace.

Everinne reached for the door that would lead her into the cold afternoon, when a low, gravelly voice sent a chill of unease racing down her spine.

"Going somewhere?"

Swallowing the knot of anxiety that formed in the back of her throat, Everinne turned to face Kralv Oldrich. He stood a few feet from her, as though he'd simply appeared out of thin air, and her panicked gaze latched onto the gleaming walls, but they gave nothing away. She curtsied out of fear of repercussions and not out of respect, taking note of the way he was dressed in warming layers, like he'd recently come out of the cold. His vest was a thick brocade, stitched with gold thread, and he wore gray wool pants. A shawl of gray fur lined the overcoat he wore, and though it was long, it was barely wide enough to stretch across the broad expanse of his chest. She thought one of the onyx buttons would pop off at any moment.

Everinne didn't care for the way his dark eyes seemed to absorb her, nor did she enjoy the way his tongue wet his papery lips as he sauntered toward her.

Refusing to cower, she locked her spine into place and gave him an answer she hoped would appease him enough so he would leave her alone. "I was only looking for Prince Atlas."

The kralv nodded, scraping the back of his knuckles across his trim, graying beard. "Mm. He has a tendency to run off when he thinks no one is looking."

Everinne's brows pinched together in concern. She wasn't sure what the kralv meant by such an insinuation, but she imagined whatever he was hinting at, it certainly wasn't good.

"Have you decided on a date for the wedding?" he asked, easily whipping her from one topic of conversation to the next without giving her a chance to recover.

"Ah, no, Your Imperial Majesty." She clasped her hands together, covering her engagement ring with her palm, leaving her amethyst with the dagger ready to spring in full view, just in case. "We haven't had a chance to discuss it."

"I thought as much. A spring wedding would be lovely." His large hand cut through the air in a dismissive wave, and his mouth curled into a sardonic smile. "But then again, the fates would favor one on the Winter Solstice as well."

Everinne startled and backed away from the kralv. "The Winter Solstice? But that's—"

"Days away?" Kralv Oldrich interjected. "Yes, I know."

He tilted his head, his gold crown embellished with black diamonds and etched with a wolf head glinting like a beacon in the dim light. Then he did the unthinkable, he offered her his hand.

"While we wait for Atlas to return from his pleasure parlor, you can come assist me in the dungeon."

She balked then, shrinking into herself as his words took root inside her, worming their way like a disease into her heart. "I'm sorry, what? Did you just say pleasure parlor?"

The kralv chortled, his massive frame trembling like a mountain on the brink of collapse as his hand fell to his side. "Don't tell me you thought it was just a rumor?"

At her shocked silence, he arched a wiry brow. "I take it you've never seen it, then? Consider yourself lucky. It's one of the more discreet parlors where patrons lounge on silk and satin pillows, drink copious amounts of whiskey and wine, and fall under the prince's sexual spell."

Kralv Oldrich scoffed, his upper lip curling into a sneer. "Vile place. Nothing but a frenzied orgy most of the time."

Everinne's stomach soured, and she bit back the urge to heave. She didn't want to think about the possibility of Atlas between the thighs of another female, even though she'd foolishly told him to do exactly that. She clutched the hem of her sweater, twisting it with her damp palms. The kralv had rendered her speechless in the worst way. She wanted to deny his accusations, to claim that Atlas would never partake in such activities, at least not since he was going to be marrying her. Except she couldn't find him. The bond was foggy, a distant pull she could scarcely hold on to, and there was no sign of him anywhere.

"Come along. You can ask Atlas to show you his parlor when he returns." The kralv snared her elbow and she staggered forward, letting him lead her without question. Guards materialized on both sides of her, and gradually, Everinne's heart tumbled as her chest hollowed out. "And if he refuses, then I will take you there myself, so you can see exactly who it is you're *really* going to marry."

* * *

The dungeon was just as awful as before. It reeked of urine, sweat, and the pungent, metallic tang of blood. Something dripped in the permeating darkness, the steady plopping noise enunciated by the pervasive quiet that seemed to linger between the hushed groans of despair.

Everinne's only consolation was that Aisling was no longer behind the metal bars. Hopefully, Veros had safely taken her to the Astralplane, and with any luck, she would be free from Prava and the Mystic Obscura. If Kralv Oldrich had even noticed she was missing, he made no show of it. He simply strode through the dank corridor, his chest puffed, his hands curled into meaty fists capable of pulverizing flesh. Maybe he was too consumed with other things, like being an asshole ruler intent on ruining the lives of his people, to realize Aisling was gone.

The cell Everinne stood before was smaller than all the rest, yet it housed two occupants—one male and one female.

The male looked absolutely terrified. He was tucked into the far corner, his knees pulled up to his chest, where he rocked in time to the haphazard beating of his own heart. The clothing he wore was nothing but scraps—the brown pants were shredded around the ankles and his threadbare sweater had been torn at the upper arm, where a festering wound bloomed against his discolored skin. His eyes were wide and bulging, his face gaunt as though he hadn't eaten in days, and his lips were moving. No words were spoken, at least none that Everinne could hear, but she imagined he was likely repeating some kind of prayer over and over in an effort to save him from whatever fate awaited him.

However, the female...she looked ready to rip off the face of anyone who took a step near them. Her eyes were wild, an unnatural shade of yellow, and they flashed with raw loathing. She bared her teeth like a feral animal, pacing the short length of the cell, waiting to pounce. Her navy pants were tucked into a pair of scuffed boots, there was a small gash on her thigh where her blood soaked the cotton fabric, and her ivory blouse was covered in filth. She gripped the bars with such strength, Everinne thought for sure she would bend the metal until it bowed like a tree branch. But the cell held firm, containing the female and her seething rage.

"Everinne." The kralv spoke her name like a curse. "I'd like you to meet Alevka and Wilhelm."

She cringed, hating the way he introduced them like they should be familiar with one another. It was some sick, twisted way of making the use of her magic more personal. More vengeful. Even though she held nothing against them.

Kralv Oldrich gestured to the cell, and the female hissed like a rabid beast. "These two are withholding information from the crown."

"What sort of information?" Everinne didn't dare look at him. Instead, she kept her gaze focused on the male...the human male, she realized belatedly. She stole a glance at the female who was, surprisingly, also human.

There was a huff of annoyance and the kralv sighed. Heavily. "That's what you need to find out."

Everinne shifted, uneasy on her feet. The woman, Alevka, was glaring at her now, her dark brows drawn in suspicion.

"But Your Imperial Majesty," Everinne began, the beating of her heart suddenly too loud for her own ears. She knew where this was going, she knew what he wanted from her, but it was agony, a kind of self-inflicted pain knowing what she was capable of doing. Unknowing if she'd be able to control herself, or if the darkness inside of her would take over. "I don't have that kind of power. Reading minds, hearing thoughts...those are not types of magic I possess."

"I know that, Everinne." He stalked toward her, gripped the hollow of her cheeks with his thumb and forefinger, and fear licked at the corner of her mind. Tightening his hold, he jerked her face up, as the acrid stench of sulfur and smoke caused her eyes to well with unshed tears. "That is why I need you to force them to talk. Compel them. Do whatever it takes to get me the answers I seek, do you understand?"

Kralv Oldrich shoved her backward, his lack of patience with her etched into the severe lines of his face.

"He wants you to torture us, *milazk.*" Alevka scraped her fingernails against the stone wall of her cell, the sound enough to make the guards standing watch shudder. "You can try, of course, but your tainted magic will never clear your name. You will always be the prince of pleasure's whore."

Everinne faltered. Her lungs squeezed, compressing the air until she could no longer draw breath. She hadn't been called that in...years. The foul nickname had stuck to her like grime she could never clean from beneath her nails. The orgasm gifted to her courtesy of Atlas's magic had been the only thing everyone talked about for months. She couldn't go anywhere without overhearing intentionally loud whispers full of snark or callous remarks. Some were even bold enough to chastise her to her face, though they were usually female, and almost always jealous. Then for a while, it seemed as though most of Starysa's elite had all but forgotten about the incident.

Apparently not.

Wilhelm, the male who was still huddled in the corner, suddenly stopped rocking. His round, dull eyes shot to Everinne. His face was a mask of emptiness when he said, "That's the one?"

"Yeah, I'd remember those eyes anywhere, all glazed and lusty." Alevka pointed a crooked finger in Everinne's direction and snickered. "The prince didn't have to lift a finger, I don't think he even *looked* at her. But she came apart all the same, moaning and crying out like a common harlot."

Alevka's words were like a swift punch in the gut.

Everinne balled her hands into tight fists, clenching her jaw until it ached. She remembered too clearly how Atlas's magic made her feel, how his quick dismissal of her left her burning with shame. Time had been a burden, moving so slowly, and she'd bottled up that mortification for so long that it fermented into loathing. Except now it no longer mattered, because Atlas was her mate. Still, the sting of the memory did not ease.

"That was years ago."

"Everinne is going to be the future princess." Kralv Oldrich's droll voice hung from the dungeon's cold walls like mold. "Mind how you speak to her."

Alevka only grinned wider, sticking her tongue between her teeth. "The prince of pleasure and the princess of pain, how fitting."

Tension spread between Everinne's shoulders and crawled along her neck. "You don't know anything about me."

"Don't I though?" Alevka taunted, her fiendish grin widening. Her yellow gaze flicked to the kralv, then back to her, and she sneered. "I know your magic is as dark and merciless as your soul. You hurt and terrorize, you inflict agonizing pain at the whim of the kralv because you lack a backbone."

"That's not true," Everinne countered, but the lie scalded her tongue.

"Yet here you stand." Alevka gestured grandly to Kralv Oldrich, her rasping laugh grating against Everinne's fraying nerves. "Doing the bidding of the kralv, while your betrothed buries himself between the thighs of any willing female. And trust, there are *many*."

"Lies," Everinne hissed as she teetered on the edge of all-consuming rage. Her power awoke at the tremor of violence, simmering through her veins, slipping from the tips of her fingers. Emotions churned through her like a torrent, volatile and restless. Anger at the audacity of this woman, as though she knew *anything* about Everinne or the truth of Atlas's nature. Frustration with herself at being caught beneath the kralv's thumb and unable to escape. And worst of all, regret. Because she knew her magic was strong, her control was lacking, and she wanted revenge against Alevka for the seeds of doubt she'd planted.

"You don't believe me?" Alevka ran her tongue along her teeth. "What makes you think he'll be loyal to you? I've seen you at the parlors, especially the Grand Cru, hanging from the chandeliers, taking home every male who buys you a drink. A sloven fae who is touched by death and thinks the world owes her sympathy. The prince sleeps around to find release from his sexual magic, you fuck and forget their names just to convince yourself you're still alive."

Her final insult left Everinne untethered.

Power erupted from her in dense, pulsing waves, and the cloying scent of midnight lilacs was so thick it was almost suffocating. She lashed out, capturing Alevka's mind, piercing her thoughts with violent claws of magic. They sank deep into the mortal's feeble head, ripping through her innermost secrets, forcing her onto her knees as her body twisted and contorted in agony. Her screams were filled with a harrowing kind of terror. They scraped the walls of the dungeon, so horrific, they would haunt the dreams of the dead.

But Everinne did not relent.

She scoured the woman, shaping her with blades of pain so she scratched at her own skin, desperate to escape the torment, willing to tear her own flesh from her face. Pulsing violence thrummed throughout the cell, swift and predatory.

From some dark, cavernous swath of space, low laughter sounded.

Kralv Oldrich.

Everinne had played right into his hand. She recoiled, hating herself for being unable to see through his schemes. He was a mastermind of his twisted games, and she was his target.

She would seek out the information the kralv sought, and then she would withdraw. Then she would find a way to break the invisible chains he kept wrapped around her neck.

Again, she pushed, delving deeper into Alevka's head, flipping through her mind like a storybook, tearing out the pages of images she considered useful. Everinne caught glimpses of

Rizenrok Forge, wooden barrels full of gems that sparkled like a midnight sky caught on fire, and lurking in the shadows of the mountains was a pair of golden, honey-colored eyes.

Without warning, Alevka's body jerked, then convulsed, her mouth opening and closing helplessly as soundless sobs were choked from her. She collapsed onto the damp floor of the cell, arms and legs twitching once or twice before a profound stillness settled over her limp body. Tears of crimson stained her sallow cheeks, blood dripped from the corner of her open mouth. She was like a smoldering flame, snuffed out completely by the breath of death magic.

The silence rattled Everinne's bones.

Pinpricks of ice prodded along her forearm as an inky vine snared around her wrist and a fourth blood rose bloomed, the tattoo marking another life she'd stolen.

A hoarse, shuddering whisper floated from the corner of the cell, where Wilhelm stared at her in abject horror.

"*Nevtorh.*" He curled into himself, hunching over, and squeezed his eyes shut.

Monster.

The word struck Everinne in the heart, stabbing her like a blade of damning.

She dropped her head and looked at her open palms, where tiny threads of black and violet slithered between her fingers. The hands of a killer. Of a monster. Wrapping her arms around herself, she stumbled back a step. Her heart thudded loudly in her ears, loud and unforgiving, a steadfast reminder of what she'd done. She grabbed the sleeve of her sweater and tugged it down, hating the way the fresh ink marked her skin. A cloak of despair draped itself around her shoulders, enveloping her in misery. Again, her gaze dipped to the contorted, lifeless body on the ground, and a depth of understanding tangled her stomach into wretched knots.

For the first time, Everinne had controlled her magic.

And she'd shattered someone's mind with it.

Nausea swam through her, and she swallowed the scalding rush of acid burning the back of her throat.

Kralv Oldrich's rumbling voice sliced through the disorder of her thoughts.

"Tell me, Everinne." His footsteps echoed through the bleak dungeon, scraping the stone walls with purpose. "What did you learn from our dear friend Alevka?"

She cringed, unable to bring herself to look him in the face. Her eyes remained cast downward, where the rough, damp floors were coated in moisture, where she caught glimpses of his towering reflection in dark puddles.

"They...they've discovered a new stone at the mines." Her voice grated against her own ears, hoarse and husky. "They sparkle like a midnight sky caught on fire and are worth far more than the rubies. Miners have been stealing them, guards have been beating them for it."

Pressing her back into the cold wall behind her, she let it catch her weight as her knees weakened. The words shuddered out of her. "And there's a sinister kind of magic lurking in the mountains. Something demonic."

"Mm, nightfall diamonds. Quite rare indeed." Kralv Oldrich heaved a sigh. "Pity."

Her gaze darted to him.

"That was information I already knew." He lifted a shoulder in feigned nonchalance and waved a dismissive hand in her direction. "I suppose I didn't need your help after all."

"What?" she rasped, disbelieving. "You...you had me torture her for no reason. You knew she had nothing to hide. You did this on purpose."

The kralv's mouth twisted into a hideous smile. He patted her cheek twice, ensuring the second smack stung.

"No *milazk*, you did this. It was your power. Your control." His hand fell away, and a look of smug superiority settled over his hardened face. "You did this all by yourself."

"No." Everinne shook her head, plastering herself against the wettish stone. "No, no, *no.*"

But no matter how many times she spoke the word, it didn't erase the truth glaring at her from the dungeon's floor. All those nightmares that haunted her, the ones she drove away with endless late nights and copious amounts of alcohol, came flooding back with a vengeance.

Callum's face appeared in her mind's eye, his warm brown eyes turning violent and murderous. She would never forget the fiery pain of his dagger as it plunged into her side, or the way he yanked it out with wild cruelty, only to aim for her heart next. His hand was locked around her throat, his touch cold, his grip tight. He'd made it impossible to breathe, even more difficult to fight him off, as shock and utter devastation injected fear into her veins. If she didn't fight him, she would die at his hand. Scarlet stained her clothing and bed, the metallic tang of her own blood filling her nose. Tears spilled down her cheeks as her magic ravaged his mind, as intense spasms of pain ricocheted through him.

Even with her heart breaking, even as tiny rivers of blood spilled from his ruthless eyes, she would never forget the words he whispered into her ear with his dying breath.

I will find you, temny feya. And I will end you.

Temny feya.

Dark fae.

Indistinct voices floated above her as the nightmares of her past consumed her.

"Get her out of here." Disgust dripped from the kralv's tone, but Everinne was too far gone to care.

She crumpled to the ground, her vision fading until there was only the penetrating darkness of her own mind, and the more she stared into its void of nothingness, the more she swore it was staring back. The scent of midnight lilacs was heavy here, the heady florals caused her veins to pulse and her head to pound. There was also a disturbing kind of silence, interrupted rarely, and only by her own disembodied voice. Self-doubt crawled through each crevice of space, carving out what remained of her confidence. It was a kind of personal sabotage, the way she so quickly turned on herself. The way her heart so easily bought into the lies her mind told her.

Temny feya.

Temny feya.

Temny feya.

The darkness attempted to swallow her then, slowly coiling around her arms and legs like the vines of deathroot, meant to suffocate her.

Everinne choked out a sob and her magic pressed in on her, cocooning her in ribbons of silky black and violet, barricading her from her intrusive thoughts until the nightmares, until the horrors of her past, could no longer reach her.

She pulled her knees to her chest, scraping her teeth along her bottom lip as her mind finally quieted. Only then did she try to speak.

"Atlas."

With a tentative, featherlight touch, she reached for the bond, the invisible thread tying the two of them together through dreams and realms.

"Atlas," she whispered again as a pinched breath escaped her tight lungs.

It hurt to breathe. It hurt to think. It hurt to exist.

She didn't know how long she sat in the dark, trapped in her own mind, repeating Atlas's name to herself over and over, until after what seemed like an eternity, tiny glimmering bands of gold slipped through the binding swath of black and violet. Lifting her gaze to the seeming endless expanse of rippling magic, she watched as Atlas finally appeared.

Not so long ago, she'd seen him here before. He'd safeguarded her heart and gently entered her mind, saving her from the chaotic storm of her emotions. Except this time, her feelings were not volatile. They were melancholy and subdued, because this time, the repercussions of her actions belonged solely to her.

Atlas waded through the darkness the way one might move toward the shore after swimming once the tide started to turn. He was pristine, glowing as the wisps of gilded light moved around him, with him. His dark blond hair was tousled, mussed with loose and wavy curls. The shirt he wore was the color of cream and his pants were a dark emerald, the colors so bright, so brilliant against the gloom. An aura danced above him, his magic shimmering and beautiful, illuminating even brighter when his eyes landed on her and he smiled.

He held out his hand. "Come with me."

She reached, then hesitated when his gaze flicked to the new tattoo marking her arm. "I did something awful."

"It's okay, I'm here now." His eyes slid to her face and held. "I know what he's doing to you. What he's forcing you to do. I will not let him do it again."

He. Kralv Oldrich.

"I did it on my own this time." Her gaze fell. She couldn't look at him, couldn't bear to see the disgust he would harbor once he realized she'd killed someone of her own will. "I hid behind my magic for so long, but maybe it's not my power that's the problem. Maybe it's me. I deserve to be alone."

"So long as you are mine, you will never be alone." Atlas stretched out his arm and the bond warmed. Hummed in a comforting melody. "I want you. All of you. The broken, the chaotic, the reckless, and damning. The beautiful, the audacious, the wild, and tempting. Beyond the skies and seas, Wildheart, I want you."

Everinne nodded. Breathless. "Beyond the skies and seas."

She clasped his hand, and the bond tugged fiercely, yanking her free from the gathering darkness. There was a crush of magic, of florals and spice, and then she toppled into his waiting arms.

Blinking, she found herself sitting in Atlas's lap on his bed, his arms woven tightly around her, the frigid cold and pervading reek of the dungeon nothing but another painful memory. She must have been carried to his bedroom, deposited onto the bed like unwanted garbage by some guard employed by the kralv. But Atlas hadn't rejected her, he hadn't disowned her even though she'd shown him the truth of her power, even though she had no idea how to break herself free from the kralv's hold. The longer she remained his puppet, the more harm she would cause, the more innocent lives would be lost.

Despite all the horrible things she'd done, Atlas hadn't abandoned her.

Everinne wrapped her arms around his neck and buried her face in his chest. She breathed in the scent of him, the familiarity, the beckoning of her soul.

"You came," she murmured softly.

Atlas's grip did not lessen as he pressed a kiss to her cheek and whispered, "You called."

Forty-One

Atlas kept Everinne close to him, never letting her out of his sight. After his father's little stunt in the dungeon where he coerced her into torturing a mortal for information he already had, Atlas had no intentions of letting the kralv anywhere near her again.

So, he kept her gloved hand tucked safely in his as they trudged through the snow-laden streets of Starysa. The city reminded him of a tranquil winter wonderland, were it not for the fact that the air seemed charged with a strained edge of friction, as though every soul was simply holding their breath, waiting for the inevitable. Whatever that might be. Even the music pouring from the numerous parlors was muffled instead of jubilant and the patrons were mellow, their drunken laughter dulled and hitched, as no one was too keen on drawing unwanted attention to themselves. Most of the shops had already closed for the evening and while there were a number of taverns and lounges open, the windows were all dark and moody, the glowing lights from within barely an acknowledgment to the hour. Clumps of snow fell from the darkening skies, the thick layer of clouds blotting out the full moon so there was only a streaky haze of silver light.

The night was bitter, a damp kind of cold, and Atlas had received reports of waves in the Ladova Bay frosting over as they peaked and capped. Only the continuous flame of the Zemni Boheme offered a shred of warmth, but even that was fleeting, as they weren't lingering in the city's center. Tonight, they were heading into the Marzena.

Caedian and Veros walked in front of them, bundled in warming layers, their boots crunching lightly against the frozen ground. Caedian stalked with purpose, constantly on alert, his hand hovering above the hilt of his sword, while Veros strolled along beside him with his hands tucked into his pockets. Atlas couldn't be sure, but he could've sworn Veros was whistling. The wind carried the faint sound back to him, the tune reminiscent of an old-world lullaby.

They rounded a corner where the cobblestones narrowed, becoming more uneven, where the faerie fire flickering in the curving lamp posts didn't quite reach.

If the streets of Starysa were lacking in citizens before, they were absolutely desolate now. Not a soul wandered down the serpentine alley, because what they would meet at its end was nothing short of abysmal.

The entrance to the Marzena stood before them. It was a towering gate with rusted bars and sharpened stakes that reached into an arch, where the metal was twisted and mangled to mimic the shape of serpents ready to strike. Beyond it, there was nothing but a tunnel made of ancient stone that descended into a pit of darkness.

Atlas looked over at Everinne. "Are you sure about this?"

She nodded, suppressing a shiver. "Yes. It's the only way."

He tugged her knit, fur-lined hat over the small points of her ears, admiring the tiny dagger earrings that dangled there. "If you're sure?"

"I'm sure." Her cheeks and the tip of her nose were pink from the cold, and her wind-bitten lips curved into a smile. "Besides,

Zoryana is more important than a blood pact with the Mystic Obscura."

She wasn't wrong, but at the same time, he didn't know the kind of repercussions she would suffer if she was late for her performance. Or worse, if she failed to show completely.

Veros tossed a look over his shoulder as the gate creaked open, announcing their arrival to anyone who might be loitering nearby. He shared a look with Caedian, then nodded toward the gaping opening of the Marzena. "Are we doing this?"

Everinne stepped up and Atlas went with her. "We're doing this."

Veros jerked his head in the direction of the tunnel. "Let's go then. I don't want us to be down here all night."

Venturing into the Marzena was nothing like Atlas expected.

It was a labyrinth of tunnels. Some were cavernous, stretching wide like the streets above them while others were excessively narrow, making it so that only one person could move through the space at a time. Bronze lanterns floated along the ceiling, suspended by magic. The dim amber light quivered often, dousing most of the Marzena into long, harsh shadows, and making it difficult to navigate. They passed a handful of drunken fae, their eyes glazed as they shuffled and toppled into one another. A few vampires stood next to a random wooden door that seemed to open into the side of the tunnel. But then they knocked four times, spoke something in a language Atlas couldn't understand, and the door swung open. Pulsing music and the potent scent of stigs filled the dank air, and the vampires strode inside, the door slamming shut behind them.

Despite the flowery smell of stigs and aged alcohol hanging in the air, there was an underlying stench as well. Acrid and foul, it seemed to seep from the stone, to ooze between the crevices.

"No wonder the witches don't like to come here," Caedian muttered, his pale gaze darting toward every movement. "This place reeks of corrupt magic."

Corrupt magic. *That* was the smell.

Carved into the tunnel walls were the market's notorious shops, the grimy windows showcasing all kinds of remarkable, exotic wares.

Beside him, Everinne drew up short. "Here."

Her gaze was fixated on one of the cluttered window displays, and Atlas peered inside, unable to note anything worthwhile or extraordinary. There was the usual collection of baubles—spelled mirrors, enchanted glass spheres, bundles of dried herbs, and sachets of tea. Jewelry was displayed as well, an assortment of necklaces and rings, as well as some daggers inlaid with sparkling gemstones. But nothing that looked like it could be some sort of key in helping them locate Zoryana and the other hunted immortals.

"Why here?" Veros asked, sauntering closer for a look. He arched one dark brow in interest. "What caught your eye, Ever?"

She rubbed her lips together and stole a glance behind her to where Caedian stood, his steely gaze trained on anyone or anything lurking in the shadows.

Everinne blew out a soft breath.

"The female...in the dungeon." Her hand drifted idly to her forearm, where Atlas knew a fresh tattoo marked her. "In her mind, there were images of the mines."

"The fire ruby mines? The Rizenrok Forge?" Atlas's brows pinched together in concern.

There had been no talk or discussion of the mines recently at all. As far as he knew, and all his father had mentioned, was that the mines were meant as a means of punishment, but the truth of the matter was that they were a slave camp. Everyone who was found guilty of an offense was sent to Rizenrok Forge, it was why the dungeon was often empty. Sentences served there were either fairly brief or exceptionally long, depending upon the crime against the crown.

He stole a hasty look at Veros, whose eyes reflected an unnatural kind of worry. Even Caedian had moved closer, his pale gaze suddenly clouded with concern. "What of them?"

"There was a discovery of a new gemstone, rarer than fire rubies, a jewel with more sparkle. More value. The prisoners were trying to pocket them, to keep them secret from the guards. I imagine some of them thought they could use this new stone to buy their freedom."

A new gemstone meant there was an increased chance Atlas's father would send more people to mines, whether they were guilty or not. "What does it look like?"

Her bottom lip trembled, but then she bit it before swallowing hard. "Like a midnight sky caught on fire. Black like obsidian, yet it reflects the sparkle of the stars."

"Was there anything else?" Veros asked, edging closer.

"No. There was nothing else. Not before I..." Everinne's face shuttered and her shoulders dropped.

Atlas grabbed her hand and gave it a reassuring squeeze.

Caedian tapped lightly on the filthy glass window. "So, why this shop?"

Everinne pointed to a glittering black gemstone cushioned on a pile of navy velvet. It was shaped like an oval, polished and smoothed, and held all the fire of the stars in its gleaming surface.

"Because *that* is a nightfall diamond." She looked up then and met each of their intent gazes. "If this shop has a stone this rare, then they must know something we don't."

"Fair enough," Veros mumbled. "Alright, let's go in."

They entered the shop together, with Atlas keeping Everinne's hand entrapped in his own. The inside of the store wasn't nearly as grimy as the window. There were leaning wooden shelves lined with an array of trinkets, anything from velvet bags filled with rune stones, to tarot cards, to bundles of sage wrapped with twine. Altars held bowls of bones and sand, and there was a table where half-melted candles burned into pools of colored wax. Books with weathered spines and faded edges were stacked precariously high. One wrong move and the entire pile would tumble to the floor. Tinkling bells seemed to echo throughout the cluttered shop, and the welcoming scent of ripe pomegranates and fresh sea mist filled the cozy space.

Atlas stepped around a large blue vase overflowing with oddly shaped branches and dried flowers when a woman—a witch—appeared before him. Her hair was silvery white, like moonlight, and fell past her shoulders in bouncy, tightly coiled curls. Icy blue eyes lined with dark kohl pinned him with a look of subdued curiosity, and her red lips were pursed in question. She wore a black skirt with a slit that reached her thigh, dark red leather boots to her knees, and an ivory lace sweater tugged over a snug black bodice. Silver bangles dangled from her wrists—two of them were decorated with wolf charms—she wore at least half a dozen necklaces of varying lengths, and large hoops hung from her ears.

She fisted her hands on her hips and cocked her head to the side. "Something I can help you find?"

Before Atlas could respond, Everinne squeezed herself in front of him and faced the witch head on.

"I know you." Her statement was met with calm resolve.

Surprise registered briefly in the witch's eyes before she blinked it away. "You do?"

"Yes. You're Belladonna." Everinne smiled then, wide and beautiful. "You own the atelier in the shopping district."

The corner of the witch's mouth lifted into a wry grin. "I do." *Belladonna.*

The name triggered a distant memory in Atlas's mind, and he startled. "Wait. Belladonna...as in, Aran Ruhdneah's Belladonna?"

"Well, I wouldn't say I'm his." Belladonna shimmied a little and crossed her arms over her chest with an air of disdain. "He made his choice long ago, and as you can tell, it wasn't me."

So it *was* her. This was the notorious witch that won the heart of the High Prince of Faeven. Last Atlas checked, Aran was still madly in love with her. Unfortunately for Aran, he'd yet to make such a declaration, and it appeared as though Belladonna had every intention of holding it against him.

"Ah." Atlas lifted a finger and winked. "But he wears the wound you gave him like a badge of honor."

Her dark brows furrowed. "Wound?"

"You stabbed him once, didn't you?"

A blush stained her cheeks. "I...yes. I mean, I did, but it was an accident."

He shrugged, lifting his hands. "A forgivable offense in matters of love."

Belladonna fumbled for words then, and Caedian wasted no time derailing the conversation.

"Why are you working down here, in the Marzena?" he asked, his gaze skimming their surroundings, his voice tinged with suspicion. "If you own an atelier in Starysa."

For the first time, Belladonna appeared nervous. She glanced toward the door, her pale blue eyes peering into every corner of the shop. "Above ground is no longer safe for my kind. It is easier to run a storefront for the occult and obscure and not draw attention to myself down here than it is to always look over my shoulder."

"Valid reasoning," Veros mused, and Belladonna's gaze narrowed in mild interest, as though she'd seen him before. "Tell me, have you seen anything unusual or suspicious as of late? Or overheard any talk of hunters or vanishing immortals?"

Belladonna bristled. "Who's asking?"

Atlas leaned in casually, flashed his most charming smile, so his dimples were on full display. "Your prince."

She startled, her eyes widening in shock as she looked between the group of them. Then she dropped into a practiced curtsy. "Forgive me, Your Imperial Highness. I didn't recognize you. It's a pleasure to make your acquaintance."

"The honor is all mine." Atlas bowed, not missing the way Everinne watched him with mocking amusement. "But if you wouldn't mind telling us what it is you know? It's a matter of great importance."

"I understand, Your Highness." Belladonna pretended to

busy herself by tidying a satin tray full of crystal spheres, each of them enclosing a different season. "I can only tell you what I know to be truth."

"And that is?" Everinne pressed quietly.

Belladonna met her gaze and held. "The Mystic Obscura is not what it seems."

"Obviously," Veros drawled, and Belladonna cut him with a scathing look.

"It breeds danger and dark magic. The demonic and necrotic. They bind those who enter with blood, damning them to a lifetime of servitude. Of performances. Then traffic them to places unknown." Belladonna shook her head and lowered her gaze. "The Mystic Obscura is treacherous. A plague unto all of Prava."

Atlas's heart tumbled into the pit of his stomach, where it roiled with acidic dread. Next to him, Everinne's complexion waned, and he quickly slid one arm around her waist to keep her upright.

"Trafficked," Veros repeated, the word ringing in their ears as numbness coupled with alarm settled between them.

The immortals were being trafficked. Hunted with purpose. It was far worse than anything Atlas ever could have imagined.

"Who?" Caedian demanded. "Who's hunting them?"

Belladonna ducked her head, and a curtain of curls shielded her face. "The spawn of the one they call—"

The walls trembled and glass shattered as the tray of crystal spheres Belladonna was holding smashed to the ground. Overhead, the lights flickered, and the earth beneath their feet started to quake.

Belladonna grabbed Atlas's shoulder, her nails digging into the layers of his coat.

"Run, my prince." Her eyes widened as the towers of books fell and the tinkling of bells was suddenly silenced. "Run."

* * *

Atlas grabbed Everinne's hand and hauled her out of Belladonna's shop into the pitch of the rumbling tunnels. Every lantern had been snuffed out and the stench of rotten, foul magic was more pronounced than before. He blinked, furiously trying to see into the endless swath of darkness, but it was like losing his sight completely, leaving every other sense fully alert and heightened.

The pounding of Everinne's heart beat in time with his own, their labored breathing echoing into the vast nothingness. Wisps of her hair tickled his cheek as she stumbled forward blindly, tumbling into him. He caught what he hoped was her waist, the layers of winter clothing making it difficult to keep a firm grip on her.

"Atlas?" Her voice danced past his ear, and he turned toward the sound, hauling her closer, letting her familiar scent consume him.

"I'm right here." His eyes slowly adjusted, and he could just barely see the outline of the side of her face. He reached out, carefully, until the tips of his fingers grazed her cheek. "I won't let anything happen to you."

That was one promise he would die trying to keep.

"Let's go." Veros's stern voice bounced off the tunnel's arching walls and Atlas couldn't pinpoint the direction. Whether the Lord of Time was in front of him or behind him, he couldn't be sure. "We have to get out of here."

There was a grunt of agreement that sounded from everywhere all at once.

"I can't see shit," Caedian grumbled, but it was the unsettling stillness following his complaint that set Atlas on edge.

The ground ceased its relentless trembling, yet the dismal light of the floating lanterns had not returned. If anything, the surrounding darkness seemed to thicken. The hairs along the back of Atlas's neck stood on end, and in the gaping mouth of the tunnel, there was scraping noise that sent a shiver of unease racing down his spine, like that of nails being dragged across a surface of rough stone. Everinne shuddered into him, and he held her closer, one hand reaching for his sword because this time, he'd sworn to be prepared.

In the distance, further into the Marzena, a set of fiery red eyes appeared.

Atlas shoved Everinne behind him and drew his weapon, the hiss of metal sliding against the sheath reverberating through the passage.

"On your guard," he warned as another set of angry red eyes appeared.

Then another.

And another.

There were so many now, Atlas lost count. A chilling, chittering noise flooded the Marzena, like the skittering of a thousand beetles, and only as the flaring crimson eyes edged closer did Atlas realize what they were truly about to face.

"What the—" Caedian's question died as Veros's shout of warning split through impregnable darkness.

"Demons!"

The foul stench of ash and brimstone slammed into Atlas as dozens of creatures descended upon them. Necrotic energy snapped through the air as the demons scoured the walls and crawled along the ceiling. They were no taller than a small child, but their skin was black like tar and fire burned in their eyes. Long, shiny claws protruded from their hands and feet, their faces were smashed and flattened, as though they'd been beaten, and rows of pointy white teeth gleamed like vampire fangs.

At once, the Marzena erupted with the clash of battle—roars, growls, and the squelching sound of swords meeting demonic flesh.

"Stay with me!" Atlas called over his shoulder to Everinne. "No matter what, don't let go!"

He grabbed her hand, fending off a swarm of demons with the other. They slashed at him, their dagger-like claws shredding through the thick layers of fur and wool, yet never sinking deep enough to reach his skin. The glint of his blade cut through the dark, piercing them with ease, but even as he struck one down, another took its place.

They were vastly outnumbered.

"Atlas!" The fear in Everinne's voice sent a spear of panic into his heart.

If she unleashed her magic now, if she lost control, it could kill them all.

"Where the fuck did they come from?" Caedian boomed as a howl of agony splintered through the air. "There's too many of them!"

His Captain of the Guard was right.

If they wanted to survive this, they would need to—the bond lurched and Everinne's scream tore open his heart.

Atlas was yanked backward, his arm wrenched in pain as something tried to pull Everinne from his grasp. He whipped around to face her, to hold on to her, but those gloves, those fucking gloves, gave him no traction.

"Ever!" he shouted, dropping his sword so it clattered loudly, using both of his hands to maintain a steady grip. He dug the heels of his boots into the ground, clasping her forearm and tugging. He gritted his teeth against the sting of claws as they bit into his legs, his shoulders, his neck. Searing pain burned through him as they tore through his clothing, finally reaching his flesh. The scour of their claws was fiery and hot, like a blade fresh from the forge. Agony splintered through him, but the pain would be nothing if he lost Everinne.

The horde of demons grappled him, smothered him, suffocated him. His knees were starting to buckle, and his boots were sliding against the damp ground.

"Atlas!" Everinne screamed, and tremors of fear ricocheted down their bond. "Don't let me go!"

"I won't!" The words were a hoarse promise, slipping through his clenched jaw. But her arm was sliding through that damn coat and the fucking demons were plucking at his fingers like violin strings, loosening his grip. His palms skated down the soft fur of her sleeve and he winced as another demon pounced upon his back, grabbed a fistful of his hair, and snapped his head back.

Atlas spat out a vile curse as pain exploded through his head, pounding at his temples, then down, ripping at his spine.

Another hard tug from the vile demons and his hands slid to Everinne's wrist, where the glove she wore was starting to slacken.

He felt her sobs in his bones, they rattled him, upended him.

There was a suffocating crush of demonic energy, and the reek of vile, corrupt magic pressed in on him from all sides. It was tearing them apart, dragging her away from him into the fathomless darkness.

"Everinne," Atlas ground out her name, ready to grind his teeth to dust, as the glove slipped from her hand.

Her answering scream was cut short, silenced by some unseen force.

The demons vanished, evaporating as though they were made of nothing more than ash and air. Atlas dropped to his knees, grasping the singular glove in his hand as each hollow, ragged breath was carved out of him. The mangled lanterns floating along the ceiling of the Marzena flickered to life, the faerie fire in them producing a waning amber glow. Wounds littered his body, but they were only insignificant tears of the flesh compared to the sensation of having his heart ripped out. His gaze trekked over the floor, and he grabbed his fallen sword, clutching the hilt with one bloody fist.

"I will find her."

He lifted his gaze to where Caedian and Veros stood watching him, their faces marred with filth and blood, their expressions mirror images of defeat.

"Mark my words." Atlas shoved up from the ground, vengeance coursing through his blood, scalding him from the inside out with rage. "I will find her. And then I will kill him."

Veros cocked his head to one side, ignoring the trail of scarlet seeping down his chin. "Him?"

Atlas flashed a merciless grin. "Jarek."

Forty-Two

E verinne didn't want to wake up.

Nightmares or not, she knew that if she opened her eyes, she would be trapped within the Mystic Obscura. The faint chords of music and the dissonance applause of a crowd were just loud enough to be heard over the erratic beating of her heart. But nor could she stay in the dream world, because it was only a matter of time before images of the wicked Marzena and the throng of demons flooded her mind. Before she was reminded, over and over again, of how she was torn from Atlas's arms, then gagged with a cloth that left her mind fuzzy and caused her vision to swim.

She shook away the awful memory.

Better to be locked inside the Mystic Obscura than lost within the wicked wood.

Her eyes fluttered open, slowly adjusting to the low glow of light pulsing from a crystal lamp. She glanced down and gasped— she knew she'd been bound to a chair, the rough cords of rope rubbing her ankles and wrists were quite unforgiving, but what she hadn't expected was to have been changed into a costume. Because that meant someone had removed her clothing, had touched her and dressed her, while she'd been unconscious.

Something sick and twisted caused tiny beads of cold sweat to pebble along the back of her neck.

Her damp palms gripped the arm of the chair as her gaze raked over her newest performance costume. She'd been made to look like a ballerina. The bodice was a blush pink and lined with silk magenta ribbons. It was strapless and entirely too snug, shoving her breasts up to almost her face. A tutu of the same soft pink jutted outward from her waist, where tiny iridescent beads studded and traced her curves. Her feet had been fitted into pointe shoes, just like the dancers at the ballet, with one terrifying difference.

The toes of her shoes were attached to a pair of jeweled daggers, the pink satin resting on top of the flat edge of the weapon, right by the embellished hilt. If she was going to dance, she would have to do so on the tips of two sharp blades.

Trepidation took hold of her lungs and squeezed.

There was a click of a tongue and Everinne's head snapped up.

From the darkened corner of the room, Jarek emerged from the shadows. Tonight, he was dressed in his usual attire of all black, the shirt was fitted, the pants were tapered. Chains were cuffed to his boots, and a cape of sleek raven feathers fell from his shoulders, pinned in place by a pair of matching skulls with onyx eyes. He sauntered toward her, grabbed a palette of makeup from the vanity shoved against the far wall, then crouched in front of her.

His cologne, the scent of warm woods and amber, was barely enough to disguise the horrid reek of his magic.

Everinne held her breath.

"Can't have you performing tonight without everyone seeing that pretty face of yours, now can we?" He dipped his finger into a swatch of pale gold paint with shimmering rainbow flecks, streaking it across the apples of her cheeks.

She stiffened at his touch, struggling to free herself from the bonds he'd tied around her wrists and ankles. "Let me go. I can put my makeup on myself."

Another click of his tongue. "Unfortunately, you lost that privilege since you didn't show up for work tonight. I had to send my minions to track you down, though it was easy enough since my imprint is on your arm."

Everinne scowled. "What imprint?"

"My ring," he clarified, showing her the back of his hand, where a skull ring glinted in the low light, its ruby eyes glowing like fire. "The one I marked you with in the Marzena a couple nights ago. I should've branded you sooner, honestly. It makes it so much easier to hunt you."

Hunt.

Realization turned the blood in her veins to ice.

Jarek was the hunter. He was the one hunting the fae, hunting vampires and witches. He was the reason the immortals were disappearing. Suddenly, her tongue felt thick in her mouth, and the sickening sensation of dread wormed its way into her stomach.

"Your performance tonight will be a form of punishment," Jarek explained, oblivious to her inner turmoil. "Mostly for your failure to keep your blood oath and also for helping Aisling escape my clutches."

His golden gaze narrowed and demonic power flared bright, snapping and crackling along her skin. "Make no mistake, I will figure out what you've done with her. And once I do, I will ensure both of you regret it."

"You'll never find her," Everinne spat out.

He chuckled then, fraying her nerves even further.

"I'm sure you thought the same thing about Zoryana. She was too perfect to pass up. Of course, it was so easy when you led me right to her hut in the Deszvila Forest." He dipped his thumb into a pot of ruby lipstick, snared her chin, then dragged his thumb across her mouth, smearing the vibrant color. "A witch with the ability to absorb emotions? How could I say no?"

"If you hurt her—"

"She will suffer whatever fate awaits her." Jarek leaned closer then, grazing the side of her face with his knuckles, trailing the cool press of his rings into her skin, all while his other thumb continued to stroke her lips. "But you...I have plans for you, pet. You continuously deny me, and yet my obsession with you only seems to grow. Fear me, run from me, it makes no difference. I'm a fan of the chase, you see, and one day I will make you mine."

"Fuck off." She jerked away from him, her back slamming into the chair. "I will never be yours."

"So much disgust, yet you already know the gentleness of my touch." His hand fell from her cheek, following the column of her neck, and then even lower so his fingers traced the swell of her breasts. He hooked one finger into her bodice, wedging it between her cleavage. Then he tugged, yanking her forward. "Who do you think dressed you, *milazk?*"

If her hands weren't bound, she'd gouge out his eyes with her own nails. Cold rage fired through her, empowered by his audacity, by his absolutely revolting claims. "You fucking—"

Jarek grabbed her throat then, squeezing painfully so that her lungs screamed for air and tears filled her eyes, slipping down her cheeks. "Mind yourself. There is no one here to rescue you. No one will hear you scream. No one will hear you cry and beg." His smile was laced with malice. "Only me."

Everinne thrashed in the chair, her body convulsing and twisting, desperate to break free from his hold. Her throat burned, raw and hot, and she thought for sure he would crush her windpipe. A stabbing ache formed in her lungs and just when she thought Jarek had every intention of ending her life, he eased his grip. It was just enough for her to suck in a greedy breath of air and then he lowered his face to hers, so close, she saw the exact moment the golden rings around his eyes darkened with power.

The terrifying power of a monster. A wielder of shadows. A summoner of demons.

"Let this be my final warning, pet." Jarek toyed with the silver dagger dangling from her ear, then leaned closer, scraping his teeth along her jaw. "I will brand you. I will mark you in every way possible. And if for some reason I cannot..."

His grin turned wolfish.

"Then I will find someone to do it for me."

* * *

Glamour ensconced Everinne, it shimmered over her clammy skin and ruffled the skirts of the tutu fanning out around her. She stood on a round stage overlooking the grand audience above the menagerie, so close this time, the whispers of those who watched could reach her. They stared in mild interest as she balanced upon the blades strapped to her pointe shoes, swirling their glasses of sparkling wine and whiskey, casting curious glances her way when a haunting melody began to play.

She tried to remember the dances she'd seen the handful of times Veros had taken her to the ballet. The ballerinas moved with such fluid grace, twirling and lengthening their bodies, that watching them dance was like witnessing music come alive. Stretching her arms overhead, she raised her chin, determined not to falter. The sooner she finished this performance, the sooner Jarek would release her, and she could think of a way to get herself out of the Mystic Obscura and back to Atlas.

Without warning, intricately carved mirrors appeared on the outer edge of the stage, sprouting up like flowers. Each one was crafted of gold, the metal twisted to resemble curling vines and blooming petals. They were tall and elaborate, and she might have found herself fascinated by them, were it not for the fact that it wasn't her reflection they revealed.

All of them displayed the image of a hulking, shirtless male. Loose black pants dipped low across his waist, held in place by a knotted belt. His broad chest was chiseled and ripped, laced with corded muscle and throbbing veins. Inky tattoos of skulls, lost souls, and monsters she couldn't name crawled up his arms and over his torso. He stood with his arms crossed, intimidating and monstrous, but perhaps what Everinne found the most unsettling was the giant animal skull he wore on his head. It reminded her of a wolf, yet ivory antlers sprouted from the skull, the tips of them blackened like they'd been rubbed with soot and ash. Beams of crimson and deep gold light spilled across the stage, dousing them in the hues of a blood moon.

A roar of discourse sounded from the audience.

"Dance!"

"Do something!"

The heckles startled Everinne, and she tore her gaze away from the alarming male, carefully guiding herself instantly into a series of delicate steps, mindful of the daggers attached to her shoes. Each movement was a precarious balancing act as she let her arms float through the air, while her fingers pretended to weave the wind. She bent at the waist, swooping low while the music led her on a breathtaking journey of the dark and depraved. Her back arched with the dramatic notes, and she extended her arms, gradually unfurling them like wilted flowers desperate for sunlight. With painstaking slowness, she twirled once, the dull thump of the daggers digging into the stage sending pinpricks of apprehension needling up her spine. Her toes throbbed and her calves burned.

She spun once more, a little faster this time to the swell of a woeful melody, when a hand slid around her waist.

Panic shot through her as she came face to face with the male wearing the wolf skull.

He dragged her close, not caring as the sharp blades grated across the stage floor. His grip was fierce when he snared her wrist, inserting himself into the dance with her. She dared a furious glance up at him, and in the gaping sockets of the skull, she caught a glimpse of golden, honey-colored eyes.

"Jarek," she hissed.

"And here I thought you'd be pleased to see me." He grabbed her leg and hiked it up, then stepped into her space, forcing her to bend away from him as he dipped her. "You need a partner for the Dance of the Macabre."

"The what?" she snapped as he righted her with ease, his fingers digging into her waist as he kept her pressed tightly against him.

"It's a seductively morbid dance based on an archaic fairy-tale," he explained, coaxing her into a series of spins and turns that sent her toppling toward the edge of the stage, only for him to haul her back into his powerful hold. "The story is about a balle-rina who ran off into the wicked wood to escape her betrothed. But she soon finds herself lost and in the company of none other than Raum, the demon of the night."

Everinne's mind whirled as the story unfolded around her, as each pivot in his arms left her lightheaded and weak, until she could do nothing but follow his lead.

"Foolishly," he continued, cupping the back of Everinne's knee and locking it around his waist, "the beautiful ballerina made a deal with the demon."

Jarek positioned his hand at the small of her back while the other was fused snugly to her thigh, certain to leave bruises. "Raum claimed he would free her of her impending martial vows on the condition that she promised him a dance."

His nefarious chuckle caused her skin to pebble with goose-bumps. She shivered, and he leaned forward, the rough bone of the skull grazing her cheek.

"The problem, you see, is that the ballerina failed to declare a length of time. So, Raum forced her to dance for an eternity. Sometimes she danced alone in the wicked wood, other times he joined her." Jarek's fingers dug into her flesh, sending a spike of fear into her heart. His intentions were clear. "Either way, she became his puppet, dancing only for him until her feet bled, until her bones grew weak and weary, until her heart gave out."

Everinne shrank back, tried to untangle herself from his arms, but his touch was like cold iron. Deadly. Lethal. "And I suppose he made her dance with daggers strapped to her shoes as well?"

Another low, menacing laugh. "No, pet, that was my own personal preference."

"Bastard." She bit the word off, planting her hands against his chest in an effort to shove away from him, but he snatched her wrists and lifted her arms over her head.

The fangs of the wolf skull gleamed like polished ivory, and for one terrifying moment, she thought he intended to bite her. But then he twirled her, forcing her into spin after spin so the colors of the Mystic Obscura bled together, the cheers of the audience became a painful thrum in her ears, and her thoughts muddled together, leaving her confused and disoriented.

"You will become my puppet, Everinne." Jarek's threatening promise whispered past her as her legs began to wobble and the quickening twirls disoriented her so she collapsed into his waiting arms. "Mine to own. Mine to possess."

"N-no..." she mumbled. Everything around her was incoherent. The lights. The music. All of it was a messy blur of sound and color. Only his words were clear, and they struck a chord of terror in her heart. "Not you. Never you."

"Yes," he crooned, turning her away from him.

He captured her waist and hoisted her over his head. Everinne's back bowed instantly to avoid being stabbed by the horns protruding from the skull as his words drifted up to her. Tingles of painful demonic energy crackled around her body, jarring her so she extended one leg straight up, coercing her to hold a beautifully broken pose.

She was the ballerina. He was the demon of the night.

A tear of determination slid down her cheek.

Everinne would *not* let him win.

But Jarek's final words reached her over the raucous applause, and her confidence faltered.

"I will be the one to haunt your dreams now."

Forty-Three

A tlas sent Veros and Caedian back to Starysa, though it wasn't without argument. Veros had absolutely refused to leave the Marzena without his sister and Caedian had no intentions of abandoning either of them in the labyrinth below the city. But Atlas held his ground. Getting into the secret entrance of the Mystic Obscura was a feat all its own, and they would draw far less attention if it was just Atlas going instead of all three of them.

Not only that, but he needed eyes above ground, too.

If word got out that Everinne had been taken and somehow circled back to his father, there was no telling how the kralv would react. Either he'd punish Atlas by pursuing the missing immortals and blame him for Everinne's disappearance, or worse, he wouldn't respond at all. He would continue to ignore the happenings within the walls of his kingdom and Everinne would be left to suffer the consequences of his inactions. Then again, Oldrich was currently using her to his advantage...perhaps he'd see her capture as a personal slight.

Atlas didn't particularly care to consider the possibility of having to ask his father for help, but if Reine refused to release Everinne, he might be left with no other option.

The sloping entrance to the Mystic Obscura was dimmer and danker than Atlas expected. It was not dripping with grandeur like the main hall, nor was it cloaked in mystery like the rune-laced door in the alley. It was mostly a thrown together path of crumbling brick in a poorly lit passage. Bronze sconces lined the walls, though they were few and far between, and the flames illuminating the way were a menacing red, flooding half the tunnel in crimson shadows. Eventually, however, the uneven ground smoothed out into lacquered shimmering marble, the steady glow of a brightly lit hall came into view, and the soft click of his boots went completely unnoticed.

In fact, no one paid him any mind at all.

There were a number of fae, vampires, and even a few mortals sauntering down the corridor toward the Marzena, and not a single one of them even looked in his direction. Apparently, they didn't give a fuck if his hair was matted with blood, if his wounds were leaving a smearing trail of scarlet in his wake, or if he was carrying a sword in one hand. His trials were none of their concern. Instead, their eyes wore the familiar glaze of overindulgence, their drunken laughter grated against his nerves, and they staggered and stumbled into the walls and each other.

In another time not so long ago, he would've been a willing participant in such revelry.

But not anymore.

And likely, never again.

Atlas ignored the group of them whose speech slurred as he passed and instead refocused his attention on the gentle tug of the bond tying him to Everinne.

She was in here. Somewhere.

He could feel it. Could feel her. The steadfast resolve flowing through her veins, the faint undercurrent of disquiet that edged on the brink of panic. The lick of fear that caused her heart rate to spike every so often. Though her emotions were tempered and calm, the bond was taut with tension, as though it might snap at any moment. He rubbed his fist over his heart to soothe the unwanted sensation, followed it around a darkened corner, and found Reine standing in the middle of the hall, waiting for him.

She canted her head to the side, and ribbons of silky brown hair fell over one shoulder. Her dress was sleeveless black satin, the neck was high, and the rest of it molded to her figure all the way to the hem, where it flared slightly. Atlas wondered how she could move, much less breathe, in such a gown. A gilded bangle in the shape of a serpent coiled around her wrist and upper arm, hoops dangled from her ears, and gold necklaces wrapped around her throat like a scarf. Heavy kohl lined her amber eyes, and she'd painted her lips a deep red shade. He scowled when they curved into a saccharine smile.

He aimed his sword at her jeweled throat.

"Where is she?" Atlas demanded, disregarding their usual customary greetings.

Reine was nonplussed. She remained calm, not even flinching at the sight of a blade pointed directly at her. She fucking curtsied.

"Everinne is doing her job, Your Imperial Highness."

He could throttle the damn witch.

"I'm afraid that's not a good enough answer, Reine." Another step brought the tip of his blade to where a tiny sliver of umber skin was revealed between layers of gold. "Let's try this again, shall we? Where. Is. She?"

She huffed out a breath of frustration as though he was wasting her time, then clasped her hands together before her. "Very well. She is performing on a stage."

"Against her will," he ground out.

"Per her contract." Reine arched a smooth brow at the suggestion. "She gave me a drop of her blood willingly, Your Imperial Highness."

"And did you withhold the importance of that drop?" he countered, his rage growing with her placid responses. "Did you have her think it was only to gain entrance into the Mystic Obscura, and nothing else?"

A rosy hue flushed her cheeks and she floundered briefly,

looking as though she was trying to pluck the correct response out of thin air. "I only told her what she needed to know."

"You're lying, Reine." Atlas made a sort of *tsk*ing noise and tapped the point of his sword against the stack of necklaces wrapped around her neck, smirking when her eyes widened in shock. "You kept that information from Everinne on purpose so you could lure her into your clutches. And you know how the crown views dishonest bargains."

That one was a bit of a stretch.

His father couldn't care less, but Atlas...unjust bargains were cause for retribution.

Still, his words had the desired effect.

"Your Highness, I concealed that information because I had no choice." Reine backtracked, the words fumbling from her like she'd forgotten how to speak properly. "I cannot...the words won't—that is, I don't..."

"You're spelled." Atlas lowered his weapon, sheathing it as his side, and his gaze narrowed. "Who? Who is trying to keep you silent?"

"Those whose powers extend far beyond this world."

She stole a hasty glance over her shoulder then, as though she thoroughly expected to catch someone eavesdropping on their conversation, and Atlas's gaze tracked to the walls, for he imagined they whispered as well. Reine stepped closer and dipped her chin, her voice dropping.

"My hands are bound, Your Highness. I am no different from those whose blood I collect." She lifted her arms slightly and showed him her empty palms. "I, too, am trapped. Merely a pawn in a game with more weight than my life, and to me, the opponents are unknown."

Part of Atlas wanted to believe her, because he knew such ancient powers existed. But for him, there was only Everinne. She was the only one who mattered to him. For her, he would gladly forfeit his own life.

He shook his head, dismissing Reine's claims, then pinned her with a ruthless glare. "Let her go."

"She broke her blood oath."

"An oath you failed to mention!" His temper flared, fury igniting in his blood. "What is it you want then in exchange for her freedom? Whatever the cost, I'll pay it."

"It's not that simple, Your Highness." Reine fiddled with the serpent bangle crawling up her arm. Tension draped around her shoulders, causing them to sag. She was unsettled. Anxious. The restlessness spread through her like a disease. "I cannot release her. Nor can I give you the answers you seek."

Fucking skies.

"Then who can?" Atlas demanded.

Reine's amber gaze locked onto him as she spoke words he never expected to hear. "No one."

Forty-Four

Everinne was officially trapped within the Mystic Obscura.

After her ballet performance with Jarek, she'd taken off those godsforsaken pointe shoes and sprinted through the menagerie down to the lower level of the parlor, hoping to find the secret entrance to the Marzena. She'd been willing to take her chances in the eccentric market, but she'd been unable to find the exit. The only room she found was the shoddy dressing room where Jarek had bound her to a chair. It didn't matter how many halls she explored, how many corners she turned, she was simply running in circles. Every path, every direction, led her right back to that same damning room.

She would never get out.

There would be no escaping him.

Exhaustion left her weary as she approached the door to the forgotten dressing room. Her toes were throbbing, sore from having been pinched into those horrible pointe shoes, and her muscles felt as though they'd been ripped from her bones, shredded and useless. She ached *everywhere*. Her skin was too heavy, her hair felt like a crown had been speared into her skull, and the tutu hung from her like the limbs of a dying tree. And she

446

was so tired. The hour must have been late, but there was no way to determine the time of day since the Mystic Obscura lacked windows or any other glimpse into the outside world. She rubbed her eyes with the back of her hands, smearing iridescent powder and kohl all over her skin.

Giving in to defeat, Everinne slumped against the door of the dressing room and pushed it open.

She knew Jarek was waiting for her before she even stepped inside. His penetrating gaze haunted every fiber of her being, unraveling all of her layers, peeling back her flesh to the vulnerability of her soul. He lurked in the corner, the malicious gold of his eyes watching her, tracking her like a predator to prey. Again, he donned all black. The creepy skull was gone, but the memory of it was seared into her mind.

Stalking into the dimly lit room, she intentionally left the door open, hopeful someone might stumble upon them. But Jarek flicked his wrist, and it slammed shut behind her.

She jolted and glared up at him, refusing to give him the satisfaction of having startled her. "What do you want, Skulls?"

He cocked his head to the side, a swath of smooth brown hair falling in front of his face. "Ah, back to the adorable nicknames now, are we?"

"No." A rod of spite skewered itself between her shoulders and she locked her spine in place. "I just hate saying your name."

"Just wait, *milaszk.*" Jarek sauntered forward with a bundle of black lace tossed over one arm. "Soon you'll be screaming it."

Everinne gritted her teeth until her temples started to throb. His threats filled her with unease, mostly because she was quite certain they were promises not yet kept. Her magic hummed and simmered, straining to lash out, until the anticipation of the pain she could cause him gave her pause. She could do it, she could unleash the might of her power on him, make him writhe and beg for mercy. He would crumple and contort in heinous pain, the fearsome demon summoner fallen at the feet of a lowly fae. And if she was feeling particularly vindictive, she could shatter his mind.

Another blood rose would mark her arm, but the price of the tattoo would be well worth it.

Suddenly, Jarek's hand shot out and he grabbed her wrist, lifting her hand. Wisps of shadowy black and violet seeped from her fingertips, and he flashed her an evil smile. She stepped back, away from him, but he matched her. Crowded her. Pressed against her until the back of her thighs met the edge of the vanity and she could no longer put any kind of space between them. Jarek brought her hand close to his face, and she watched in horror as his tongue darted out, licking the air, tasting her magic.

"So beautifully violent," he murmured, then inhaled deeply and groaned. "Your magic is a summons to my soul. An aphrodisiac to the senses. Go ahead and give me your worst. Watch what happens when the touch of death is met with the chaos of the demonic."

"Get away from me." Everinne jerked, yanking her arm free from his grasp. "You unhinged bastard."

Jarek just laughed, cold and calculating. He shoved the bundle of black lace into her arms. "It's time for your next performance."

"I already performed." She crumpled the fine fabric in her hands. "I'm not going out onto another stage again."

He leaned back then and ran his tongue along his teeth. Folding his arms over his broad chest, he arched a singular brow. "Who said anything about a stage?"

"I..." She glanced down at the lace. "What are you talking about?"

Jarek rummaged through a polished cupboard next to the vanity and produced a decanter of honeyfire and a single glass. The amber liquid gleamed with a sheen of gold, and when he gave the bottle a swirl, the alcohol burned even brighter. He spun to face her, uncorked the crystal decanter, and the scent of honey, warm spice, and something else permeated the air.

"Change into the lace, Everinne."

"I will do no such thing." Fury swelled inside of her. She would not be manipulated. Not again. Kralv Oldrich already controlled a piece of her life, she would not give up all she had left. "You don't own me. I'm not your fucking property. I might be stuck at the Mystic Obscura, but I work for Reine. Not for you."

"Is that what you think?" A bemused expression softened the hard lines of his face. "I'd have thought you would've figured it all out by now. No matter."

He waved away the thought with a dismissive hand, and Everinne's stomach clenched in apprehension, sweat slicking her palms. She already knew Jarek was the one hunting the immortals, but what else was missing? What had she overlooked?

"The lace, Everinne," he commanded, a harsh edge roughing his tone. "If you cannot change of your own accord, then I shall do it for you."

He reached for her, and she lurched from his grasp.

"Fine!" she snapped, slapping his arm away from her. "I'll change. But don't fucking touch me."

"Suit yourself." Jarek poured himself a glass of the honeyfire, then pulled out the chair in front of the vanity and dropped into it. He extended his legs, crossing one ankle over the other, then took a slow sip of his drink. He raised the glass. "Carry on."

"Are you going to *watch* me?"

"You're most entertaining." His shrug was careless. "Yet if you insist, there's a partition behind you, in the corner."

If she had a dagger, she would plunge it into his heart.

Everinne whipped around toward the darkened corner, throwing the black lace over her shoulder. She carefully unfolded the partition, ensuring she was safely hidden behind the panels of silver mesh. It wasn't exactly thick enough to keep her completely from his view, but at least it wasn't sheer.

She glanced down at her poor feet. They were red, swollen and blistered, but she was grateful they weren't bleeding. She yanked the wretched tutu off next. It landed in a crumpled heap around her ankles, and she kicked it away. The silk ribbons binding the bodice were a struggle, and she eventually just tore at the soft fabric with her nails in an effort to free herself from its confines. The façade of a ballerina was suffocating. Strangling. By the time she ripped the bodice off, she was panting, each breath labored and painful.

"Are you sure you don't need any assistance?" Jarek drawled, and Everinne's hands coiled into fists at her sides.

She whipped around, a stream of vile curses ready to spill from her lips, when she caught sight of him through the partition. He was seated in the chair, but the absolute stillness of his body caused her pulse to jump. Needles of fright pricked her spine. His head was dipped low, his brown hair swept over half of his face, and the light gold of his eyes was focused directly on her. Like he could see *through* the partition. Like every inch of her was visible to him, despite the layers of thread and mesh. He gripped the arm of the chair with one hand, his knuckles white, and in the other he held the glass of whiskey. Except now it was empty.

Everinne froze, icy fear consuming her veins.

Naked behind the partition, she felt entirely too exposed. Even though she knew, *she knew*, there was no way he could see her. Not fully. Maybe a vague outline, but not the entirety of her body.

Jarek sucked his teeth, his gaze sliding to the empty glass before refocusing on the flimsy partition dividing them. "You're taking too long."

"I'm not!" she yelped, snatching the black lace off the ground. "I'm almost done."

She held up the outfit and scowled.

It was a bodysuit of sorts, and though it would cover every inch of her, it left absolutely nothing to the imagination. She pulled it on, her lip curling at the way black lace roses were strategically placed, barely enough to cover her most sensitive areas, showcasing her curves for everyone to see. The soft fabric melded to her skin, so it resembled glittering paint instead of lace, and Everinne's lip curled in disgust. Even the tattoo marking her forearm looked as though it was part of the costume.

She slipped into a pair of spiky black heels, wincing as her toes were pinched yet again, then turned only to find the partition had vanished.

And so had Jarek.

"What the..." Everinne glanced around the dressing room, but there was no sign of the demon summoner anywhere. His stench had evaporated, and she could no longer sense the tormenting pressure of his gaze.

Plucking a small towel from the vanity's counter, she scrubbed away the excess makeup from her previous performance. Jarek had smeared lipstick, powder, and paint all over her face earlier, and if she was expected to perform again, she certainly wasn't going to do so looking like a sullen, morbid fae. She stole a glance in the faintly illuminated mirror and bit back a strangled scream.

The makeup she wiped off was gone, but she didn't recognize the female in the mirror staring back at her. Her eyes were lined heavily with kohl, golden powder was dusted across her eyelids and the apples of her cheeks. Shimmering crimson painted her lips and gilded dagger earrings dangled from the tips of her ears while diamond studs replaced the amethysts she usually wore. She turned her head from side to side in a daze, unable to comprehend how it happened. Even her hair had been pulled into a high ponytail, fastened in place by a golden ribbon.

Everinne looked at the towel in her hands, then back at her reflection.

Glamour.

It was the only possible excuse.

Suddenly, a distinctive tug pulled on her heartstrings, and she jumped upright. The bond warmed, a soothing familiarity.

Atlas.

Atlas was *here.*

He'd come for her.

Spinning around, she started for the door. She was going to tumble right into his arms, and he would carry her out of this hellish nightmare. Then she would be safe. They would find a way to break the chains the Mystic Obscura had wrapped around her. They would cut the leash to the invisible collar the kralv had bound around her neck. Then she would finally be *free*.

Everinne yanked open the door, tears of elation clinging to her lashes, and was devoured by the wicked dark.

Forty-Five

"Are you certain this is a good idea?" Caedian asked, his silvery brows drawing together.

"No." Atlas shoved a hand through his hair. In fact, he knew it was a very bad idea, but as of now, it was his only option. And Reine's statement had cemented that notion. "But there's no other way. I told you what Reine said, she can't release Everinne. But if my father can guarantee her freedom, then that's a chance I'm willing to take."

He stood with Caedian and Veros in one of the darkened corridors of the palace outside the throne room where his father was currently holding court. The witching hour was already upon them, the moon high in the night sky, yet still Oldrich had not yet retired. All Atlas needed was a few moments alone with him, a scrap of time to plead his case, to ask his father to use his authority to get Everinne out of the Mystic Obscura.

"Are you truly guaranteeing her freedom, though?" Veros asked, shoving his hands into the pockets of his pants, the gold chain to his timepiece glinted softly in the low light. "From the clutches of the Mystic Obscura to the kralv's iron fist hardly seems like a fair trade."

Caedian nodded in agreement. "From one prison to another."

"What else would you have me do?" Atlas threw his arms wide and faced Veros, his temper rising. "You're her brother, yet you've adamantly been against every suggestion I've thrown your way since I got back from the Marzena. It's almost like you want her to suffer, like she deserves nothing less."

Veros was in his face a second later. "That's not fucking true, and you know it."

Caedian stepped between them and caught Veros's fist before he could throw the first punch.

"You want to know why I've been so composed and so level-headed throughout this whole fucking ordeal? It's because she *is* my sister." Veros shrugged Caedian off, pacing away from them. "Because I know that one wrong move, one mistake, could cost her life. I have *seen* this, Atlas. Minute by fucking minute, I've watched this scenario unfold and there is not a damn thing I can do to stop it."

"I'm going to—" Atlas started, but Veros plowed on, refusing to let him get a word in.

"There is *nothing* you can do that will alter the course of her destiny. Or your own. Choices have already been made, and time doesn't give second chances." Veros pulled out his timepiece, carefully spinning the gold chain around his finger so it ticked and whirred. "Whether it be the will of gods, or stars, or fate, I cannot say. All I know is the past is what was, the present is what is, and the future is what will be...and when you walk into that throne room, whatever you say or do will not change the outcome. The motion has already been set."

"Fuck." Atlas roughed a hand over his face, hating that his two closest friends were right. If Everinne got out of the Mystic Obscura, she was just trading one prison for another. "It's the lesser of two evils. In the Mystic Obscura, Everinne is untouchable. I can't get to her, I can't see her, and that fucking demon summoner is there. I've seen the way he looks at her, and I want to gouge his eyeballs out with a serrated blade."

Dejection smothered him, threatening to snuff out the

glimmer of hope he still carried. "In the palace, though, I can protect her. It won't be easy and I'll have to watch my back, but at least I'll know where she is at all times."

When Veros spoke, his voice was a near-silent whisper. "What if you can't protect her?"

"Then I'll die trying." Atlas met the intensity of his stare without flinching. "Right now, Oldrich sees Everinne as a means to an end. To him, she's a weapon. She's useful. And he won't want to lose that to anyone, especially not Reine and Jarek."

Caedian considered his plight, running his knuckles along his sharp jawline. "That's a fair point."

"The only way I can get my father to help," Atlas ventured, his next words souring on the tip of his tongue, "is by convincing him that someone else has the one thing he wants."

Seconds of tense silence pulsed between them, until finally, Veros conceded.

"Fine." He inclined his head, but there was a look of warning in the depths of his turquoise eyes. "You know where to find us if you need us."

Atlas nodded and Caedian bowed stiffly before he and Veros turned and headed down the corridor, leaving him alone with his thoughts and wavering confidence. He waited until they were out of sight before he made his way to the throne room. Two guards shoved open the intricately carved wooden doors depicting a lone wolf traversing through a thick forest, and the hinges groaned, announcing Atlas's arrival.

His father either didn't notice or didn't care.

If Atlas had to guess, it was the latter.

Kralv Oldrich sat upon an obsidian throne that shone like the darkest night kissed by moonlight. He cupped a goblet of red wine lazily, swirling it about while the contents sloshed dangerously close to the rim. His boot tapped a jovial rhythm on the granite flooring, the tempo just slightly off in comparison to the musicians whose less vivacious tune carried up into the arching ceiling above. A handful of nobles loitered near the bountiful tables overflowing with food and wine, their mediocre conversations hushed while they pretended to enjoy the gilded splendor. It was all a bit excessive, considering the company was meager, and the kralv wore an expression of tedious toleration. Upon first glance, he looked drunk and bored, with the way he slouched in the throne and stroked his beard. But his dark eyes were clear and keen, never missing anything.

Atlas approached the throne and bowed deeply. "Father."

Oldrich propped himself up on his elbow and took a hefty gulp of wine. "What do you need, boy? It's unlike you to call upon me unless you're in want of something."

Atlas's jaw popped.

He rarely asked for anything. It was always his father who was making demands of him.

Atlas smoothed the front of his navy shirt, as though he couldn't be bothered with the kralv's insults. After all, he'd grown accustomed to them over the years. "I've come to speak with you about my future bride."

Those seemed to be exactly the right words to say.

Oldrich straightened then, a gleam sparking in his nearly black eyes. "Is that right? What sort of trouble has the girl gotten herself into this time? Has she passed out in one of the parlors from too much drink? Or have you already caught her with her legs spread for someone else?"

Atlas's nails bit into his palms until he thought for certain he would draw blood. Agitation tore at him, threatening to release his increasing temper. He cleared his throat, cautious of his tone. "None of those things."

"Then tell me what she's done, and I'll take care of it." His father waved a dismissive hand and took another long drink of wine. "I realize her name is already being cursed by every eligible female in Prava, but I'm sure we can whip her into shape in no time."

I'm doing this for Everinne.

Atlas reminded himself of that over and over as he stood

before his bastard of a father. Everinne would be in the palace, with Atlas, likely in his bedroom. And it was a far safer location than the Mystic Obscura.

"She unknowingly entered into a blood contract with the Mystic Obscura." He kept his words soft, for his father's ears only, and his posture rigid and unapproachable, in case anyone looked in their direction. "I spoke to Reine, but she refuses to release Everinne, even though she failed to mention the truth of the terms before collecting a drop of Everinne's blood."

"I see," Oldrich murmured, and all the previous mocking amusement drained from his face. "This is a serious matter indeed."

"Which is why I came to you." Atlas dipped his chin in a show of respect. "I figured if anyone could free her, it would be you."

The words were bitter on his tongue, but a little flattery never hurt.

His father considered his request, stroking his beard once as his bushy brows pulled together in a stern line. He glanced up at Atlas, canting his head to the side, a look of concern etched into the rugged lines of his face. "What did you offer Reine in exchange for Everinne's release?"

"Anything." His shoulders rose and fell in defeat. "Everything."

Oldrich's gaze narrowed. "And she still refused you?"

"Yes." Something about their conversation caused Atlas's skin to prickle with awareness. The hairs on the back of his neck stood on end, and the unnerving, unsettling sensation of being watched burrowed into his subconscious. The kralv was being too obliging. Too understanding.

"Very well." Oldrich stood then, depositing his empty wine goblet on the arm of the throne. He puffed out his chest, tucking his hands behind his back. "We can't have the future Princess of Prava trapped in an unpleasant blood oath, now can we? I will see that she is freed immediately."

Too easy.

The entire transaction was incredibly too easy.

His father gripped his shoulder. "However..."

Ah, there it was. The infamous catch.

"I imagine the cost for her freedom will be quite high, therefore, I must ask you to grant me a small favor. If you will." Oldrich increased the pressure, a warning to obey.

As if Atlas had a choice.

"What sort of favor?" he asked.

The kralv released him, a wry smile twisting across his face. Then he chuckled, which was never a good sign. "Oh, nothing outrageous. We can discuss the specifics later."

"I'd rather discuss them now," Atlas countered, rocking back on his heels. No way was he going to let his own fucking father try to wrangle him into an unjust bargain.

"Really?" Oldrich stepped down from the throne so they were on the same level. An untrustworthy glint sparked in the pits of his black eyes. "I would've thought you'd be keen on freeing your beloved from the clutches of the Mystic Obscura."

Fuck.

Atlas scoffed. "She's not my beloved."

"Don't lie to me, boy," Oldrich sneered, closing the distance between them. He reeked of stale alcohol, smoke, and sulfur. The rancid scent clung to him like death. "I see the way you look at her. I've seen it for years. Originally, I would've chosen anyone else for you. She's a complicated mess, that one."

Atlas locked his jaw to keep from growling.

Everinne might be a mess, but she was *his* fucking mess.

Oldrich continued speaking, oblivious to his son's inner rage. "But then, Maxim told me the most curious bit of information about her."

Maxim.

Maxim was his valet, he trusted him. Spoke freely in front of him. Oftentimes forgot the fae was even around.

No.

Oldrich snapped his fingers, and his guards moved with precision, silencing the musicians, ushering the remaining nobles out of the space—some of them still carrying drinks or plates of food —so the onyx and golden grandeur of the throne room was empty and devoid of life. Cold, just like it was the day Atlas's mother died.

"You see," Oldrich continued, grabbing a hunk of roasted meat off one of the large platters and chomping noisily as he chewed. "Once I learned Everinne possessed the power to torture and kill, I knew there was no one better suited for my son."

Atlas fisted his hands at his side. Anger flowed through his veins, crashing into him like the hostile waves of an ocean during a squall. He was the steadfast shore, and he would take the lashings no longer. "So, you forced her into a bargain."

"A marriage," Oldrich corrected, pointing the chunk of meat in Atlas's direction. "You can't tell me it's been so awful. I can smell her on you, all those forbidden, sugary sweet layers of temptation."

Atlas took one threatening step forward, and his father's guards closed in on him.

"She was feisty to start, refusing to cooperate." The kralv tossed the meat onto the table and grabbed another goblet of wine. "I may still need to work on that, come to think of it. But once I saw her greatest fear was anything happening to *you*, she crumbled fairly quickly."

Atlas had never known this kind of fury. He'd hated his father plenty of times, had wished he could toss aside his kingdom and crown and sail across the Ladova Bay for realms unknown. But now, more than anything, he wanted his father's blood on his hands. He wanted to slit his throat and watch the life drain from his eyes, watch as Oldrich gasped his last wheezing breath, knowing that his own son had been the one to end his wretched life.

His hand hovered above the hilt of his sword. "And what do you get out of this arrangement?"

"Free use of her power?" Oldrich mused, swirling his wine. "The ability to torture. To inflict pain and suffering. To kill."

"You fucking bastard."

Atlas lunged for him, but the guards were faster, tackling him to the ground. His knees slammed into the hard granite, sending spears of pain shooting up his legs. One of the guards twisted his arms behind his back, binding his wrists in shackles of cold iron. Searing agony radiated up his arms, the stench of lightly charred flesh lingering in his nostrils. The damning metal took effect quickly, dulling his magic until it was nothing more than a mediocre hum in his blood, weakening him so that he barely had enough strength to hold up his own head.

"So valiant," Oldrich chuckled. "Such an admirable quality. Too bad it's wasted on a male who only thinks with his cock."

Of course. Everything always circled back to the fact that Oldrich thought Atlas was a flaw upon their family name. He'd been accused of sullying their blood line with sex magic, of being irresponsible and incompetent. On more than one occasion, the kralv had made it quite clear that the crown would *never* pass to Atlas. He was too unworthy. Too weak.

"Don't worry, Atlas." Oldrich stepped forward, lifting Atlas's chin with the leather toe of his boot. "I'll free your pretty little bride. And she'll do exactly as I say, because if not, she'll be forced to watch her *mate* suffer my wrath."

Atlas glared up at his father, seething, and made one final vow. "I'll fucking kill you for this."

The kralv shrugged, the corner of his mouth twisting to one side in a look of disinterest. "You can try."

Oldrich reared back and kicked Atlas in the face.

The sound of bone crunching echoed in the space between Atlas's ears. Thick blood filled his mouth, seeped out from between his lips, sticky and warm. Nausea swept through him and his balance wavered. The last thing he saw was his father's smirking face as he lifted his goblet of wine.

"*Dravska.*"

Forty-Six

Everinne was dead on her feet.

She was still breathing. At least, her chest rose and fell, and there was a constant thump—the beating of her heart. But bleeding skies, she was so weary. Fatigue drained her to the point of delirium, where she was lost between reality and the edge of her own mind. She wandered through the bleak fog, her thoughts nothing more than the soft flutter of butterfly wings, flitting in and out of the darkness, then vanishing forever.

Time did not exist in this place.

Only the impenetrable dark.

Hours may have passed, or perhaps it was only mere seconds. Everinne had no way of knowing. She gazed into the pitch, unable to discern if her eyes were open or closed, for the darkness was everywhere. Dense and heavy, it absorbed all sound, all feeling. Her body was numb, and when she lifted her hand in front of her own face, she saw nothing. Here, she was made of shadow. She melded with the darkness, she let it bleed into her bones until they were one and the same.

Sleep tugged at her, its lulling presence remaining just out of reach. So, she drifted in a fever state, maniacal yet lucid. Rational yet disoriented.

A masculine voice sounded, its rough baritone a scrape against her mind.

"Looks like someone paid for your freedom."

She knew that voice, feared that voice.

Jarek.

"A pity," he mumbled, and she shrank into the pitch as his breath skated past her ear. "I rather liked it when you weren't able to escape me."

His open palm pressed into the small of her back, shoving her forward, and searing light blinded her from every direction. She threw her hands over her face, shielding her eyes against the harsh glow. The suffocating darkness faded, leaving her exposed and bare. Peering through the slits of her fingers, blinking slowly, Everinne gradually recognized her new surroundings.

She was in the palace—the throne room. A decadent chandelier of twisted gold hung from the vast ceiling, the quivering lights of faerie fire engulfing the space in a soft glow yet giving no warmth. Long draperies of black and gold brocade framed the sculpted windows, where glistening snow piled upon the sills. The inky sky beyond gave no hint of the hour, whether dawn was on the horizon or if the moon had yet to rise.

Everinne lowered her hands and found herself on the dais beside the throne. The kralv to her right, Jarek to her left. She had no idea how she'd gotten there, or what kind of polluted magic Jarek had used to bring her to the palace, but she stood between them in nothing but that revealing black lace bodysuit that molded to every curve of her flesh.

She wrapped her arms around her chest, hugging herself in the hopes of maintaining some sense of decency.

Before her were numerous guards, most of them stationed in pairs. They barricaded the entrances to the throne room, and six of them formed a strict line behind three kneeling figures, all with black burlap sacks thrown over their heads to hide their identity. One of them, a female from the sound of her weeping, shook and trembled, her small frame rattling like the panes of a window during winter's coldest night. The figure in the middle, likely a male given his haughty posture, was reclining on his knees, as though he was already resigned to his fate. It was the third one, however, where Everinne's gaze lingered. For of the three, he was the only one chained in iron, obviously the only one capable of posing some kind of threat.

The bond wavered, such a feeble recognition, it was hardly noticeable. A quiet murmur of hearts, nothing more. If Atlas was in the palace, she could barely sense him.

Her heart plummeted into her stomach.

Atlas wasn't here. The bond was stronger when she was trapped in the Mystic Obscura, when she could've sworn he was just on the other side of that dressing room door. He probably had no idea she'd been returned to the palace. And now, Kralv Oldrich had bought her freedom with the intention to keep using her to inflict more pain.

Unless...

"Everinne, my dear." Kralv Oldrich rapped his knuckles on the glossy arm of his throne, where a ferocious wolf with molten silver eyes was engraved into the ebony wood. His dark gaze raked over her and he smiled, slow and methodical. "How lovely it is to see you again. I hear you've gotten yourself into quite the predicament."

She faltered beneath his unnerving gaze and stole a quick glance over her shoulder, only to find Jarek staring at her, his expression one of cold calculation. He rolled his neck, the crack of bones splintering through the room, and when he flexed his hands, the skulls decorating his fingers gleamed with diabolic energy.

Everinne looked back to the kralv, lounging upon his throne with lackadaisical authority. "I...I'm not sure what you mean, Your Imperial Majesty."

"Blood magic?" He gestured vaguely in Jarek's direction. "I would've thought you were smarter than that to get caught in something so treacherous."

"Yes, well." She shifted on her feet, angling herself toward Kralv Oldrich and away from Jarek's penetrating gaze. The palace would always be safer than the Mystic Obscura. "It would appear I made a grave error."

"Quite so." The kralv stood then, his beastly frame towering over Everinne, and she suppressed a shiver. He closed the distance between them in one stride, and it took everything in her power not to shrink away, not to show fear. "I'm going to make you a deal, Everinne. In exchange for your freedom from the blood oath, you will use your magic on one of these innocent souls."

He tossed his arm out toward the three hooded figures surrounded by guards.

All the blood drained from Everinne's face, and she stumbled back a step.

"What?" she asked, breathless.

"And to make it even more interesting," the kralv continued, fully aware she heard him correctly the first time, "I'll let you pick which one."

"No. I can't." Everinne shook her head, refusal and determination rolling her shoulders back, filling her with fire. "I won't."

"Choose me." Atlas's pleading voice was a soft murmur through the walls of her mind, like a mountain stream whose song was silenced by frost.

Her gaze latched onto the three captives kneeling across from the dais. "Atlas?"

The one chained in iron flinched and her heart stopped.

That was why the bond felt distorted and muted. Atlas was locked in cold iron.

Rage ravaged her.

"Atlas!" Everinne jolted forward, but the kralv's hand captured her shoulder and hauled her backward, his grip fierce enough to grind her bones to dust. She tried to twist away from him, to break loose of his hold, but the more she struggled, the more he increased the pressure, until her knees almost buckled out from underneath her.

"You're running out of time, Everinne." Kralv Oldrich's threat grated on her nerves. "Unless you'd rather I choose for you?"

"No!" She knew what he was implying, knew the warped intention of his mind. He wanted her to hurt Atlas, wanted her to inflict her devastating magic upon his own son.

And she was fucking sick of it.

Everinne could put an end to this madness. She could over-power the kralv, she could be stronger, unleash the full might of her magic so that claws of pain tore into his veil of fear. It was a dangerous, treasonous thought, and she welcomed it. Relished in it. Her power was born of darkness, an endless well of pain and violence. When those wisps of violet and midnight poured from her, bones of the living wept, tears of suffering turned to ash, and the sweet silence of death lingered in her wake. Her magic was exactly as High Priestess Rozalie had claimed, a blessing to those in need of protection, a curse to those who deserved a fate worse than death.

Again, Atlas's pained voice entered her mind, a caress to her senses. *"It's either myself, Veros, or some unfortunate maid my father wants to punish for not coming to his bed."*

Everinne's heartstrings snapped.

Kralv Oldrich had her brother, too, and she swore then he would know her wrath.

"So, choose me, Wildheart. Whatever you throw at me, I can take."

"No," she whispered, then faced the kralv. Glaring up at him, she held her ground. "No. I refuse. There must be another way."

Jarek grabbed the back of her neck, ripping her away from the kralv's cruel grasp.

"Oh, there's another way." He inhaled deeply, snaking an arm around her waist, his fingers dipping below her navel. "And it involves me claiming you while your precious mate watches."

Fear licked up Everinne's spine, and from across the throne room, Atlas roared.

He thrashed and fought, surging forward to reach her, the black sack slipping from his head to reveal golden green eyes laced with fury. He was feral with rage, baring his teeth like he was a caged beast ready to rip out Jarek's throat. Veros struggled alongside him, his hood falling away as he lurched toward the dais.

"Damn that boy and his temper," Oldrich muttered, snapping his fingers so the guards pounced, restraining Atlas further. The kralv whirled on them, jabbing a finger into Jarek's chest. "You, however, will remove your hands from her at once. We had a deal."

Everinne's mouth fell open in shock, but Jarek released her.

"I want what I was promised," he spat.

"And you'll have it." Oldrich raised one hand, his steely gaze narrowing on Everinne. "But not until I ensure she's thoroughly broken."

A demonic kind of growl, a primitive snarl, erupted from Jarek. "She is mine to break."

"NO!" Everinne screamed, power erupting from her as her magic awoke, flooding her veins. She was as fearless as the night, for when the forest's dark heart had shown its teeth, she flashed a vicious smile of her own. "I will never bend to you, or any male, ever again. I am not a puppet. I am not a pawn. But I will be the last thing you see before you die."

Swirls of violet and black swarmed the throne room.

In the distance, she heard Atlas and Veros calling for her, begging for her to stop. But she did not listen. She would never let another rule her, own her, ever again.

"You dare defy me?" Kralv Oldrich boomed, his thunderous voice echoing up into the vaulted ceiling.

"I will *never* stop defying you," Everinne hissed, taking one menacing step toward him. "I will fight you, every day, until I have nothing left."

"Then I shall be forced to break your will." The kralv crossed his arms and his lips twisted into a smug smile. "And your mate will suffer the consequences of your transgressions."

Everinne released her caged power. Slashes of violence lashed out, snapping and gnashing like the jaws of a ferocious monster. It swirled around her, dense and heinous, a frenzied wall of pain and suffering. This time, the agony would be sweet. She would delight in the kralv's screams, marvel in the way his mind would shatter at her hands, watch as he crumpled into a husk of a body at her feet. Kralv Oldrich was a poison, a disease plaguing his own kingdom. And Everinne was going to purge it.

Except his screams never reached her ears.

Instead, it was Jarek who stepped through the intense cruelty of her magic, his honey-colored eyes gleaming with desire, a sadistic smile tugging at his lips.

"Your lust for death is most enchanting, *temny feya*." Jarek grabbed her arm with one hand, then pressed his skull ring into her shoulder, searing the metal into the same place he marked her once before. "You performed so well tonight. Take a bow."

Everinne screamed as the skull burned into her skin, as pulsing heat spread through her, charring her lungs, scalding her throat. Beads of sweat slid down her back and her knees softened. Darkness clouded the outskirts of her vision, slowly consuming all color and light until there was nothing left. She swayed, light-headed and dazed, her body toppling into Jarek's arms.

"Atlas."

She reached for her mate one final time before the bond, and the rest of the world, went silent.

Forty-Seven

"**E**verinne!" Atlas roared her name, hating the way she was limp in Jarek's arms, the way her head lolled like a broken doll.

Cold iron seared into his skin, stifling his magic further, making it impossible to even summon his wings. He strained for her, ached for her, but every movement was like slogging through wet sand. Strenuous and taxing. It didn't matter how hard he fought, his muscles would not work. Fatigue riddled his bones, and the powerful metal clamped around his wrists and ankles rendered him useless.

"Let her go," he seethed, because at least the fury in his voice had not yet failed him.

"Calm yourself, boy." Oldrich motioned toward the guards standing watch behind Atlas. One of them stalked forward, snatched Everinne from Jarek's arms without a word, then swiftly carried her out of the throne room. "She'll wake up eventually."

"Where are you taking her?" Atlas demanded, but from the corner of his eye he saw Veros slump, as though he already knew.

Oldrich snorted in annoyance, his chest puffing out, while he blatantly ignored his son's question. "I need you to understand something, Atlas. You will *never* wear the crown. Prava will *never* belong to you."

He stomped down the dais, his boots clicking against the polished granite, each step an enunciation of his blatant tyranny. Pausing in front of Atlas, he looked down the length of his nose at him, like he'd stepped in something foul. "When Everinne returns from her little adventure, broken in mind and soul, you will wed her as planned. You will plant your seed in her. And once she births a healthy heir, you will be free from your responsibilities."

Atlas tilted his head back, spasms of pain ricocheting down his spine as he craned his neck to glare up at his father. "What the fuck are you talking about?"

The kralv suffered him a sigh.

"I will no longer have any need for you. But since the gods and goddesses do not look kindly upon the slaughter of one's child, I've come up with a compromise." Oldrich snapped his fingers. "Remove the iron."

A guard hauled Atlas to his feet. The clanking of metal rang in his ears as the iron chains were removed and the moment they fell away, he was renewed, as though the very essence of life flowed through his veins. His magic and strength were restored, his heart pounded, his lungs expanded, and calm rage wound him tightly with tension. The bond tying him to Everinne was still intact, their heartbeats intertwined, the pull of her soul called to him like an ancient song full of eternal promises.

Yet all he wanted was to kill his father, to plunge a blade into his chest and carve out his heart, then crush it with his bare hands until it was nothing more than a pulpy mess. But he could do none of those things. He'd been stripped of weapons, and worse, Everinne had been taken. Again. Until Atlas had the answers he sought, he would keep his father alive, and then he would end the bastard's life.

Kneeling beside him, Veros looked up, caution flashing in his turquoise eyes. There was a hollowness there, a silent grief that bled into the gold around his pupils. Atlas had known Veros for *years*. He remembered it clearly, the day he first arrived at the palace, just like he remembered when Veros rescued Everinne from the Deszvila Forest, before it devoured their village. Before it stole the lives of their parents. Only then had Atlas witnessed such a deeply harbored sorrow in Veros, only then had the Lord of Time worn a mask of despair.

Until now.

Whatever they were about to endure...it would be devastating.

"What compromise?" Atlas rubbed his wrists, his fingers grazing the sensitive skin where his flesh was left charred and burned from the iron. "I only agreed to an unnamed favor."

"Exactly." Oldrich's gaze slid toward the dais, and Jarek strolled forward, his cloak of black moving around him like slithering shadows, the skull rings he wore emanating a reddish, evil glow.

Alarm needled its way into Atlas's spine, suspicion and mistrust keeping him on edge. Wary and alert. He glanced at his father, guarded, and his voice dropped. "What have you done?"

"I did what is best for the longevity of my kingdom." Oldrich tucked his hands behind his back and turned, climbing the few granite steps of the dais. He seated himself on his throne of obsidian—the engraved wolves seeming to snarl at his presence—and leaned back, rapping his knuckles across the curving arm. "You see, not so long ago, the fire ruby mines began to suffer. As you know, the rubies are one of Prava's main sources of wealth, and the jewels make for excellent trade."

Atlas glanced down at Veros, who was staring straight ahead, his mouth pressed into a firm line.

"What does any of this have to do with Everinne?" Meeting his father's complacent gaze, Atlas dared one step forward. The kralv's guards remained in place, only Jarek met his advance.

Oldrich disregarded him once more, instead he reached into his pocket, and pulled out a glittering black stone. "Without the rubies, there would be no wealth. Then one of the mining prisoners discovered this."

He lifted the gem and held it high, so the waning light of the chandelier reflected a thousand stars against the stone's polished surface. The jewel looked exactly like the one Everinne pointed out at the witch's shop in the Marzena.

"It's a nightfall diamond. Rare and desirable. And its value is excessive." The kralv cradled it in his palm, coiling one finger around it at a time, hiding away its beauty. "Unfortunately, mining for the diamonds is quite dangerous."

"The immortals," Atlas breathed, shock radiating through him. He knew his father was vile, but never did he think the kralv would stoop low enough as to send innocent lives to Rizenrok Forge just for more wealth. They were citizens of Prava, *his people*, and he'd betrayed them. "You're not hunting them. You're enslaving them."

That was why Oldrich continuously brushed off Atlas's concerns, that was why he attempted to distract him by forcing him to marry.

"Rather brilliant, don't you think?" Oldrich chuckled. "The demon summoner so graciously agreed to grant me an endless supply of bodies to mine for nightfall diamonds."

Atlas's gaze shot to Jarek.

He stood utterly still, his hands folded before him, his expression one of quiet contemplation. His jaw ticked. There was a flicker in his gaze, barely imperceptible, but Atlas noticed it all the same. Jarek knew the entirety of the story, whereas Oldrich only seemed to be aware of the most intriguing chapters.

The kralv had been fooled.

"In exchange for what?" Atlas spun on his heel to face his father. "What did you promise him?"

The kralv smirked. "Your soul."

Atlas reared back as though he'd been slapped. "Are you fucking serious?"

"Quite. Though I couldn't give up my only son, not without ensuring I had a proper heir." Oldrich leaned forward, his knuckles whitening over the arms of the throne, his brutal aura looming like a storm of tyranny. "Which is why I will raise your son or daughter to be the next kralv or kralvina. And you will become the next Zolvost."

"What?" Atlas rounded on Jarek and stalked toward him, his malice expanding. He met the demon summoner's cold glare head on. "You're going to turn me into a sex-crazed demon? That's your plan?"

Jarek said nothing, but Oldrich answered for him instead. "You must admit, it's rather fitting."

Atlas raked his hands through his hair, pacing before the dais. This couldn't be real, it had to be some kind of fever dream. Maybe he'd indulged in too much honeyfire and his sound, rational mind was suffering the repercussions of exorbitant intoxication. His fists clenched at his sides, squeezing until his nails bit into his palms. He squeezed his eyes shut and when he opened them a moment later, he found Veros staring at him in solemn resignation.

He'd known. He'd known this would happen and could do nothing to prevent it. Because he was bound to the power of time.

Atlas sent a scathing look at his father, ignoring the way Jarek was closing in on him. "And what of Ever?"

The kralv shrugged and lounged back against his throne. He waved one dismissive hand through the air. "I intend to have her thoroughly broken and then I'll use her as I see fit. I'd wed her myself, but I can't have all of Prava loathing me for stealing my son's betrothed."

Atlas lunged for him, darting up the steps of the dais. It didn't matter if he was without a dagger or sword, he would rip out his father's heart with his hands.

His father's answering laughter rattled through his mind as a blast of fiendish energy slammed into him. Without warning, he was airborne. The surge of power threw him down the stairs so his back smacked soundly against the granite floor and glowing skulls danced in front of his eyes. Pain cracked up and down his spine, and his breath wheezed out of him, leaving him gasping for air.

"Not so fast, playboy prince." Jarek's shadowy outline came into view, his eyes pulsing red beneath a drawn, dark brow.

"You can't change me yet," Atlas rasped, the words slipping between broken ribs and punctured lungs. He rolled his head, pinning his father with a look of retribution. "Your plan will fail. Everinne will never wed a demon. Our family bloodline will die with me, and you'll never get your precious heir."

His father flashed a cruel smile. "She will do exactly as I say... because you're her mate."

It was all the warning Atlas had before Jarek's demonic powers consumed him. The air crackled and hissed, pressing in on his chest so he thought his lungs would collapse. Blood boiled through his veins as his bones elongated, forming new tendons, distorting his body into that of a hulking beast. Silver claws emerged from his hands and feet, and the sound of ripping fabric and tearing flesh pounded against his skull. Pain magnified and he writhed in torment, suffering beneath Jarek's corrupt magic. Atlas's chest expanded, his arms and legs bulking to an immense size, carving him with solid, corded muscle. Before his eyes, he watched as his skin morphed into a hideous red shade, like the charred flames of an inferno. Curving onyx horns protruded through the top of his head, and when Atlas opened his mouth to scream, the agony worse than anything he'd suffered before, a serpent-like black tongue lashed out from between his lips.

The crush of demonic magic was too much, it slithered into his mind, absorbing his thoughts and dominating his emotions.

He was losing, the demon emerging from inside him would become his master, and he would be forced to obey.

Atlas snarled, repeating one name over and over while he was restrained, powerless inside the body of the Zolvost who craved lust and blood.

Everinne.
Everinne.
Everinne.
Terror riddled Atlas when the demon responded.
"Mine."

Forty-Eight

An annoying, rattling sound woke Everinne from what felt like a month's long slumber. Or perhaps it was the fact that she could no longer feel her fingers and toes. Shivers wrecked her frozen body so she shuddered compulsively, unable to retain any warmth. Her eyes flew open, and it was only then she realized the rattling sound was coming from her. She clenched her jaw, but not even that was enough to keep her teeth from chattering.

She found herself curled onto a rickety wooden bench at the mouth of a gaping cave. Frigid wind slapped at her cheeks, tearing at the threadbare clothing she wore—the thin brown top and pants with shredded hems did nothing to keep away its bitter sting. Iron shackles were clamped around her wrists and ankles, dampening her magic, leaving her weak and faint. She eased herself up, her gaze drifting skyward to where jagged mountain peaks capped with snow carved an indigo sky.

Everinne knew those mountains.

The Karmorva Mountains sculpted Prava's northernmost border, their rugged interiors filled with veins of sparkling fire. Except maybe not anymore. Now the majestic mountains would be exposed for nightfall diamonds.

Tears pricked at the corner of her eyes and a knot of emotion strangled the back of her throat. She tried to swallow it, pretend it wasn't real, but understanding had already lodged itself in her heart. The stench of dried blood and cold sweat hung in the air, mingling with the scent of raw earth, pine, and fresh snow. The wind howled, drowning out the cries of anguish and despair coming from inside the mountains.

Kralv Oldrich had sent her to the Rizenrok Forge.

Boots crunched loudly against the frozen ground and Everinne jerked upright, her iron shackles clattering together.

A guard stood before her, but he wasn't dressed like the ones back in Starysa. Whereas they wore black and gold, this male was dressed in all gray leathers. Intricate runes were carved into the armor protecting his chest and he wore a cape of the same dull color, the hood thrown over his head to conceal most of his face. A studded belt was wrapped around his waist and from it hung a corded whip of braided leather. Dark scruff lined his angular jaw, but the rest of his face was hidden from her view. He cracked his knuckles, one at a time, and only then did Everinne see that he wore a gold signet ring embellished with a fire ruby on his pinky.

"Why am I here?" she asked, her voice scratchy and coarse, even though she already knew the answer. It was a pathetic attempt, but at least if she could get this guard talking, then perhaps she could suspend time, maybe even delay the inevitable.

"First rule." He spoke with icy precision, his tone lacking any warmth. "You don't get to ask questions."

The guard reached for his whip and Everinne cowered on the bench, curling into herself as the long strap of leather unfurled toward the ground.

"But since you asked so nicely." He rolled his wrist, spinning the whip around and around, so it kicked up dirt and dust, so the sound of it hissed into the wind, and caused Everinne's heart to stutter. "You're here to be broken and I'm going to be the one to break you."

She cried out, but in one swift movement, the guard raised his arm and the whip cracked like lightning through the air. Stiff leather connected with Everinne's shoulder, lashing at her flesh through the thin material of her shirt, drawing blood.

Everinne screamed. The wicked wood awoke. And somewhere in the back of her mind, a demon roared.

Acknowledgments

I know that didn't end how you were expecting. Honestly, it wasn't how I pictured it ending either, but here we are. Don't worry, I promise I'll piece your broken heart back together in the next book.

A thousand thanks to my Discord, my readers who have waited so patiently for their sex fae book (IYKYK). My endless gratitude to my beta readers—Ashley, Kristin, Ali, Robin, & Cat.

Thank you to Kimberly for creating such beautiful chapter headers. To my amazing cover artists, Yosbe Designs (the paperback & ebook) and Angela Chen (hardcover) for such beautifully intricate designs. I can't wait to work with both of you again for book two. To my amazing editor Emily, thank you always for helping me produce the best books possible.

For my sanity, I owe an obscene amount of gratitude to Ashley, Chyanne, Lindsay, & Diana.

And to Morgan, I love you infinitely. Thank you for reading this beast of a book and loving it with your whole heart.

To my family, I love you fiercely. To Nate, for supporting this crazy dream. And to my girls, I hope you know you can be whatever you want in this world.

Finally, my readers. Thank you for reading my stories. For loving my characters. For letting my worlds live in your minds and hearts.

About the Author

Hillary Raymer is a fantasy romance author. She's a wanderer, a storyteller, and believes in happily ever afters.

She has an unfinished Bachelor's Degree in English, because she ran off and married a Marine halfway through college. She loves the mountains and the beach, but would also like to live in a place where it was autumn year round. Currently, she lives in Virginia with her husband, two daughters, and two cats. When not writing, Hillary enjoys reading, doodling, and buying more plants she doesn't need.

Join her Court here https://www.facebook.com/share/g/1Zke8ybqNr/

Also by Hillary Raymer

The Faeven Saga

Crown of Roses

Throne of Dreams

Realm of Nightmares

Void of Endings

The Starstorm Series

All the Chaos of Constellations

All the Sacrifice of Shadows

All the Pain of Promises

www.ingramcontent.com/pod-product-compliance
Lightning Source LLC
Chambersburg PA
CBHW061536190726
48289CB00004B/1063